Unweaving the Thread

First published in 2001 by
Marino Books
an imprint of Mercier Press
16 Hume Street Dublin 2
Tel: (01) 661 5299; Fax: (01) 661 8583
E-mail: books@marino.ie

Trade enquiries to CMD Distribution
55A Spruce Avenue
Stillorgan Industrial Park
Blackrock County Dublin
Tel: (01) 294 2560; Fax: (01) 294 2564
E.mail: cmd@columba.ie

© Monica Tracey 2001

ISBN 1 86023 140 3

10 9 8 7 6 5 4 3 2 1

A CIP record for this title is available
from the British Library

Cover design by SPACE
Printed in Ireland by ColourBooks,
Baldoyle Industrial Estate, Dublin 13

UNWEAVING THE THREAD

MONICA TRACEY

In memory of my parents,
Owen and Annie Gallagher

CIRCLING

We have reached the Irish coast and will shortly be landing at Aldergrove Airport. Our captain has told us that it is raining, there are strong winds and the ground temperature is forty degrees. My baby opens wide, terrified eyes and howls. I stick a bottle into his mouth and relax as his gums close over it. Yellow spokes of light fan out to the left below us. Shore Road, Antrim Road, Crumlin Road? Names crowd and jostle in my head. The line weaving up towards the airport, what's it called? Hannahstown? Or is it the Glen Road? Or Ligoniel? I can't remember.

I have never come back in winter before and never in darkness. Either the slow passage of the Liverpool or Heysham boat up the lough to the docks in the early morning or ragged Antrim fields appearing under banks of broken cloud. I am returning to my family and friends and a place I will slot back into with ease, yet I am casting names like chicken feed on the roads below me.

I glance at my watch as the plane prepares to land half an hour behind schedule and all my certainties vanish. I want it to swoop back up into the sky and circle the way planes sometimes do in films. To give me time. To let me keep my options open. To decide if I really want to go to a job interview this evening at seven o'clock and to another one on Friday, or return to London with this child who had not been part of the bargain.

My brother-in-law, Tim, waits at the barrier. He says we'll have to get our skates on and there's a roadblock just outside

Andersonstown. Traffic trickles into a queue. A soldier scrutinises Tim's papers. Another stands, rifle pointing six inches from the side window. No time to go into my sister's house for a peaceful handover. Raindrops spatter the baby's angry face as Bridie carries him inside, out of the wind that whips round her porch.

Tim deposits me outside the parochial house at ten past seven.

'You left Ireland in 1954. Why do you want to come back?'

Yellow light from an anglepoise lamp reflects on the priest's glasses. His nose is large and pitted, a network of thread veins; his shoulders hunch round a bull neck. Ash falls on his black chest and over my application form. He flicks a cigarette in the direction of an ashtray on his desk.

'Because it's my home.' I can't see behind the gleam of his glasses. I fumble for words. 'I was born here. Grew up and studied here . . . ' My voice trails away. The baby's screams still jangle my nerves.

The man behind the desk waits. I'm filling in the edges of the jigsaw, the green of the grass, the blue pieces of sky. He wants the shapes that slot together in the middle.

'You have three children. How will you manage if you have another baby?'

I jab my nails into the palm of my left hand; a flush of anger sweeps over me.

It's four hours since Sally left us at Heathrow. I wish I was out of the haze of smoke that stings my eyes and catches my throat. How will I answer his question? 'The last child was a mistake. There won't be any more.' 'Why don't you mind your own bloody business?'

He moves sideways, out of the glare of the interrogation lamp. The eyes behind the spectacles are marbled glass, the colour of hens' eyes. Two women on his right wait, mute as fish.

'I'm getting on, Father. I'm not likely to have any more children,' I mumble and flush again at my reply.

'You're thirty-eight years old. I see you have an infant aged two months. You can easily have another child, several other children.' The words reverberate from linoleum to ceiling.

My application is folded at the section dealing with marital and family status. I could turn the tables. Give them a sob story. Or I could tell him what I think of him and his Nosy-Parkering.

He is a clergyman. On a pedestal. Beyond reproach. And I am a mealy-mouthed coward.

Rain slaps against black window-panes behind his head. Bridie will find the bottle and nappies in a bag I pushed inside the door. She'll know what to do. In the weighty silence of the parochial house parlour, I hear my son bawling.

The priest pushes my application form to one side, leans back on the arms of his chair and lights another cigarette.

'Have you any questions, Sister?' He swivels to his right.

'No questions. Thank you, Father.' The figure that was introduced at the start of the interview smiles a marshmallow smile. She's headmistress of the school where the vacancy has occurred. It's the first time she has spoken.

'That will be all. We'll let you know.'

I dash through slanting rain to Tim's car and a newsflash on the radio. Another bombing in Belfast. The IRA claims responsibility.

'Well, did you get the job?' Tim asks.

'Did I hell!'

Mammy ushers us into the living room that smells of fresh paint and paint stripper and is completely bare apart from the kitchen table. Scraps of wallpaper cling like butterflies to naked plaster and lie in confetti piles on the floor. She stares me up and down.

'That short hair suits you. You were far too old to have it trailing down your back like a gypsy.'

'I know. I should have had it cut years ago.'

She and I perch on the table in front of the fire and Michael sleeps between us in a borrowed carrycot. She glances at her youngest grandchild. 'I'm glad you called that child after your father, God rest him. If he takes after his grandfather, he'll be all right.'

Mammy doesn't believe in slobbering over babies. She'll open a bank account for Michael as she has done for each of her grandchildren and top it up twice a year out of her pension.

'Well, did you get the job?'

'No. My face didn't fit.'

'You would be better working in Carrig than travelling up to the city. I'll see Canon Doyle after Mass tomorrow. He thought a lot about your father. He couldn't pass you over. Not when you think how much time your brother Brendan spends on those football teams and the youth club. He'll put in a word for you.'

'I don't need anybody to put in a word for me. There were good references attached to my form but yer man up in Belfast didn't even bother to look at them. He was only interested in finding out how many more children I intend to have. As if that was any of his damn business.'

'Show a bit of respect when you talk about a priest, madam. He's God's anointed, or are you too grand to remember that? Living among a pack of heathens in England hasn't done you much good. Your manners or your morals.'

'And just what's that supposed to mean?'

Five minutes home, my mother and I, legs dangling, shins roasting, are set for a row.

'Whatever you're up to, I don't approve of it. It's not right for a woman to up sticks and leave her husband. Your father and I had our differences but we respected our marriage vows. Your husband's a decent man. You should count yourself lucky.'

'Who said anything about leaving him? All I'm doing is applying for a job. I miss Ireland. I miss my own family. I miss *you*, for heaven's sake! What's so odd about that?'

'It's a bit late in the day for all that, Mary Ann. You listened to nobody when you went off to England chasing after an English Protestant you hardly knew. I warned Eva time and again about going out with Englishmen and Yanks but she paid as much attention to me as you did and look what happened to her.'

'That's not fair, Mammy. Poor Eva couldn't help herself. Sure, she was a bit touched.'

'Maybe she wasn't the only one.' Mammy eases herself off the table, throws a shovelful of coal on the fire and banks it with slack from a bucket she keeps near the hearth. Then she plucks a tiny shovel from a brass companion set and sweeps ash and coal dust on to it. She pokes the fire, till tongues of flame flare through the slack. 'He's got another woman, hasn't he?' she asks, her back to me.

'Another woman! Where did you get that notion?'

'I can read you like a book. And you with a new baby.'

'What's the point of me saying anything? You'll believe what you want to believe.' I wish I had a cigarette. The shops are closed and it's pelting outside. I gave up smoking years ago.

'I never liked him. His eyes are too close together. You can never trust a man with eyes too close together.'

She waits for me to fight back. I lean over the carrycot and try to remove the baby's matinée jacket without wakening him.

'He'll have no luck. You wait and see.' After a pause she adds in a voice with the ring of the last trump, 'The sins you do in two-by-two, you pay for one by one. Is it some slut he works with?'

The phone in the cupboard under the stairs rings and Michael cries out.

It's Sally, checking that we have arrived safely.

The floorboards creak as Mammy paces to and fro with Michael. A trail of curdled milk inches over her shoulder and down the back of her black cardigan.

'Was that him?'

'No, he's working in Bristol this week. He works away a lot these days. It was his mother. The children send their love.'

'Bristol, is it?' Mammy gives me a hard look and goes into the kitchen. She returns ten minutes later with the teapot, two cups, a plate of soda bread and eggs cooked in a cup. She always cooked eggs in a cup for me if I was ill or if she thought I needed pampering.

'I've been thinking, if you have really made your mind up to come home, you had better take the Carrig job on Friday and you don't need to go throwing money into another house. There's a home here for you and the children. They will be much better off growing up in Ireland than in a godless country. David will have to grow his hair long and stop talking with that English accent. He could be shot, you know, if he was taken for a British soldier'. She balances the teapot precariously on the grate shield and the rim of the grate. My offers of help are ignored. It's half past nine. A long time since I left London this afternoon.

'You can go out to school every day and I'll look after that youngster.' She nods towards Michael. My head aches. Her voice is the rapid fire of a machine gun. 'You can keep your head down and behave yourself and let nobody know anything about you. I haven't looked at a man since your father died and neither will you. You'll bring your children up in the fear and love of God. You have had your life. They are what matters.'

I have had my life. Women grow old early in this country.

My reflection in the bedroom mirror surprises and pleases me. No flying hair blinding me or whiplashing my face. No husband, nobody dictating how I should look. It's barely a week since I went to Franco's in Muswell Hill and watched his scissors chop my waist-length hair that had only ever been trimmed since the night Joseph scalped me in Moynagh. My neck felt naked as black coils slithered to the floor and Franco shaped what remained into a style not unlike Bridie's after that Good Friday.

Joseph's cut-throat. The crackle of nits in the grate. Bridie's hair and veil blazing in the Good Friday procession. The perm that rotted Eva's hair.

Eva! She's back in my head again, only this time I can't get her out of it. The hovel where she lived and where I last saw her was just a little way from here.

I don't want to think about Eva.

All that was a long time ago. I was only a child after all.

1

Every so often a nurse wearing a stiff headdress bobbed into the doorway. Each head in the room rose; jutted forward in expectation. She barked a name. One child and an adult stood up and followed her. The rest slumped in silence. Except Eva. She was on her feet again, padding the speckled terrazzo floor, glowering at silent rows of parents and children on wooden benches. I wished she would act her age. But Eva had no idea how old she was. Mammy said she could be twenty-five or -six. Nobody knew for sure. It was her first time at the eye hospital and she thought I had been done out of my turn. I tried to explain to her that my name might be called next or that maybe we would have to wait till ten or eleven o' clock, or even twelve. There was no knowing. I was seven years old and I had been coming every week since I was three, so I knew the ropes.

'I won't tell you again to sit down and keep quiet. This is a waiting room, not Smithfield Market.' The nurse reappeared and shouted at Eva but sitting quietly was not in Eva's nature. She darted back to me, leaned across a woman with a runny-nosed child in her arms and grabbed my shoulder.

'You sit there like a good girl and I'll be back in a wee minute.'

'Where are you going?

'To see a man about a dog.' She was already halfway to the door.

If I had known then how little time I would have with Eva I

would have cherished every moment we spent together that day instead of feeling ashamed of her. Ashamed of her loud voice, her flat moon face and her skelly eye that wandered over your shoulder instead of looking straight at you. I hear myself say 'skelly'. A square of Elastoplast covered my right eye and eyebrow and part of my cheek, and my left eye squinted towards the bridge of my nose. The doctor had tried clipping a black patch to my glasses but I peered over it and round it. I never for a minute saw any link between Eva's skelly and my lazy eye for I was tenderly reared and came from a respectable family. Eva never had a mother to take her to the eye hospital, only a skinny father with a face as shifty as the ferret he kept for hunting rabbits.

When my turn came I was instructed to climb on a high metal stool and look through a machine at pictures of a lion and an empty cage. I had to move them till the lion fitted exactly inside his cage. Not a whisker, not a fraction of his tail outside. Then I fitted two tigers one on top of the other. This was much better than reading black letters printed on white charts, first with my right eye, then with my left. I was taken into a darkened room. Another doctor shone a light into my eyes and said to come back next week. I returned to my seat and waited for Eva.

The last couple, a boy in horn-rimmed glasses and his mother, left the waiting room. I began to wonder what would become of me if Eva couldn't find her way back, or if she had been bitten by the dog and was bleeding to death in the street. The nurse came in. She glared at three squashed chocolates oozing out of their wrappers, at a coil of orange peel and sweet papers under the front bench and at me cowering at the back.

'It's nearly one. You have no business sitting there by yourself.' She swept papers from the benches. Before she flounced out she called from the door, 'I'll be back in five minutes to lock up.'

To shut me in as I had shut the lion in his cage. Her anger smelled stronger than the sweat of the bodies that had waited all morning. I raced from the room and crouched in the bricked entry outside a door marked Out Patients. Tears welled behind my new plaster. I pulled the bottom end away from my face to let them trickle through.

'Cry baby, cry! Stick your finger in your eye.' Eva hauled me into the street.

'Look what I brought you.' She waved a poke filled with dolly mixtures at me. 'You can have them if you stop bawling and if you don't tell your mammy on us.'

'You had no right to go away. You're supposed to be minding me.'

'Get up behind me and stop whingeing.' She climbed on the low wall in front of the hospital and I followed her, my eye fixed on her wobbling backside, my cheeks bulging with dolly mixtures. We were trapeze artists on the high wire performing feats of daring above cheering crowds. We were parrots soaring up into the damp Belfast sky. Yellow and blue and green splashes of colour against the grimy buildings in Great Victoria Street; chirping, tottering along the little walls towards Shaftesbury Square.

'We're going the wrong way, Eva. The station's back there,' I shouted into the back of her tweed coat that flapped in the breeze like the wings of a scuttling hen.

She kept on going, up and down and round the corner till she ran out of walls. Then we hop-scotched to the Great Northern. Every time my foot touched a line between the paving slabs Eva shouted 'Slipsy' and I gave her a dolly mixture. Her size eight lace-ups hit nearly every line.

We had a carriage to ourselves. We sat with our backs to the engine so that smuts would not get in our eyes and sang at the top of our voices. Eva's fist thumped the beat on the windowsill.

Will you come to my wee party will you come?
Bring your own cup and saucer and a bun.
Mussolini will be there, throwing bananas in the air
Will you come to my wee party will you come?

'*Mussolini*'s my favourite word, Eva.' I nestled into the crook of her arm.

'Promise you won't tell on us and your mammy will let me take you every week and we'll have a great time, the two of us' She squeezed me hard. 'You're a lovely wee girl, Mary Ann.'

I nodded and tightened her arm around me. Only Eva and my father thought I was lovely. Mammy said I was no oil painting.

She took a tiny blue bottle of 'Evening in Paris' out of her pocket and dabbed perfume behind her ears, on her wrists and on the backs of her knees. She said that's what film stars did.

'You stink, Eva. You smell like Marley's pub,' I told the heaving pillow of her chest. 'Mammy says people only wear perfume to hide other stinks.'

The train rattled past row upon row of streets of terrace houses that climbed uphill from the railway line. Past the high chimneys of the linen mills and bleaching greens covered with broad strips of linen. Through stations, backs of houses, embankments and wintry fields.

'One for sorrow. Two for joy.' Eva pointed at two crows perched on a telegraph pole. We jumped to our feet and scanned every pole along the line. 'There's two more. Three for a girl. Four for a boy. I'm going to have a boy, Mary Ann, a baby boy. Isn't that great?'

'Those are crows, Eva. You have to see magpies. Magpies are

black and white and you hardly ever see them.'

'Them were black and white. Honest to God.' She rocked a pretend baby in her arms and started to sing in her high, cracked voice:

Rockabye baby on the tree top.
When the wind blows the cradle will rock . . .

'Where will you get your baby from?'

'From the shops. But I have to get a man first.'

'Why do you have to have a man?

'Because they won't give you a baby till you have a man. I'll put wee blue dresses and romper suits on him in the summer and a white furry coat when it's cold and I'll wheel him out in a big black pram. A big shiny pram. And you can help me mind him.'

'When the bough breaks the cradle will fall.' I screwed up my eyes and saw Eva's barefoot baby lying on the seat opposite, the born spit of her, with the hem of a blue dress peeping out from under a white fur coat.

Mammy waited at the station.

'Thank God you're back safe, the both of you. I thought you had been murdered.' She reached out her arms as I jumped from the train. 'What kept you?'

'We missed the train, Mrs Ward, and we had to wait a long time for the next one.'

We didn't call at Ginny White's for a pennyworth of liquorice all sorts. Mammy said 'Cold day, today,' to Mr Rossi who stood in the doorway of his ice-cream parlour but didn't stop for a chat. Maybe she didn't want him to see her putty-coloured face and the swollen body under her tent coat. Maybe she didn't want to hear him telling me once again how beautiful she had been on that Christmas Eve when my father proposed to her in one of the horse-boxes over three scoops of vanilla ice cream with raspberry cordial. Eva and I linked her and we walked slowly past rows of net-curtained mill houses along the Dublin Road and the big villas that had been built for grandees in the last century, and on up the hill to Rathbeg Avenue and our new house. It took us over half an hour because Mammy had to stop often to rest and get her breath back.

Smoke from three mill chimneys scudded over the sky and disappeared into black clouds that started to spit on us. By the time we reached home we were soaked.

Mammy lay in the downstairs bedroom which Eva had spring-cleaned last week. It was only used if somebody was ill or if Mammy's uncle, Father Tom, came to stay. A strawberry-coloured eiderdown, so fluffy you could jump up and down on it without leaving a trace, had been laid over the white bedspread. Mammy asked me to put two pillows under her feet.

Varicose veins bulged and writhed over her legs like fat worms and an ulcer wept through her crêpe bandage. Where her ankles had been were blobs of blue-veined fat. Eva told me one day that if one of the purple clots on Mammy's legs moved up over her heart she would die on the spot.

'I shouldn't have let Eva take you to the hospital but I didn't want you to miss your appointment. Don't tell your daddy. He'd say it was the blind leading the blind.'

Mammy closed her eyes and lay so still that I wondered if I should look under the bedclothes to see if the purple stains were still in the same place. The sockets under her eyes were the colour of mustard and I could see the shape of her skull beneath the taut skin on her cheekbones and forehead.

'Are you going to die, Mammy?'

'Everyone has to die some time, Mary Ann. You know that,' she whispered. 'Death comes like a thief in the night.'

I lay down beside her and traced the curves and squiggles among the embossed leaves of the beige wallpaper. I watched them swell and burst into tropical flowers growing along pathways that curved through a dense jungle. Distant tom-toms drummed with the monotony of a tap dripping.

Brightness shattered the November dusk. Banging. Clattering. My sister Bridie had switched on the light. She threw her schoolbag in before her and burst into the bedroom. In the kitchen my father yelled 'Where is everybody? The fire's nearly out.' He rattled cinders from the range and banged the kettle and saucepans from the sink to the top of the cooker.

'Mammy, Daddy picked me up from school,' Bridie shouted. She pointed at me. 'Is she pretending she's sick?'

My father rolled up pages of the *Irish News*, put them in the bedroom grate, covered them with sticks, which he criss-crossed to let the air pass through them, and placed small pieces of coal on top. He bent down, struck a match and blew till flames licked round the sticks. They stretched and roared and the newspaper he held in front of the grate flew in a blaze up the chimney. He turned out the light, which hurt Mammy's eyes. The shadows of two wooden candlesticks on the chest of drawers grew tall and thin against the wall and bent across the ceiling. They were painted green and had yellow flowers with white centres climbing over them. The same flowers which Mammy had stuck over a crack in the mirror above the fireplace. The crack was not exactly in the middle so your reflection had a lopsided look.

Bridie impaled a slice of bread on the end of the toasting-fork. When the bread browned and curled towards the fire, she turned it. A white three-pronged image was printed on each side. Butter melted on a dish inside the fender.

'Tell us a story, Daddy.'

My father unhooked a poker from the brass companion set and poked the fire. We watched flames flickering through scarlet caverns and castles, crawling over trees and black rocks and waited for him to point to the characters of his story.

'Once upon a time when pigs were swine and reindeer were as plentiful as blackthorn bushes there lived a king who was very . . . '

'Mick, Mick. It's time,' Mammy cried from the bed. Pain racked her face, contorted her body.

'Get to bed at once, you two.' My father placed a metal guard round the fireplace. 'Never mind washing. Say your prayers and go straight to sleep.'

He bundled us upstairs to the cold of our bedroom. We heard his lorry rev and skid out of the drive and ages after, we heard sounds of people coming and going downstairs and Mammy's low cries. She hadn't even called out that day when the window she was cleaning crashed down and crushed two of her fingers.

'If Mammy dies we will only ever have toast to eat,' I whispered. 'Daddy can't even boil an egg.'

'All you ever think about is your stomach,' Bridie said. She was ten months older than me and treated me like dirt. 'Anyhow, Mammy isn't going to die. The doctor will make her better. That's what doctors are for.'

Who would look after us? Who would make our clothes and embroider the costumes we wore when we danced at the *feiseanna* if Mammy didn't get better? And what about the three down-and-outs from the Nazareth Home for Destitute Men who came every Saturday for their dinner and went away with sixpence each and a brown paper bag filled with soda bread, a pair of socks and maybe some of my father's old jackets or trousers?

And Eva? She was all right as long as she had Mammy to look out for her and tell her if her clothes were on back to front. Who would help her rear her baby if Mammy didn't get better? I was too small.

I cannot see Eva without Mammy. Eva cleaning and stoning fruit. Mammy weighing sugar, putting blobs of runny jam on saucers, her eyes alert for the crinkled moment of setting. Eva, Bridie and me, tongues stretched to lick the saucers. Eva following Mammy along the clothes line, passing coiled washing to be shaken out and pegged. Eva waltzing up the garden path with my father's frozen shirt for a partner, her breath hanging in the space above the collar. And the sheet dance she and Mammy performed before ironing. The pulling and stretching. The gathering and folding. Advance and fold and back and gather up. Perfect oblongs, even sheets made out of flour bags. Eva only seemed like Mammy's shadow. A tiny woman could not cast such a big, raw-boned shadow.

Every Friday when she finished her jobs she had a bath and washed her hair. It was checked, just like ours, to make sure all the shampoo was out and that the final rinse was in rainwater to make it shine. Mammy bought her four vests and four pairs of knickers, or 'unmentionables' as we called them. Interlock vests with built up shoulders and knickers with elastic in the legs.

'It's not decent for a grown woman of your age to go out without undergarments, Eva. Apart from everything else, you could get a cold in your kidneys.'

When we were alone with Eva she taught us to samba and rumba in time to music on the wireless. She said the sailors at the dance halls in Belfast could throw their partners up into the air and catch them. Our ceiling was too low.

Mammy stayed in bed for days. The doctor came often and a woman in a white apron shooed us away from the door. My father didn't go the quarry. He sat at the table, his head in his hands. I didn't know that big men cried.

'What's wrong with Mammy? Can we see her?'

He said we were to play quietly and he carried the cradle back up to the loft. He had brought it down a week or so before and he had whistled 'My Bonny Lies over the Ocean' as he polished it. We sneaked into the downstairs bedroom. Mammy's waist- length hair lay damp and unplaited over the pillow; her lips were pale as mushrooms. She said we should put on clean clothes and wash ourselves, and turned her face away.

Eva took Bridie and me to the graveyard. She led us past the white angel over Canon Donovan's tomb, past the broad plot reserved for the nuns, past mounds of earth with wooden crosses and withered flowers to a small triangle of ground hidden behind a privet hedge. Among leaves and twigs was fresh red soil. Eva said our baby brother was buried there because he hadn't been baptised and so was Mrs Brennan from Hill Street because she had cut her throat. It was no use explaining that we didn't have a brother. Mammy had told us not to argue with Eva. She wasn't as cute as the next person. Bridie said that dead-born babies had original sin on their souls and were not fit to be in God's presence. Neither were people who committed suicide because they had turned their backs on God.

Bridie and I wouldn't let my father out of our sight. We perched on the edge of the bath and watched him open his cut-throat and swish it back and forth along the strap which hung on a nail beside the wash-hand basin. When we misbehaved he threatened to take the strap to us and we were afraid that some day he might. He rubbed his shaving brush in soap and lathered his face and neck. He scraped foam from his cheek and piled it on the side of the washing basin. It was flecked with black like snow when it has lain for a few days at the edge of the street.

'Why is your moustache still black when your hair's nearly all grey, Daddy?'

'Because my moustache is sixteen years younger than the hair on my head.'

He stretched his neck, peered into the mirror. Bridie stroked her neck.

'Why do you have a lump in your throat, Daddy?'

His razor paused halfway through the swathe it was mowing. 'Do they teach you nothing at school? Well, it was like this. After Eve ate the apple she tempted Adam and made him have a bite but he was a decent fellow and couldn't bring himself to swallow it. It stuck right here.' The razor nicked the spot. Blood reddened the foam on his throat.

'Don't cut your throat, Daddy,' Bridie screamed and clasped both arms round his leg.

'I wouldn't if you two would give me a bit of peac.' He raised the cut-throat high above her head. One side of his weather beaten face was bearded like Santa Claus; a trickle of blood dried on his neck.

'Thou O Lord will open my lips and my tongue shall announce Thy praise.' That night the three of us knelt on cushions on the kitchen floor in front of the Sacred Heart lamp. My father and Bridie said Mammy's decades. None of us could remember the order of the Litany, though we had heard her recite it every night. After we said three Hail Marys that Mammy would be spared to us my father told us to go to bed. He was still on his knees when Bridie and I left the kitchen.

We removed the bolster we kept down the middle of our bed to stop toes or nails or fists invading the other's territory, to stop us punching and clawing each other till we drew blood. We lay stock-still, not a shoehorn's space between us, listening for the death rattle in Mammy's breathing. Listening for the thief that comes in the middle of the night.

2

If word ever arrived in Carrig about a war that England had been preparing for long before September 1939, it did not reach Bridie and me. Each morning at school we prayed for General Franco to beat the communists because he was a Catholic and they were atheists who wanted to stop people believing in God. We prayed for peace as well, but I assumed that meant peace in Ireland. Nobody bothers to explain things to you when you're seven. All the same, if they knew about the coming war, why did they bother widening the road that summer? A summer that smelled of hot tar. Bridie and I stationed ourselves as near to the sprayer as we dared, inhaling it by the lungful. It trickled from under stones and gravel and settled into thick pools. We crouched by the roadside stirring the glossy surface with sticks and drew up clingy strands that thread-veined our legs and hands. Eva's shoes stuck in it and came out with a loud slurp with gravel and dust clinging like crusty scabs.

But long before a new tarmacadam road and footpaths could be laid, an army of workmen had ripped out the iron gates and railings which the newcomers to Rathbeg Avenue had erected only two years previously. They lay on the ground or were propped against gable walls, waiting to enclose the shortened properties of their owners.

On that hot summer day Bridie and I had more serious matters preying on us than imminent war in Europe.

'I wish I had never been born,' she announced out of the blue. We were sitting on a rug in the front porch watching the same workmen tear out tiny green and yellow hedges that had hardly had time to take root, let alone grow.

'Sister Pius says that at the end of every day your guardian angel writes your good deeds in a white book and your sins in a black book and they're all totted up on the last day. I'm going to hell for sure.'

Eva had taught us both to say, 'You baldy-headed bugger, will you pass us down the suggar' and Bridie had been slapped for passing dirty notes in class. I was wondering what other sins she had committed when she turned towards me with narrowed eyes.

'And so are you.'

That Bridie should never have been born was more appalling than the thought of joining her in hell. She was my mirror. My role model. Not an odd-looking child with one brown eye and rush-straight hair, but a slim girl who had two blue eyes. Laughing Irish eyes, Mammy's English friend, Mrs Bradshaw, called them and she had auburn hair that curled round her face and fell in ringlets over her shoulders. Without Bridie I was less than a puff of smoke. Her birth, achieved only after novenas, pilgrimages and 'investigations', had ended my parents' seven barren years of waiting and been hailed as a miracle. She had paved the way for me to arrive hard on her heels and given hope for the sons who had not as yet materialised.

Claudette Campbell glided out of next door's drive on roller skates. A new dirndl skirt flared up over her backside; blonde hair swirled around blue cotton shoulders as she circled in front of our house. Bridie and I wore checked dresses made by Mammy out of remnants. Claudette Campbell was lucky. Protestants didn't have guardian angels snooping on them, consigning them to hell.

'I'm practising going backwards.' She paused on the tip of one skate before reversing down the road.

'I hope she backs into a bus,' Bridie muttered. Claudette was a year older than her and her best friend out of school. We were the only children on the road who went to the convent school; who wore the green costume of the McCarthy School of Dancing every Saturday and who were allowed to play outside on Sundays.

'I hope she falls and breaks her neck.'

'And her nails.'

Mrs Campbell manicured Claudette's hands every Friday, cut and shaped her nails, pushed back the cuticles with cotton wool dipped in hazel water and rubbed cold cream into her skin. My father cut our nails with the clippers attached to the end of his watch chain. 'That will stop spuds growing in them,' he'd say and chopped them down to the bone.

'Sufferinjeezus,' spluttered Eva. Crumbs exploded from her mouth, spattered her face and the biscuits and milk on the tray she was carrying. 'Lady Muck will have a fit.'

Eva's voice was pitched an octave above ours. My mother said it was a legacy from her time in the spinning room, having to shout above the noise of the machines. She hadn't lasted long at the mill because she had two left hands and was accident-prone and the damp atmosphere did for her chest. She came three times a week to help with the housework.

Eva pointed at three workmen who had started to demolish the six-foot beech hedge which surrounded Lismore, the big mansion opposite us. The hedge, that had isolated Major and Mrs Dalton from the brand new houses that had sprung up around them, was being flung on the back of a lorry together with the foot-high privets of the 'blow-ins'.

Everybody admired Major Dalton. A perfect gentleman, always

a polite 'Good morning' or 'Good evening' and what a handsome figure he cut in his army uniform with his brown moustache and swagger stick. And Mrs Dalton, the image of Jeannette McDonald? Well, handsome is as handsome does. Wouldn't any woman look rested if all she had to do was paint her nails and rest herself.

Eva flopped down between us as bit by bit, like the Sleeping Beauty's castle, the front and side of the huge Virginia-creepered house was revealed. Eva worked alternate days for Mrs Dalton so the unveiling of Lismore did not have the same impact on her. The Major always gave her a shilling extra at Christmas and a half-crown for the Twelfth party. He told her nobody could scrub a floor better than she and she would make some man a good wife. She dreamed that Mrs Dalton would die and she and the Mayor would get married and live happily ever after in Lismore.

Rumours of the widening of the road had created a brief Dunkirk spirit among the neighbours, though Dunkirk was yet to happen.

'We will be exposed, Mr Ward,' Mrs Dalton complained to my father.

I was impressed that she knew his name. Bridie pointed out that a lorry with the words 'Michael Ward, Slieve Dubh Quarry' written on it was often parked in the drive, until Mrs Campbell objected because it was letting down the tone of the avenue.

'We will have no protection from crowds and straying cattle,' Mrs Dalton crossed slim hands over her bosom. 'We shall be naked without our hedges.'

My father swallowed hard. His Adam's apple wobbled.

'We can't stand in the way of progress,' he said. 'It will be for the best in the long run, you'll see. Safer for the children.'

I suspected that, being childless, this might not be a priority with her.

Mammy said it was hard for Major and Mrs Dalton to be deprived of their privacy. Those jumped-up nobodies who thought they had come up in the world by moving to Rathmore Avenue couldn't understand how the gentry felt. Mammy knew what it was to live in reduced circumstances. Her first married home, a pokey two-up, two-down with outside lavatory in Enfield Terrace was a far cry from the big farm she had been reared on and a modern box wasn't much higher up the social ladder.

For my father, whose family in Mammy's words was 'poor but decent', our double-fronted home with bay windows and garage was his pride and joy. He wanted to call it 'Ard na Gréine', but Mammy said it was a lot of nonsense to give a name to an ordinary house on a road. Others could call their homes 'Sion Mills', 'Ypres' or 'Hilly Fields'. We were Number Six.

If my father was hurt by the neighbours' reaction to the quarry dust that blanketed his car and made him look as if he had been dipped in a bag of dirty flour, he said nothing. You could have set your clock by the weekly blasting. Twelve-thirty every Thursday. First a slight shaking in the ground, a tremor like the start of a small earthquake. Then boom! Mrs Campbell said the blasts made her Royal Doulton and Crown Derby tinkle and jump in the china cabinet. She was terrified that one day she would find them in smithereens. And she was sick of the layer of dust which covered her lawn and furniture in dry weather or if the wind blew from the east.

I must have been about five when my father let me see a blasting at Slieve Dubh. I clutched his hand where we stood about a quarter of a mile from the quarry face above which stretched the jib of the well drill. There was a muffled thump as the plunger set off the high explosive. The earth shuddered. The face bellied out like an overblown balloon as it shattered into a thousand cracks and a stream of rock crashed to the quarry floor.

My father loved working in the earth, whether it was at the quarry or digging our garden. Once, after drilling and blasting a new bench, he found a tunnel that ran down underneath the field behind our house. Here it joined up with another one which went all the way down through the centre of the Earth and came out in Australia. He took Bridie and me into the field to a certain spot which he paced out. Forty paces north of the path in our back garden and twenty paces east. We had to close our eyes. We peeped through ever widening fingers as he bent down and removed a circle of earth; and there was the entrance to the long, narrow tunnel that came out at the bottom of the world.

'Look down,' he said to Bridie. 'Can you see the blue sky and the tops of trees?'

'I can't see anything, only mud and black.'

'That's because you're not looking right. Lie really flat and half close your eyes till you get used to the dark. Now can you see the light?'

'Yes, yes, Daddy. I can see it now.'

'Look right through the sky. Can you see those Australians standing on their heads?'

'Why are they standing on their heads, daddy?'

'Because the Earth is round. That's why. They would fall off if they didn't. Look at the woman in the green hat and the old fellah with the baldy head.'

We saw them all. Sometimes we couldn't see anything. He said it must be raining in Australia and the clouds were dark or else he had made a mistake with the time and it was night down there.

Bridie and I often climbed into the back field and we counted paces just as he did but, without him, we never once found the circle of grass that hid the entrance to Australia.

'You only think you can see Australia,' said Claudette Campbell when I opened my big mouth and started boasting. She went on riding her bicycle in a circle and called out, 'You're all that daft you will believe anything and your daddy's daft as well.'

She went crying to her mother, though her knee hardly bled at all, after I knocked her off her bicycle. But she was wrong. We did see Australia and even now, if I half close my eyes and peer into the dark, I can still see it, even though I know the entrance to the tunnel has been sealed forever.

3

Bridie and I usually walked to ten o'clock Mass with my father. Him in a dark suit, us in best dresses and sun-bonnets or in matching coats and hats which Mammy made on her treadle sewing machine. He walked up the middle aisle to the third bench from the front and ushered us in before him. With his gold cuff links and his watch chain hanging in two golden loops from the pockets of his waistcoat he looked every bit as rich as Doctor McFaul, and he was much taller and more handsome.

On 3 September we went in the lorry. The date sticks in my mind because Mammy, who had come back from eight o'clock Mass, told us the world was on the brink of destruction and that, barring a last-minute miracle, today would be remembered as one of the blackest in history. Rain sheeted against the windows, too fast for the wipers to push it back. I wondered if God was going to send another deluge to punish us even though he had promised never to flood the earth again.

'We live in troubled times,' Father Doyle said. He didn't shout at the latecomers skulking in the back of the church nor did he refuse to go on with Mass till they filled the empty seats at the front. 'The devil has broken loose from his chains. He is a raging lion roaming the earth seeking whom he can devour.'

Water dribbled from coats, shoes, galoshes and umbrellas and trickled down the aisle. I thought of the lion at the eye hospital bursting out of his cage. The devil I saw had the purple gums and yawning mouth of the mangy lion at the zoo in Bellevue. His stench was more overpowering than the reek of sodden clothes, candle wax and chilled sweat, and his roar was louder than the Metro-Goldwyn-Mayer lion in the picture house.

'We are tottering on the edge of a precipice,' said Father Doyle from the pulpit. Nobody coughed or whispered or cleared their throats. 'Let us pray in silence for peace in the world.'

Bridie and I clutched the arms of my father's raincoat and clung like leeches.

A light burned in our kitchen. Mammy was glued to the wireless. A man's voice announced that a state of war existed between His Majesty's government and Germany as from eleven o'clock today, 3 September 1939.

'That was Chamberlain,' said Mammy. 'The Germans marched into Poland on Friday. Warsaw has been bombed and Hitler is trampling over the Poles.'

At his place at the top of the table my father carved a beef roast.

'Millions died in trenches in the last war and this one will be worse. There will be famine and the blood of a whole generation of young men will be spilled.' Mammy piled roast potatoes, beans and carrots on our plates. Blood swirled out of the beef and marbled the gravy.

Mrs Dalton's plans to have a high fence constructed round Lismore had to be shelved for the duration. Once again, without so much as by your leave, the gates and railings of Rathbeg Avenue were ripped up, cast on the same lorry that had carried off the hedges and were never seen again. My father's quarry was never busier, supplying materials for barricades to stop German tanks from mowing down the shops in Main Street and Castle Street; building air-raid shelters at every school and government building. At first nervous eyes scanned the skies for the *Luftwaffe* when practice air-raid warnings and the all-clear disturbed the peace of Carrig. Soon their wailings became as commonplace as the pealing of the Angelus bell at midday and six o'clock or the banging of Orange drums every Saturday night

Major Dalton went off with his regiment to fight Hitler. Nothing much seemed to change in his wife's life. Young officers as handsome and dashing as the major with moustaches and swagger sticks came and went in staff cars. At all hours. My mother and Mrs Campbell tut-tutted and pursed their lips over the back fence.

'Isn't it disgraceful and the poor Major risking life and limb fighting for his country.'

'Take it from me, Mrs Campbell, it was a bad day for us when they took that hedge down.'

They agreed that the English had different moral standards though the only other native of England we knew was Mrs Bradshaw. She was a neighbour from our previous house in Enfield Terrace. A tiny woman, she had been a chambermaid at Buckingham Palace before her marriage. In her purple cape, black sateen dress, diamond earrings and buttoned boots she was my idea of royalty. She held court in our sitting room – kitchens were for cooks and scullery maids – tea cup in hand, little finger extended at the polite angle. Her sole topic of conversation was the Royal Family. She had suffered with her friend, Queen Mary, at the time of the Abdication.

'David was not level-headed like his brother Bertie. He was always a foolish boy but so attractive and a gentleman to his fingertips. That's why he allowed himself to be taken in by that divorced hussy from America. Thought she would be Queen of England! Queen Wallis! I ask you. Well, Queen Mary soon put a stop to that, I'm glad to say. Queen of England indeed! Over my dead body!

Get along, Mrs Simpson, get along.
You thought you were the Queen of England
You were wrong.

She stamped her foot as she chanted and went on to tell us about a certain princess.

'A dirty, lazy beggar! Wouldn't even wipe her own BTM. Can you imagine, girls, she had a special maid to wipe her BTM!'

As we were not encouraged to mention or even think about that part of our bodies, we frowned our vigorous disapproval.

It was Mrs Bradshaw's idea to have us vaccinated on the leg, not on the arm. 'You won't see a vaccination mark on the arms of any of the debutantes when they are presented at court,' she told us and we wouldn't give her the satisfaction of asking what debutantes were. We had learned at school that the feast day of the Circumcision on 1 January commemorated the day when Jesus was taken to the temple to be cut on the arm. In summer, mill girls wore only sleeveless braskins to work and I assumed the grainy imprints tattooed on their upper arms showed where they had been circumcised.

Apart from Mrs Bradshaw's official visits we were allowed into the sitting room only to drink tea with Mammy on holiday afternoons or if we had guests on Sunday evenings. The pink velvet curtains were closed tight when the sun shone to stop the speckled grey carpet fading or the top of the piecrust table blistering. The centre of the table was inlaid with diamond-shaped pieces of lighter wood. Four legs curved out from under the mahogany top, ballet dancer legs that held a baby table somewhere between their calves and ankles. The baby was a replica of its mother, with inlaid centre and fluted like her, its sheen protected from sunburn and wrinkles and from the abuse of Sister Augustine's keys.

Sister Augustine put her keys on the table at the start of our music lessons. Because some of her fingers were dead she had to chase the keys across the surface and her nails and the metal made tiny scratches on the wood. Mammy could never fathom where the marks came from. Not all of Sr's fingers were dead and not always the same ones. I would have liked to touch them, just once, to see what a corpse felt like but nobody was allowed to touch nuns or watch them eat. Bridie carried in a tray with cake and ham sandwiches for Sister Augustine during my lesson. She waited till Bridie left and moved her chair back out of my one-eyed line of vision. I stared at her reflection in the black wood of the piano. A blurred echo, stuffing the sharp oval of her coif, drinking tea like anyone else. I wasn't clever enough to play without looking at the music and hit white notes instead of black ones. Sister squeaked and spat wet crumbs of cake over my back. She lived in a home for elderly nuns, the rest of whom were bedridden or only able to totter round the grounds. One day Mammy had seen her studying the chocolates on the sweet counter in Woolworths and bought her a half-pound bar of fruit and nut, mixed fruit drops and mints for her cough. She was so cold and tired that Mammy took her home, gave her beef tea and bacon and eggs and we turned our backs while she ate. Sister Augustine came every weekday at half past three to be fed and warmed and Mammy bought her combinations like my father's to keep her extremities warm. Nuns were forbidden to set foot in a lay person's house, even their family home, so she pretended to the mother superior she was going to church to pray for a few hours. She told us her mother had persuaded her to become a nun because she said married life was hell on Earth. Like being handcuffed to the devil.

To show her gratitude to Mammy, Sister Augustine taught

Bridie and me to play the piano every day after school. We were both tone-deaf. Sister Augustine emitted thin nun's screams at what we did to the Minuet in G and the 'Blue Danube'. She taught us 'I dreamt I dwelled in Marble Halls' and 'Danny Boy' which Mammy insisted we perform for visitors on Sunday nights. Later on, we entertained them with duets. Bridie always played faster than me so we never finished together.

To celebrate the arrival of troops to Carrig, Eva announced that she was going to give up her metal curlers and have a permanent wave. Curlers cut into her head and stopped her from sleeping and she needed to look her best at all times. Day and night.

She came to our house straight from the hairdresser's though it was Saturday and her day off.

'They were talking and laughing and not taking any notice of us,' she sobbed. 'They left the stuff on too long and they didn't switch the thing off in time.'

Mammy helped to undo her headscarf. There were bald patches on her head and her hair looked like chewed elastic bands.

'The barefaced cheek of that pack. I'll sort them out.' Mammy threw her apron over the back of a chair and put on her coat. 'Sit yourself down by the fire, Eva. Bridie will get you a cup of tea and a bit of fruitcake.'

She stormed into 'Marlene Bell, Hair Stylist', leaving the door wide open behind her.

'Eva Patterson is as valuable a customer as anybody else so don't you think you can get away with treating her like dirt.' Mammy zinged the bell on the counter and held out her hand. 'You can hand over the money you stole from her.'

The only sound in the salon was the wind blowing in from the street and water gurgling out of a wash-hand basin. Marlene's jaw dropped open. 'Consider yourself lucky, she's not claiming compensation.' Mammy added before Marlene could get a word out, 'Not yet.'

She counted the money. 'The next perm Eva has will be free, gratis and for nothing and it will be done under my supervision,' was her parting shot to Marlene, her assistant and two women who had stuck their heads out from under the driers to hear what was going on.

Back home, Bridie had hidden the remains of Eva's hair under a turban. Mammy showed her how to pull bits out and stretch a sausage curl over the forehead like the women in the munitions factory.

'There's the money Marlene Bell owed you. Hide it where your father won't be able to get his hands on it,' Mammy said to Eva after assuring her that her hair would soon grow. Thicker and stronger. She and Eva picked over ends of material at the half-price stall at the market and settled on four yards of slightly flawed, blue-and-white flowered material to make a dress fit for the dances at the barracks. A dress to please Gordon, Eva's soldier from Birmingham.

Eva stood barefoot on a mat on the kitchen floor. She inched round while Mammy pinned the hem of her dress. It had revers and puffed sleeves and pins in the bodice where the buttons would go.

'You be careful, Eva. Don't let your young man take liberties with you.' Mammy spoke through a row of pins sticking out between her lips. She knotted a tape measure round Eva's thick waist and swayed back on her heels. 'Soldiers are here today and gone tomorrow and many of them are married men with families back in England.'

I had heard Mammy confide over the fence to Mrs Campbell that she worried about what might happen to a girl like poor Eva going out with any Tom, Dick or Harry.

'Have a titter of wit, Mrs Ward.' Eva patted Mammy's head. 'Gordon's not married. He would have told us. Him and me's getting married on his next leave.'

'Stand up straight and turn slowly. Bridie, bring the bathroom mirror for Eva to see the length.'

'Could I not have it a wee bit shorter?'

'It's quite short enough. Decent girls keep their knees covered. You don't want to look like those brazen heelers I see flinging themselves at the soldiers.'

Eva sashayed over the green and cream tiles. A smile lit up her face. It was a pity about her skelly and scalped head.

'You look gorgeous, Eva,' said Bridie. 'Like Carmen Miranda.'

'You will be the belle of the ball. Now take it off and be careful of the pins.' Mammy eased the dress over Eva's shoulders. She put a blanket and a sheet that were triangled with scorch marks on the table and pressed the hem.

Waterloo Bridge wasn't the best introduction Mammy could have had to the cinema in the company of her children. Eva had already seen it with her soldier.

'It's so beautiful, so sad. I cried my eyes out,' she told me and Bridie. 'I didn't see much of it though. Being with Gordon an' all, you know.'

An outing to the picture house was arranged. The Saturday afternoon matinée. To sustain us during the performance Mammy packed a basket – a cake-tin filled with butterfly buns and shortbread, home-made treacle toffee, eight apples, a bottle of lemonade and four mugs. I think she had been under the impression that the film was about Napoleon whom she admired because he was proof that even a poor man could become emperor of France. When Robert Taylor started kissing Vivien Leigh, she hauled off my glasses and proceeded to polish them on the sleeve of her cardigan. All I saw with my lazy eye was two blurred heads, close together.

'Don't you dare try to take your eye patch off,' Mammy snatched my hand from my face. During the kiss which lasted through a whole verse of 'Auld Lang Syne' played at a snail's pace, she rustled the grease proof paper in the cake tin, offered a choice of shortbread or butterfly buns and cracked the toffee on the arm of her seat.

Next time the lovers embraced she reached across, prodded Eva and asked in a voice that could be heard all over the stalls, 'Is there much more of this nonsense?'

Eva's mouth hung open, an angelic smile covered her face. The usherette shone her torch on Mammy and told her to keep quiet or she would have to leave.

'We shouldn't have let her come with us,' I muttered to Bridie's shoulders that were shrugged away from me and Mammy.

There was no kissing for a long time and Mammy settled down. We had two butterfly buns each, an apple and a drink of lemonade. I held the mugs while Mammy filled them. Vivien Leigh lost her job as principal dancer with a ballet company because she had missed a performance to say goodbye to Robert. She and her friend were starving. Through tears we saw her standing on Waterloo Bridge gazing sadly into the river. Then off she went with a man. Mammy leaped to her feet.

'This is filth. Disgusting,' she shouted, grabbed Bridie and me and shoved us into the aisle. 'Eva, we're leaving. Are you coming or are you not?'

Eva didn't move. She was up there on the bridge waiting for Robert Taylor while Vivien Leigh walked off with a man she didn't know from Adam. People all round shouted for the usherette to throw us out.

'Did you not enjoy the show, Mrs Ward?' the commissionaire asked as Mammy flounced out of the cinema.

'No I did not and we won't be back.

Bridie and I refused to walk beside her. We dawdled yards behind her, scuffing our shoes on the kerb and swore we would never allow her to disgrace us in public again.

Eva was supposed to iron only sheets and pillowcases. Never shirts or blouses.

'Keep testing the iron, Eva,' Mammy called to her. 'Make sure it doesn't get too hot.'

I was standing on a newspaper on a chair. Mammy had let down the hem of Bridie's cast-off First Communion frock and was pinning a frill round the bottom when Eva screamed and pointed at twin holes in Mammy's pink satin slip and at tar bubbling on the iron. Mammy had never had satin before. Only Celanese that drooped and laddered like lisle stockings. We had never seen Mammy wear the slip. Low-cut with lace inset and narrow straps, it was fit for a film star. I had imagined her wearing it at a ball, her hair falling down to her waist and my father in his best suit with his watch-chain gleaming over his waistcoat. It would never happen. Father Doyle said English dancing was sinful.

'Let that be a lesson to all of you. Always test first on a corner of the material.' She turned to Eva. 'Stop that noise. It's not the end of the world. What need did I have for such grandeur? Now hurry and clear this lot away. It's Mrs Bradshaw's day. She will be here any minute.'

Mrs Bradshaw was annoyed at being received in the kitchen. Before she sat down beside the white range she flicked a few threads of cotton from the armchair.

'I'm sorry,' Mammy said to her. 'The Holy Week processions

are next week. The girls will be at the front strewing flowers and I have to make sure they look their best.'

'For her wedding to Bertie – King George, girls, when he was Duke of York – Elizabeth Bowes Lyon wore a dress of ivory silk crêpe embroidered with seed pearls.' Mrs Bradshaw looked straight through Bridie, whose turn it was to stand on the chair. Mammy pinned sleeves into her new white dress and arranged her First Communion veil on her head. It was made of stiffened organdie and stood out from her head.

'She had two trains, one fastened to her hips, the other floating from the shoulders.' Mrs Bradshaw's thin hands described the flow of the trains. 'She was only a commoner from Scotland but King George was glad to find anybody to take Bertie off his hands.' Mrs Bradshaw paused to sip her tea. She leaned forward. In hushed tones, as if she was letting us into a state secret, she added, 'His stutter, you know. Poor Bertie, I used to feel so sorry for him. He always stammered worse when the king was around.'

Sister Aquinas, the headmistress, chose the girls who were to strew at the processions on Holy Thursday and Good Friday.

'Mary Rooney, Sarah Gallagher, Bridie Ward, Eileen McKillop, Maureen Crossey, Mary Mulholland.'

Six girls went to front of the class. I waited for her to call 'Mary Ann Ward'. To leave my desk and stand where I had stood last year.

'It is a great honour to be chosen to strew before our Divine Lord. Tell your parents I expect you to look worthy of that honour. Baskets filled to the brim with fresh flowers, white ribbons and dresses we can all be proud of.'

Tears scalded my eyes. Splashed on my hands. Sister paired the strewers. Eileen McKillop was Bridie's partner.

'Choose a flower. Place it against your lips. Let it fall.' Sister Aquinas backed across the front of the class, a crow picking an imaginary flower from an imaginary basket, bending the beak of her coif over it, opening her fingers. Each time she bent, the cane that was hooked round her wrist trailed with her skirts on the floor. The chosen six followed Sister round the classroom, picking, kissing, letting go. Eileen McKillop walked in my place. Her black ringlets tumbled round her face when she bowed.

Sister Pius whispered to Sister Aquinas who pointed at me.

'I'm surprised at you, Mary Ann. A big girl crying like a baby. You can't expect to be a strewer every year.' Everyone in the classroom stared at me. Sister Aquinas towered over my desk breathing camphorated fumes. 'We can't have you tripping like last year. Remember how Father and the Blessed Sacrament had to wait while you gathered your flowers off the aisle.'

'I won't trip, Sister. I can see really well now. I don't need to wear an eyepatch. Or glasses. Honest, Sister.'

'You can serve our Divine Lord just as well by walking behind Him and singing. God has given you quite a nice little voice.' She paraded to the door and called, 'Bridie, ask your mammy if Eileen may borrow your other strewing basket.'

I didn't want to serve God. I wanted to strew flowers my father grew specially each year for Easter. Only the best for our baskets. Daffodils with perfect trumpets. White narcissi with orange hearts. Tulips he pampered and coaxed to make them flower in time and primroses that he wove round the handle. I prayed that Eileen McKillop would break her leg. That her ringlets would frizzle and drop out the way Eva's hair had.

'*Vexilla regis prodeunt,*' bellowed Father Doyle from under a silken canopy which was held up on poles by four men from the St Vincent de Paul Society. An altar boy walked in front of him swinging the thurible from which poured a smokescreen of incense.

I refused to sing but I mouthed the words in case Sister was looking. My eyes were riveted on the strewers walking backwards immediately in front of the Blessed Sacrament. On Eileen McKillop carrying my basket.

'*Fulget crucis mysterium*,' sang the choir and the congregation. Those up near the altar stopped singing. Gasps of fear raced through the front of the church. Parents covered their mouths in fright. Bridie's veil and hair were alight. Flames licked around her head, like when the Holy Ghost came down in tongues of fire and sat on the heads of the apostles. Then I saw Bridie's terrified face, the shrivelling mess of her veil, her knuckles clenched on the handle of the strewing basket. She had brushed against a stand of lighted candles. Father Doyle with the Blessed Sacrament stopped in his tracks.

The stink of burning hair mixed with the smell of incense, flowers and soap scoured children. Swift as lightning, Sister Aquinas ripped the blazing veil from Bridie's head, quenched her hair with the sleeves of her habit and covered her head with a man's handkerchief. Her nod ordered Bridie not to hold up the procession any longer. Nobody disobeyed Sister Aquinas. Bridie raised a narcissus to her lips and let it fall.

'Eat your food, Mary Ann, and stop playing with it,' scolded my father. 'You don't want to be sick and miss trundling the eggs on Easter Sunday.'

With the back of a spoon he moulded my champ into a bird's nest and dropped a lump of butter into it. We always had champ on Good Friday.

'Stop dreaming. Look at Bridie's nice clean plate.'

Bridie smirked at my father. Her eyebrow and eyelashes were singed. Her beautiful ringlets had been cut to match up with the side of her head where the hair had been burned.

I dipped a forkful of champ into the well of melted butter. It stuck in my throat. I had prayed that something would happen to keep Eileen McKillop out of the procession and the devil had answered my prayers.

4

The summer after Belfast was bombed Mammy took me by bus to her family's place in Moynagh. Bridie was to stay at my father's home in Donegal and I was to be dumped with Mammy's sisters and brother. To escape the blitz, we were told. If it weren't for lorryloads of soldiers moving through Carrig, the blackout and the newsreels at the picture house you wouldn't have known there was a war on.

'Why can't I go to Donegal too?'

'You'll do what you're told.' Mammy pushed me into the inside seat of the near-empty bus. 'Your Aunt Annie isn't fit to look after two of you. It will do you good to stand on your own two feet for once and not in Bridie's shadow. Children in England and Belfast have been sent to live with total strangers. You should be thankful to have family in the country to take you in.'

I sulked most of the way to Moynagh and refused the bull's-eyes she tried to bribe me with. The bus bumped along a narrow road edged with hawthorn hedges. It stopped to pick up women laden with bags and baskets. Women with freckle-faced children who smelled of grass and turf fires. Out-of-breath women wearing worn-out coats over trailing dresses and old-fashioned lace-up shoes and lisle stockings like Mammy's. Their hair, same as hers, was plaited and pinned into a bun at the nape of the neck and their ruddy faces had never seen cold cream, let alone lipstick or powder.

I closed my ears to the instructions Mammy was giving me and looked out at cattle grazing in rushy fields and the dreary sameness of the straggly towns we passed through. My father's half-crown sweated in the palm of my hand. He would take Bridie out every day with Mickey the Post to deliver letters round the islands. Everyone would pet Bridie, say what a grand girl she was and how like her granny, Bridget Rua, she looked with her fine head of red hair. They would ask had I started to grow yet and go on admiring Bridie.

'Daddy never goes to Moynagh,' I muttered.

'That's not true.' Mammy shifted round to look me in the eye. 'He has never missed a funeral, more out of respect for the dead, I admit, than out of love for any of them. Your daddy got a very bad reception when I first brought him to Moynagh after we were married. My parents were angry with me too for not giving them the chance to vet him beforehand.'

She opened the bag of bull's-eyes. I took three, but she didn't notice, she was so pleased I had stopped sulking.

'When my father heard your daddy was reared on a couple of acres he threw back his head and scoffed, "My daughter grew up on two hundred acres of the best arable land in Ireland, not rocks and heather like your lot in Donegal".'

'Were you not furious with him, Mammy?'

'I knew what to expect. My family suffered from delusions of grandeur. They thought they were a cut above buttermilk because they had clergy on both sides of the family and a marble tombstone in the graveyard. Anyhow, your daddy would make two of any of them.' She lowered her voice when the woman in front of us turned sideways to listen.

'It had poured for weeks before his first visit to Moynagh. The priest had granted a dispensation to allow the hay to be saved on Sunday. Your Uncle Joseph guided the horses and the mowing machine round and round the fields till all the crop was cut. Then your daddy and the servant men turned the drying hay and raked and stacked it. They worked till the sun turned their faces and necks the colour of raw meat and every inch of their bodies itched from hayseed and dust. Joseph supervised from the shade of a tree.'

When Mammy got going she talked in chapters. She answered the question I was going to ask.

'Joseph was to be ordained the following year. He couldn't be expected to get his hands scarred by thorns and thistles or blistered from holding a rake or a pike. When a priest elevates the Host at Mass or gives absolution, you can take it from me his hands aren't like a labourer's. One of the men said to me as I doled out their supper when the last of the haymaking was done that they would never have managed without your daddy. That he shifted more than two men.'

"Ellen was content to pick a quarry digger for a husband. He fulfils the function of his state in life which is the most we can expect from him," was Joseph's comment and he cracked his fingers at me and pointed to his empty cup.'

I could see Mammy pour the tea, add milk and sugar, stir it and place it before him, the handle facing into the angle of his thumb and forefinger.

'Why do you and Agnes look after Joseph as if he was a cripple?' I asked when she paused for breath.

'It's what he expects. It's the way my mother reared us.'

'And did Daddy just sit there and say nothing?'

'Oh no! Your daddy's not a man to let anyone walk over him. He told Joseph that, for all his education, he was nothing but an ignoramus and an ungrateful pup and he would not spend another night under the roof with him as long as he lived.'

Mammy's eldest sister Agnes and little Maisie were waiting with the pony and trap when we got off the bus. Mammy climbed up beside Agnes and I was put in the back with Maisie. She was two years older than Mammy but was not much taller than me. She blethered away and kept prodding me and laughing whenever we passed anyone on the road. I paid no attention to her for I couldn't understand her way of talking and I wanted to hear what Mammy and Agnes were whispering about. Agnes stopped the horse while Maisie jumped out and opened a rusty gate. We turned into a lane rutted with potholes and overhung by dripping trees. Mammy said that the outbuildings showed what a prosperous farm it had once been. One of the doors hung off the barn. Moss greened what was left of the roof of the outhouse next to it and purple flowers and high grass grew among wooden stalls.

'We had six horses stabled there when I was young, Mary Ann, and your great-grandfather rode to hounds with the gentry.'

I wouldn't give Mammy the satisfaction of looking. A duck and a handful of ducklings sailed through the scummy water of the pond in front of the house and waddled out with muddy bellies. It was less than two hours since we had left Carrig but we might have travelled back to the last century.

A green door at the far end of the low whitewashed house opened into what had once been quarters for a servant man and his family. Beside the open fire in the kitchen were a bellows wheel and a metal crane where pots could be hung. Stairs behind a brown door led up to the loft where the family had slept. Cobwebs and twenty-year-old dust curtained that stairway and it reeked of dead birds and mouse droppings. Mammy had slapped us last summer for opening the brown door and had made us swear on our prayer books never to go up there again.

I followed Mammy through the porch leading into a whitewashed passage that ran along the front of the house. It smelled of mildew and chicken feed. I was sick with loneliness for Bridie, for my father and Eva and our lovely home in Rathbeg Avenue.

Joseph sat by the range reading a newspaper. A black range with taps on both sides of the grate and racks for plates or for airing clothes above it. It had been the talk of the country when my great-grandfather had it brought up from Dublin to impress Miss Fisher, his English wife. (She was never called anything but Miss Fisher.) When the range was first installed neighbours had called daily with a few eggs or a loaf of caraway bread to inspect it and to size up the grand foreign lady who was mistress of Moynagh. Water no longer flowed from the taps because the boilers, like the oven, were cracked and black with soot and debris.

You could tell Joseph, Mammy and Agnes were related. They were short and had the same dark hair and eyes and the high cheekbones that Mammy said were a sign of good breeding. So were their small ears and their high insteps.

'You remember Mary Ann,' she pulled me forward. Had I been a calf for sale at the market he would have shown more interest. 'She's fond of reading, Joseph. Maybe you would let her have a look at your books while she's here.'

Last time Bridie and I were in Moynagh, we went into his bedroom every morning with Agnes while she made his bed, brushed the floor and emptied the chamber pot and shaving-water down the drain outside. Two of the whitewashed walls were lined with the books he had needed in Maynooth. Brown and green and black books with gold writing on the spines. Books about theology and canon law. Poetry and story books. Books written in Latin and Greek. He must have known we opened some of them, for he gave strict instructions that Agnes was to do the cleaning on her own.

'Keep her away from my room,' he said to Mammy. 'Women are better off without reading. It puts notions in their heads.'

Before we left Carrig Mammy had told me to keep out of Joseph's way. He was a bit strange but it wasn't his fault. He had been on the run from the Black and Tans when he was young. They had hounded him like an animal whenever he came back from the seminary. And I had to understand that a spoiled priest was like a fish out of water. A man of his education had nothing in common with the gombeens who gossiped and played pitch-and-toss at the cross roads every evening and it wasn't his fault that he had no interest in farming. She said he was a genius who could have been a doctor or a lawyer but their mother had insisted he become a priest. He left Maynooth shortly before he was to be ordained. His mother never forgave him and refused to recover from the disgrace.

When Joseph went to drive the cows into the byre for milking it was as if the low ceiling of the kitchen had been hoisted up a couple of feet. I sat on the settle-bed. It reminded me of one of the horseboxes in Mr Rossi's ice cream parlour. The same dark wood, the bolt-upright back and it was just as uncomfortable. I poked my fingers through the air holes and wondered how Agnes had managed to sleep in there when she was young with the lid closed as if she was in her coffin. Mammy unpacked the presents she had brought. Wraparound aprons, black with purple and green patterns, for her sisters, a green cardigan for Agnes and a Fair-Isle one she had knitted for Maisie. Agnes said it was like Christmas and Mammy shouldn't have gone to all that expense but Mammy believed in paying her way and never arrived at anybody's house with one arm as long as the other. She and Agnes pushed Maisie's arms into the sleeves of her cardigan, worried was it too tight across the back, would she dirty it too quickly and maybe a dark colour would have been better; and they turned up cuffs because Mammy had made the sleeves long in case the cardigan shrank in the wash. Maisie was only to wear it to Mass and change into an old one when she came home. She grinned at herself in the small mirror on the windowsill, turned round to have a look at her back, patted her hair and stroked the soft wool. She hugged her arms in front of her chest when Mammy told her to take it off and removed it only when Mammy promised her a slice of the fruit cake she had brought. Four pairs of black socks and a woollen scarf were put on the chair beside Joseph's bed. Agnes said he would be pleased though he wouldn't let on and Mammy insisted that she had not brought them for thanks.

Then Mammy cross-examined Agnes while she made the tea. So the Kernaghans had finally found somebody to take poor Mary off their hands. Was he a decent sort of fellow at least and how much of a fortune had he asked for? And how much was the offering at Dan O'Reilly's funeral, God rest his soul? Was Agnes making a decent living from the milk, butter and eggs? Maisie sat beside me on the settle watching her sisters, laughing, nodding her head and joining in with them. I was asked to get four mugs, four plates and saucers from the dresser.

'That dresser was filled with the loveliest willow pattern anybody ever clapped eyes on, till the Tans burst in and smashed everything they could lay their hands on. Bad luck to them.' Mammy told me that every time we went to Moynagh.

'All that's dead and buried, thank God,' said Agnes. 'You don't want to fill the child's head with those old stories.'

Mammy talked about the Black and Tans and the famines of '47 and '48 as if they had happened yesterday. Agnes clasped a farl of wheaten bread against her floury chest. She cut it into thick slices and made the tea.

'You don't know how lucky you are to have your own butter. All we have is two ounces a week. Can you imagine that?' Mammy plastered a week's ration of butter on two slices. 'Butter will fatten you up, Mary Ann. Your daddy won't know you when you come back.'

'Read the cups, Ellen,' said Agnes when we finished eating. 'See if there's a big farmer in there for Maisie and me.'

Mammy shook the cup three times and peered at the tea leaves. I couldn't bear to hear whatever yarn she would spin to her sisters and I thought she should have more sense than to build up hopes in them. I left the kitchen, driven out by their shrieks and laughter, and their three heads ringed round Agnes's cup.

I stood at the gate of the broad meadow at the top of a lane going down to the bog. Since my grandfather's death, not a cow or even a goat had been allowed to graze there. If a flock of goslings or baby turkeys wandered in, Agnes or Mammy had to force themselves to shoo them back to the yard. They were afraid of the *buachalán buí* that had been growing wild in the broad meadow since the accident. They ripped them out of the other fields and set fire to them. I loved the coaxing faces on their yellow flowers and their heavy smell. According to Mammy, what happened to her father was no accident. It was cold-blooded murder.

She and Agnes told the story of their father's death so often I could recite it by heart. He was a bad-tempered man and fond of a drink. Every spring he swore the foulest oaths as his plough steered a wide arc round the fairy thorn that grew in the middle of the broad meadow. In summer he cursed the dense shadows it cast.

'That bloody tree gobbles up any fertiliser I spray on the crop. It's coming down. By God it is,' he often threatened, 'and I'll have a straight run from one end of the field to the other.'

My grandmother begged him not to tempt the wrath of the fairies. She might as well have talked to the tree itself. Besides, he hadn't spoken a word to her for years. One morning she was in the kitchen making bread. She had cut the dough into farls and was bending over the range to put them on the griddle. She saw her husband with an axe in his hand as plain as if she was at his side beyond in the broad meadow. He had chopped a great wedge out of the trunk of the fairy thorn. He had only to touch it for the whole tree to topple. He looked up as if somebody had called him with a look of terror on his face that was to haunt my grandmother till the end of her days. Whatever he saw, the axe dropped from his hand and he stumbled like a drunkard into the path of the tree. She left her bread to burn and raced so fast to him you would have thought every demon in hell was after her. All she saw as she ran was the empty space on the skyline where the tree had been. He was on his back in the middle of the field. The leaves and branches of the fairy thorn covered his body like a shroud.

It was many years later that Mammy told me her father had been fortifying himself all morning with whiskey and that an empty bottle was found under his body.

The day before she was due to go back to Carrig without me I made up my mind to wade through the grasses and weeds of the broad meadow, to where the dead thorn tree lay. I wanted to provoke Mammy. To frighten her and make her slap me so hard she would feel sorry and take me back home with her. Home to our white-tiled bathroom and lavatory and away from the stinking shack at the bottom of the orchard where there was a wooden bench with three holes cut out of it. Away from squares of newspaper for wiping your backside and from bluebottles gorging themselves on fresh Number Two.

A haze of thistledown and dandelion clocks floated over the meadow and turned the blobs of *buachalán* to gold. Their drowsy scent floated around me. My heart pounded in my throat and I was afraid my knees would buckle under me. I knew that if the *buachalán* sent me to sleep the fairies would steal my soul and leave one of their own children in my place. I turned to run back but I tripped and fell. Down, down through a sea of blind greenness. I staggered up and stumbled towards the verge of the broad meadow. Tow grass knotted round my feet, tripping my every step. Fairy hands were grabbing me, pulling me down into their home in the Beyond. I screamed but the grasses swallowed the sound.

Mammy grabbed the shoulder of my pinafore and a fist full of my hair and dragged me back to the house.

'How many times do you have to be told to stay away from there?' She shook me by the ear. She slapped my legs till the track of her hands stood out in red and white weals. 'Just look at the cut of you.' My pinafore was green with grass stains; thistledown and hayseed tangled my hair.

'Don't you think enough harm has come to this family?' Then she held me so tight that her huge stomach muffled my sobs and my eyes and nose dried on her apron.

I never saw any fairies in the flesh but they were all around. Agnes had often pointed out their three-toed footprints on the solid skin of milk left to sour in crocks in the dairy and showed me the shapes their greedy hands hollowed out of clotted cream. Not pretty creatures with gossamer wings and magic wands that flitted through my storybooks granting wishes and bestowing gifts. These were evil spirits that stole milk and butter from the dairy, that shot darts into cows in calf so they could lay claim to the newborn calves, that coveted and stole human children.

Mammy poured a noggin of water from Saint Kieran's well down my throat. It was supposed to ward off the '*drochshúil*' as well as being a cure for bad health which was what they called consumption in that part of the world.

'And what do you think happened to poor Maisie?' Mammy demanded. Maisie was calling 'Chuckky, chuckky' as she scattered grain to the hens scraping round the door. She shouted something to Mammy. All I could make out was 'Ag, Ag, Ag.'

'You can go and wait for Agnes at the gate but don't open it till she comes,' Mammy told her.

She trundled down the lane to swing on a bar of the gate, a child with a crumpled face in a forty-two-year-old body.

'The summer Maisie was born was the wettest in living memory and my mother had to work with the men in the field whenever the rain stopped to save what little of the harvest they could. In her exhaustion she must have left Maisie under a *buachalán* and the fairies stole her and left that poor creature in her place.'

It was the first time I had heard an explanation for what was the matter with Maisie though I knew that being wrong in the head was as much of a slur on a family as consumption.

'Is that what happened to Eva?'

'No, Eva would have been all right if she had had half a chance in life. Probably her mother or whoever was minding her put too much laudanum in her bottle to keep her quiet when she was a baby. It was a common practice for women who had to work in the mill or in the field. That's why you get a lot of people of Eva's age and older who are a wee bit touched.'

It broke my heart to think about her. Eva, Bridie and me polishing the bedroom floors, skating round the beds at top speed with bits of blanket tied round our feet. Eva waltzing up and down the hall with the sweeping brush, singing 'Daisy, Daisy, give me your answer do.' How she refused to believe I had German measles because I wasn't covered in swastikas the way Lord Snooty in the comics had been.

'Tell Eva I'll write to her and I'll see her soon.'

'Now you know there's no point in writing. Sure, poor Eva never learned how to read or write.'

5

'You are to behave yourself and do what Agnes tells you.' Mammy heaved herself, her bag and a basket of butter and eggs into the Belfast bus. 'You will be sent for when the time comes and please God there will be a surprise waiting for you.'

I lay in the big bed I had shared with her in what had been my grandparents' room. A crucifix with a china Christ guarded my head. Fat drops of blood glistened on the crown of thorns, dripped from hands, feet and side. Above the fireplace hung a photograph of all the family except Sister Mary Francis who hadn't yet been born. Agnes, Mammy and Maisie stood behind their grim-faced parents. White pinafores covered their dark dresses. My grandfather's hand rested on Joseph, sitting cross-legged in front of him. My grandmother held a baby on her lap. Thomas, who died when he was small. We weren't allowed to mention his name.

I prayed for Mammy's 'special intention' and that Bridie would have a rotten time in Donegal; and I tried to sleep. But in the corners of the room and in the attics, the ghosts of the house waited for the last glimmer of day to be swallowed up in darkness before doing their rounds. Spirits so ancient nobody could put a name on them. My grandfather who was said to have thrown off the weight of the fairy thorn and come tapping on the windows in search of a drink. Miss Fisher whom Mammy had often seen rise from the bed where I lay, wander up and down the passage and pass through closed doors into every room of the house. Not the beautiful young woman in a low-cut dress of blue velvet whose auburn hair glowed against her pale skin in the portrait above the fireplace in the parlour but a demented figure in a long nightdress. Mammy surmised she was looking for the baby girl who had died three days before she herself did. Poor Miss Fisher, I would have thought she had seen more than enough of Moynagh in the few years she spent there without coming back from the dead.

Mammy had inherited the gift of second sight, passed on to her from her mother. Bridie and I prayed it would skip a generation. Sometimes as she doled out porridge at breakfast she would say, 'I heard the banshee crying last night. There will be a death in the family.' Or, as she cracked eggs into bacon fat she would remark – matter of fact, as if she was asking would we like another slice of fried bread or a sausage – that she had smelled 'the clay' or that she had dreamed of rats. It was a sure sign of imminent death and she even named the next corpse. She was always right but, in fairness, we did have a lot of elderly relatives. When her predictions came true my father said it was pure coincidence and what she heard was a dog howling or a couple of cats fighting on the roofs.

From the loft above me where Mammy and Sister Mary Francis used to sleep, feet scuffled and pattered between the floorboards. Creatures rustled and whispered in the chimney, waited to slither through cracks in the ceiling and walls, to crawl out of coats hanging on a nail behind the door. The bedclothes fluttered, shivered. Ripples so slight they were barely visible. Miss Fisher's ice-cold ghost sliding out from beside me to start her wandering? A dull thud. A load of soot thumped down the chimney. It blackened the fireplace and the threadbare carpet. The stench clogged my lungs. I jumped out of bed and raced to the kitchen.

'You have far too much imagination. It was only birds nesting in the chimney that dislodged the soot.' Agnes washed my feet in a tin basin. She said to sit opposite Maisie while she blew the dying fire. Sparks flew and flames, orange and vermilion, curled round the sods of turf she threw into the grate. She heated milk in a saucepan, cut three slices of bread and made bowls of pinady for me and Maisie.

'You had best sleep with me and Maisie. You're far too small to be down there by yourself.' We said the Rosary, a much shorter version than Mammy's, and Agnes stuck a candle into a blue candleholder. Maisie took a chipped enamel chamber pot from behind a curtain at the bottom of the settle bed and the three of us proceeded to the maroon-coloured door in the passage. Thatch fringed a low window that barely let the remains of the day pass through. Apart from one chair, the only furniture was a cupboard which stood at the highest point of the room. A Saint Brigid's cross, made by Maisie for the feast day in February, yellowed on the wall beside the bed. My two aunts undressed in the gloaming; wraithlike, almost girlish figures releasing aprons, pulling dresses over their heads, lowering white shifts over their shoulders. Shifts that smelled of scorched bread and hawthorn hedges and of women who hoped for nothing more than a dry day for the washing tomorrow. Agnes removed her hairpins. Dark waves fell halfway down her back, the streaks of white clouded by the near darkness. I lay close to her, listening to Maisie's unfathomable whisperings and her sister's reply.

'It will be all right. I won't let you fall out. Go to sleep, there's a good girl. We mustn't waken the child.'

The three of us turned together. Ghosts tapped without let up at the uncurtained window. It didn't matter. Agnes laid her arm across me. I snuggled into her and fell asleep.

Joseph went to the crossroads every morning for the *Irish Independent*. One day he brought back an English paper to see what lies the people in England were being told. He asked me to read it to him.

'Skulking German warships battered. In their biggest ever daylight raid the RAF shot down thirty Nazi planes. A German division was wiped out,' I read.

'Propaganda! The British public are that gullible they'll believe anything,' he roared and knocked his pipe into the fire so hard that most of the tobacco fell out. 'Read something else.'

'The Queen celebrated her forty-first birthday to day. She spent the day quietly in the country with the King and the two . . .'

'God almighty.' He stood up and banged the table where Agnes was making bread. Agnes steadied the dancing baking bowl. 'There's supposed to be a war on. The *Luftwaffe* have bombed the hell out of Britain and they print rubbish about laughing Lizzie and stuttering George having a party.'

'Whose side are you on, Joseph?' I asked. 'Who do you want to win the war?'

'Ireland's a neutral country. I'm not on any side.'

'It's a neutral country all right, but Joseph knows which side he's neutral on,' Agnes said and carried on kneading dough on the table, dusting it with flour and shaping it into rounds.

The following morning Joseph returned with two exercise books. I had to write about what I was doing every day in one and show it to him in the evening. I cut the 'Curly Wee and Gussy Goose' cartoons out of the *Independent* and stuck them into the other exercise book with flour and water paste.

I sat on a wooden bench in the dairy and read to Agnes as she rammed the plunger into the churn. Up and down. Up and down for hours. A steady rhythm until yellow flecks appeared in the milk. Then gently till a lump of butter gleamed on the surface. When the family was well off they had a donkey which walked round outside the dairy on a stone circle and turned the churning mechanism. The remains of it still stuck through a hole in the wall, two rusted arms reaching into the space above the butter table.

'They used to blindfold the donkey to stop him getting the head staggers.' Agnes wiped sweat from her face and poured two mugs of buttermilk. 'I do the donkey work now, but nobody bothers to blindfold me.'

'Why did you not get married, Agnes?' It was easy to see her up to her armpits with children.

'Husbands don't grow on bushes. Times were hard and I had no fortune.' She salted the butter. Wooden spades shaped it into rectangular slabs for use in the house. 'Men round here only look for money in a wife. Your mammy did well to leave home when she did or she would have ended up buried alive here like me and Maisie. And poor Mary, I often think she only went to the convent to escape from it all. She wasn't that religious.' She sculpted the rest of the butter into circles and stamped each with a shamrock mould to sell at the market. 'Anyhow,' she went on, pouring buttermilk into a crock for the house and into buckets for the pigs, 'somebody has to look after Maisie and Joseph.'

'Mammy and Joseph don't like each other. Do they?'

'They like each other well enough but they daren't show it,' Agnes flopped down beside me and drank her buttermilk. 'Your Mammy was a far better scholar than him and they both knew it. She wanted to be a teacher but my parents thought it was a waste of money to educate a girl so he was the one that went to college and in the end he made nothing of it. It's a pity he didn't marry but he won't now. It's a sad thing when a family name dies out. Joseph and Maisie and me are the last of the name.' She stared into the mug as if it was a crystal ball and she was prophesying the end of a dynasty. It's a mercy she didn't see what would happen to Moynagh and the whole family.

Maisie milked on a four-legged stool, nestling her cheek and shoulder into the cow's flank. She squeezed the teats. Milk squirted and frothed into the bucket. When she finished she dipped her finger in the milk and made the sign of the cross on the side of the cow. I crouched beside her. It looked so easy. I asked if I could have a go. She led me by the hand from the byre. Her cheek was creased and sweaty from the cow's hide. She took off her cardigan and put it round my shoulders. The finger on her lips told me I must be quiet and not upset the animal. She hunkered near me, pulling her skirt clear of the drain full of pee and cow dung. The teats were leathery and slack. I squeezed and pulled. Not a drop of milk emerged. The cow fidgeted, raising one foot, then another. Maisie stroked the slobbery face and sang 'Whist now. Whist.' I reached for the teat again. The swollen udder quivered and danced away from me. The cow swung her tail. It was matted with hardened dung and left a red mark across my face. Maisie caressed the brown flanks, crooning like a mother over a cradle. The cow pawed the ground for a few seconds. Maisie sat down on the stool, coaxing, singing and milk thrummed into the bucket.

Dear Mary Ann,

I am having a great time. Mickey the Post takes Daddy, me and Maggie Anthony John out round the islands every day. We had tea and soda bread on Rutla
nd and Inishmore and Inishfree and Mary Manus cooked barnacles for us.

Aunt Annie lets me get up and go to bed when I like and Patsy Cunningham from Glasgow sleeps with me sometimes in the bedroom next to the kitchen. She has white patent shoes with pink satin bows.

All the Scotchies are over for their holidays. We play at the Port till dark and then sit round the fire in Partlan's. It is better than last year when you were here.

Write and tell me what you are doing in Moynagh and remember me to Joseph, Agnes and Maisie.

Your loving sister,

Bridie.

PS I want to stay in Donegal forever.

PPS I have learned how to swim.

The taste of barnacles, salty as dulse, tender as mushrooms, watered my mouth. Only the nagging of crickets in the hearth and the plop plop of rain falling into mud outside the window broke the silence. I was heartsick of Moynagh. Of the smell of boiled cabbage and rotting bracken. Of mists hanging in veils over damp hills and of the house where every cupboard, every corner brimmed with secrets.

Would I write to Bridie that the big event of the week was going to Mass in Ballyroe on Sunday in the trap, Agnes in her tweed Sunday suit and hat with a mangy fox round her neck. A fox with glass eyes and a wicked mouth propped open by a piece of bone. But Bridie knew about that. Or would I write that the best part of the day was eating pinady by the fire and falling asleep beside Agnes, knowing that tomorrow was another day nearer home.

But I would never tell her, or anyone, what happened the following day. Not having the vocabulary to explain to a man behind a grille in a darkened box, I made one bad confession after another. By the time I got married, secrecy had become a habit with me.

It was the first time Agnes allowed me to carry the tea by myself to the men cutting turf on the far bog. She waved to me from the field beside the house where she was spreading the washing on the hedge. I strutted through the long acre and down the lane that was so narrow the hedges formed an archway above me and I was almost happy. The basket in my left hand was filled with slices of caraway seed bread. I had lathered butter on each slice and sprinkled sugar over them the way Agnes had shown me. I held the wire loop of the tea can out from me so the japs of tea wouldn't scald my legs.

I hated passing the dug-out boghole. The body of a dog floated on murky waters. Pinkish white and swollen like a balloon filled to bursting.

'Mary Ann, Mary Ann, come here. I want to show you something.'

The voice calling from the bushes belonged to a jobber from Mayo who had hired himself to Joseph for the turf cutting. Agnes didn't like the way he looked at Maisie and he had too much to say to her.

The wire handle of the tea can bit into my fingers. I walked on. Faster. The Mayo man stepped out and blocked my path.

The can juddered in my hand. A pink rod spouted from his trousers like a giant tortoise head jerking out of a shell. His hand was coiled round it but it twitched as if it had a life of its own. Where to run? The boghole and the dead dog on one side. A wall of briar and hawthorn on the other. Back to Agnes down the green tunnel? He could run faster than me. Would catch me from behind. Throw me down where nobody would hear. My feet took root in the soft earth. Part of me saw or remembered his face, black with stubble, the missing tooth in his grinning mouth. But it was the thing I couldn't take my eyes off. The purple snout of its face. The bleary eye in the middle. Coming straight at me.

'You like him. Good girl. Give him a kiss. Come on. Come on. Open your mouth. Open your fuckin' mouth, for Chrissake.' One hand yanked my hair. Pushed my face against it. It was alive. Dribbling. Prodding the corners of my mouth. His other hand sent the basket flying. Grabbed between my legs. Pushed them apart. Reached inside my knickers. Scratching, jabbing into me. Screams pounded in my head, in my lungs. Thundered against clenched lips and teeth that the thing was trying to force apart. It wasn't the thing or knife-sharp fingers tearing at my insides that unlocked my mouth. Not him, but tea scalding my bare leg.

My scream splintered the morning.

'Fuckin' bitch,' yelled the man. He jumped back. Tea steamed on his trousers. Tea I had been trusted not to spill. The rod had shrivelled and hung flabby against his buttons.

'You dirty scut.'

I hadn't heard Joseph's feet on the sodden ground. The flat spade he used for slicing turf hit the man square on the side of his head. He tottered and dropped like a felled tree into the boghole. One by one, Joseph released my fingers that were frozen to the loop of the can. He towered over the boghole. I wiped my face with my sleeve. It was covered with white snot. A drowned face emerged through the bog-water, level with the corpse of the dog. Two hands reached up.

'If I catch you within ten miles of my land I'll stick the graip through your guts,' Joseph thrust his spade towards the head as if he was going to slice it from the neck.

'Stop crying, there's a good girl. Get yourself back to Agnes,' he said to me and started to walk towards the house.

'Keeping her for yourself. Fuckin' pervert.' The crumbly sides of the boghole muted the voice but Joseph heard it. He turned and charged like a wild bull. Then he stopped in his tracks.

'Why should I even my wits to scum like that, Mary Ann?' It was the first time he had called me by my name. I waddled behind him, my legs wide apart to stop them sticking together.

'There's no need to tell your mother or father about this. No harm's been done. Agnes will see to you and you will be as right as rain.'

'Mother of God! What happened to her?' Agnes' hand flew to her mouth when she saw the bruises on my arms, my scalded leg and the skirt of my dress half ripped from the bodice. 'Where are her glasses? Has she broken them?'

Joseph whispered, 'Dirty beast! – exposing himself. See to her first and bring the tea yourself.'

'Are you all right? Will we take you to the doctor? Show me where he touched you?'

'He never touched me. Joseph didn't let him.'

'Your legs are scratched. Let me see. There's a good girl.' She moved to raise my skirt above my knees. Her gentle hands were close to the spot where his had been.

'He never touched me. He never touched me. It was briars that scratched me. Leave me alone. I want to go home.'

Agnes put a spoonful of honey in the milk she warmed for me. She knew what briar scratches looked like. 'You must let me see where he hurt you. You must tell the truth. Please, Mary Ann. There's blood on your dress and on your legs. Let me take off your dress and wash you.'

'He didn't hurt me. I fell running away from him. Leave me alone.'

I loved Agnes. I didn't mean to yell at her. To push her away. I pulled the filthy dress over my knees. Blood had seeped through the cloth. Slobber had stiffened on the bodice. I curled into a ball on the floor. Between my legs swelled and throbbed. I stank of him – of tobacco breath and the fishy, sour milk smell of him. Of my own terror.

Agnes made fresh tea, buttered and sugared bread. I was glad when she left but frightened he would come into the house while I was alone. I wanted to sit in a basin of cold water to cool the burning. But Agnes might come back, see me and ask more questions. If I was at home I could lock the bathroom door, open my legs in the bath and let the water flow in and wash his fingers and the smell of him out of me.

I was glad Mammy wasn't here. She wouldn't be put off like Agnes. She would hold me down. Examine me. Fix me with ointments and medicine. Cover me up as if she was putting a stone back over the creatures she had found crawling underneath it. Sister Mary Francis told Bridie and me that the nuns in her convent slept with their hands folded outside the covers, even in winter, in case they committed a sin by touching themselves in that place while they were asleep. Saint Dympna had preferred to be hacked to pieces and the early martyrs allowed themselves to be eaten by lions rather than be touched impurely. I could have jumped into the boghole and saved my soul but I had stood like a tailor's dummy and allowed the Mayo man do what he liked.

I crept from the house and hid in the high grasses of the broad meadow. Nobody would look for me there. My mother had taken me away from home and left me in Moynagh to be safe from Hitler's bombs. Out of danger. Out of harm's way. My father used to say that I was more precious than the sun and the moon and the stars. That he wouldn't let the wind blow rough on me.

I lay down. I didn't care if I fell asleep and the fairies stole my soul. I would be better without it. It was black with sin. I didn't care if they took me to their home in the Beyond. It couldn't be worse than here.

6

Even though I had been invited into Joseph's room, I hovered in the doorway.

'Come in. I won't bite you,' he said.

He picked three books bound in green leather from one of the top shelves and placed them on a table before me. *David Copperfield*, *Oliver Twist* and *Great Expectations*.

'Charles Dickens, one of the greatest storytellers in the English language, possibly in any language. Now which of these would you like to cut your teeth on?'

I chose *Great Expectations* because it didn't have a man's name in the title.

I had been kept indoors for four days and made to lie inside the settle bed as if I was an invalid. Compared to Pip's life with his sister and the bleakness of the marshes where he met the convict, Moynagh with Joseph, Agnes and Maisie seemed almost cosy. Agnes always accompanied me to the privy. The young man, whom Magwitch had said would rip out Pip's heart and liver and roast them, lurked behind every bush watching his chance to grab me. His face floating on the bog-water haunted me day and night.

It was good to have something to do apart from cracking the white balls that grew on the bubble bushes in the lane or helping Maisie look for eggs the hens laid in the fields. I read all day and long after the oil lamp was lit. By bedtime Miss Havisham's decaying body and Estella's beautiful face had eased the Mayo man's features to the edges of my mind.

'She'll ruin her sight,' Agnes said to Joseph. 'Her eyes are bad enough without her sitting like an ashy-pet from morning till night with her head in a book.'

'She needs something to occupy her mind. It's a pity those parents of hers didn't think about that before they dumped her on us.'

'That's not fair. Ellen is forty-one. She has been warned to rest. If she loses this one she may not have another chance.'

'Another chance for what?' I asked.

'Ask no questions and you'll hear no lies,' said Joseph.

The following Monday he took me to school across the hill.

'You are to study hard and be a credit to your family,' he called back to me puffing behind on his Sunday-suited shadow. 'You are not to mix with the Grogans. The whole family is rotten with TB. I don't want your mother to say you caught it here. And keep away from the Flynns and the Raffertys. They're a gang of tinkers that would steal the eye out of your head. And they're alive with vermin.'

Master McNamee shook hands with Joseph.

'So you are Ellen's child,' he said to me. 'Your mother and I were in the same class here at Saint Kieran's. She had a brain as good as any man's.'

He told me to sit at the front of the senior class. I was proud of Joseph and the way the master spoke to him as an equal.

'De Valera's right to hold on to the ports and keep out of the war after the way England has crucified this country for the past eight hundred years,' said the master.

'I'll never forget him telling Chamberlain when the war broke out that the Irish of all nations knew all about force being used by a strong nation against a weaker one.'

'The British say they're fighting this war for the rights of small nations. What about this small nation?'

'What indeed. Well, if Dev had gone to war he wouldn't have got many recruits here if he had tried to force conscription on us. And that's a fact.'

'They don't dare to bring it in, even in the Six Counties. The lot of them would be straight over the border like scalded cats if they did.'

'Fight for John Bull? Myself, I would see the last Englishman drown before I'd lift a finger to save him.'

I saw Joseph's spade jabbing at the Mayo man and fear with dirty fingernails goose-pimpled my skin. I wondered if the quicksands of the boghole had sucked him into its depths. If his bloated corpse would rise rise to the surface one day to float beside the dead dog. Or would he be waiting for me every day. Round every corner.

The master taught all the children in the school in one big room. Infants on the right. Seven-year-olds and upwards on the left. A bamboo cane hung behind his desk. He didn't walk about with it hooked over his arm like Sister Pius or test its swish on the desks or in the empty air. He never used it but we knew it was there.

When my north London pupils ran amok in my disastrous first term at Redwood School I wished for the gift the master possessed which had made us sit in rapt attention. We had no fear of him. Maybe we feared losing his approbation. Like being excluded from the sight of God.

'Stand up, Mary Ann. This is Mary Ann Ward from the North where there's a war on. She is going to attend school here at

Saint Kieran's while she's in Ballyroe.' He turned to the blackboard. Every eye in the room bored through me. Many of the children were barefoot. I wished Agnes had not made me wear my best dress, the blue one with cap sleeves, and that she hadn't tied a blue ribbon round my hair.

The master wrote the date on the board and below it the title: 'An Experience I Shall Never Forget'.

'You have three-quarters of an hour to write your compositions,' he said and went to the other side of the room to hear the small ones reading.

I wrote about the Blitz as if I had been awake in Belfast, not far away and fast asleep in Carrig. I had heard about the bombing on the radio and seen the ruins of German cities on the Pathé news. I wrote about the sound of Messerschmitts and Junker Eighty-eights flying over in waves and about the pptt pptt of the ack-ack. Of searchlights probing the night sky and silver barrage balloons that made the enemy aircraft fly higher. It was easy to describe the sandbagged air-raid shelter my father had dug under the garage and to imagine fearful nights huddled there while buildings collapsed or were swallowed up in craters.

The master read my composition to the class and said he had learned a lot about rationing, the blackout and the troop invasion. My father used to read the *Belfast Telegraph* to us each evening and my mother listened to every news bulletin on the wireless, including the graveyard voice of Lord Haw-Haw: 'Germany calling. Germany calling.' She kept the radio turned down low in case the neighbours or my father heard. He got angry if he caught her, said she would be better off saying her prayers than listening to Nazi propaganda.

I was a heroine to the rest of the pupils, a refugee from a distant war-zone, even though Ballyroe was only just inside the

Irish Free State. I talked about eggs steeped in jelly to keep them fresh and about the gas masks we carried in cardboard boxes to school and my accounts lost nothing in the telling. I told them how we took a boat from Warrenpoint to Omeath and risked imprisonment by smuggling butter, sugar and sausages to keep ourselves from starving. I was glad Bridie wasn't with me, stealing the limelight, saying 'No, she's got it wrong. It wasn't like that,' and then going on to tell bigger and better lies than me.

Children crowded round me on the way back from school. Over Knockmore Hill and along the main road. They fought for a place beside me; hung on my every word, touched the softness of my dresses and stroked my fleecy cardigans. Even Tom Grogan, who was twelve, waited for me with questions about U-Boats and the British soldiers.

'You're fierce clever for a girl,' he said. He was very good looking with what Mammy would call the hectic flush of TB on his cheeks.

Every morning a crowd of children waited at the gate till I arrived like a princess in a different dress with matching hair-ribbons. My best friend was Eileen Grogan, Tom's sister. Four of her sisters and her father had died of TB in the last nine years. I went to her house every day after school. Her mother spent most of the day in bed. On my second visit her aunt gave me a slice of chocolate Swiss roll with a white sticky filling. Eileen and Tom had soda bread sprinkled with sugar. The Swiss roll was wrapped in cellophane paper and produced each day. Only for me. The last slice, which I ate ten days later, tasted of mould and the slimy filling had disappeared into the cake.

Every night I longed for morning and a new day. Of all the years I spent at school those first three weeks at Saint Kieran's were the happiest.

When I think of that time I see myself in vivid technicolour, moving through a black-and-white background peopled by clamouring children all scrambling to be close to me, to absorb some of my brilliance. And I'm glad I had my brief time of glory, especially these past months when I feel that all colour has drained from me and I have become little more than a shadow, so insubstantial you could punch your hand through me and think you were punching air.

Friday afternoons were best. For the first hour, while the master went over compositions with each pupil, we read from piles of school readers that dated back fifty years. My mother's name was written on the inside cover of one of the books. Ellen McKenna, 1910. And, word for word, the stories and poems she recited to us as she baked or sewed or put us to bed. Disappointment hit me when I realised that Mammy wasn't the first person to say 'Neither a borrower nor a lender be' or 'Breathes there a man with soul so dead.'

On the wall beside the blackboard hung a picture which showed a huddle of children crouched close to a hedge and a schoolmaster teaching them while a young boy who was keeping watch at the top of the field pointed at a group of Redcoats.

'In the penal days,' explained the master at the start of the history lesson 'the Irish people were forbidden under pain of death to send their children to school, to practise their religion or to speak their own language. Such was their thirst for learning that they risked their lives by sending the children to be taught in hedge schools. Learning that, you take for granted sitting in comfortable desks in a fine warm building.'

The infants sat cross-legged on the floor, their necks craned to look at him, and senior pupils in a semicircle around them listened motionless to stories that Mammy had taught myself and Bridie. How Irish monks had converted Europe after the Dark Ages; how maggots had eaten Cromwell's insides while he was still alive to punish him for slaughtering the populations of Drogheda and Wexford; how the natives of Ulster were evicted from their homes and chased to hell or to Connacht.

Dear Bridie,
I am having a great time at Saint Kieran's. It is much nicer than our school in Carrig and the master is a brilliant teacher. I have lots of friends and I always get the best marks for . . .

Something fell on the sheet of writing paper. A moth or one of the midges that swirled like lunatics round the oil lamp, knocking themselves dizzy or committing suicide against the heat of the globe. An insect, far bigger than a midge, crawled across my exercise book. Blood in its stomach shone pink through the gray armour plating of its skin. I recognised the shape of the head. The splayed legs. A head louse.

Every Friday night at home Mammy locked her knees round my head and raked it with a fine-comb that she scanned after each raking. If anything moved on the close packed teeth or if she spotted nits clinging for dear life to a single hair, she plastered Bridie's head and mine with stinking liquid and the Friday fine-combing became a nightly ritual. Heads trapped in the stocks of Mammy's knees, us wriggling and whingeing till my father threatened to put a bowl over our heads and cut round it if we didn't sit still. What if Nitty Nora, the school nurse, had spotted the bugs before Mammy and we were doused in public with lice killer whose stink would set us apart like lepers? We would be labelled 'the dirty Wards'! Like the girls we called 'the dirty ones' whose bare bums showed when they bent over, whose red-rimmed scabs wept and spread and never healed, who queued up at Christmas for their free issue of boys' boots. Whose job it was to clean the lavatories, sprinkle tea leaves on the floor and sweep the classrooms when school ended. What if the neighbours in Rathbeg Avenue found out and stopped their spotless children playing with us and muttered among themselves, 'Dirty Catholics, what else could you expect? They should have stayed where they belong with their own kind.'

Maybe it wasn't really a louse. Just an insect that lived in the turf near the fire. Or a discoloured cockroach like the black ones that scuttled out of sight when we came into the kitchen. I shook my head over Bridie's letter. A shower of lice fell out. I cracked them with my fingernail smearing the page with red.

'Agnes, Agnes. I think I've got bugs.'

Agnes pulled my head near the lamp and ran a comb through it.

'God help us, child. You're walking. Did you sit beside those filthy Raffertys? You must have.' She squashed the procession of bugs that marched across the table.

'She will have to have her head shaved and doused with sheep dip. The whole lot of us could be infested for all we know.' Joseph got up from his rocker by the fire. He returned from his room and clicked his cut-throat open. It flashed long and straight in the lamplight. 'I told you to keep away from that pack of vermin but you know better than anybody else. Just like your mother.'

Slish, slash went the cut-throat round the back of my head. Skeins of hair were flung on the fire. They whispered, crackled, rose in orange flames like the tongues of fire that had haloed Bridie's head on Good Friday. Slish. Slash. All my hair, that Mammy used to bind with red, green, blue, yellow and white ribbons to try and make me less of a plain Jane, fizzled and bubbled on red turf.

Joseph wiped the cut-throat, swished it back and forth on his shaving strap, tested it against his fingers and ordered Agnes to lather my head. I dashed out from under the blade and buried my head between the folds of Agnes' wraparound apron.

'Don't let him touch me!' I bawled into her cardigan. 'I'll tell my daddy on him!'

'Best leave her be.' Agnes moved his hands from my arms. 'I'll wash her head with carbolic and rub paraffin into the scalp.'

I didn't look in a mirror and I didn't weep when I felt my head, sharp as stubble after corn has been cut. God had got even with me. He knew I hadn't been sorry when Bridie's hair had gone up in smoke. That deep inside me I had been glad.

He had paid me back. Maybe now He would leave me in peace.

The Raffertys, the Flynns, the Nolans were bloodhounds, sniffing raw carbolic, the whiff of paraffin. Fingers poked my ribs, picked my cardigan down to its skin. Farmers' children in boys boots and labourers' children in grass-stained gutties edged away from me in the classroom, gathered in groups at the far end of the playground. Barefoot tinker children with snotty noses who stank of the pigsty swarmed around me, pulling me in amongst them, batting me like a rag doll from one to the other. Not just a princess shorn of her crown. Not even one of them. They formed a circle round me and pushed me back in when I tried to escape. One by one they pulled the skin down from under their eyes and flashed the red insides at me.

'They're putting the *drochshúil* on her. Keep away from her!' One of the infants, who had crept up to look, squealed and took to her heels.

While the little ones chanted their six times tables to the master, the whispered litany 'baldy head, scaldy head' buzzed in my ears. 'Nit-head, bug-head' hissed round and around me.

'Your granny was a murderer. Your granny killed Gilmour. She should have swung. Killer. Murderer.' Maggie Flynn walked backwards over Knockmore Hill, her runny nose two inches from mine. 'Gilmour. Murderer, killer, should have swung,' spat into my face. 'Joseph is a loony. Should still be in the loony bin,' rasped through broken teeth. Her brothers, cousins, the Flynn tribe walked on my heels, shoved me up against the pus on her stye.

'Loony bin. Bastard. Murderer.' Lies, poison spilled from her mouth.

I closed it with my fist. Rammed 'loony bin', 'Gilmour', 'murderer' down her throat. Nails clawed my face. Gouged my cheek. I punched again. And again. Punched her nose and the red-edged wetness below it. Blood streamed. Fell in dust balls on the road. She screeched. Blood poured through her fingers, reddened the grime of her hands. She stared at them, unbelieving.

'Arragh Maggie, you let the townie best you,' scoffed her friends and pushed her into the ditch.

I walked away from them, not daring to run. Proud of the blood on my fist and my stinging face. Clods of earth hit my back. Stones whizzed past my head. I closed the gate and raced down the lane to Agnes.

She sat outside the door plucking a white Leghorn. She knew I didn't like to see her chasing a hen for the pot, that I hated the squawking when she caught it and the legs that kept on jerking after she wrung its neck.

'Would you just look at the cut of you,' she called to me. 'You look as if you've been in the wars. What have you been up to?'

'I had a fight with Maggie Flynn. She started it. Honest, she did.'

'Joseph told you to have nothing to do with the Flynns. They're a bad lot.' She plucked downy feathers from the hen's breast and put them in a sack to be kept for stuffing pillows.

'She said my granny was a murderer. That she should have been hung.'

Feathers dropped from the hand plucking dimpled skin. Picture-book fairies, they swirled and floated round our knees and danced across the street into the slimy water of the duck pond.

'She wouldn't stop so I punched her on the nose. She's a rotten, stinking liar. Agnes, why would they say my granny was a killer?'

She didn't answer. Eyes wide open but unseeing, she went on plucking, not noticing the feathers falling past the open mouth of the sack, drifting towards the duck pond.

'The women in Ballyroe were jealous of my mother. They thought my father should have married a woman from his own townland. He'd been courting Bessie Ryan for years. It was her he wanted to marry. But he needed my mother's fortune to redeem the place.' She plucked stiff feathers from the wings.

'You'd be better off making yourself a couple of pens with those than raking over what's best forgotten. Pump a bucket of water and wash yourself. You look as if you've murdered some-body.'

'I want to hear about my granny, Agnes. What happened to her when she came here?'

'Where would I start?' She held the hen by the feet. Its limp body dangled between her knees. She told me that the first time her father took my grandmother to Mass he went to tether the horse in the chapel yard and told her to go in and sit on the women's side. A crowd of women blocked her way to the church. They jostled her and bad-mouthed her, said she would never have any luck for stealing Bessie Ryan's rightful husband.

'My mother was a strong woman, cold as ice. She didn't wipe their spittle from her hat or her face. Let it dribble over her hair and coat, even when she went to the altar. The women never forgave her for the telling off they got from the priest. They were jealous because she came from a two-storey house with a slate roof and her brother was a parish priest in Dublin.' Agnes stopped talking as if she had given me an explanation.

'But Agnes, why would they say she was a murderer? What made them say that?'

The hen slipped from between her knees and lay half-bald on the street, its glassy eyes staring up at me.

'It was when wee Thomas died they started those rumours. They gave her no peace. Chanting and jeering at her when she took the pony and trap to market and when her back was turned they tipped her basket. Dozens of eggs were smashed over the street.'

'What happened to Thomas, Agnes? What did he die of?'

'He was about a year old. Not quite walking. A lovely wee boy. My mother had never had time for Maisie or your mother or for any of her daughters but she carried him round on her hip wherever she went, talking to him, showing him things, and my father couldn't get enough of him. He sat with him on his knee in the evenings and took him out across the fields, small as he was, to see to the cattle and the crops.

'Nobody saw Thomas crawl out of the house that day. One minute he was on a mat under the table, next minute he was gone. We searched high up and low down. In every corner. In all the outhouses. My mother called the men in from the fields to hunt for him. I found him. There.' She pointed at the metal pump that stood like a soldier in full armour, down from the house below the duck pond.

'They got the pump after,' she went on after a few moments. 'I went to the well for water. I pulled the lid back. The wood was rotten and it was a bad fit. He must have cowped the lid and then it fell back after he slipped in. He was lying down there on his face. Way down there, in that dark hole on the black water. Floating on the surface with his wee shift spread out around him. To my dying day I'll see him, his body stretched across the water. So small. So small.' Agnes rocked to and fro on her chair, her hands over her face. Maisie rushed out of the house.

'Whist, Ag, whist, whist.' she stroked her face and talked to her as she had talked to the cow in the byre. Blood dripped from the cut in the hen's neck and bluebottles swarmed over the ground where it lay.

Agnes wiped her eyes. 'Two of the servant men got Thomas out. My mother took him in her arms and laid him dripping on the kitchen table. She lined us all up and made us take a good look. "You were all forbidden to go near the well," she said. "That's what happens when you are disobedient."

'My father had been to a fair in Clones that day. One of the men ran to the gate when he heard him coming back. He jumped off the horse at the door and tore into the house with the whip in his hand. When he saw Thomas lying on the table he gave a roar like a wild animal and he threw himself on the wee body. Then he ordered each one of us to go outside and he dragged my mother by the hair and made her stand in front of us.' Agnes stared at the ground a few feet from her. I stared too and waited for her to continue. 'He raised the horsewhip and lashed her across the face, lashed her arms, her breasts. Her lip split open and blood poured over her bodice. She didn't even try to protect her face, just stood there, still and silent as she had been when she carried Thomas from the well. I think my father wanted to kill her. He had drink on him. He always drank after a fair.

'The servant men grabbed at the whip. "You'll kill her if you don't stop and you will have nobody to rear the children," one of them shouted and they wrestled the whip from his hands. My father never spoke to my mother from that day till the day he died. She went on attending him hand and foot. A baby boy was born dead the next year and Mary Francis two years after. When he was told he had another daughter he didn't even bother to look at her. He shook his head in disgust. "Another pratie-washer," was all he said and went on raking the hay.'

Agnes picked up the white Leghorn and plucked it bald. A long time passed before she spoke.

'It's time you went home, Mary Ann. God knows we'll miss you but this is no place for a child. There's been nothing but trouble in this house.'

She went into the kitchen for a basin. She cut the claws off and handed them to me. If I pulled the back tendons I could make them walk but I had no heart for seeing dead legs move. Then she pulled out the insides. The gizzard full of grit and tomorrow's and the day-after's eggs and next-week's eggs among tubes and blood.

I crouched beside Agnes and pricked my nose against the stink of the hen's guts. The Raffertys and the Flynns had said nothing about my granny murdering Thomas but I would ask no more questions till I got home. Mammy was like her mother, not soft like Agnes. She wouldn't rock to and fro, and sob 'Oh God. Oh God. Oh God.'

She might shout at me for asking but she would tell me who Gilmour was.

7

'In undera God, child, what did those savages do to you?' My father held me at arm's length before he picked up my attaché case and bag. The conductor handed him the basket of butter and eggs I had left on the bus.

'I had bugs, daddy. Joseph cut off my hair.'

'Bugs! Ah well, bugs never did anybody any harm. Why did Joseph cut your hair instead of Agnes?' He touched the scar on my face. 'And how did this happen?'

'I had a fight with Maggie Flynn. Joseph was nice, Daddy. He gave me books written by Charles Dickens to read.'

'Did he now? He's the dickens of a fellow himself, is the bold Joseph.' He opened the door of the lorry. 'So, who won the fight?'

'I did. I made her nose bleed so much she had to stop.'

'You're a fine girl, Mary Ann.' The furrows disappeared from his brow and from the bridge of his nose. He smiled for the first time. 'It's good to have you home again. Children are better in their own house. The whole family. You, your mammy, Bridie and me and . . .'

No perfume was sweeter than the throat-catching smell of quarry dust in the lorry. My fingers stroked the grey film that coated the dashboard as my father drove out through familiar streets of mill houses and up past the smooth lawns, shrubs and flowers of the mansions on the Dublin Road. The nightmare of Moynagh was behind me. A dimming memory. Maisie calling

'Bye, bye, bye, bye, bye,' to the departing bus, still clutching the bunch of dog daisies and wild roses she had plucked this morning for me to take home. Agnes's eyes brimming through her goodbyes 'We'll miss you, Mary Ann, your company and your chat. The place will be as silent as the grave with you gone.' The two half-crowns she had saved out of her butter money for me and Bridie lay forgotten in my pocket. And Joseph. I hadn't seen him this morning but his books, *Bleak House*, *Nicholas Nickelby* and *Dombey and Son* weighed down my attache case. 'Every time you see *Bleak House* on your bookshelf you'll remember Moynagh,' he had said last night.

'There's a great surprise waiting for you when you get home. No I'm not telling you. I'm under strict orders to say nothing and not spoil it.' My father started to sing to the tune his fingers thrummed on the steering wheel:

By the short cut to the Rosses
A fairy girl I met
I was taken by her beauty
As the fish is to the net
The fern uncurled to look at her
So very fair was she –

'We'll all go to the Rosses next summer. You, your mammy, Bridie and me and . . .' He put a finger to his lips, then went on singing

With her hair as bright as seaweed
New drawn from out the sea.

Donegal, where the fairies were kindly and frothy as the foam on the sea where they lived; not wicked like the spirits in Moynagh with hearts as black as the dark earth that was their home. Donegal, where the short cut to the Rosses wasn't just the road to fairyland. It was the road to heaven. The car turned into Rathbeg Avenue. Our lovely house. Too young for ghosts dragging sleepless sorrows. Too far from Moynagh for the Mayo man to find me or for Maggie Flynn's fists and taunts to reach. The flower beds in the front lawn still glowed red and pink and yellow roses smothered the trellis between us and the Campbells.

'Ward's mansion, Daddy,' I waited for him to stand beside me in admiration.

'Never mind that. Just you see what's inside.' He bundled me to the back door.

Mammy didn't rush out to greet me, to inspect me, to ask was I hungry and did I need a cup of tea and a piece of cake to tide me over till dinner time.

'I'm home, Mammy. It's me. I'm home,' I shouted.

She didn't move. She sat on a low chair in the kitchen. On her lap, in a white nightdress, lay the smallest baby I had ever seen. His fist was stuffed at his mouth and he made the same snuffly noises as the piglets in Moynagh searching with blind eyes for the sow's teats. A sweet sour smell hung around Mammy and the baby. The smell of the dairy. Of Maisie's hands after milking.

'Where did you get the baby from, Mammy? Is it ours?'

'Of course he's ours. The doctor brought him.'

'In his black bag. I'm allowed to hold him.' Bridie posed behind the baby, a guardian angel on a Christmas card. A burnished angel, her hair bleached to a light copper and her skin tanned by sea and sun. 'Don't touch his head,' she shrieked. 'The bones haven't closed yet.'

My hand froze inches above the hollow of pulsing flesh under a fuzz of black hair on the baby's skull.

'What's his name?'

'He's to be called Brendan after his grandfather,' said my father. 'If he's as good a man as him he'll be all right.'

'You could plant potatoes in the dirt on your neck,' Mammy said. 'Did you forget how to wash yourself when you were in Moynagh?'

I stood back, angry and hurt. They had brought this creature into the house as soon as my back was turned. I was bursting to tell my mother how well I had done at school, how I could read faster than any of the thirteen-year-old boys. But she didn't want to know. All she had eyes for was that baby. I could tell by the way she gazed at him that she saw a priest's collar round the folds of his fat neck. And my father, down on one knee before him, had already emblazoned 'Michael Ward and Son' in big letters on the side of a new fleet of lorries. Nothing would ever be the same again. I knelt beside my father and pretended to worship his son. It was what was expected of me.

'Do you want yer oul' lobby washed down, Mrs Brown? Do you want yer oul' lobby washed down?' The cracked voice, louder and louder, burst through the back door.

'Eva, Eva. I'm back.'

She hugged me tight, wet my face with slobbering kisses. She held me out from her. 'Look at you, would you just look at you, all grown-up after your holidays. You're gorgeous with your short hair, Mary Ann. Honest to God you are.'

'I was so scared you would have married Gordon and gone to England and I would never see you again.' My arms barely reached round her waist.

'Gordon? Who's Gordon?' Eva's face was blank.

'Eva's got a new boyfriend. His name's Ronnie. He's from Glasgow. He's daft about her,' said Bridie. 'Do you really like her hair, Eva? Do you not think she looks like a chewed rat?'

'Any more remarks like that, young lady and I'll tan your backside for you. You should be glad to have your sister home again,' snapped my father. He gave Eva two shillings. 'You can take these two for an ice cream in Rossi's to celebrate Mary Ann coming home and to give their mother a bit of peace.'

Eva grabbed hold of the baby and danced round and round with him. He turned a deep shade of red and started to howl. 'He wants his diddy, Mrs Ward.' Mammy turned her back to us and fiddled with her jumper. The baby guzzled, slurped and choked like a newborn calf and I realised to my horror that she must be suckling him.

I'm sure she was pleased when Bridie and I went out with Eva. We linked arms, Eva in the middle, and raced downhill to Rossi's ice cream parlour. We sat in the horsebox where my father had proposed to Mammy and we each had a scoop of vanilla and a scoop of chocolate ice cream in a metal dish shaped like a chalice. Mr Rossi wound up the gramophone and put on the record he always played when we came in.

'Beniamino Gigli,' he said. 'I play this for your mamma, Bridee, Marie Anna, when I see your papa open the red box with the ring. So beautiful she was, so beautiful.'

Bridie and I boasted about the brilliant summer we had had and Eva described the dress she wanted Mammy to make her for her wedding to Ronnie. Floor-length white silk with a net train and we would both be bridesmaids in pink satin and I would give her a silver horseshoe.

On the way home we splashed about in puddles to see if Mammy would notice that our socks and sandals were soaked. 'I'm glad you're back. I'm sick of that baby,' Bridie said. 'You would think he was something special the way those two go on about him.'

Hot water swirled through the suds in the bath. Mammy scrubbed my neck till I thought she would take the skin off. She examined the scratch on my face.

'You will carry that mark to the grave. You must have kept picking the scab to leave a scar like that. Why were you fighting with Maggie Flynn anyhow?'

'She called Joseph names and said horrible things about your mammy.'

'What sort of names? What did she say about your granny?' She grabbed hold of my arm.

'I don't remember. Honest I don't.' Her grip tightened. Her nails dug into me. 'Agnes said she was stupid and I was to pay no attention to her.'

The noise of the baby screeching brought her up from her knees beside the bath. She hurried to the door. I turned on the hot water tap and emptied shampoo into the bath. The baby screamed blue murder.

'Who's Gilmour, Mammy?' I called when I knew she had reached the top of the stairs. I closed my eyes and lay on my back imagining I was Greta Garbo floating in bubbles.

'What did you say? Who told you about Gilmour? What did they say about him?' She pulled me to a sitting position.

'A crowd followed me from school shouting, "Gilmour, Gilmour." What did they do to Gilmour?'

'The baby wants you, Mammy. Can you not hear him bawling?' Bridie shouted up the stairs.

'Let him bawl. It will expand his lungs. Can I not have a few minutes alone with Mary Ann on her first night home?' She closed the door and rounded on me 'What else did they say?'

'It was horrible. They followed me all the way over Knockmore hill chanting "Gilmour, Gilmour" as if it was a dirty word. That's all. You're hurting me, Mammy; your nails are sharp.'

'It is a dirty word. A filthy word. Don't ever let me hear you say it again. He was one of the most evil men ever lived. He tried to destroy our whole family but he didn't get away with it.' She picked up the bar of soap and lathered my back but I could tell by the way she rubbed the same spot below my shoulder that her mind was with Gilmour, not on scouring seven weeks' grime from me.

'Did he die, Mammy?'

'He died like the rat he was and he was buried like a rat.' Mammy didn't speak badly about anybody, except Cromwell and the Black and Tans. The scum of England, she called them. Sewer rats. Jailbirds, all chosen because they had records for grievous bodily harm. Given a pardon so they could come over here and murder and torture innocent people.

'What happened to him? How did he die?'

'I'll tell you another time. I'm tired. I can't talk about him now. People in Ballyroe have long memories and they don't have enough to think about.' She stroked my wet head. 'I'll take you to Marlene Bell's tomorrow and see what she can do with your hair. Now, I had best see to that brother of yours before he brings the roof down. You lie there and have a good soak.' Her face bending over me looked much older than I remembered.

I bumped into Eva on my way home from school.

'You've been crying. What's wrong?' she asked.

'Sister Paul caned me.'

'What did she want to go and cane you for?'

'For laughing during catechism and making Bea King laugh.'

'I'd like to go up and pull the oul' hood off her. You should get your daddy on her. Better still, get your mammy on her. She'll ate the face off her.' Eva spat on her cuff and wiped my face. 'Come on into Wooly's and I'll buy you a slider.' She showed me her wages from Mrs Dalton.

She bought a slider for me in Woolworth's and for herself a poke with raspberry cordial drizzled over it. Greedy bites polished off my slider. Eva broke the bottom off her cone, filled it with ice-cream and handed it to me. Ice-cream flowed through the open base and down her chin. She mopped it with her cuff. She walked towards home with me sucking the last dribbles through the bottom end.

'Come on and get some conkers,' she said and we went into the chestnut field,

I told her it was too early for conkers, that we would have to wait another few weeks. She bent down and picked up a prickly chestnut fruit. We split it open. In a white cocoon lay a milk-coloured chestnut, smooth and beautiful as a pearl in the heart of an oyster. Eva said it was her lucky charm and she would always carry it with her. I sat on my school bag at the top of the field and Eva pulled her coat tight over her bum. She stretched her legs straight in front of her. Legs with measled patterns scrawled over her shins. We pushed off with our hands and tobogganed down the hill.

'Don't tell Mammy I got caned. She'll kill me,' I called as I whizzed past Eva.

'I will so. That oul' nun has no business touching you,' she shouted after me. 'You're only a wee girl.'

I realise now that it wasn't me Sister Paul wanted to punish in the empty space between Standard Four and Five. It was me she forced to kneel before the picture of the Sacred Heart but it was my father she wanted on his knees. It was his spirit she needed to break. My back ached and my neck hurt but I wouldn't give her another chance to say 'Up straight, Mary Ann Ward! Our Divine Lord hung on the cross for three hours to redeem mankind, and you can't even keep your back straight for ten minutes.'

I held my breath till my lungs were full to bursting. I wanted to crash unconscious to the floor, my lips black and my face the colour of ashes. To waken up outside in the cold air. I wanted her to feel the fear I felt when she called Sister Aquinas to hold my head and she came towards me uncoiling the noose of her tape measure.

'Hold still, you bold girl. Hold her still, Sister. Just because some country schoolmaster or other thought she could write a half-decent essay she thinks she's too good for this school.'

On the other side of the room Bridie's class recited 'Thirteen times eleven are 143. Thirteen times twelve are 156. Thirteen times thirteen are 169.'

I could have sat stone-still at my desk as I did at ten o'clock when she took the first measurement and noted it on a clean page. I could have let her chart how fast my head was swelling every hour as a nurse charts a patient's temperature. And I could have made an Act of Contrition in front of the two classes to atone for my indiscipline instead of kneeling there, my lips glued together.

'Did you know, girls, that the father of the Ward girls sent me a letter today demanding special attention for his daughters? They are not to be chastised like the other pupils in this school. He has set his authority above mine. The same Mr Ward who boasted to me only last week that this brilliant daughter had won some competition or other. Showed me a cutting from the newspaper. Any wonder her head has swollen?'

Oh, Sister, my father didn't set himself above you. He revered and respected you. You were on a pedestal, you who had consecrated your life to God and your pupils. It was thanks to you I could recite the principal towns of the thirty-two counties of Ireland, the coalfields of England and Scotland and most of *Hiawatha*. That Bridie and I could teach him square root and the parts of a flower, tell him about Julius Caesar and Vasco da Gama. And he was grateful to you for coming into school early to teach us the Irish script. He could only speak Irish. He wasn't educated like you. He was a humble man, Sister. I think it was the blood that made him angry.

'Girls, what is the worst, most deadly sin?' you asked. 'No, not murder.'

'Adultery, Sister.'

'No, not adultery either. A sin more hateful, more shameful even than adultery.' You scanned the faces of your pupils and waited. You pointed a finger at me out there on the floor. 'It is pride! Pride that caused Lucifer, the brightest of all the angels, to plunge from heaven to hell. For the sin of pride, for setting herself up above the rest of you, for refusing to ask forgiveness, Mary Ann Ward will kneel before Our Blessed Lord until she learns humility.'

I shiver at the ice in your voice as I did then.

She didn't tell them how she lost control yesterday when I moved my hand and the cane whished against her habit. She didn't tell them that she made me hold my hand steady, that she took a new, unsoftened cane from her cupboard and swung it from behind her shoulders. Swish, swish, swish till her face went red and beads of sweat like tiny pearls fell on my hand as the cane fell. That it welted my hand and wrist and broke the skin on my wrist. Swish,

swish, swish. That she didn't see the watery blood even when it turned blood red.

At twelve o'clock when the school was empty, all the other nuns went to the big convent for their lunch. She told me she could wait all day if necessary but kept watching the school clock. The minute hand jerked to one minute past, two minutes past, three minutes past. I remembered Sister Augustine telling Mammy that every nun must be in her place in the refectory before Reverend Mother could say grace. I felt strong then as she weakened and my back stopped hurting. From her desk she took a toffee with gold writing on its green and black wrapper. She bent down beside me. Her skirts brushed my knees.

'You're a big girl, Mary Ann, you're nearly ten.' She clasped my hands in both of hers. The tip of her coif ruffled my hair. 'Old enough to do what you're told. Isn't that right?'

'Yes, Sister.'

'That's a good girl. Now say with me 'O my God I am very sorry.'

'O my God I am very sorry that I have sinned against you . . .'

She rubbed my knees, went into the cloakroom with me and helped me put on my coat.

'Run along home now. Don't be late.' Her voice was honey. Sweet as the toffee with gold writing on its black-and-green wrapping.

She rushed past me and I walked through the school gates, unmarked.

Bridie and I made a figure of Sister Paul from the remains of ginger-bread mixture Mammy left in the bowl for us. A naked figure. No currant buttons down her front. No currants or slice of cherry on her bald face. When she was cooked and her body had swollen into a shiny mound we put her in the middle of the table, did a war dance round her, skewered holes in her eye sockets and plunged the bread knife through her heart.

We stopped dancing when we heard my father come in from work.

'You are a right pair of cannibals,' he said. 'Who's the unfortunate victim?'

We told him.

'That's a terrible thing to do to a decent, hard-working woman after all the extra time she has given to you. You should be ashamed of yourselves.' He bent over and inhaled Sister Paul's warm, gingery perfume. 'All the same I wonder if she tastes as good as she smells.'

Bridie gave him half a leg. It was brittle and crunchy like toffee, whereas the body had the soft sweetness of sponge cake

'I'm nearly finished,' hissed Bridie. 'You'd better hurry up. You're far too slow.'

'I can't hurry up. I'll lose my place.'

'I'm sick of this. Just stop playing. Come on. *Now.*' Four hands crashed almost simultaneously on the piano.

Mr and Mrs Bradshaw sat glassy-eyed on armchairs on either side of the sitting room fire while Bridie and I entertained them with Schubert's *Rosamunde* overture arranged for four hands. My father stood proudly beside the piano to turn the page when Bridie nodded, as if we were giving a recital at the Ulster Hall.

The card table was already covered with a white cloth on which Mammy had embroidered a crinoline lady in pink dress and bonnet surrounded by pink and blue hollyhocks on daisy stitch stems. On it she had placed a plate of ham sandwiches and a silver cake stand with slices of cake on the top tier and currant bread with gooseberry jam underneath. The two cups, saucers and plates for herself and Mrs Bradshaw were part of her china teaset. Miss Fisher had brought the walnut table from England to Moynagh. My grandmother had given it to my mother to save it from the woodworm that had tunnelled through most of the furniture there. Its four curved legs were spindly and graceful as a newborn foal's. If you looked carefully you could see the twin faces of two devils in the grain of the wood. Whiskery faces with wild masses of hair covering the bumps of their horns.

Mammy backed through the doorway carrying a teapot and two white delft mugs and white plates for my father and Mr Bradshaw.

'The Japs have bombed Pearl Harbour. They have destroyed the American fleet and dozens of planes,' she announced in her newsreader's voice. We were used to being greeted by her when we came home from school with items of news such as 'The *Bismarck* has sunk the *Hood*. There has been terrible loss of lives,' and we would drop our school bags to the floor and say three Hail Marys for the repose of the souls of those who had died.

'That'll put paid to Roosevelt's Neutrality Act,' said my father. 'Maybe the Yanks will get off their backsides now that they've sampled what Britain has been putting up with for the past two years.'

'Do you remember Churchill saying to Roosevelt way back in February: "Give us the tools and we will finish the job"', said Mr Bradshaw. 'Maybe this will shame him into action. Lovely bit of ham, Mrs Ward, you can really taste the pig.' He had been a regular soldier, a sergeant, in the Irish Guards and had tried to join up but he was too old.

'I expect the next troop invasion in Carrig will be the Yanks,' said Mammy, 'as if there aren't enough soldiers here turning the girls' heads.'

The Yanks did join the war. US forces invaded Carrig in the early summer of the following year. Big soldiers with crew-cuts and uniforms made from smooth khaki waved at us from the backs of jeeps and lorries, showered us with candy as we walked or cycled to school, called 'Hi honey, hi baby!' in loud, drawling voices. Mammy went down on her knees and thanked God that her daughters were too young to become camp followers in this war and prayed we would be too old for the next.

I remembered Pearl Harbour long after other battles were forgotten. Not the wreckage of ships and planes, but the shattered gates of heaven and the sun reflecting all the colours of the rainbow on fields of splintered pearl.

8

When Bridie and I were small we carved our names on Keadue Strand. Each day we dug deeper and deeper till we were waist high in shell-lined holes and gouged 'Mary Ann' and 'Bridie' in giant letters across the beach. Every morning we raced to the shore to search for them among shells and seaweed and worm casts and cried to find no trace of them.

If there was one year of my life I could wipe out forever as the tide erased our names, it would be the year that followed. I would go straight from the December the Japanese bombed Pearl Harbour to January 1943. Not because of the terrible events in Europe and the Far East and the battles in North Africa. Not even because of what Mammy suffered. I wasn't responsible for any of those things. I would still have my squint but that is a price I would gladly pay a hundred times over. I tell myself what happened to Eva wasn't my fault. I was only ten years old. But in the catechism it is written that a child reaches the use of reason at the age of seven and is capable of distinguishing between right and wrong.

Tides flowed and ebbed. 1942 did happen, like every other year.

I can't bear to think about Eva. Maybe if I concentrate on the first seven months of the year I can skim so quickly over August and the weeks that followed that no one will notice.

It started so well. That Tuesday in January when Mammy left the baby with Mrs Bradshaw – even though she hated babies, especially boys – instead of taking him with us to the eye hospital. Mammy's excitement on the bus. She hoped I'd be seen quickly. We were going up the Ravenhill Road to look at a rug that had been advertised in the *Belfast Telegraph*.

'I hope it's still there,' she said. 'It will go lovely in the front room.'

She described it to me. Deep red, rectangular with swirling patterns and it was han made in India. It was expensive but it paid to go for quality. She had the right money in a brown envelope on which she had scribbled the address: 17 Sycamore Avenue.

The head doctor at the Ophthalmic Hospital, Mrs Lynn, told me to sit on a high chair. One by one, a group of students peered with lights into my eyes. After they had given their verdicts and accused me of all sorts of defects, she said, 'There is nothing wrong with this child. She has perfect sight. Her squint is cured.' And she told me to throw my glasses and patch in the bin.

Going up the Ravenhill Road itself was strange. We were Antrim people. We never crossed the Lagan. We found Number 17, a large Victorian house in a tree-lined avenue. The rug was exactly as Mammy had described it to me, newer than she had hoped.

After Mammy had paid for it the owner of the house asked how we had known it was for sale.

'I saw your ad in last night's *Telegraph*,' Mammy replied.

The woman shook her head and said that wasn't possible. She showed us a piece of paper with her address, a description of the rug and the asking price. 'It hasn't been in the paper yet. I have just this minute written out the advert. I was going to advertise it at the weekend.'

Brendan was in the pigeon loft with Mr Bradshaw at the top of his long, thin garden. I loved to sit up there. To search the sky with Mr Bradshaw for homecoming birds, to hear him talking to them, calling them by name, taking the rings off their legs and clocking their time. To hear them answering him and see them sway towards him, their claws coiled round his fingers.

'How do they know the way home from England and all those foreign places?' I asked him one day. 'How come they don't get lost?'

'It's what you call a homing instinct, Mary Ann. All creatures have it, some more than others. Take me. I travelled all over the world when I was in the army but at the end of the day, Carrig was the only place for me, and back I came like a homing pigeon.'

He pointed at a mauve-breasted bird strutting about on red talons. Every so often it raised lashless eyes and called what sounded like 'Bucket of coal, bucket of coal' and puffed out his feathers.

'What's he saying?'

'That's a love call he's making and he's preening himself to attract his mate, the way a young man does before going out with his girl. I always leave at least one broody hen at home to encourage the males to come back quickly.'

Brendan sat on Mr Bradshaw's knee. In one fist was a chewed biscuit, the other clutched a tuft of the old man's white hair. He called 'Coo coo' and reached towards the pigeons in their cages. I held my arms out to him but he buried his face in Mr Bradshaw's pullover. I was just as glad when I spied a trail of shimmering green liquid slithering down the sleeve of his jacket. I loved the tea Mr Bradshaw brewed in a billycan on his Primus. Darkening layers of brown stained the inside of his white mugs and the Rich Tea biscuits he kept in a tin with a picture of Windsor Castle on the lid, tasted of birdseed. Enfield Terrace was in a poor part of the town. There were still lavatories in the yard but the gas mantles Mammy remembered from the time our family had lived next door to the Bradshaws had been replaced by electric bulbs.

'It's wonderful what you see if you look up at the sky,' said Mr Bradshaw. 'I remember in the last war we were stuck in the trenches in France. One of the men pointed up. There above us was a flock of storks flying in such perfect formation they might have been a squadron of fighter planes. All those great birds with their legs stretched out straight behind them, making arrows in the sky. Then another flock of them swept past. And another, in perfect Vs. We stood up to watch them and for a few minutes I think we forgot there was a war on.'

'How could you tell they were storks, Mr Bradshaw?'

'It was easy. Every last one had a baby wrapped in a shawl hanging from its beak.'

Storks. Doctor McFaul's black bag. And Eva thinking she'd get a baby from the shops if she had a man. Mr Bradshaw was telling me how salmon come back to the river where they were born to lay their eggs when Mammy called from the back door that I was to come down and have my tea in the parlour.

'You had better go. That sounds like a royal command from her highness. Tell your mammy I'll keep the baby up here. The best place for us,' he stood up with Brendan in his arms. 'Do you know, Mary Ann, I would rather be up here in the pigeon loft than in Buckingham Palace.'

I wondered was he referring to his wife's former place of work or to her front parlour. Mrs Bradshaw had created a miniature stateroom, or at least my idea of one of the chambers in Buckingham Palace in her front room. The deep red – or claret as she called it – of the velveteen drapes was repeated in heavily embossed wallpaper and in an almost threadbare carpet. Pictures of royalty whom she had served covered the walls and were reflected in the huge mirror above the fireplace. Queen Victoria in widow's weeds and a picture of a young Prince Albert. Edward the Seventh and Queen Alexandra.

'Poor Alexandra, she did not have to go seeking her sorrows. Did you know that all fashionable ladies of her day limped because the queen did?' Mammy and I looked impressed.

The stories Mrs Bradshaw could tell about Edward! But an ex-employee of the palace was sworn to a secrecy as strict as any of the priests of the Roman church. Dear Queen Mary and Bertie and David and poor plain Alice who was palmed off on old doddering Lascelles. More like her father than her husband.

Mrs Bradshaw offered a plate of chocolate marshmallows, each one encased in red fluted paper. My teeth cracked the layer of dark chocolate, sank through sticky mallow into raspberry jam and a circle of biscuit. Mammy spread her new rug on the floor for us to wonder at; to exclaim how well it looked in Mrs Bradshaw's parlour.

I admired my unspectacled face in the glass on a picture of the Bradshaws on their wedding day, him in the uniform of the Irish Guards, her in a tight-fitting dark dress, and I postponed for a moment the pleasure of eating a second marshmallow. I couldn't have been happier.

A few weeks before we were to go on holiday Bridie and I were put out in the hall while Mammy talked in a serious voice to Eva. She asked a lot of questions but we couldn't hear the answers.

'God help the poor creature; somebody has taken advantage of her,' Mammy said to Mrs Campbell. 'She doesn't even know what's happening or who's responsible.' We had hidden under the open window of the downstairs bedroom to listen to them talking over the fence.

'Could it be her father? It's not right for a halfwit like her to be alone in the house with him.'

'Whoever it was, she will need to be looked after when her time comes.' We could tell that Mammy was annoyed. She didn't like anyone calling Eva a halfwit.

'Eva's going to have a baby,' Bridie whispered.

'She can't. She hasn't got a man.'

I knew about Virgin Birth and the Immaculate Conception and that Jesus was born nine months after the Annunciation. All that was the result of miracles and easy to understand, but I hadn't the remotest idea of the mechanics of ordinary, run-of-the-mill reproduction.

Mammy often took Eva aside to talk to her when we were out of earshot. All we could see was the blank look on Eva's face and Mammy's hands going up and down the way they did when she was trying to explain something.

The quarry, like all the factories and public works, had to close for the Twelfth. Eva was excited about walking in the Orange procession and couldn't understand why we were not allowed to go with her to the party in the Field. Two years previously Bridie and I had watched the procession from the corner of Castle Street. We tapped our feet to 'The Sash My Father Wore' and 'The Oul' Orange Flute' and wished we could play in the girls' pipe band and wear red, white and blue uniforms. We loved the way the pipe major danced along in the procession, twirled his baton and passed it through his legs and round his back but we cowered behind the phonebox when the lodge banners appeared, followed by rows upon rows of grim-faced men in hard hats and dark suits.

What if they recognised us for what we were and yelled 'Papishes, Fenians' at us and the crowd chased us and threw stones at us. One of the banners displayed a picture of Oliver Cromwell. Bridie whispered that it was a terrible thing to see the butcher of Drogheda carried through our town. A brute who had read the Bible while the streets ran red with the blood of the infants he had ordered to be quartered.

Mammy always liked to be away before the celebrations got under way. She said the place didn't really settle until after Black Men's Day.

My father showed his son with pride to all his relatives in the Rosses; carried him on his shoulders from house to house. The neighbours exclaimed that Brendan was the born spit of his grandfather, Brendan Conal Dominic Mór, that he had his grandmother's nose and the shape of her head, and the hands of a fisherman. Mammy gave me a look that said those Donegal people could talk till the cows came home but Brendan was a McKenna from the tip of his dark head to his high insteps.

Every morning my father took Bridie and me out in the boat with Mickey the Post to the islands. We played round the Port while the two men loaded the mail, groceries, hanks of wool, rubber boots and the pair of us into the boat. Rutland, Inishmore, Inishfree. Shores too treacherous or too shallow for the big boats. We played with the island children, had soda bread and tea by the fire while Mickey and my father delivered the mail and read letters for eyes that had grown too old to read or had never learned how. They helped fill in forms and talked about the crops while Mickey diagnosed ailments, prescribed remedies and conveyed news and gossip from island to island. A visit lasted as long as it took. Mickey had all the time in the world. 'We'll be a long time dead,' he said.

We stayed overnight on Inishfree with Mary Manus, our second cousin once removed. She was little and stooped. At night we climbed a ladder to the space where she slept above the far end of the kitchen. Her husband, Bartlan, was tall and stooped. At night he climbed into the settle bed.

'You won't find it at all strange being in your coffin,' I told him before he closed the lid.

The narrow channels between the islands were often choked with seaweed that sprawled over the water, bulbous and shining, like monstrous toads. My father raised his oar out of the water. 'Jesus, Mary and Joseph,' he murmured and crossed himself and we wondered if we were to be marooned there forever. Mickey's knowing oar coaxed apart fronds of sea-grass and sea-reeds that were tangled under the water. He said they were the long green hair of the fairies of the deep. If you looked at them they would reach out and wrap you in an embrace you would never escape from. Mickey fixed his eyes on the gap between two mountainous walls; his oar caressed the jagged edges of hidden rocks and he inched his boat out to the open sea.

Bridie showed off her swimming and I walked in the sea and made breaststroke motions with my arms that fooled nobody. Evenings, after the pub, a crowd of men gathered in my uncle's house to chat and tell stories. I sat next door with Bridie and a group of women in Kitty Peadar's listening to tales they told of the herring gutting in Scotland and in the English ports while knitting needles clicked and fingers flew. Fingers eaten by salt from the kippering. Mammy went to bed early every night with Brendan. People said she was a bit peculiar but what else could you expect from a Monaghan woman, born so far from the sea.

We left Donegal in a hurry. Mammy sat pale and silent through the journey on the steel bus, the narrow gauge railway and the

Great Northern Railway. That night she was rushed to the hospital in Belfast in an ambulance. Next morning my father gave us tea and bread. No porridge. No bacon and egg. He told us Mammy would be away for a few weeks. We were to pray for her and stop asking questions. Mammy's ailments always excluded us, as if some mystery or shame was attached to them. Brendan crawled round the house crying 'Mamma, mamma,' his cheeks on fire with new teeth that were pushing through his gums. His sobbing often wakened us and we heard my father walking up and down the kitchen, singing and trying to put him to sleep. In the morning he clattered about and burned the porridge. He said we were worse than useless but he wouldn't allow Bridie get up during the night with Brendan.

It was the hottest summer of my childhood. And the bleakest. It was said you could fry an egg on the pavement. My father yelled at us for pushing the pram through melted tar and leaving black tyre marks on the polished floor in the hall and said he would have to take the strap to us if we didn't mend our ways.

Eva too disappeared from our lives. We never questioned her absence as we didn't separate her from Mammy. We talked a lot about her and skipped to the song she taught us:

My Aunt Jane, she called me in.
She gave me tea out of her wee tin.
Half a bap with sugar on the top
And three black balls out of her wee shop.

The old men from the Nazareth still came on Saturdays. Paddy Fogarty, Tatsy Rice and Jimmy who didn't know his second name. My father gave them money to make up for the soup and wheaten bread they had been expecting.

I heard Mrs Campbell tell a neighbour she had been to the hospital. Mrs Ward had had everything taken away but she was not mending. She would come home in a box. Mammy didn't come home in a box. She and another patient in her ward caught typhoid and were transferred to Purdysburn Isolation Hospital. She was there for months, or maybe it only seemed like months. My father went to Purdysburn many evenings to wave up at her window. Some days he would wait on the bank opposite the hospital for hours and not see her. He took us all in the ancient car he had bought and pointed at a distant figure at an upstairs window. The nightgowned figure raised and lowered its hand for a minute and disappeared. I wondered if it really was Mammy or a dummy with a moving arm, or just somebody who was paid to wave at watching families to keep them quiet.

I became friends with Betty McFaul at Miss Fletcher's, my new piano teacher. The reverend mother had received an anonymous letter telling about Sister Augustine's visits to our house and she was no longer allowed to leave the convent unaccompanied. Betty McFaul went to the convent preparatory school. Her mother, Mrs Doctor McFaul, didn't want her to mix with the commonality and pick up a backstreet accent. Perhaps because Mammy was in hospital or because Betty lay down on Miss Fletcher's floor and kicked until her mother agreed, I was invited to play at their home in South Street. We had tea in their huge first-floor drawing room, served by the maid, Kathleen Ryan, whose father worked at our quarry. 'How often do I have to tell you to scrape the butter on, Ryan, and scrape it off again!' Mrs McFaul complained to Kathleen. 'We must all do our bit for the war effort.' The cold drawing room and Mrs McFaul's vulture eyes made me uncomfortable but I was thrilled to have a new friend, especially one who lived in such a grand house.

To get to the McFauls' we had to pass Eva's house – a one-storey building with a long bit of rough ground in front. A narrow strip where grass and weeds choked the living daylights out of each other. Nobody saw inside Eva's house. It skulked behind filthy curtains as if it had been pushed out of the way for shame's sake and two stunted trees, waist high in briar and nettles, cast blackened shadows over it.

For my second visit with Betty to her home, I wore the brand-new blazer Mammy had bought before she was taken into hospital. As we passed Eva's house her voice cracked the air.

'Mary Ann! Come here, Mary Ann.'

I didn't want to stop for I could tell something was wrong with her but there was no way I could pretend not to hear the racket she was making. Her enormous shape filled the doorway. Pregnant women weren't encouraged to go out flaunting them-selves in those days so I wasn't used to their bloated bodies. I had never seen anything so repulsive as the figure shambling towards me. Men's shoes slip-slapped along the path. The laces had been taken out and the tongues lapped over feet that were puffed up like baps. Her right hand was splayed over the bulge in front of her. With her left she clutched the small of her back as if she was trying to stay upright and not topple over, like one of those celluloid dolls that wobble about on weighted bottoms.

The expanse of her belly mesmerised me. It rippled and moved as though something was alive under her filthy man's shirt. Something that kicked and elbowed, trying to burst through. Her father used to call at our house to collect Eva's wages. That was before Mammy started to take her to the grocer's as soon as she was paid. The cloth bag he carried on his back writhed and slithered, just like Eva's belly. He said it was his ferret. One day he opened the bag and showed us its mean, foxy face and darting body.

Eva grabbed the lapel of my new blazer.

'Mary Ann, get your mammy. Tell her she has to come.'

Her face too was swollen. You would have thought her whole body had been pumped up into a great barrage balloon. I felt sorry for her but she scared me. Her rolling, skelly eye. Her vast bulk. Her hand tugging at my blazer.

'My mammy can't come, Eva. She's in hospital.'

'She said she would come if it was sore. Tell her she has to come. Now. It's awful sore.' her moon face twisted and tears flowed over it in dirty channels. She stopped to get her breath. One hand clutched her back. The other clung to my blazer.

'She can't come, Eva. She's very sick. She's not allowed out.' I was shouting as loud as her, trying to get it into her thick skull.

'Tell your mammy, please Mary Ann. She will come if you tell her it's awful sore.'

I was fed up with her. What right had she to think Mammy would leave hospital for her when she didn't come home to her own children. Bridie had cried all night with toothache. It had persisted even though she put oil of cloves on the tooth and lay with a sock filled with warm salt against her cheek, and my father still had to walk the floor with Brendan to shut him up. Eva should have been ashamed, slopping around in dirty clothes. She hadn't even bothered to wash her greasy hair, let alone rinse it in rainwater. I tried to explain that typhoid was much worse than scarlet or diphtheria. Bridie and I had been allowed to stay in the fever hospital in our own town when we had scarlet but they had stuck our mother out in the heart of the country, miles from anyone. Bridie said no one could even speak to her for fear of catching it. The nurses had to leave her food outside the door and run away before she opened it. Same as they did with lepers. But I couldn't make Eva understand.

'She will come if you tell her. She promised. She promised.'

'Hurry up. Mamma's expecting us,' Betty called from the gate and started to walk on towards her house.

Something warm splashed my leg. Pee poured down from under Eva's skirt. A flood, thick and fast like when a cow lifts its tail. I jumped back but my patent shoes and white socks were spattered.

'You're disgusting,' I screamed. 'You should be ashamed of yourself.'

'I couldn't help it. It just come.' Eva stood like a moron, both feet in the pool. I wanted to shake her, to pull her onto dry land, but I was afraid Betty would come back and see me.

'It doesn't just come. You're not a baby. And you're not even wearing knickers. You know Mammy said you had to.'

'I couldn't help it. Honest. It just come.' Pain distorted her features. She bent over, doubled up. 'It's awful sore. Awful sore.'

'Do you need the doctor? Will I tell Doctor McFaul you're sick?'

She straightened up. 'No, I don't want him. Your mammy took us to see him. He shouted at us. Your mammy took the face off him. I want your mammy,' she howled.

I thought of putting my arms round her and helping her into the house but the steaming puddle between her and me had widened and narrow streams ran in all directions from it. And Betty McFaul's head moved past the end of the row of houses.

'Tell your mammy, Mary Ann. Tell her I need her. It's awful sore,' rang in my ears as I turned away. I closed the gate and watched Eva lumber back to the doorway, swaying from side to side the way her father did when he had been to the public house.

'Who's that? How do you know her?' asked Betty.

'She's just a skivvy. Used to scrub floors for us. She's a bit soft in the head.' Even as I spoke I was ashamed of myself.

Mammy did at last come home. I wanted to know if she was hollow inside and why had they taken everything away. She said children should be seen and not heard. Bridie and I never let her out of our sight. We handcuffed ourselves to her on her first trip to town. As we turned into Main Street a neighbour of Eva's, Mrs Bailey, stopped to ask my mother how she was keeping.

'Wasn't it terrible about poor Eva?'

'What about Eva?'

We could feel our mother's arms tense through the thick material of her coat.

'Why don't youse two wee girls go and have a look in Robinson's window?' We clung on like barnacles.

Eva was dead. Mrs Bailey whispered, her lips close to my mother's ear, funnelling words through cupped hand. Snatches of conversation escaped – 'Lying there for days. All by herself. Haemorrhage.'

'What about her father? Where was he?'

Mrs Bailey's eyes shot to the top of the lamp-post. Her lip curled down.

'On the blatter.' Out of the corner of her mouth.

'And the baby?'

She shook her head. Right to left. Left to right. A slow pendulum. More whisperings, more shielded hushings: 'Cord round its neck – hadn't a chance – didn't even know to cut the cord.'

Eva did know how to cut cord. We kept cord in the second drawer in the scullery. We took it off parcels and tied it in skeins.

I saw her baby in a white furry coat and blue romper suit. I wondered if the shop had wrapped him in brown paper and how did she get him without a man.

Mammy shivered. Her thin face was ashen.

'I'm tired, children. I'll have to go back.'

Arm-in-arm, the three of us turned half circle.

She sat for a long time by the range, warming her hands on the cup of tea Bridie made her. 'Eva's soul will have gone straight to heaven,' she told us. 'She was as innocent as a newborn baby.'

I thought of the babies buried behind the hedge in the graveyard, the babies who still had original sin on their souls and were not fit to be in God's presence, and I wondered what had become of Eva's baby.

Mammy took a long drink of tea. We were afraid she was going to cry, though her eyes were dry. Then she said, 'God help poor Eva. She had a sad errand to this world.'

9

I would catch sight of Eva in the washhouse, turning the handle of the mangle or on her knees on a chair at the sink, rubbing shirts against the washboard, skating from room to room on bits of blanket. When I reached out to touch her she slipped like water through my fingers. Something would brush against my sleeve, skim the back of my head. Eva's hands that had rubbed camphorated oil over my chest, pushed me on swings in the park? I turned and called 'Eva,' to the empty space behind me. Mammy still asked her to pass the starch or the blue bag, to keep testing the iron and scolded her for adding too much salt to soup.

'Can you see Eva, Mammy? Are you not frightened of her?'

'Of course I still see Eva and why should I be frightened of her? Can you imagine anyone less frightening?'

Bridie's two friends Betty McFaul and Claudette Campbell and I sat round the table. Teeth, tongues and eyes inspected each morsel of the barmbrack and apple tarts Mammy had baked for the Halloween party, searched for sixpences and the ring wrapped in greaseproof paper she had baked in them. Brendan had to be held in Bridie's arms to bob for apples that hung on string from the clothes-rack on the kitchen ceiling. My father said the noise we made would wake the dead in Dublin. Then he put a basin of water on the floor for apple-ducking. Betty had first go. Her face grazed the water, jabbed at dancing apples. Brendan pushed her head underneath and Betty said Mammy mustn't slap him because he was still a baby.

It was my turn to kneel over the basin. Eva's tear-streamed face bobbed up to float among red and green apples. Even after Brendan stuck his head right in and splashed water over the floor, it rose to the surface, wrinkled and distorted. We threw salt in the fire and Eva took shape among the crackling flames. Bridie and the others pointed with the poker at the faces of different boys from the Christian Brothers' School and at Claudette's boyfriend who went to the Royal High. At midnight Bridie prodded me to get up and look with her in the mirror for the reflections of our future husbands. I pretended to be asleep and pressed my hands hard against my eyelids, but Eva's double image still quivered among stinging red and orange lights.

Next evening and throughout All Souls' Day we visited the church and said seven Our Fathers, seven Hail Marys and seven Glory Be's to release a soul from purgatory. My parents had lists as long as their arms of souls waiting to be let into heaven. We trudged through the heavy doors and down the steps with other figures that November fog had turned into formless ghosts, and back in again to kneel among the mumble of Hail Marys and Glory Be's. I didn't pray for my grandparents or for Sister Augustine who had died three weeks previously. There were enough people to take care of them. Each visit I offered up for Eva, in case the last one hadn't worked. And I begged God to ask her to forgive me.

Afterwards, when I thought I saw Eva bringing in the washing from the garden or peeling potatoes in the scullery, I closed my ears and my eyes. On my monthly visits to Betty McFaul's home I sat in the back of her father's car, dizzy with the smell of ether and Mrs McFaul's perfume and my own importance. I looked straight ahead when we passed Eva's house and I buried her in the deepest crevices of my mind.

Bridie had won a scholarship to the Grammar School. She got out half an hour later than me and she made new friends, so I had no one to walk home with. I often invited girls from school to our house but I was never asked to theirs.

'Will you go to the wavin' or the windin' or the spinnin' when you lave school?' May Mulholland asked me. When I said I would go to university and be a war correspondent or a radio announcer, my classmates edged away from me. They allowed me to turn an end of the rope but not to skip. Outside the school gates a row of girls from my class linked arms across the breadth of the footpath and I had to walk in the gutter beside them or trail behind.

It was a relief when Sister Aquinas kept me behind after school to tutor me for the scholarship. She taught me to work out how long it took for trains travelling in opposite directions to pass each other and how many tiles were needed to cover a hearth or the walls of a bathroom. She explained vulgar fractions, πr^2 and why Archimedes jumped out of his bath. I learned about infinity and decimals that would go on recurring forever if I didn't put a dot on them. She gave me Bridie's old essays to learn by heart and said I was to pray and go to Communion on the first Friday of nine consecutive months.

On my last lesson before the exam she told me how the Wild Geese, after their defeat by William of Orange, had to go into exile and fight in armies over Europe. Suddenly, that woman whose heart I thought was made of stone walked over to the window and recited:

The swallow flies in the summer
and the gull returns to the sea
But never the wings of the Wild Geese
will flash over hill and lea.

'Mary Ann, can you imagine a sadder fate than to be banished from the green land of Ireland?' She gazed out at the rubbish tip, then raised her eyes to where the Lagan Mill chimney bisected the sky before turning to look at me.

I stared at my book. It was probably more serious to see a nun cry than to watch her eat.

Mammy took Bridie and me on her annual visit to Sister Mary Francis. She brought a fruit cake big enough for each member of the community to have a slice, a cardigan and three long-sleeved vests. We hated those visits. The convent that smelled of Mansion polish and boiled cabbage and the silences when Mammy and Sister Mary Francis stopped sniping at each other.

'Why do you wear a wedding ring, Sister, when you're not married?' I asked.

'Because I'm married to Christ. He is my bridegroom.'

'And are all the nuns married to him?'

'Yes, er yes. They are.'

'That's polygamy. It's a sin to have more than one wife,' said Bridie.

'Did they chop off your hair before or after they made you take off your white dress, Sister?'

'Children should be seen and not heard. Why don't you teach those two some manners, Ellen?'

Then Mammy told us about the time her mother took her and Agnes to their Aunt Margaret's profession when she entered the Carmelite order. A procession of young women in white wedding dresses left the chapel through a heavy door. After what seemed hours to a child of seven, she saw a group of figures, dressed in brown from head to toe, walking backwards into the church. Mary Francis tut-tutted and said Mammy must have been stupid to think they were walking backwards. She should have known that a Carmelite nun's face must always be covered once she was professed. Mary Francis said it was time for us to leave. She always sulked if her sisters talked about what had happened before she was born.

I didn't need Bridie to tell me that Claudette Campbell had only asked me to tea to get back at her. Claudette had accused Bridie of being a scholarship girl whose parents were too poor to pay for her education. Bridie had said it was just as well Claudette's parents had money because she didn't know a B from a bull's foot and was too stupid to pass an exam.

I breathed in the fragrance of carnations in a glass vase in the Campbell's dining room and Claudette's Californian Poppy wafted across the table to me. Our house smelled of wheaten bread and soda farls cooling in the kitchen and buttermilk going sour in an earthenware crock under the sink. The scarlet tips of Mrs Campbell's fingers presented me with a china cup and saucer.

'Pass the sandwiches, Claudette. We have a choice for you, Marianne. Would you mind if I call you Marianne? I don't know what came over your parents to give such an old woman's name to a wee girl.'

'It's like that song about the Lammas fair in Ballycastle. You know, Mummy, the bit where it says 'Would you treat your Mary Ann to some dulse and yellowman?' Ugh. It's so country.' shuddered Claudette.

Instead of spitting at her, I accepted two triangular morsels displayed in crustless symmetry on a paper doily. I didn't like cucumber and Mammy wouldn't give fish paste house room.

'I'd love you to call me Marianne, Mrs Campbell,' I rolled my new name and a fish paste triangle round my mouth. Marianne Ward! Headlines in *The Times* and the *Belfast Telegraph*.:

Another on-the-spot report from Venezuela from our foreign correspondent, Marianne Ward. Our intrepid reporter scorns danger to bring us a first-hand account of the shipwreck. Marianne Ward nibbled a cucumber sandwich at a reception in her honour at the White House. 'Thank you, Mr Roosevelt,' she said when the president, to thunderous applause, pinned the award for valour on her lapel. 'No, I never think of the risks, only the story.'

The dining room looked out on the garden where Mrs Campbell and Claudette, and the other neighbours, sat on sunny days in deckchairs, their skin turning from tan to golden brown, while Mammy elbowed pallidly through soapsuds and wholemeal flour. The lawn, like all the other lawns in the avenue, was a velvet island in a sea of flower beds. All other gardens except one! Ours was knee-high in potatoes, carrots, cabbages and beans. Six apple trees reached for the sky through tangled raspberry, gooseberry and blackcurrant bushes. Broken china embedded in the cement of the path, spelled out Bridget, Mary Ann and Brendan.

'Clau-deh-eh-ette, perhaps Marianne would like a fairy cake or a slice of marble cake.'

Each syllable of her daughter's name lingered like the notes of a love song. Whenever we fell out with Claudette, Bridie and I used to chant:

Claudette Campbell had a cat.

It sat upon the fender.
Every time it caught a rat
It shouted 'No surrender'.

How did Mrs Campbell stick that marble cake together without any of the joins showing? Protestants were so artistic.

'Take Marianne up to your bedroom and show her your new "bellay" outfit. I'm just going to pop into the kitchenette and slip on my pinny.'

'Pinny, fairy, kitchenette, "bellay".' Gossamer floated from Mrs Campbell's crimson lips and hovered in the air. Pinnies, light and frilly, for flower arranging or feather dusting to be popped on or slipped off. Mammy enveloped herself in her braskin first thing in the morning. She wrapped it round an old jumper and skirt in winter, over petticoat and vest in summer. Braskins were for scrubbing floors, digging potatoes, boiling jam. When the hooter sounded in the mill every evening at six, floods of weavers, winders and spinners poured into the streets. They walked, arm in arm, row upon row, their curlers glinting in sunlight or streetlight, their braskins stiff with grease and sweat.

I envied Claudette each and every one of her possessions from her single bed with its floppy eiderdown to the clothes on her back and the rings on her fingers. Every time I came into the Campbell home I wished I had been born on this side of the fence. Being a member of the one, true church was too much of a responsibility. Mammy used to tell us how the native Irish during the Famine preferred to starve to death, their mouths green from eating grass, than take the soup and hairy bacon available to those who gave up their faith. I would have been first in the bacon queue.

Claudette held a pair of ballet shoes against her face.

'Don't you just love them to pieces?'

I nodded vigorous, lying love. Ballet was the one thing I didn't envy her. I was a champion Irish dancer. Dancing was the only thing I did better than Bridie. I had won three gold and two silver medals at feiseanna. Mammy made my costumes – the dark green of the McCarthy School and the white with green embroidery for set dances – and she spent weeks embroidering them with intricate Celtic designs.

'Have you asked Marianne to your birthday party next Saturday?' Mrs Campbell smiled her way into the room.

I caught the horror on Claudette's face that her mother missed.

'That's settled then, dear. Nothing fancy, just a party tea for you two and a few girls from the "bellay" school. Very nice class of girl does "bellay", Marianne.'

They stood like sisters waving at the doorstep. Mrs Campbell draped her arms round her daughter's shoulders. Arms empty of babies, washing or shopping-bags. Being an only child looked great.

'She lives next door. I told you about her.' Claudette cast my Ashes of Roses into a pile of birthday presents.

Four pairs of eyes took in my lace-up shoes, ankle socks, check dress made out of a remnant from Anderson and McAuley's. I had never seen girls like these close up. Round-faced and fair like Claudette, in their smart shop-dresses.

'Is she the one that goes to the convent?'

'What's her name?'

'Marianne. I'm called Marianne.'

'No she's not. She's called Mary Ann,' said Claudette.

'Mary Ann! Mary Ann!' The four girls howled with laughter.

Lemonade in painted glasses tasted like gall. Meat and fish paste sandwiches turned to sand in my mouth. I thought of pictures in my school reader of sickly Victorian orphans gazing through leaded windows at merrymakers feasting inside, and I envied those orphans their freedom to move away.

Mrs Campbell slipped in from the kitchenette and popped the birthday cake on the table. 'Marianne won the cup for jig and hornpipe at the All-Ireland festival in Dublin this year.'

Cake jammed in Gloria's mouth. Had Mrs Campbell announced that I was a belly dancer in Baghdad the effect couldn't have been more dramatic.

'You dance for them after tea, dear. Show these girls how good you are.'

Back in the sitting room space was cleared.

'There's no music. I can't dance without music.'

'I'll play a jig. Jig jig, jiggetty jig!' Linda rifled through the music stool.

'I need special shoes for the jig.'

'Those look pretty special to me,' smirked Norma.

'We want the jig jig, jiggetty jig,' the four girls shouted, stamping their feet.

'I don't want to dance, Claudette. Please don't make me dance.'

'Dance,' she hissed, her back to the group.

'The Dusty Miller' stumbled and stuttered over the keyboard, then picked up momentum. Four figures on the sofa and armchair waited. I danced to the faltering music fixing my gaze on the upstairs window of the house opposite, well above the sniggers of the audience. 'The Dusty Miller' gathered speed. I followed. The contents of the china cabinet chattered in time to the quickening tempo. Faster and faster went the music, drowning the giggling on the sofa. Out of the corner of my eye I saw shapes leaning against each other, jabbing handkerchiefs at eyes and mouths. I raised my eyes to the roof of the house but they wriggled into the edge of my vision. The music raced. Breathless, stiff with tension, I tripped over my feet, struggled to lift them from the carpet. With a clash the music stopped. Linda, convulsed with laughter, fell on the keys.

'Don't stop. Finish the dance even if the roof falls in. Don't ever stop or you will have to start from the beginning,' Miss McCarthy's voice commanded. Programmed to go on to the end, I moved to the beat in my head while my hands by my sides tapped time. Above jeers and peals of mirth, I danced each step as though I was performing at the *Ard-Fheis*. A blue dress bobbed beside me. Blue and gold sandals thudded the carpet to whoops of encouragement from the onlookers. When the dance was finished I raced through the front door.

'Look what the cat brought in.' Bridie heard me sobbing at the back of the house 'Must have been a great party. Would your posh friends not let you play with them? Serves you right for being so full of yourself.'

'Go to your room and do your homework. This minute,' Mammy told her.

She strapped Brendan into his pram. Then she put a bottle in his mouth and a rattle in his hand. She led me through scattered bricks to the rocking chair, sat down and drew me against her.

'There, there, it's all right. You're home now.'

She crooned and rocked me in her arms as she would an infant. I smelled carbolic soap on the water-wrinkled hands that stroked my face and the rustiness of rainwater in the coils of her plaits. Brendan slurped and banged against the side of the pram and tomorrow's porridge spluttered on the range. My sobs subsided and tears fell till they had soaked the shoulder of Mammy's braskin and the broad strap of her vest.

10

If Joseph had addressed the letter to him, the head of the household, not to Mrs Ellen Ward, maybe my father would have reacted differently. Oh, he would have blustered, called Joseph a lazy good-for-nothing and waited to be coaxed. In the end he would have given in. He always did. Bridie and I had learned from a young age how to handle him, to wait for the right moment, to butter him up and make him think that what you wanted had been his own idea. Considering all the years he and Mammy had spent together, we wondered why she had never learned such a simple lesson.

The edge of the letter rimmed her apron pocket for a whole day. It was still in its brown envelope the following morning. It lay opened on the sideboard when we came back at teatime.

Dear Ellen,

You know our father left the farm saddled with debt. The bank is threatening to foreclose and take possession of the land and buildings unless we come up with five hundred pounds. I believe Michael has done well since the war started and I would appreciate it if he would lend the money till such time as I can pay it back.

I will go to England as soon as the war ends to seek employment. Tell him I am not asking for myself but for Agnes and Maisie.

Your brother
Joseph

A state of hostility was declared. My father didn't speak to us,
nor did he play with Brendan when he carried him round the
garden. Mammy and he spat words we had never heard across
the dinner table. Mortgage. Bailiffs. Grippers. Debtors' prison.
She stirred her resentment into the rice pudding, walloped it
into mashed potatoes. She demanded to know if he was prepared
to sit back and see her two sisters pitchforked onto the street
without a roof over their heads. He said he didn't work ten hours
a day to hand over his earnings to a jackass who had never given
him the time of day. It was only a loan, Mammy insisted. Her
people had never been beholden to anybody. Did he expect Joseph
to go down on bended knees to him?

'Only a loan! Till such time as he can pay it back! And he
hasn't even the common politeness to ask me in person. Has to
go hiding behind his sister's skirts. I've known cheek but that
beats Banagher. It would kill that wastrel to throw off his coat
and do an honest day's work. Well you can tell Mister God
Almighty he's not getting one penny from me.'

Why could Mammy not have waited till he had seen the brown
crust of the rice pudding, till he had smelled the spice of nutmeg
and let its buttery smoothness slide down his throat?

'You have no right to talk like that about Joseph in front of
the children,' she shouted. 'Was it his fault that his cattle died of
the red water and he had to go to the bank for a stock loan? He
has had nothing but bad luck in life, what with having to leave
the seminary, and his illness.'

'So it's luck he needed, is it? Was it luck that sent me tramping
round Scotland at thirteen years of age, looking for work when

he was lying about wasting his time in Maynooth? And I suppose I never had a day's illness in my life?' He slammed his knife and fork down on half a herring and a dollop of potato and left the table.

Apart from the odd cough we never remembered him being ill. He often told us about the time he went to the chemist for medicine for a sore throat. The chemist sat him down in the dispensing room, gave him a glass of whiskey and cut out his tonsils with a pair of scissors and he went straight back to finish his day's work on the roads. And when he was laying tarmacadam on the drive up to a golf course near Edinburgh a golf ball hit his leg with such ferocity that it lodged in the flesh. If he had stopped to have it removed, the tar would have hardened and a day's work would have been ruined. By the time he had it seen to, the golf ball was embedded in his leg. It was still there, over twenty years later, stuck to the bone about four inches up from his left ankle.

'Get a move on. There's not much fear that you two will burst a blood vessel. At the rate you're going the dishes won't be done till morning,' Mammy snapped.

I dried cups and plates that Bridie handed me. Through the scullery window I watched my father gouge the earth with a fork, seize a potato plant, shake it and fling potatoes not much bigger than golf balls into a metal pail. In his haste, he upset the pail and scattered them over the furrows they had been loath to leave. He stomped to the other side of the garden and started to break up a rough bit of ground. Not the measured, turf-cutter slicing of each sod, the turning over with the fork, the rhythm of the shaft in tune with the song on his lips. His spade had hardly sunk into the earth till it was out again and sods stiff with scutch grass, plantain and dandelion roots were hurled unsorted at a pile of debris ten feet from him. Veins bulged over his neck and temples. Sweat poured in rivers down his crimson face.

I thought of King Conor Mac Nessa, Ireland's first martyr. How, on the first Good Friday, he asked his seers why the world had been plunged into darkness. He was told that in a far off land a just man who was the Son of God was being crucified. He rushed with his sword into the forest, slashing branches off trees, saying that was what he would do to the killers of the just man. A fireball, that had been lodged in his head in a battle many years previously, burst and he dropped dead. And I remembered Eva telling me about purple clots that could move up from Mammy's legs and choke her heart.

'Don't burst a blood vessel, Daddy,' I whispered to the closed window. 'Don't get too angry or the golf ball will move up over your heart. Don't let it burst out of your brain.'

Evenings, he took to his bunker in the armchair beside the radio and camouflaged himself with the *Belfast Telegraph*, stretched to its full width. The sniping continued and the return fire.

'Are you going to lend the money and redeem the place or are you going to have it on your conscience till the end of your days that you let your own children's flesh and blood go homeless?'

'Can a man not have peace and quiet in the home he pays for? You watch your tongue, Missus, and get on with your duties or you might find yourself out on the street with them.'

I shot a look of terror at Bridie. The worry of whether I would win the scholarship to the grammar school or be an additional financial burden on my father paled at the prospect of Bridie replacing my outcast mother as mistress of the house. She rolled her eyes, shrugged her shoulders and went on reading *The Prisoner of Zenda*.

My father folded the newspaper across his lap. 'No, I will not see your sisters without a home. I have a lot of respect for Agnes when I think of what she has had to put up with from the rest of you. We have an extra bedroom and you are always whingeing about having too much to do since poor Eva died. Agnes can come here to live. She is more than welcome.' He raised his hand and his voice to silence Mammy who had jumped to her feet. 'As for Maisie. There are convents that look after the likes of her. God help her, sure what difference does it make to her where she is. If money is needed for her keep I will see to that. As for that half-lad of a brother of yours, he can rot in hell for all I care.'

He disappeared behind the paper. End of discussion. 'Hamburg Hammered Once Again. Sicily Attack Going Well,' the front page of the *Telegraph* proclaimed. Bridie and I stared open mouthed. We had never heard our father string so many words together at one go.

'If you want to finish Maisie off, you're going the right way about it. She knows a lot more than you and the likes of you give her credit for. And Agnes wouldn't come here. She would be under the sod in six months if she had to leave Moynagh. And another thing . . .'

Screams from Brendan cut Mammy in mid-flow.

'I'll go, Mammy.' Bridie and I collided in the doorway.

'How much longer can we stick those two yapping at each other,' she said as we dragged ourselves upstairs.

'It's not as if they stop when they go to bed.' Debt, mortgage, bailiffs, charity bounced off the walls of their bedroom at night and resounded in ours.

Brendan's cot shook. He was on his feet gripping the bars of his cot to support his rage.

'You shut up or the bogeyman will get you,' shouted Bridie from the door.

'Cruelty will come for you and take you away in a potato sack.' I charged across the bedroom and prodded his belly with devil's horns I had made with my fingers until he fell down laughing.

Bridie kicked off her shoes and slid head first under the cot. I followed her. We called up to Brendan that the toes tickling his face and belly were the bogeyman's fingers.

'Five hundred pounds is an awful lot of money to give anybody. Do you think Daddy will pay in the end?' Brendan grabbed hold of my toes and started to chew them.

'Oh, he'll pay all right.'

'He says he won't. He said he'd see Joseph in the workhouse first.'

'He says he won't, but he knows he will. That's what's making him angry.'

He did pay off the debt and every year he paid the Land Purchase Annuity due on Moynagh. And Mammy paid every day of the rest of their life together. Electricity bills, demands for ground rent, new plant for the quarry sparked off another row. The misdeeds of Mammy's family – her father's drunkenness, her grandfather's gambling and squandering as he tried to ape the gentry and Joseph's delusions of grandeur – were all raked up. She fought back tooth and nail. What a tragedy it was for her poor sisters that the sins of the fathers' should visit the children and real charity meant not counting the cost.

A letter to say that I had passed the scholarship brought a

temporary ceasefire. My father gave me a half-crown and said I wasn't the dimwit Sister Aquinas had led him to believe. He gave Mammy money to kit me out in J. and S. Donnelly's High Class Ladies Outfitters. Green blazer, gaberdine, jumper, two cream blouses and a bottle-green velour hat with a cream and green ribbon round the brim. Mammy bought a black button-up cardigan for Sister Aquinas and four books of stamps as thanks for tutoring me.

Mrs Donnelly's only daughter, Myrna, said she wished she had a quarter of my brains. She was in charge of the gown department that had 'Chez Myrna's' written in black and gold Gothic script above the entrance. She was nineteen and as popular as she was beautiful. I would gladly have traded three-quarters of my brains for Myrna's eyelashes, her violet eyes and her hourglass figure. Her mother had seen Myrna Loy in *Pretty Ladies* when she was pregnant and had been to every one of her films since that. Father Doyle had refused point blank to call a baby after a Hollywood actress and christened her Bridget but Mrs Donnelly saw to it that 'Myrna' appeared on her birth certificate. The Donnellys had just moved into 11 Rathbeg Avenue on the opposite side to us and christened it 'Shangri La'.

Newspapers showed the Abbey of Monte Cassino in ruins after Allied bombings. Mammy said it was a godless act and the Allies should be ashamed of themselves. De Valera refused to close the Axis ministries in Dublin so all travel between Eire and Britain was suspended, giving Joseph another excuse to put off looking for work. There was tremendous excitement in the avenue when Major Dalton was spotted stepping out of a staff-car. He hadn't been seen him since the war started and many folk assumed he had been killed or taken prisoner. He was as charming and courteous as ever. More distinguished, even. Greyer and thinner. He was now a colonel, commanding the third battalion of his regiment.

'Do you think this war will drag on much longer, Colonel?' my father asked him.

'No, I don't think so. The tide has turned for us. It will all be over within the year.'

I opened the bedroom curtains on the morning after the colonel went back to the war and saw a figure in white lying at the back of 'Lismore' – Mrs Dalton in her nightdress sprawled motionless on cold flags.

'Mrs Dalton's dead, Mammy. Come quick.'

She put Bridie in charge of Brendan and hurried across with me. In a very low cut satin nightdress that could have passed for a ball gown, Mrs Dalton was a magnificent corpse. Tragic and mysterious like Ophelia or the Lady of Shalott. Blood had dripped on the path from a cut on her left cheek and her skin was the colour of buttermilk. Mammy bent over her, an ear to her blue veined breast, fingers on her pulse. She sniffed, a hound scenting the fox; then stood up to her full four feet eleven inches.

'She's drunk. Blind drunk. Disgraceful. At this hour of the morning and her poor husband gone off to fight for a better world for us all.'

I knew only too well what Mammy thought about women and drink. It was perfectly all right, commendable even, for a man to have the occasional jar. Women who indulged were another matter. 'There are as many handbags as hard hats in the pubs nowadays and that is the cause of the ruination of this country,' she used to say.

'Go into the house and bring me a big bowl of water.'

I was surprised Mammy would even think of giving water in a

bowl to a grand lady like Mrs Dalton who lolled in the crook of her arm. She slapped the poor woman's face, short quick slaps on alternate cheeks. Then she threw the contents of the bowl over her. Mrs Dalton woke up and rubbed her face. Hair dripped over her shoulders. Her eyes were red and puffy, and a dark smudge was all that remained of the pencilled arch of her left eyebrow.

Mammy and I put her arms round our shoulders and half-dragged her to a chintz sofa in her sitting room.

'I need a drink,' slurred Mrs Dalton.

'That's just what you are going to have. I am going to make you a good strong cup of tea. Mary Ann, find a coat and cover her up,' said Mammy, averting her eyes from bare shoulders and a cleavage that plunged to Mrs Dalton's midriff.

I moved away from her and from the sweet-sour smell of stale alcohol and wandered around the room. The walls were crammed with pictures – hunting scenes, pictures of houses, churches and boats, men in uniform and disdainful women gazing into the distance. The furniture was old and dark and two bookcases lined the fireplace wall. I had never seen so many books except in the Public Library.

Mammy came in with a cup of mahogany-coloured tea into which she stirred three spoonfuls of sugar. Mrs Dalton winced.

'Drink every drop; then clean yourself up and go for a walk in the fresh air.'

Mrs Dalton drained the cup.

'I'll come across this afternoon to see how you are.' Mammy called from the doorway. 'We will remember your husband in our prayers every night and ask God to bring him safely home.'

'Don't you breathe one word about this to anyone,' she said as we crossed the road. 'That poor creature is all on her own here. Her husband's away at the war and she has no children or family to turn to. Is it any wonder she hits the bottle?'

That afternoon Mrs Dalton appeared at our front door with a huge bunch of flowers. She wore a green silk dress and was made up to the nines but her eyes were red and dark circled. Mammy whipped off her apron and hid it under a coat on the hallstand. She ushered Mrs Dalton into the sitting room. Visitors were always received with two bars of the electric fire. Bridie and I followed.

'How can I thank you for your kindness to me this morning, Mrs Ward. You too, Marianne. I feel I owe you an explanation.'

She looked tragic, yet elegant; silk-stockinged legs crossed at the ankles, the face of a wounded Madonna.

'Nonsense. You don't have to explain anything.'

'I need to talk to someone and you have been so good to me.' Mammy motioned her to an armchair in full view of Miss Fisher's serpentine table and the picture of the home where she had been brought up in Devon but our visitor made no remark about either or them. 'I must tell you why you found me in that state. You see, last night my husband confessed that he has been having an affair for years with a friend of mine in Sussex. I suspected something but didn't want to believe it.' She dabbed her eyes with a lace handkerchief. 'He's been spending his leaves with her. As soon as the war is over he plans to divorce me and turn me out of my home.' Tears welled in my eyes. 'I am at my wit's end.'

My mother pointed the door to us. Mrs Dalton rose and blocked our retreat.

'Let them stay. Let them know that men are deceivers. Young girls should be warned.'

Her eyes flashed. Her voice quivered. She was Emmeline Pankhurst, Anna Karenina, Scarlett O'Hara.

'She's bewitched him, the damn fool. Turned him against me. I am to be thrown out of my home. To find alternative accommodation. Can you imagine me in some ghastly little modern house?'

She paused to shudder. Bridie and I, in our eight-year-old home, shuddered in sympathy.

Mammy's feelings about drinking women registered very low on the Richter shock scale compared to her opinions of 'bad characters'. Flogging was too good for them.

A bottle of whiskey, reserved for the parish priest's annual visit or severe colds, was produced from the china cabinet.

'God help you, Mrs Dalton. How many men can you trust? The colonel seemed like a decent man. The bad rascal! How could he do such a thing to a lovely woman like yourself?'

Colonel Dalton did not set up house with his London floozie. On D-Day, at the Normandy Landings, his battalion led a successful assault on an unexpectedly well-defended stretch of the French coast but a stray mortar bomb put an end to his brilliant military career. And to his philandering.

Mrs Dalton looked sensational in the black silk dress and veiled hat she wore to the investiture at Buckingham Palace where she received from King George the DSO awarded posthumously to her husband. The *Carrig Herald* published a three-column account of the colonel's outstanding bravery and leadership and a picture of his widow holding his medal, grief-stricken but dignified.

Mammy and Mrs Dalton became friends, exchanging stories of their very different but equally loveless childhoods. Mrs Dalton learned that, as a triplet, she possessed singular healing powers. She had been unaware that she could cure warts by preparing food for the afflicted. Bridie and I were invited to take our wart scabbed fingers to 'Lismore' for tinned-salmon sandwiches and Bourbon biscuits. Despite frequent treatment, the warts persisted but salmon sandwiches and chocolate biscuits beat rubbing them with a live snail and burying it under a cabbage.

Girls who were only a few years older than me and Bridie were having the time of their lives. The soldiers of two armies to choose from. Well-fed Yanks who bulged with money, candy and silk stockings and British soldiers in rough-textured battledress and hairy greatcoats.

Myrna Donnelly, who had cold-shouldered British Tommies and local admirers alike, fell in love with Eddie Jakabowski, a lieutenant in the US army. A Clark Gable lookalike, he was the only son of a Texan rancher on whose land oil had started gushing ten years earlier. Myrna entertained her customers with photographs of Eddie's parents and their home, the likes of which had only ever been seen on the screen at the Alhambra.

Mr Donnelly was dispatched to Warrenpoint on the train every Sunday where he took the boat to Omeath. He returned with butter, steak and sausages smuggled from the unrationed Free State for Eddie's tea and the odd bottle of spirits for himself.

'Making an eejit of herself,' scorned Mammy 'for a foreigner with a name she can't even pronounce, let alone spell.'

Eddie arrived in a jeep to escort Myrna to dinners, balls and social evenings at the officers' mess at Langford Lodge. She wore different outfits on each occasion, most of which were slipped back on the clothes rail in Chez Myrna's the following morning. The sound of the jeep bringing her home could be heard at midnight, at one o'clock. At all hours.

'Mary Ann, get up quick and look.'

I craned out of the window of our bedroom. A bomber's moon stood high in the sky. Eddie held Myrna close. He cupped her face in his hands and kissed her. Then Myrna buried her head in his khaki tunic and Eddie stared down the avenue.

'That's lovelight gleaming in his eyes,' said Bridie. She and Claudette read Mrs Campbell's *Home Chat* and *Woman's Weekly* every Saturday.

Lights went on in 'Shangri La'. We ducked back into bed.

After a hectic courtship an engagement was announced. The event and slipping on of a five-star diamond ring were to be celebrated with Eddie's fellow officers after champagne at 'Shangri La'. On the night of the party Bridie and I hopscotched on the pavement opposite the Donnelly residence.

'Come on, in and watch me getting ready,' Myrna shouted through her bedroom window.

We sat on her bed in our school uniforms while Myrna, in a pink satin dressing gown, dipped into an array of creams and lotions. She powdered, painted and rouged her face before stepping into the ball gown which her mother held out for her. A fairytale princess shimmered before us. From her waist floated layer upon layer of gossamer lace in shades of blue, from azure to the sky at midnight. A low-cut bodice revealed Myrna's smooth neck together with a considerable expanse of powdered bosom.

We stood in the doorway with her parents as Eddie handed Myrna up into the back seat of the jeep and climbed in the front beside his driver.

'Just like *Test Pilot* with Clark Gable and Myrna Loy,' Mrs Donnelly sniffed and blew her nose.

'Myrna Loy and Melvyn Douglas in *Third Finger, Left Hand*,' said Bridie.

Myrna's courtship was cut short when Eddie's regiment was called to fight Hitler and crush the troops of Emperor Hirohito. She scanned the faces of every US soldier on Pathé News, from the Normandy landings to the shores of Iwo Jima. Only his letters kept her going. Letters from which great hunks were all too often obliterated by the censor's blue pencil. They also brightened the lives of many of the young women who came into 'Chez Myrna's' to browse, to shop or share their loneliness.

'I feel really sorry for Myrna,' Bridie said. She was reading in the paper about the Yanks and their battles against the Japanese who preferred to die rather than surrender. 'She doesn't know if she will ever see Eddie again.'

Mammy looked up from the sewing machine and the shirt she was making for Brendan out of one of her old dresses. 'There's hope from the ocean but none from the grave,' she said. 'There are plenty of women in England who won't ever see their husbands again. Myrna Donnelly could have had her pick of the decent Catholic men in her own home town but she had to take up with a cowboy from the Wild West who doesn't even believe in the Pope.'

11

8 May 1945: VE-Day. It was all over. We went with my father to the bonfire in the main square. A group of Belgians soldiers – boys not much older than me – stood beside us. Two of them asked my father's permission to dance with Bridie and me. I danced with Michel, aged eighteen, from Liège, who asked to walk home with me. He pulled me close to him when other couples bumped into us and whispered '*Tu es si belle, Marianne,*' into my neck. My father glared at Henri who had danced with Bridie and stood with his arm round her shoulders during the firework display. He said we had had enough excitement for one day, that it was time we were in bed and he marched us home.

Bonfires crackled behind us. The strains of 'Tipperary' 'Roll Out the Barrel' and 'The White Cliffs of Dover' followed our sullen progress back to Rathbeg Avenue.

'*Tu es si belle, Marianne,*' I said over and over again into my pillow. I dreamed I wore a dress with layers of blue net like Myrna Donnelly's and that I was gliding round the Town Hall dance floor in Michel's arms.

On 16 May Mammy hushed us to silence during Éamon de Valera's calm but passionate reply to Churchill's attack on Irish neutrality in his victory broadcast:

> Could he not find in his heart the generosity to acknow-
> ledge that there is a small nation that stood alone not for

one year or two, but for several hundred years against aggression: a small nation that could never be got to accept defeat and has never surrendered her soul?

'That will fix the old bulldog,' cheered Mammy. 'Does he think we have all lost our memories?'

My father switched off the wireless and said we should be grateful the war was over and he would thank Mammy to make his tea instead of trying to start another one.

Agnes wrote that Joseph had gone to England and had found work in Coventry.

'A man with Joseph's brains and education will be snapped up over there. He will have got a job teaching Latin and Greek in a boys college or in a seminary,' said Mammy, pleased he would have a chance to make his mark.

'Coventry was flattened. More likely he'll be labouring on a building site,' said my father and added that he didn't care if Joseph was breaking stones as long as he paid back the money he owed.

Though not a square inch of Carrig had been touched by enemy action, the fields sl

oping down behind our house became a building site. My father bought two more lorries, ex-War Department, and hired another four to deliver materials for temporary roads and house foundations and road surfaces. A housing estate was constructed on the flat land below us and started to sprawl uphill on the field behind our garden.

'Why don't you look where you're building your roads and footpaths, Daddy? Brendan will never be able to look down to Australia,' I said to him.

'That housing estate is our bread and butter. It will keep the wolf from the door for another few years. Maybe I'll find another tunnel for Brendan at the next blasting,' he answered. And they covered up forever, under piles of rubble and concrete, the dark tunnel that went all the way down to Australia.

Railings and a gate once more enclosed our front garden. Mrs Dalton had a six-foot fence erected. To shelter her from the prevailing wind, she explained. The owner of the local saw-mill, Robert Jefferson, a well-set-up bachelor, personally supervised its construction. He often worked overtime. On the late shift. He and Mrs Dalton could be seen driving through wrought-iron gates in his black Armstrong Siddeley and a handsome couple they made.

She called on us with important news one day. Lismore was to be sold. After she and Mr Jefferson were married they would move into his Victorian mansion in the depths of the country. My parents knew the house, in secluded grounds, miles beyond the octopus reach of our fast expanding town.

My mother held strong opinions on a vast number of subjects from Charles Stewart Parnell's adultery to Dr Crippen; from dried eggs to the seams the schoolmaster's wife drew with a crayon on the backs of her legs. Her views on the remarriage of widows were unequivocal.

'One man in a lifetime is more than enough. Any woman who lumbers herself with another husband is man-mad or needs to have her head examined.'

It was different for widowers. They needed a woman to look after them, cook their meals, run a proper home for their children. As Mrs Dalton was English and badly done-by, my mother's rules didn't apply to her. She was magnificent in pink and white and she glowed with the excitement of a teenager in love for the first time.

'I cannot begin to tell you how happy I am. I never knew what it was to have a real man until I met Robert. So virile, so passionate, so . . . '

Bridie and I leaned forward, agog. At which point my mother ordered us to take Brendan for a walk and watched till we passed through the front gate.

VJ-Day ended Myrna Donnelly's anguish. It transpired that Eddie had been shot in the leg by a stray American bullet as he was about to capture the beachhead at Anzio and he had finished the war without further conflict or blemish at a recuperation centre in East Anglia.

Myrna announced to her parents that she had to go to London to see about updating stock. She confided to Bridie, me and anyone who happened to come into Chez Myrna's that she was going to have a few days with Eddie to finalise wedding arrangements before he was shipped back to the United States.

A radiant bride-to-be returned to busy herself with her trousseau and wait.

And wait.

Barbara Crossey, fiancée of Lt Larry Stretzl, got the call from Uncle Sam and embarked at Portsmouth. Young Carrig women who were to marry American soldiers were summoned and left with bursting suitcases for a new life in the New World. Boats sailed from Liverpool, from Southampton, from Portsmouth crammed with GI-brides. But no letter arrived from the US War Office, on behalf of Lt Jakabowski, with travel pass and documents for Myrna. And from the lieutenant himself there came not a letter, not a postcard, not a word.

News did reach the Donnellys via Mrs Barbara Stretzl. The ranch she and Larry lived on in Texas bordered the Jakabowski acres. Everything Eddie had said about the oil and the big house was true. He had just neglected to mention one item – or four, if you counted his three children.

Myrna's bloom faded. Her step lost its bounce and the flesh melted from her.

'Poor Myrna, she looks as if she's in the last stages of TB,' Mammy said. 'She won't be long for this world if she goes on like this.'

Brows puckered. Heads nodded in sympathy.

Mrs Donnelly appointed another assistant until her daughter recovered from 'a chesty cold', and it was as if the earth had opened up and swallowed Myrna.

'Gone to finishing school in Switzerland to complete her education,' mumbled her mother.

'She was finished before she left. She could teach the rest of us a thing or two,' ran the whisper round the town.

Rumour, deadly as poison gas, spread in and out of the houses in the avenue and swept like a tornado through the spinning rooms, the reeling rooms and into every corner of the weaving rooms.

Myrna Donnelly had gone to the bad.

Myrna Donnelly for all her airs and graces was no better than a common streetwalker.

'I'll say this and I'll say no more.' Mammy lowered the clothes rack from the kitchen ceiling. We waited while she covered its wooden bars with sheets, pillowcases and liberty bodices. 'If Mrs Donnelly saw fit to call her daughter after a Hollywood tramp she shouldn't be too surprised when she behaves like one.'

One February morning Mammy got word that one of her sisters was dying. No telegram or letter arrived but she had been smelling the clay for days and she had heard the banshee keening for two nights outside her window. To crown it all, she had been wakened by three death knocks – the Holy Souls confirming her worst fears.

'Pray it's not Agnes,' she said before she set out with Brendan for the bus, 'for what would Maisie do without her? Make sure your daddy's dinner is on the table when he comes home at six and behave yourselves.'

'Your mother's very headstrong,' my father said, 'When she takes a notion I might as well try to turn the tide as try to control her.'

Maisie was dead when Mammy arrived. She hadn't moved when Agnes tried to waken the warm body beside her. No one, not even the doctor, knew the hour of her death. Except Mammy. She fixed it at five o' clock on the dot, the time of the Holy Souls' warning.

Next day we drove to Moynagh with my father. Maisie, already coffined, was laid out in the parlour. Though in her late forties she was dressed, not in a shroud, but in the blue-and-white of a Child of Mary. A mother-of-pearl rosary was draped over her stubby hands. The same look of contentment covered her face as when she pottered from henhouse to byre, or out to the fields, or sat by the fire at night listening to me and Agnes and Joseph. Birds nesting in the chimney flapped and squawked and sent showers of soot down over the fireplace. Somebody said it was Maisie's soul, newly released, flying up to heaven. A dusty hawk in a case perched on a marble-topped chest of drawers above the coffin, together with a framed photo of Fr James McKenna, my great uncle, who had died in the Philippines, and the Infant of Prague in a glass dome which released a snowstorm when you turned it upside down.

My father stood at the bottom of the coffin, eyes down, his lips moving in prayer.

'She's gone to a better place,' sobbed a neighbour, 'the poor innocent creature. She didn't know what sin was.'

Between me and Maisie's innocence sprang the Mayo man with the wild rubbery stalk leaping out of his trousers and I found no prayers for Maisie. 'Please God, make him go away. Dear God, take him away,' I begged.

A taxi brought Sister Mary Francis and a companion, Sister Vincent, from the convent in Dublin. Nuns weren't allowed to travel alone. Their skirts sent dust balls snowballing along the wooden floor, rising against cinnamon-coloured skirting boards, drifting down to regroup in corners. Sister Mary Francis dropped tears over Maisie's hands and Sister Vincent said 'Eternal rest grant unto her, O Lord,' in a jolly west-of-Ireland voice, shook hands with the rest of us and said how pleased she was to see us. All the family kissed Maisie and said their goodbyes. My mouth skimmed above hers. Above the cold taste of death.

Before the undertaker nailed down the lid we had to withdraw to the kitchen. Mammy explained that it was a custom in the family to allow Miss Fisher time on her own to tend the corpse. I glanced up at her portrait which dwarfed the yellowed photograph of my grandmother. I hoped she would be dressed in her blue velvet gown when she tended Maisie and that she wouldn't scare the wits out of her by appearing red-eyed in the nightdress she wore to roam the house.

The priest shook holy water into the grave and my father, the only male member of the family present, cast the first spadeful of red earth on the coffin.

'She's gone back to her own people. Back to the earth where they belong,' said Mammy.

'Will you give over with that superstitious nonsense.' Sister Mary Francis turned like a tiger on her. 'Maisie was my sister. As much a sister as you or Agnes. Can you not let her rest in peace. Today of all days.'

Sister Vincent placed her barrel of a body between Mammy and her youngest sister and told Mary Francis to remember her calling and behave in a way that befitted a member of the Mercy Order.

When we got back to the house a meal was laid out on the parlour table – cold ham and chicken, bread, cake and tea. Everyone struggled for a place near the fire that had been lit by Mrs Brady during the funeral. Windows steamed, walls sweated and damp glistened on cinnamon wainscotting. My father poured whiskey and porter for the men.

'Could I offer a glass of sherry to any of the ladies?' he asked picking up a bottle of Bristol Cream.

'You could try offering us some of your Bushmills, Michael,' Sister Vincent filled a tumbler with whiskey and knocked it back.

My father said that before driving north he would take the two nuns to the convent in Clones where they were to spend the night. Agnes asked Sister Vincent would she like a slice of onion to take away the smell of the whiskey and Sister Vincent said she would rather have another glassful to help her sleep in a strange bed.

When all the mourners had gone, Brendan was put down for the night. Agnes took a box of papers and photographs out of the top drawer in the sideboard: my grandparents both dressed in dark clothes on their wedding day, Father Tom at his ordination and at the Eucharistic Congress in Dublin and Joseph in soutane and clerical collar. Almost a priest.

'Why did Joseph leave Maynooth?' asked Bridie.

Mammy and Agnes exchanged glances. Agnes stood up and

put turf on the fire and asked did we want tea.

'Did he fail his exams? Did he not believe in God?' Bridie persisted.

'Of course he believed in God and he was top of his class in theology and classics,' Mammy snapped at her and said it was time we were all in bed.

'Was it to do with Gilmour?' I asked.

Agnes stopped in the act of dipping a tin jug into a bucket of water.

'Yes, it was. They're old enough to know,' Mammy stared at Agnes whose shrug of agreement was barely perceptible. 'He brought misfortune to this house. He hunted Joseph from morning to night as if he was a criminal. Lay in wait to ambush him,' she paused waited for her sister to help her out but Agnes, teapot in one hand, caddy in the other, said nothing. 'Joseph had no interest in politics. Not at that time.' Agnes put the teapot on the range to warm and dropped three spoons of tea into it. 'Gilmour and his murderers combed every inch of the place looking for him. We hid him between the floorboards up in the far loft. He lay there for days. We hardly dared bring food up to him. If the Tans had found out they would have set fire to the place and him in it.'

'It wasn't just Joseph they were after. It was any Irishman that didn't lick their boots,' said Agnes.

'But after the Treaty why did Joseph not go back to Maynooth and finish his training?' asked Bridie.

'All those years of being on the run had affected him. Well wouldn't it affect any sane person? Buried alive up there in darkness with only mice and vermin for company. Thinking that every new day might be your last.' Mammy pointed in the direction of the far attics. 'Wouldn't it drive anybody mad? But the authorities in Maynooth showed no mercy. When Joseph came out of hospital they wouldn't have him back. They had been snooping. Found out about Maisie. Tried to pretend there was insanity in our family. That he wasn't fit to be a priest.' Her face flushed and her voice rose to a shriek. 'There never was a hint of insanity in the McKennas. There were clergy on both sides.'

'Would you give over, Mammy, and Mary Ann, you shut up and stop asking stupid questions.' Bridie led Agnes to a seat by the fire and wiped her cheeks. Mammy huffed and puffed and told her not to be so cheeky but I could see she was concerned about Agnes.

'When you're at it, why don't you tell them what sort of hospital he was in? It was Monaghan lunatic asylum.' I had never before heard Agnes raise her voice in anger. 'Blame Gilmour. Blame our mother. Blame the Superior in Maynooth. Why not blame Joseph for a change but don't ever let me hear anyone blame Maisie.' She took a pair of tortoiseshell rosary beads from a hook on the dresser and said 'God help her, she'll find it strange in heaven after Moynagh for she never spent a night anywhere but under this roof, though there were those that thought she should be hidden away. We'll kneel down now and say the Rosary for the repose of her soul.'

Mammy distributed beads to us and bowed her head, not raising it to correct Agnes when she said the joyful mysteries even though it was Tuesday.

I climbed into the hollow that had been moulded over the years by Maisie's body and listened to Agnes undressing in the dusk. The swish of her best silk blouse and the sigh of flesh released from her Sunday corset. Unsnapping of hooks and popping of fasteners, followed by the thwack of twill and laces and whalebone. A corset screen blackened for a moment the space between me and Agnes before landing with a thud and a jangle of suspenders on the wooden chair.

'Daddy says you should come and live with us. There will be plenty of company and maybe you won't miss Maisie so much.'

'When I leave Moynagh it will be feet first and I hope I always miss Maisie.' Agnes put her arm over me and we both rolled into the middle of the bed. 'She was great company, you know. She knew so much by instinct. She heard sounds we couldn't hear and she was in touch with things the rest of us couldn't begin to understand.'

Maisie always found eggs the hens laid away. When baby turkeys were lost she knew exactly where to look and nobody could soothe cows in labour like her or nurse calves and piglets that didn't look as if they would survive their birth. At times she would stop brushing the floor or shelling peas, and a faraway smile lit up her face.

'What can you hear, Maisie?' I would ask her but I never understood her answer. It was fairy music Agnes told me, sweeter than the wind whistling through rushes or in the heads of bog-cotton.

'I've heard it said,' she went on, 'that fairy music is so beguiling that even the angels in heaven stop whatever they're at and lean down to listen. Those who catch even a few notes of it, break their hearts because they can't enjoy it forever.'

'I'll ask Mammy if I can stay with you for a week or so to keep you company.'

'And what about your schooling? No, child, I have to get used to being without Maisie. Maybe you and Bridie will come down with your mammy when the days turn.'

I woke to the squawking of chickens and the sound of Brendan calling 'Chukky chukky'. The loft smelled of Maisie, of milk that had dried into her clothes, of cow sweat, of the rushes she had plucked to weave fresh Saint Bridget's crosses the evening before she died.

'Did Granny murder Gilmour?' I asked. It was Wednesday evening. My father was playing cards at Mr Bradshaw's.

'That's a wicked thing to say. You two should stick to your books and mind your own business.'

Bridie placed her pen beside her exercise book and leaned back in her chair. 'Well did she or didn't she?'

Mammy took off her glasses, folded the *Telegraph* and put it on top of the wireless. 'It wasn't murder. It was self-defence. The Bible says "An eye for an eye and a tooth for a tooth."'

'Why was he trying to kill her?' I asked.

'It was nearly dark when the Tans arrived. They searched the house, turned beds upside down, smashed the crockery and anything they laid eyes on. They even went up to the attics and tramped over the spot where Joseph was hiding. We thought our last hour had come. Before they left Gilmour said to my mother "We'll be back in daylight. I'll find him if it's the last thing I do." She sent Agnes and me across the field to make sure they had gone before she allowed Joseph to come down and go out for a breath of air.'

Picture Agnes and Ellen, home for two days from her job of nursemaid to an English family in Cootehill. They race like hares past the circle of stones the donkey treads during the churning and through scabbed apple trees. They slip through the rotting gate into a field that is still sodden despite a week's watery July sunshine. They move parallel to the Auxiliaries' tender in the lane and crouch inside the hedge at the gate. They hear Packie Flynn's oaths as he falls and staggers towards the spot two miles along the road where his tribe have their camp.

They don't hear his curses or his foul language or the noise of a bottle smashing. They listen only to the growl of the tender now two feet from them, as it prepares, at a snail's pace, to turn out of the road. English voices swear at Packie Flynn. Threaten to run over him. They hear him slither into the ditch before the vehicle with its load of jailbirds takes the road to Ballyroe.

Breathless, they tell their mother the coast is clear and Joseph is released from his tomb. Mary McKenna guides the stiff body of her son down the stairs to the pump and waits in the shadows under the eaves of the house. And watches. She hears Gilmour's footsteps. The light tread of an assassin. She hears the click as the hammer of his revolver is retracted.

Years of groping in the dark at Moynagh have heightened her senses. Years of learning to avoid her husband's fists have made her invisible. She sees or she remembers the stocky figure of Gilmour. Black jacket, Sam Brown and holster, fawn breeches, woollen socks. In pitch darkness he pads towards the groaning pump handle; towards Joseph's gasps as cold water pours over his head.

Mary McKenna has lost one son on the spot where Joseph's head is bent under the mouth of the pump. She will not lose another. She sees Gilmour aim, step closer to his invisible target. Silent as a cat she moves, but the blow the edge of her spade lands on his head is struck with the strength of an ox. Blow upon blow is rained on Gilmour till the body stops twitching. She tells Agnes to bring Joseph's coat and what bread there is in the house and she orders him to run all night over the fields and hide during the day.

Maisie is instructed to throw buckets of muddy water from the duck pond over blood that spouted in a fountain from Gilmour's head after the first blow. The sound of a creaking pump would carry too far on a still night. Mary Francis is posted in the field near the road to keep watch. Agnes, Ellen and their mother drag the body to its hiding place.

Bridie was the first to break the silence when Mammy stopped speaking.

'What did you do with his body?'

I couldn't speak. A cushion cover had come loose and was twisted in my hands. I saw Joseph's spade hit the side of the Mayo man's head and I knew what would have happened to him if he hadn't fallen into the boghole.

'We disposed of it in the last place that trash from the back streets of England would think of searching.'

She drew back the curtains and stared out into the night. We watched her, too awed to speak. She turned round and said she would answer no more questions. She had already told us too much. We knelt before the lamp under the picture of the Sacred Heart and swore we would never breathe a word of what we had heard to a living soul, not even our father.

Some time later she told us the Tans came back at dawn and wrecked what they had missed the last time. All the treasures Miss Fisher had brought from England, except for the china and ornaments they had buried in the potato field; and they smashed the furniture that had been part of my grandmother's dowry. The card table in our sitting room had been put in the hen house and covered with old sacks and bags of meal. Other families in the district suffered. Their sons were rounded up and beaten – and the McKennas were blamed for what happened.

Rumours flew round the neighbourhood and fingers were pointed, though nobody could prove that an old woman, her two prim daughters, a child and poor simple Maisie could have had anything to do with Gilmour vanishing off the face of the earth. And what decent person would admit talking to, let alone believing the word of a drunken tinker like Packie Flynn?

'I expect Gilmour was just listed as a casualty of war when

the truce was agreed the following day.' Mammy shrugged her shoulders and added, 'They partitioned the country into the Irish Free State and the Six Counties with what old Craig called a Protestant parliament and a Protestant people and they thought they had solved the problems of Ireland for once and all. As if Irish people would ever stop fighting to get back their six lost fields.'

12

It never entered my parents' heads that I would mitch from school. That I would mitch to go to the picture house with a member of the opposite sex, who was not only English but a Protestant as well, was inconceivable. It was no use Alan assuring me he was Church of England, turned atheist. Anyone who didn't go to the convent or the Christian Brothers' school, or attend Sunday Mass at Saint Malachi's church was a Protestant or what Tom Ryan called a relapsed Catholic. As for being an atheist, in Carrig you were a Protestant atheist or a Catholic atheist.

I pulled my fringe over the latest batch of spots and scowled at the bumpy nose that the chill of the bedroom had turned to shining red. Alan was the double of Alan Ladd, only half a foot taller. I asked myself once again what on earth someone as gorgeous as him saw in me. I scraped a circle through the frosted forests on the window-pane. Icicles hung from the eaves of houses and a fresh coating of snow whitened piles of slush on the edges of the road. With any luck, buses from the country districts would be cancelled and my absence wouldn't be noticed among the empty desks in my classroom. If asked, Bridie would say I hadn't felt well at lunchtime.

It was three months since the wind had swept my school hat across the street to land at Alan's feet.

A gust? A puff? A sudden flurry? I don't remember. All I see is my green velour hat rise and sail across Castle Street, drop on the pavement in front of him, then dance off with a skip and a jump until his hand reaches down and stops it careering into the traffic.

For weeks before they met my parents had observed each other every Sunday at eight o'clock Mass without speaking. My father noted Mammy's modest demeanour, her country way of dressing and her serene face. He found out that she worked in J. C. Abernethy's High Class Ladies' and Gents' Outfitters, so he bought a pair of socks at her counter. He watched her wrap them in brown paper and write out the bill and, while they waited for his change and receipt to fly back on the overhead railway line from Mrs Abernethy's office, he asked Mammy where she hailed from. Every week he bought socks or handkerchiefs or a tie until the day he found she had been moved to haberdashery. He chose a posy of stiff green linen leaves and blue linen flowers on wired stems and presented it to her as she left the shop. On Christmas Eve, he reached across the marble-topped table in Rossi's ice cream parlour and put a red-stoned ring on her finger.

In their second year at Queen's University, Bridie and Tim Molloy were assigned to the same dissecting table. By the time they knew their corpse inside out they were certain they wanted to spend their lives together.

The church. A marble top. A dissecting table. Solid foundations.

The Bible warns against houses built on sand. It says nothing about building on a breath of wind, and if it did, would you listen? Would you not feel sorry for people who will never know the joy of living on air? The lightness of it. The weightless joy of it. And you take care. When winds blow roughly you learn to sway with them, to lean into them. You know that your house may rock, may shake a bit, but not for one moment do you think it could ever come tumbling down.

'Don't put it on. It hides your face. You're much prettier without it.' He pushed fair hair out of his eyes. He wore the maroon blazer of the Royal High school. I loved the confident way he had crossed the road with my hat. His English accent gave him an air of superiority, so different from the fumbling Christian Brothers' boys who hung around Bridie, tripping each other up to walk beside her.

'I'm supposed to wear it in the street.'

'What's your name?'

'Marianne. Marianne,' I repeated.

'Marianne.' he paused. 'It suits you. I'm Alan. Alan Reed, and I'm pleased to meet you, Marianne.'

'You're not from here.' I said. We had turned off Railway Street and were walking up the Dublin Road to Rathbeg Avenue. I hoped the girls in my class would see me with him. He was nearly as tall as my father and looked at least seventeen.

'I was sent over to Carrig to live with my grandmother when the Germans started bombing London. After the war my father got a job in Singapore and my mother went with him. They thought it best for me to stay on till I finished school.'

'You'd better not come any further,' I said when we reached Rathbeg Avenue. 'My parents are very old fashioned.'

'OK. I'll see you tomorrow, Marianne.'

He was waiting in the same place the next day and every day. I daydreamed through afternoon classes about him standing at F. W. Collins's bookshop and turning round when I arrived as if we were meeting by accident. We varied the routes we took and Alan camouflaged his blazer with a black gaberdine or a lumber-jacket. Saturdays, we cycled to Lough Neagh or to the coast and we often climbed up Logan's Hill to sit under whin bushes, away from fingers pointing at the Catholic girl going out with a Protestant.

The day school broke up for Christmas he gave me a box containing four pink handkerchiefs, each with the letter M embroidered in the corner. One of the hankies covered the base of the box; the other three were folded in triangles and pinned like petals to the centre. I hid them under the newspaper that lined my drawer and slid his Christmas card 'To Marianne, All my love, Alan' beneath the lino under my bed.

He had already bought the tickets for *Madame Curie*. Seats in the stalls. Not too near the pit where fights always broke out, not under the edge of the balcony in direct line of fire from orange peel and spittle and not in the courting seats on the back row. The stink of Woodbines and farting competitions in the pit drifted up to us. I filled my lungs with the fragrance of Knight's Castile soap on Alan's skin. Of romance and adventure.

It looked even colder in Poland and Paris than in Carrig. Greer Garson's latest experiment to separate radium from pitchblende had failed. Walter Pidgeon, ill and cold, had just put his arms round her to comfort her when Alan took my right hand in both of his. He traced my fingers with the precision of a sculptor memorising their shape and size. Over and over again. I held my breath. Each finger anticipated his touch, stretched out from its neighbour lest he miss any fraction of the hollow between thumb and forefinger, between the third and little finger. Wished they were longer and more tapered to prolong the pressure of his fingers on mine.

Greer Garson shouted 'It's radium. It's my radium.'

Alan raised my hand to his lips and kissed the palm and a

glow, warmer than the ball of brightness on the black-and-white screen, spread through me. I could have imagined Pierre Curie kissing Marie's palm. Going down on one knee, even. He was a Frenchman, wise in the ways of the world and sophisticated like Alan. Pat Flanagan and his mates in the hurling team would think it was sissy to kiss a girl's hand. Two small boys in front of us turned round and shouted to Alan, 'Give her a birdie. Go on. What's keeping you?' Walter Pidgeon died. Madame Curie won the Nobel Prize and I floated up above the shower of sweet-wrappers and chip papers that rained down from the balcony.

'You're beautiful, Marianne.' Alan's lips brushed my cheek as *The End* appeared on the screen.

'You're in love, Marianne,' I told the face that glowed in my bedroom mirror. The girl in the mirror parted her lips. Eyes, dark with mystery, eyes that sparked with the lovelight Bridie had recognised on Eddie Jakabowski's face, smiled in agreement. Radiantly.

The following Saturday we took the train to Belfast to see *The Courage of Lassie* in technicolour at the Imperial. I got away with buying a half-price railway ticket and we went to the cheapest seats, two rows from the screen. We had money only for two milk shakes and one doughnut that squelched jam over our lips and fingers at every bite. I hoped on the journey back to Carrig to find an empty compartment with upholstered seats like the one Eva and I had shared when she took me to the eye hospital. We stood in the central aisle of a utility train clutching a wooden post and I had to be content with Alan's hand coiled round mine and the weight of his body against me every time we lurched to a halt.

'You're too fond of gallivanting, miss,' said my father when I came home. 'In future you will stay in on Saturdays and help your mother. You're getting to be as bad as your sister. Where were you till this time?'

'It's only seven o'clock, Daddy. I was going over my maths homework with Betty McFaul and we just sat talking.' I waved an exercise book at him.

'Leave her alone, Mick. Mary Ann works hard at school. She needs to relax sometime.'

'She will do what's she's told and so will that other one. They're not too old to feel the weight of my hand. I won't have my daughters traipsing about in the dark and I won't have you contradicting me in my own house.'

Mammy told us his money problems made him bad-tempered. McClennan's the builders owed him two thousand pounds for materials he had supplied to build a new bridge. They had been declared bankrupt and as far as payment was concerned he might just as well have flushed the money down the drain. She daren't ask about the business or he would start a row that forty could fight in and throw Joseph and Moynagh in her face.

Weeks of planning paid off. Alan sat beside me on the edge of the sofa in our kitchen.

'Are you sure your parents won't come back? Your father would skin me alive if he caught me here.'

'Relax,' I moved into the space that burned between us. 'The quarry social goes on till after ten and Daddy has to stay to the bitter end. Anyhow, we would hear them coming round the back and you could nip out the front.'

Brendan never wakened once he had fallen asleep and Bridie was babysitting for the Watsons at Number twenty-four. Or at least that was what she said she was doing. I lay back into the circle of Alan's arm. We had never kissed like this. Long, hungry mouthfuls. His hands and an electric shock touched the skin under my jumper. Caressed. Explored. I would stop him before he went too far.

But not yet.

Alan tore his hand away as if he had touched a live wire. He hunched at the end of the sofa, pointed at the picture of the Sacred Heart on the wall opposite us.

'It's watching me. I swear to God it is. It's weird.' He shifted position, crouched beside the sofa. 'It won't take its eyes off me.'

'Of course He's watching you. He's God. He sees everything,' I sucked in my cheeks, pursed my lips, levelled an accusing finger at him. 'There's nowhere you can go to escape the all-seeing eye of God. No place is dark enough for you to hide. He can see even into the darkest recesses of your soul.' Sister Aquinas's funeral voice. Sister Aquinas in a crumpled pink sweater and tartan skirt. 'Do they teach you nothing in your school?'

I could have told him how I used to hide behind the sofa and turn my face into the furthest corner of the room. How I pressed my fists into my eyes till hectic lights danced on my eyelids. But He was still there, attached to my retina when I looked again, staring, unblinking. When I was a pious seven-year-old, I thought this eye-to-eye contact was a miracle, that I had been singled out for special divine attention – a sort of precursor of the Stigmata. By the age of nine and into more serious sinning, that calm, 'I know all about you' look had begun to get on my nerves.

Alan rose from the floor. He stood two feet from the picture, eyes riveted, shaking.

'Don't be stupid. It's only a picture. It won't bite you.'

I put my arms round him, unpeeled his eyes from the picture, held him close.

'God almighty, Marianne. You don't half go on. I can't stand being gawped at like that. It gives me the creeps. I'm sorry.' I felt him begin to relax. 'You're a lovely girl, all the same. All soft and silky.'

I turned out the light, took him by the hand and manoeuvred him back to the sofa. And the embers that had been dampened, smouldered and blazed. Alan's body stretched alongside mine, his hands and lips laying the ghost of the Mayo man.

'Don't move a muscle till I come back,' he kissed my forehead and stood up. 'I'm just going to turn that bloody lamp out. It's putting me off. I can still see those eyes.'

I leaped to my feet and jumped between the lamp under the Sacred Heart and Alan. I was Joan of Arc at Orleans. A Crusader, defending the Holy Places from the infidel. Charlton Heston taking on pagan Rome.

'Turn out the bloody lamp! Do you know what you're saying? That lamp gets trimmed. Topped up. Never turned out.'

Waves of exasperation and shame swept over me. What did I think I was doing here in my parents' home, of all places, with somebody who could utter such blasphemy and not even know the enormity of it. It would be useless to try and make someone like him understand that the lamp was a symbol of the faith we had kept alive through centuries of persecution.

'You're thick. You're stupid. You've no respect. You're the sort that would –' I searched for an example he might understand, '– would throw a bucket of water over the eternal flame in Paris.'

'Paris?' He was on his knees looking for his shoes. 'What have I done? What are you talking about? I've never been next or near Paris in my life.' He brushed hair out of his eyes, and stood up. 'My granny told me Catholic houses were filled with plaster saints and graven images. She didn't know the half of it. She never said anything about pictures with moving eyes and smelly oil lamps.'

'She sounds a right, dirty bigot to me and you're as bad as her. I should have known better than have anything to do with an ignorant Protestant. What's so funny anyway?'

'You call her a bigot. You should try listening to yourself sometime, Marianne.' He was half-laughing, half-smiling holding his arms out to me. 'Come here. I'm sorry for being disrespectful to your lamp.'

Anger boiled inside me. Anger at his blond Saxon hair. At the smirk curling his lip. At the condescension which centuries of imperialism had bred into him.

'You'd better go. My parents will be home soon.' He reached to pick his jacket off the floor. I got there first and thrust it at him.

'If that's what you want. I'll see you around, Marianne.'

'Not if I see you first.'

The minute the back door closed behind him I felt sorry. Sorry the sinful pleasures of the flesh had been interrupted just as I was finding out how pleasant they were. Sorry I had lost the only boyfriend I might ever have.

I arranged my books in front of me at the table. The trial scene of *The Merchant of Venice* danced over the pages. I was depraved. I had been taught that men were little better than the beasts of the field. But decent women were supposed to help them control their base urges. Not egg them on.

My parents came back. Bridie returned half an hour later, sullen and slinky. My father snarled at her, said he didn't approve of this babysitting lark or of her painting her face like a streetwalker.

'I don't care if you're tired.' Mammy gave her a hard look. 'You will kneel down and say the Rosary. Remember: "The family that prays together, stays together"'.

There had been ructions when Bridie came in the previous month at midnight and refused to say where she'd been. Apart from babysitting for poor Mrs Watson, who needed an outing and who paid well, she had been confined to barracks. She and Mammy sparred at each other like two fighting cocks on the same walk.

I overheard Mrs Campbell say, 'It must be hard for Marianne having such a gorgeous sister. Not that Marianne isn't a very nice wee girl but Bridie's a real smasher.'

'Handsome is as handsome does. Mary Ann is level-headed. Bridie's a bit too full of herself. Needs her wings clipped.'

Level-headed! What she meant was that nobody would look twice at me.

'Who'd want to stay here? I'll be out of this dump the minute I can,' Bridie muttered to me.

How could those two boring people have produced a daughter like her! Brendan and me, mousy-faced and dark, I could understand. Chips off the old block. But Bridie. Her sultry eyes and that pouty, sexy mouth! And worldly-wise. I wanted to talk to her about the night's events. Events that helter-skeltered in my head through the first three decades of the Rosary.

'Forgetting the thumbs again,' said my father when I curtailed the fourth glorious mystery. I latched on to the eyes of the Sacred Heart and tried to concentrate. Poor Sacred Heart, forever silent, five drops of blood forever falling from His broken heart. What must He have thought over the years of the way Bridie and I behaved during the Rosary? Of kicks at unguarded shins, of tongues stuck out through prayerful fingers and furtive reading of comics.

'Three Hail Marys for my father and mother. Three Hail Marys for your father and mother. Three Hail Marys for Canon O'Toole. Three Hail Marys for Sister Augustine.'

'If any more of those bloody priests and nuns die, we'll be here all night.' Beads of frustration glistened through Bridie's Max Factor.

'Ark of the Covenant, House of God.' Mammy's voice shrilled. Her eyes assumed the sorrowful look of the wounded Christ on the wall. 'Let us now examine our consciences.'

Guilty on every count! I had acted with malice of forethought, with clear knowledge and full consent of the will. Eleven years of catechism under my belt and I had tried to lure an innocent Protestant into sin and lost my temper when my lustful desires were thwarted.

'May the divine assistance remain always with us,' Mammy's voice droned on.

Divine assistance. Words she intoned, night after tedious night, hammered on my brain.

Divine assistance. Like the whoosh of the mighty wind before the Holy Ghost descended on the Apostles in the upper room in Jerusalem, it was revealed to me. Divine assistance! That's what I had received. Not once, but twice He had pulled me back from the brink of hell. Above the fireplace the Madonna, who was supposed to intercede for us with her son, gazed uninterested into the distance while her open-mouthed baby slept at her neck. God Himself had been forced to intervene.

My parents clattered in the kitchen and Bridie slammed herself into the bathroom for a ten-minute session of plucking and anointing. I eased back the lino and took out Alan's photograph. I looked, as I did every morning, for a whole minute at his beautiful face, memorising his smile, the strands of hair falling over eyes. Numb with bereavement, I kissed the shiny paper and I buried him in his cellophane wallet, under the bed between the lino and two sheets of newspaper.

'The guerrillas are closing in. The sound of aircraft above my head is deafening. The air is choked with the dust of explosives,' I declaimed to my attentive reflection. I coughed, just a little to clear the dust from my throat, recovered and tapped 'Marianne Ward, Reuters Correspondent. Caracas, Rangoon, Dar es Salaam.'

To think I might have sacrificed my brilliant future for a few minutes' lust.

Then I put my head on the pillow and cried myself to sleep.

Alan stood at Collins's window the next afternoon. I took a roundabout route through the bottom end of the town. By the end of the week the space where he usually waited was empty.

13

'Your bodies are temples of the Holy Ghost, sacred vessels to be cherished and reverenced,' the priest told the older girls on the last day of the annual retreat. 'Remember the words: "God sees me always". Carve them on your hearts. If ever you are tempted to do anything that might defile that sacred vessel remind yourself, "God sees me always" and you will be protected from the evil side of your nature.'

With a darning needle I gouged a capital G, followed by a full stop on the inside of my forearm. S and another full stop were cut so large that M and A petered out close to my wrist and there was no room for punctuation. Each time Alan's face lingered in my mind and I remembered his hands under my jumper I dug into my flesh, scratching, scraping with the fervour of a hairshirted saint, till four wounds wept blood and pus into my blouse. I would go into the noviciate once I had done my Senior and spend my life in the service of God. The idea of being a saint, revered by millions, appealed to me: of being on show in the odour of sanctity till the Last Day, like the priest whose exhumed body I had seen displayed in a glass case at Omeath.

But not yet.

The M and S of 'God Sees Me Always' disappeared after I gave up the idea of the religious life. Eventually the scabs on G and A fell off and the skin unwrinkled and turned from red to pink, to white.

I crossed the road when I saw Alan walking brazenly in the street with a girl from the Royal High, maroon arms wrapped round each other's waists. I skulked in shop doorways and watched her toss her head and swing blond hair over her shoulders. Over his blazer. There would be a picture of the Royal Family on the walls of her home, photographs of her as an infant on a fluffy rug, a hunting scene or a still life. The only religious message likely to impinge on Alan would be a reminder that 'Jesus Saves' or 'The Lord Is My Shepherd' in Gothic letters round a spray of violets.

If there were any justice in this world the new girlfriend would get boils. Huge, angry boils all over her face.

The Divinity didn't rush to Bridie's assistance.

'This is no time of night for a young girl to be out.' My father paced up and down the kitchen. 'Those Watsons take advantage of her. Out sporting themselves till all hours of the night when they know full well she has to go to school to morrow. I'll go up there and sit with her and see she gets safely home.'

Don't go, Daddy. Bridie's not babysitting at the Watsons. She's out with Pat Flanagan. Dear God, please don't let him go.

The door closed behind him.

The last time Bridie babysat, Mr Watson came back without his wife. He was worried about the little boy, he told her. His teeth had been giving trouble. Instead of dashing upstairs to see his son he followed her into the sitting room.

'I'd like you to take this,' he said, trying to stuff a pound note into her hand. 'Don't tell anybody. It will be our secret. Yours and mine.' Bridie said it was far too much, that Mrs Watson had already given her half a crown. He insisted. Put the note into her blazer pocket.

'You're very beautiful, Bridie. I can't get you out of my head. Day or night. Your boyfriend is a lucky fellow. I'm very jealous of him,' he panted, red in the face. 'But you can be good to me too.' He fell on her. Rubbed wet lips over her face. Stuck his hand under her jumper. Up her skirt.

Bridie pushed him off and he slid down onto the carpet.

'You're a dirty dog, Mr Watson. I'll tell Mrs Watson on you,' she shouted, grabbed her blazer off the back of the chair and ran out of the house.

'Did you throw his stinking money at him?' I asked her.

She reached out of bed, pulled a pound note from her pocket, smoothed its creases, held it up to the light and smacked a kiss on it.

'The wages of sin,' she said 'with the compliments of rubber-lips Watson.'

Would my father meet Bridie walking down the road with Pat, gazing so intently into each other's eyes that they wouldn't see him till they bumped slap into him? Or would he come upon them lying inside the field where the road narrowed and became a country lane? Mammy moved the porridge to the back of the range. She lowered the clothes rack and laid Brendan's clean school clothes in a pile on a chair, listening for my father's and Bridie's footsteps coming round the side of the house. For the sound of them chattering together.

I held my breath. The door burst open. My father frogmarched Bridie into the kitchen. Flung her against the table. Long red hair trailed between his fingers, clung to his sleeve.

'I'll teach you a lesson you'll not forget. Liar! Tramp!' The house shook to the thudding of his feet on the stairs. He came back, his razor strap wrapped round his hand. He hauled Bridie to the middle of the floor, settled himself the way a golfer does before hitting a shot and let fly with the strap. Her hands crossed over her bowed head caught the first blow. Mammy's hand and arm the second.

'Get out of the way,' he yelled at her, eyes bloodshot, face on fire. 'I'll thrash that slut to an inch of her life. She's no child of mine.' He raised his arm. Weaved about, a boxer searching where to land the blow that would do the most damage. Bridie cowered behind Mammy, welted hands still crossed over the crown of her head. The strap, suspended down his back, quivered.

'You're all the same, you men. You think you can settle everything with your fists or a belt. Take yourself and your strap upstairs. You too. On your way,' Mammy glared at me. 'I'll sort this heeler out. Stand up straight, madam, and look at me when I speak to you.'

I scuttled upstairs. Given the choice, I think I would have preferred the strap. Not Mammy's interrogation. Not the ice-cold lecture on ingratitude and the promise on bended knees never to sin again.

My father knelt by his bed in his unlit room. He straightened his back to call to me.

'You're a good girl, Mary Ann. You've never been any bother.'

In the dim light from the landing his shadowed face begged me to speak to him. To show disapproval for Bridie's behaviour. To be on his side. But I could still see the rage that had blazed his face and hear the slap of the razor strap on my sister's hands and head. I imagined him bursting in on me and Alan when we lay wantonly on the sofa downstairs and fear locked my throat.

'I only did what I thought best. A father has to discipline his family.' He paused. 'You must understand that, Mary Ann.'

Still I said nothing and he bowed his head till it touched the counterpane.

'Yes, Daddy. Goodnight, Daddy.'

'I hate, hate, hate them,' Bridie muttered under the blankets. 'They're still in the Dark Ages. She's worse than him. If we don't get out of here quick, we'll end up as weird as them.'

After I sat my last exam Bridie and I were exiled to Moynagh with instructions to behave ourselves and help Agnes.

Moynagh, the backend to nowhere. A pudding basin hollow, its inhabitants so inward looking they hadn't learned that they had only to stand on tiptoe to see into the next valley and beyond. Gunmetal clouds merged with the bushy trees on the skyline as Regan's taxi turned into the lane to Mammy's old home. Grass spouted through the thatch that seemed to have slipped down since last year and chickens strolled casually through the doorway at the top of the house.

'God, what a dump,' said Bridie. 'It's gone to rack and ruin. It's a nightmare.'

'We might as well be buried alive as stuck here. It will be like doing time,' I said.

'That's no way for you to be talking,' Padraig Regan rebuked us. 'Agnes does her best. This past year hasn't easy for her, all on her own and no man to look out for her, so see you keep a civil tongue in your heads, the pair of you.'

Agnes greeted us, wiping her hands in a big apron, and led us into the house. The thatch blotted most of the daylight from the passage that was slimy with snail trails.

'You can't go on living here on your own, Agnes. It would send me round the bend,' I said to her. 'Why don't you come and live with us?'

'How do you stick it with nobody to talk to from one day's end to the next?' asked Bridie. 'Does it not drive you up the walls?'

'I've stuck it for fifty years and I would rather end my days here than anywhere else. I have to keep the place going for when Joseph comes home. He'll be back as soon as he has the money to pay your father. Now, will you have one egg or two?'

A day's haymaking blistered our hands and washing in a tin basin did little to dislodge hayseed that had worked its way into every fold of our bodies. The two labourers whom Agnes paid to help with the harvesting laughed at us, informed us that we were useless townies, good only for one thing.

'You've a grand pair of diddies, Bridie. I bet you're a great coort,' the older one said when we brought their tea to the field. He stretched out with an eye on Agnes who was raking hay at the far end of the meadow. The sun had turned his nose and forehead the colour of overripe tomatoes and flamed the skin under his sparse ginger hair.

'Would you drop your drawers for me if I took you behind the hedge?' He tilted his head to look up Bridie's skirt.

'Would you drop down dead for me.' Bridie towered over him, the sun shining through the blaze of her hair. She tilted the tea-can. Boiling liquid splashed over the hand about to grab her leg.

On the way back to the house I longed to be able to tell her about the Mayo man. Would she have poured scalding tea on his stalk and laughed to see it shrivel as she had laughed at the redhead just then?

When we arrived back in Carrig a friend of Alan's told me he had gone to London and was due to start university in October. My Junior results were better than anyone had hoped but Mother Carmel's praise and my parents' delight did little to cure the lump-of-lead pain in my stomach.

We had fillet steak and tinned pears and cream to celebrate

our return. My father said he would take a day off as soon as the pressure of work at the quarry eased and go to Moynagh to fix gates and fences and put locks on the door.

'I'm a proud man to have two such clever daughters. You're a credit to your mother and me,' he told us. 'You must bring your young man home in future, Bridie, so that we can see if he's good enough for you. I have been thinking, maybe I was too hard on you. No hard feelings?'

'No hard feelings, Daddy.'

'You too, Mary Ann.' I turned away from his long, hard stare. 'No doubt the young lads at the Christian Brothers are chasing after you as well.'

He didn't go out to work in the garden as he always did after the evening meal. In a minute he was asleep and snoring open-mouthed. An old man with a puckered turkey neck and a swatch of gray hair sprouting out of his open shirt.

'So who's Alan Reed when he's at home?' Mammy turned down the heat under a pot where a piece of shin simmered on the electric cooker in the scullery.

'Just somebody that sometimes walked home with us from school.'

'He's not a Catholic. Not with a name like that.' Her elbow joggled in time with the vegetable knife that sliced carrots into thick rounds. Stray pieces danced to the edge of the chopping board. A pincer movement of her left arm headed off their escape. 'He doesn't look like a Catholic either.'

'How do you know what he looks like?' I tried to sound casual, to hide the hope and panic welling over me.

'He came straight up to the front door, bold as brass. Asked you father for your holiday address, as he put it.' She slid carrots into the pot and lined up three leeks on the chopping board.

'Did he tell him where I was?'

'No, he did not. He said you were too young for that sort of thing.' She moved the saucepan off the ring and skimmed speckled foam from the surface of the broth. 'It didn't stop him writing here. By the sound of the letters he was a bit more than somebody you met on the way home from school.'

'How do you know what was in his letters? Where are they? You had no business opening them.'

She had put a spoon between her teeth to stop her crying while she chopped an onion. Through the side of her mouth she muttered 'Your father opened them.'

'He opened my letters. He had no right. You should have stopped him.'

She took the spoon out of her mouth and wiped away tears with the back of her hand. 'Me? Try to stop him? He's your father. He has every right.'

I strode into the kitchen shouting, 'Daddy!'

'Jesus, Mary and Joseph! What's wrong?' He woke and sat up. His face softened when he saw me.

'What did you do with the letters that were addressed to me?'

He paused and frowned. 'If you mean the letters from that English Protestant I'll tell you what I did with them. I burnt them and I will burn any others he has the cheek to write.'

'You had no right. You had no business opening my letters.'

He jumped to his feet. His hand hit me so hard across my right cheek I staggered against the range. 'I had no right! I'll show you who has rights in this house.' There was no time to duck from the blow that landed on my left cheek.

Mammy made me unlock the bathroom door. She soaked two face cloths in cold water and held them against the welts that had risen on my face.

'You had no business going for your father like that and him so pleased to have you at home again. He's not a man to think before he lashes out but he'll be sorry he hit you. You had best put that fellow out of your mind. There are plenty of nice Catholic boys around. Nothing but trouble comes from mixed marriages. They're the curse of the country.'

Put Alan out of my mind. If they thought they could beat me into forgetting about him they had another think coming to them.

His granny was tall and skinny and her dyed blond hair was permed into corrugated iron waves. She wore a powder-blue two-piece and silk stockings.

'So you're the wee Ward girl that goes to the convent.' She eyed me up and down. 'No, I don't have Alan's address. He's a very busy young man. He's not interested in the likes of you. See you close the gate properly after you.'

I prayed she would fall and break her spindly legs and choke on her false teeth.

'Please tell Alan I called when you hear from him.'

I hadn't the courage to leave the gate swinging open.

14

I think my father was trying to make amends when he took us to Newcastle for the day. No wet tomato sandwiches or grey tea tasting of thermos flasks. A slap-up meal in a hotel near the seafront – vegetable soup, roast beef and gravy, potatoes, carrots and peas floating in a turquoise green liquid, followed by tinned pears and cream, or apple tart and custard, or ice cream with a dash of raspberry syrup. A white-aproned waiter appeared between courses with a silver-topped brush and a tiny silver dustpan to sweep crumbs and bits of food from the cloth. Bridie and I ordered coffee instead of tea. Neither of us liked coffee, especially bottled Camp coffee, but we wanted to look sophisticated and compensate for my father tucking his napkin into the neck of his shirt and Mammy telling the waiter and everyone else in the dining room that she hoped the soup wasn't made out of other people's leavings. She argued that two and six was far too much to leave as a tip. My father slapped a half-crown on the side plate and said he wasn't going to spoil the ship for a ha'porth of tar. He was having the time of his life eating out in a smart hotel with his family and there were no pockets in a shroud.

Like other elderly couples my parents wore hats as they walked along the promenade. My father's watch and chain were displayed on the waistcoat of his tweed suit and Mammy was dressed up in a blue and grey herringbone costume, a white, high-necked blouse and lace-up granny shoes with medium heels that would discolour and sink into the sand if she was to walk on the beach. They sat on a bench to read the *Sunday Press* and the *Universe*. We took off our shoes and helped Brendan make a sandcastle surrounded by a moat. A man wearing swimming trunks who was playing cricket with three small boys asked if Brendan would like to play with them. His wife in a blue-and-white striped bathing costume and dark glasses jumped up from the deckchair where she had been sunning herself and joined in.

'Could you in your wildest dreams imagine Mammy and Daddy playing cricket in bathing costumes?' Bridie asked

'Only if they were allowed to keep their hats on.'

'And if Mammy could wear a modesty vest and a bathing tent over hers.'

'And her Spirella corset.'

I helped my father tidy the flower beds. We dug out faded annuals and he split astilbes, day lilies and irises which he would replant or give to the neighbours. Kneeling side by side, he and Brendan planted more snowdrops, crocuses, early daffodils, narcissi, tulips and hyacinths that would bloom well into May.

'The secret is to have colour all year round. It takes a while for a garden to develop but I think we've cracked it. Next year it will be like the Botanical Gardens.' He dug out dahlias and gladioli and put them in a wooden box.

'Don't you wish we had another wee girl to strew in the procession instead of him?' I ducked to avoid the shower of soil Brendan threw at me.

'No I don't. So stop annoying the child. It's well he has me to look out for him in a house full of big women.' He took Brendan's hand and together they went to the shed to get more bulbs to plant in the beds under the windows. Bulbs that would flower in late January and February. Splashes of yellow and white and purple against winter brickwork.

Where was the banshee that night? Was she having time off, resting herself under the hedgerows of County Monaghan when she should have been belting up to the North to keen outside our windows and warn Mammy to make him stay at home? Or was she so niggardly with her forebodings that she only announced deaths in the McKenna family because they claimed to be descended from kings? And the Holy Souls? What use were they? Why did they not waken us all up with their knocking if they really knew of the danger?

We could have forbidden him to leave the house that day. Protected him till the blasting was finished. Or could we? He was a stubborn man. Would not be told. Mammy said afterwards that she begged him to be careful. She had dreamed three nights running of seeing him in his coffin.

We didn't see him dressed in the brown shroud of the third order of Saint Francis, beads wrapped round marbled fingers. Nor did we kiss his cold cheek and lick the aftertaste of death from our lips. When his remains were brought home for the wake the lid was already screwed down over what was left of his face after a 'wild' rock hit it during quarry blasting. A million to one chance.

Remains!

We hadn't noticed the blasting that day, any more than people in Railway Terrace hear trains passing but can always tell if they run late. Tom Ryan arrived in my father's car just as Bridie and I were leaving home to return to school. A red-eyed snowman, eyebrows and moustache thick with dust, dropping grey footprints on red tiles.

'There's been an accident, Mrs Ward. The Boss,' he spoke in

a choked sort of voice. 'They've taken him to the infirmary.'

We waited, unbelieving, till Mammy came back from the hospital.

'Your father's dead, children.'

She grabbed at the edge of the table and we helped her to sit down. We clung to her, willing her to take back the last word, to say she had made a mistake. Our father was too busy living to be dead. He had talked to her this morning about a contract he was going to clinch. Said he might be late home.

'Your father is late, children.' That's what she had meant.

'Your father is dead, children,' she repeated, looking first at Bridie, then at me. 'What's to become of us?' And it was as if she had shrunk and become a frightened child.

What was to become of us? He was the roof over our heads, the clothes on our backs, the food in our mouths. He held our futures in the hollow of his hands.

I went with Bridie to pick Brendan up from school, to put one foot past the other down Rathbeg Avenue and the Dublin Road, to turn into Bridge Street and up to the school gates where butterfly whispers flitted from one parent to another.

'Awful sad. You never know the minute. Such a lovely man. God help the mother.'

Mournful heads were nodded from a distance and the group inched away from us as if death were contagious. We made our way home with Brendan, full of himself in short trousers and homemade overcoat, a turnip lantern in his hand.

The house filled up quickly. Neighbours came with cakes and sandwiches for the wake. Whiskey, porter and beer were stockpiled in the dining room. Father Doyle ruffled Brendan's hair and told us God would give us strength. Our father had been a man among men and he was in a better place. I wanted to rage at him, to scream that there was no better place for him than here in his own home tying apples to swing from the clothes rack at tonight's Halloween party, shaving the inside of Brendan's lantern to stop the candle wobbling about.

A crowd waited outside in the drizzle, their faces yellowed by street lamps and by the turnip lanterns of children collecting money round the doors. The funeral car arrived and a coffin was carried into the house and placed on trestles in the bay in the sitting room. An oak coffin with 'Michael Patrick Ward. Aged fifty-four' engraved on a brass plaque.

I lay beside Brendan on his bed listening to the noise downstairs.

'Where's Daddy? Is he not home yet?' he asked again. 'Can we have the party when he comes?'

'Daddy's not coming home for a while.'

Daddy is at home. He's downstairs in a wooden box. His friends are leaning against it, resting their glasses on the lid.

'He is. He is. He said he would tell me a story after the party. You tell me a story. Go on.'

'What story do you want me to tell you?'

'The one about the whale.'

'Once upon a time a boat set sail from Donegal for America with a captain, his wife, three crew and a cow.' From my mouth fell words as lifeless as the corpse downstairs. 'When they were far out on the Atlantic Ocean a big whale came alongside the boat and banged so hard against it they were afraid it would . . .'

'Tell it right, Mary Ann. Tell it the way Daddy does. Make the noises.' Brendan sat bolt upright. His fists pummelled my shoulder. Red-faced, he tugged at my sleeve. 'Tell it right.'

His bed was a ship tossed on thundering waves, battered by the thud-thudding of the gigantic whale against its sides. The raging of the storm, the huffing and puffing of the great beast, the hiss of water spurting out of the top of his head and his hungry cries filled the room. Brendan's voice rose and fell as my father's used to. His telling overtook my faltering account. The huge jaws, so wide open that you could see his tonsils, threatened to devour each and every person on board. The captain threw the bucket and the stool his wife sat on to milk the cow into them and the monster swam away satisfied. But only for a little while. He came back, smacking his lips, roaring like a bull and walloping the boat so hard it nearly capsized. The cow was thrown into the gaping jaws. The third time the whale heaved into sight he almost leaped into the boat and the captain had no choice but to throw his wife to the ravenous creature. He did so sadly for she had been a good wife to him and he had a high regard for her. The whale reappeared just as the coast of America came into view. The captain had a good view of him in the shallow water. He took aim, killed the beast with a harpoon and the body floated to the shore.

Brendan fixed round eyes on me and waited for me to ask. 'As soon as they landed in America they slit the whale open. What do you think they found inside?' I heard the excitement in my father's voice every time he put that question to us.

'The woman sitting on the stool,' Brendan shrieked 'sitting on the stool, milking the cow.'

The bed shook with his laughter. I left him when he fell asleep and crossed the landing to my parents' room. I lay where my father had woken up this morning, wrapped my arms round his pillow and wept till my eyes ran dry.

My uncles, John and Daniel, arrived from Donegal in rough jackets and hobnail boots. Mammy opened my father's wardrobe and said John and Dan were to dress themselves in his suits, shirts and shoes and to take the rest of his clothes home with them. When Daniel walked into the kitchen in my father's Sunday suit Brendan jumped up into his arms. He touched Dan's cheekbones, his eyebrows and his chin, then he slid down, ran to Mammy and hid his face in her skirt.

My father was buried on All Souls' Day. Sister Mary Francis, accompanied by Sister Vincent, arrived in time for the funeral Mass. The quarry workers in their Sunday best walked behind the hearse. No blasting boom reverberated in the genteel homes on Rathbeg Avenue. No grey dust dimmed the sheen on Mrs Campbell's furniture or settled on her window sills that day. Tom Ryan, Mr Bradshaw and my uncles carried the coffin into the graveyard. Dan in his dark grey suit and John in navy blue. Twin ghosts of the man we buried.

The man we buried? None of us had actually seen him, had checked if it really was him. Mammy had told us many times how Cromwell's body had been filled with perfumes and scented oils but the stench of his corruption had broken through two coffins of wood and lead and it had to be cast immediately into a deep pit, lest it cause an epidemic. A wax effigy, draped in a black velvet shroud with gold tassels, had lain in state for a fortnight. After a week the dummy was propped up into a standing position. Its glass eyes were opened. A sceptre was stuck in its right hand, a globe in its left and the mugs who filed past it for two weeks were fooled into thinking it was Oliver Cromwell, the curse of Ireland, in the flesh.

Red clay shuddered on the brass plate inscribed with the name of Michael Patrick Ward and I told myself it was not him lying six feet under the ground. He had gone away to earn enough money to pay his debts and would turn up one day, fit as a fiddle, like the woman who had sat milking her cow in the stomach of the whale.

About thirty friends and family came home with us for the funeral breakfast. The two nuns ate separately at the piecrust table in the sitting room.

'Would you like a drink, Sister Vincent?' Bridie asked.

'I thought you would never ask.'

'Do you go to a lot of funerals, Sister Vincent?' Bridie filled a glass with whiskey from a bottle concealed in a tea cloth.

'Not that many. Reverend Mother sends me to make sure your auntie here behaves herself. I'm what you might call a sobering influence.' She raised her glass. 'To Mick.'

'Poor Mick. Poor orphaned children,' sobbed Sister Mary Francis. We fled the room.

Mrs Ryan, Kathleen Ryan and Mrs Donnelly served chicken, ham, tongue, cold beef and lamb followed by sherry trifle and tinned peaches. Mammy, Bridie and I sat like guests at our dining table which was extended to its full size. My uncles had drunk a bottle of brandy before the meal to take away the chill of the graveyard. When he had finished eating, Daniel stood up and sang 'The Short Cut to the Rosses' in memory of his brother. Bridie and I clung to Mammy when he sang the last verse.

By the short cut to the Rosses
'Tis I'll go never more
Lest she should also steal my soul
Who stole my heart before.
Lest she take my soul and crush it
Like a dead leaf in her hand;
For the short cut to the Rosses
Is the road to Fairyland.

Dan said it was time everybody had a drink to cheer them up, that Mick had always enjoyed a good wake and the last thing he would want was crying at his funeral breakfast. Over whiskey, porter and sherry the question was asked that no one had dared put into words while the coffin was in the house. How had the accident happened, and to Mick of all people? He had seen too many men die in quarries through carelessness and inadequate safety precautions, not only when he was a labourer in Scotland but also when he became foreman at Slieve Dubh. He had set up rigorous procedures for blasting and secondary blasting. His lorries were checked regularly and fitted with reversing lights and there had only been minor accidents after he became owner.

Men round the table competed with each other to tell about disasters they had known. Vehicles running over the edges of quarry faces, plunging into waste-filled excavations, brake failure and men crushed by reversing lorries. Tom Ryan remembered when he was working in County Down how a badly handled blast hurled a boulder four hundred yards and killed a man standing at his own back door. Jimmy Doherty, the shot firer, begged my mother's pardon for mentioning the word 'privy' at the table and told us that one day a blast had blown the wooden structure clean away and left him sitting on the seat, out in the fresh air. Mr Bradshaw gave him a look that would sour milk and informed us that soldiers in the Great War believed if their name was on a bullet it would find them no matter where they went. Mammy said none of us knew the day or the hour and we should live every day as if it was our last.

God knew. All those millions of years ago when He created the world He had stamped 'Michael Ward' on the rock that would kill him and He had sat back and waited for the day it would happen.

15

Mammy wears a green-and-brown tweed coat and green hat; the paisley scarf my father gave her for her last birthday is loosened in the heat of F. & G. McArdle's office. Mr F. McArdle's nicotined fingers flick through sheaves of papers. Light from a naked light bulb bounces off his polished head.

'Nothing!' she shouts. 'I don't believe you. My husband lived for his family. He was a provider. He would never have left us destitute.'

A tan film scums the tea which Mr Mcardle's secretary placed at Mammy's elbow ten minutes ago. She is a beige-coloured woman with chair-stuffing for hair. She staggers back from the blaze of Mammy's anger.

'Your husband was a businessman, Mrs Ward.' The solicitor has put on his reasonable voice. His voice for speaking to stupid women. 'Every business runs up debts. He borrowed heavily. He wouldn't have worried you with details. He would have pulled his affairs round but he died too soon.' His head shakes. Bristled jowls quiver in sympathy. His raised hand silences Mammy's next outburst. 'If only you had a son in the business to take over or somebody trained to carry on. As it is, the receivers are unlikely to find any remaining funds once the creditors have been paid.'

Poker-faced strangers walk through our house, open cupboards, tap skirting boards, complain about blistering paintwork. Admire the size of the rooms. Shudder at the nearness of the council estate. I want to shout, 'Our house is haunted. Eva lives in the attic. She comes down when everybody is asleep. You'll sense her bending over you. Her cool breath will waken you up. You'll see her on her knees in the hall, setting the table, raking ashes from the grates. You'll hear her sigh and you'll say it's the wind but you will never be sure. And my father. He will never leave his house. His mansion. He's in the bricks and mortar. In the apple trees and rhododendrons. In the pathways where he wrote our names and his name in broken china. Buy some other house.'

He doesn't look like a buyer, the man with a bulging stomach who wears a stained suit and has a cigarette growing on his lower lip. He's on his own. No wife to criticise, to say black-and-white bathrooms look like public lavatories; there are too many windows, too few windows. He offers the asking price. Cash on the nail. Wants immediate possession once the legal ends are tied up. No, his missus doesn't need to see it. He's a scrap merchant. Drives a red Jaguar with a dent in the passenger door.

Mother Carmel orders the lay sister who has ushered us into the parlour to bring tea for Mammy. Mother Carmel's peaked coif is covered with a veil of fine crêpe and held in place by three black-tipped pins. It's stiff as a washboard and reaches to her shoulders. Starched linen is stretched skintight over her skull and encases her neck. A silver crucifix on a silver chain leans against her serge habit.

'It is vital that the girls' education continue uninterrupted. Bridie is doing her Senior this year and is on course for an Exhibition and Mary Ann has settled into the Senior course and would have great difficulty surviving a move to another school, especially one in the Free State.' She shakes her head from side to side, a hypnotist holding Mammy in a trance.

I practise pinching my nostrils together and looking down my nose the way Mother Carmel does. Bridie looks down her nose at me. Her eyes are crossed. She winks and we both splutter into our handkerchiefs.

'Besides, Mary Ann may want to stay with us,' Mother Carmel bares her teeth at me. Her eyes are the bluish green of duck eggs. 'I am not the only one who thinks she has a vocation,' she adds. 'Isn't that right?'

Blood rushes up my neck and flares my face. She remembers my religious maniac days after the Lenten retreat. After Alan. The hours I spent in the chapel, my back ramrod straight, my head tilted at the pious angle. She sees me in a habit walking in prayerful attitude behind her during nuns recreation, snuffing out candles in the chapel with a brass snuffer on a brass rod.

I am in my cell in the dormitory. I kneel beside my bed praying to God to keep me safe through the night. Tomorrow when I am professed my hair will be chopped off by Mother Carmel and swept away with the hair of the other postulants. I'm so deep in prayer I don't notice that smoke has filled the room and flames are licking around me. My veil and habit are on fire. I hear the sound of breaking glass and Alan swoops down through the skylight. He's so bright and golden I think an angel has descended from heaven. He snatches off my veil and habit and a black cascade flows over my breasts that have burst from nuns' underwear. Alan kisses those waves in the firelight, takes me reverently in his arms and carries my limp body through the skylight averting his eyes from my naked beauty. But not before I have seen the untamed passion and love that burn as brightly as the fire devouring my narrow bed.

Mother Carmel coughs a genteel cough. She waits for a reply. 'What, Mother. What?'

Bridie chortles into her handkerchief. Mammy's eyes dart poisoned arrows at me. It's vulgar to say 'what' instead of 'pardon'. It's blasphemy to say 'what' to Reverend Mother.

The lay sister puts a tray on an inlaid table beside Mammy. A coarse veil like a headscarf covers the white cloth that fits tightly over her forehead and frames her round face. There are cracks on her splayed sandals which are flat, not medium-heeled like Mother Carmel's calf leather shoes. She offers us macaroons and shortbread on white china plates bordered with pale blue flowers. Mammy refuses. She is afraid of the sound of her false teeth cracking through shortbread, cracking the polished silence of the parlour. Of crumbs spattering the gleaming floor.

'There's a different syllabus in the South. Most of the teaching is done through the medium of Irish so a fluent knowledge of the Irish language is essential. Spoken and written. Your daughters have had enough upheaval in their life, Mrs Ward. They can continue here as boarders. It's what their father would have wanted.'

Reverend Mother reads the question on Mammy's lips. The words she cannot form without losing face.

'Mr Ward was very generous to us. We will come to an arrangement about fees. I expect both these girls, each in her own way, will contribute more to the school than the cost of their food and lodging. Rest assured, Mrs Ward, a boarding school, away from the distractions of the world, is exactly what they need.'

The snowdrops and yellow and purple crocuses my father planted in September are buried under another fall of snow. The back of

Kelly's removal van has been opened in our drive. Men wearing fawn aprons carry the three-piece suite, the piecrust table and the card table through the front door. The piano has been sold together with the dining-room table and sideboard. Brendan climbs on a box and into the back of the lorry. He pulls out a nest of tables and starts to carry them back into the house. Mammy slaps his legs, tells him he's a bold boy.

'Leave him alone,' Bridie yells at her. 'He doesn't know what's going on. He has feelings too.' She puts her arms round Brendan. They make a giant snowball, rolling swathes of snow from the lawn.

My footfall echoes through empty rooms. Curtains still hang at the four bay windows, pink velvet in the sitting room. Autumn chintz in the dining room, yellow flowers embossed on glazed cotton in the bedrooms. I look through Brendan's window and search along Slieve Dubh for the quarry, now buried in snow. The white top of Logan's Hill merges into the grey skyline. Mrs Campbell calls to say that lunch is ready. Mammy tells us to go on ahead. She'll make a final check. We tell her all the rooms are empty. Twenty minutes pass before she leaves our house. Mrs Campbell says the meal will be ruined.

Caroline sobs into a pink handkerchief with the letter C embroidered on one corner. Mr Campbell drives us to Main Street and unloads our suitcases at the Ballyroe bus stop. Mammy tells us we are only going to Moynagh to give her breathing space. It will take a while to find the right place for us, at the right price and anyhow Moynagh belongs to her now that our father has gone.

The room I woke in reeked of mildew and a hundred years of overflowing chamber pots. When I was in bed in Rathbeg Avenue light from street lamps used to shine through the slit where the curtains didn't quite meet – a slash of yellow at the window that picked out furniture, shapes of dressing gowns behind the door. A room that was safe against noises of the night.

In this place there wasn't a glimmer, not a hint of a window or door in blackout darkness. Feathers poking out of mattress ticking and threadbare blankets prickled my skin. My foot touched a lukewarm stone jar and another foot. Bridie's.

Moynagh? Bridie and me in Moynagh? In fading darkness I made out a wall lined with books and the swan neck of a water jug on a marble topped wash stand. Joseph's room. Bridie and me in his bed! Mammy had supplanted her absent brother. She had smashed the taboo and our fears that Joseph would come back from Coventry like a thief in night and find us, trespassing in his Holy of Holies.

A grey light faltered at the window revealing a hideous shape. Blurred, almost formless.

'Bridie, wake up,' I screamed, too paralysed to point. 'There's a ghost at the window.'

She opened one eye. 'It's snow, stupid. We're being buried alive. Shut up and let me sleep.'

I looked more closely at the mound of snow humped half way up against the pane and remembered last night. Padraig Regan's taxi spinning on impacted snow. Smoke belching from the exhaust. The engine coughing and spluttering. He had placed a potato sack and two lengths of cardboard under the back wheels. Mammy, Bridie and I pushed and Brendan flung himself into a snowdrift. When we reached Moynagh the gates opened a foot or so and jammed.

'There's no way I can make it to the house. I'll be lucky to get turned round on the road as it is,' Padraig said.

Snow found its way down the tops of our boots as we trudged towards the hurricane lamp that cast a yellow gleam over untrampled whiteness. The privy was half buried under snow. Bridie and I squatted, bare-bummed, outside the kitchen window.

'Did you know that if you pee your name in snow the writing will be the same as if you wrote with your hand? I read that somewhere. The *Encyclopedia Britannica* or the *Readers Digest,*' Bridie informed me. 'Maybe it only works for men.'

'What about if we write with our left feet?'

'The same, if you practise enough.'

'Or with a pen stuck between our teeth.'

We moved, side by side, giggling at the sizzle of melting snow. Mammy came to the door and asked if we intended to stay outside all night laughing like hyenas. We heard her tell Agnes it was the first time she had heard us laugh since our father's death.

'Hurry up and eat your breakfast,' Mammy shouted. 'Kelly's van will be here any minute. We have to clear the lane if it is to get down.'

'How long are we going to be in this dump?' Bridie demanded.

'Daddy wouldn't have let us be dragged here. It's not fair,' I said glowering.

'If your father was alive you two wouldn't dare to be so cheeky. You're lucky to have a roof over your heads and not find yourselves in the workhouse.'

All morning she and Agnes worked at clearing the lane, tossing shovelfuls of snow on banks that rose on either side. Each woman in rubber boots and old coat bent and raised her shovel in harmony with the other, pausing to rotate her shoulders, stretch her neck or rub the small of her back. Bridie and I half filled spades with snow which we hurled randomly to the side. We pelted Brendan with snowballs and plodded back and forward to the house to warm purple-blotched hands and sit disgruntled at the fire. Brendan called to come and see a flock of swans sailing over the lake and waddling on the muddy shore.

'They're whooper swans,' Jimmy McMahon told us. 'They come here every October from the Arctic once they have reared their babies. They fly at a powerful rate, they're so keen to get back to Moynagh. Listen.' He said they were honking to show off their voices to the mute swans that spent their whole lives here. 'Poor divils, that lot can only hiss when they're annoyed.'

'Do you think we will keep coming back here in years to come the way Mammy does?' I asked Bridie.

'No, we're stuck here forever. We'll probably lose the power of speech and end up like those dummies'.

Kelly's removal van arrived with the thaw that dripped from the thatch, from hedges, bushes and trees and turned the lane and the front street into a sea of slush. When the removal men left, the parlour looked like a second-hand saleroom, a warren of upside-down tables and chests of drawers. The sofa of the three-piece suite was upended in a corner, one armchair sat on its companion's lap, castors facing the ceiling. Miss Fisher's portrait and the picture of my grandmother disappeared behind a mattress and bed springs. Seascapes, landscapes and *The Wreck of the Hesperus* were put face down under a table and piled with pictures of Our Lady of Perpetual Succour, Saint Patrick, Saint Bridget and Saint Gerard Majella. The Sacred Heart who had scared the wits out of Alan was hung, complete with oil lamp, on a nail Mammy knocked into the kitchen wall. Agnes went with the hurricane lamp and milking bucket to the byre.

'Stop taking over, Mammy. This is Agnes's home and there's no room for her to budge with all our stuff,' said Bridie.

'Nonsense. Agnes is delighted to have the company. Why don't you mind your own business.'

In August Bridie and I had shaken the dust of Moynagh from our feet and returned to our real life in Carrig. The fragrance of summer was in our hair and our handbags swung against yellow and green dresses as we sauntered into the bus, revelling in the effect our rolling hips were having on the country lads who had gathered at the stop in Ballyroe to wave us off.

Six months later, two shapeless figures in green gaberdines, felt hats and thick stockings took the same bus to Carrig, where we turned our backs on the road leading to Rathbeg Avenue and headed towards the grey slab of the convent. Home was a curtained dormitory cubicle containing an iron bed and a locker. Our days started at a quarter to seven with the clanging of a bell and the chant 'Benedicamus Domino' from the duty nun. Her voice rose to an angry climax and the tongue of the bell was released to clamour against its brass side until she heard a muffled 'Deo Gratias' from behind the curtain. We washed in silence, went to Mass and were given permission to speak after Grace in the refectory at eight o'clock. Twelve and a half hours later we were confined once more to our cells.

After Mass on Ash Wednesday we packed our cases, each girl with a black cross on her forehead. Mother Carmel sent for Bridie and me. She had informed our mother we would leave Carrig on the afternoon bus. Sister Barbara would tell us what we were to do. Sister Barbara looked like Vivien Leigh. Nobody could understand why she had become a nun. Rumour had it that she had entered the convent after her fiancé was killed in the war. Some said he had been a doctor looking after the wounded at the front. According to others, he was a sea captain whose ship had been torpedoed by Hitler. I preferred to think of him as a fighter pilot shot down over Nazi Germany.

Sister Barbara gave us a each a bucket, a scrubbing brush, a lump of red soap and a bottle of bleach and asked us to clean all the desks in the senior classrooms, making sure we scrubbed with the grain of the wood. She lent us *Tess of the D'Urbervilles* and *Barchester Towers* to take home with us and said too much bleach would burn our hands. I would have plunged my hands into nitric acid if she had asked me. When the last desk was scrubbed our skin had wrinkled and white; stinging blisters coated our fingers. When we curtsied to Mother Carmel before leaving the convent I noticed how smooth and perfectly manicured her hands were.

'What does Lady Muck think we are? Bloomin' skivvies,' Bridie muttered as we trudged to the bus stop. 'I'd like to kick her teeth in.'

'And shove them down her throat. She wouldn't dare do that if Daddy was alive.'

'You'd think she owned us just because we don't pay the full fees.' She strode on ahead of me, then turned and asked, 'Are you still thinking of being a nun?'

'Are you kidding? I'd rather jump in the boghole. Head first.'

'Well get that stupid hat off for a start.'

We stuffed hats and gloves in our pockets and ate ice creams in the street. Mother Carmel would have said we looked like common mill-girls and expelled us on the spot.

'I'll see you later. I'm helping Tom take Mammy's cow to the bull,' Brendan flicked a stick at the hindquarters of a cow and strode down the lane with Tom McMahon and Joseph's dog, Togo.

Mammy's cow?

We dropped our suitcases in the porch. The stink of paraffin hit us between the eyes and swamped familiar Moynagh smells.

'Come and see this,' Mammy called. 'It can do anything an electric cooker does.' She turned up the wicks of a paraffin cooker. Yellow flames rose. Another twist of the knobs on the front and two funnels of black smoke shot up in line with soot marks on the wall behind. 'It will take a little bit of practice to get used to it.' She bent down, picked up a green metal box, placed it on the cooker, opened a glass door and stood back for Bridie and me to inspect and admire.

'What's this about you buying a cow? I thought we were only here for a short time,' said Bridie.

'We can't eat Agnes out of house and home. I make my own butter and she takes it every week to the market. Maybe it hasn't dawned on you that I have to look twice at every penny.'

My mother and my aunt churned together. Agnes stood, ramming the plunger into the churn that had been in the family for generations. Mammy sat on a bench turning the handle of a dainty churn which spun round like the earth on its axis till yellow specks appeared on the glass of its built in window.

'It's good to see the twentieth century coming to Moynagh,' I said to her and she said it was best to move with the times.

Brendan took us to the hen run. 'Take a look at that fellow. Mammy got him last month. He sees to it that the hens lay eggs with chickens in them. Don't ever go near him or upset him. He's fierce bad tempered.'

'Sounds like Joseph,' said Bridie 'only the rooster's better looking in his own nasty way.'

'He's not an ordinary rooster. He's a game cock. He's called Gabriel.'

Gabriel strutted about fixing a malevolent eye on us, flexing his claws, ruffling the sheen of his green-black plumage. He paused, sized up the dowdy hens that were pecking the ground at a respectful distance from him and jumped on the back of a Rhode Island red. His rear end bounced up and down over the passive bird. His glass eyes stared at a spot in the distance.

'Vicious brute. He looks as if he's possessed. I wouldn't like to get on the wrong side of him,' said Bridie.

'Mammy says he's the cock of the walk.'

As darkness fell Mammy produced a new Tilley lamp, a drawing room model with a translucent glass shade. She pumped air into it and held a match close to the mantle, not too near or the delicate material would blacken and dissolve into ashes. The light was better than we had known at Moynagh, so bright that moths and midges came from far and near to crash against the red-hot shade and ring the golden base with their corpses.

'You don't ever intend to leave,' I shouted at her. 'You've dug yourself in with your smelly cooker and your cow and that stupid rooster.'

'How could we invite any of our friends here?' asked Bridie. 'Telling them to rub their hands on the grass after they've trekked half a mile down the garden to that stinking privy. '

Mammy wondered why God had given her two such ungrateful hussies for daughters and said our father should have sent us to work in the mill at fourteen, instead of killing himself so that we could have a better chance in life than he had.

Joseph's letter arrived three hours before Togo's barking announced he was coming down the lane. Barely time for Agnes to fumigate his room. To open doors and windows and eliminate any hint of our occupancy – any whiff of Lily of the Valley, of Pond's face cream, of teenage girls' sweat. Blankets and pillows were shaken in the wind, inspected for lingering specks of Coty face powder, for strands of Bridie's red hair. Sweet papers and dirty hankies stuck to the broom Agnes stretched under the bed and a pair of knickers, a garter and a brown lisle stocking fell to the floor when it was pulled out from the wall.

A mattress, springs and two bed ends were hauled out of the parlour and a bed was erected for myself and Bridie in what had been the labourers' kitchen. We threw damp tea leaves over the floor to keep down the dust that caught in our throats as we swept the floor. We put a match to turf in the hearth and turned the bellows wheel. The draught sent flames leaping up the chimney. Moisture oozed through the walls over which we had plastered pages of the *Sunday Press*.

Out of her school bag Bridie took *Forever Amber*, wrapped in the dust cover of the *Holy Bible*. It had been passed round most of the girls in her class. She lay on the bed, removed a bookmark and started to read.

'Can I read it after you?'

'No, you're too young. Read the wallpaper.'

'It's wrong to read dirty books. They're an occasion of sin.'

Suddenly she sat bolt upright.

'Holy God. This is disgusting. *Disgusting!*'

'Let me see it. Ah go on. Let me see it.'

We were wrestling over the book when Mammy came in and asked why we were fighting. 'She won't let me read the Bible and I have to for my religious knowledge exam.'

Mammy said I had become a cheeky tinker and I should take a leaf out of my sister's book.

Joseph surveyed the furniture stockpiled in the parlour and the paraffin cooker and oven.

'It looks as if you have settled your family in for the duration,' he remarked.

'And what if we have,' Mammy snapped. 'I don't need to tell you whose name is on the deeds of this house. That said, I want you to know that you are always welcome here.'

'That's very big of you. I take it you haven't actually seen the deeds, missus, or would that be too much to expect?' He gave Mammy a quizzical look and went to his room.

'What does he mean by that?' I asked.

'Joseph can't forgive your father for being in his debt. That's all. Like all men he has to be top dog and can't stand a woman being anything but a servant.'

Joseph was pleased when Bridie asked for help with her Latin. He hummed and hawed, said he had probably forgotten all the Latin he ever knew but he drew a chair up beside her, held the *Aeneid* Book Four open in his hands. Grime circled his nails and there was a band of dirt under the split nail of the finger that traced Latin words across the page.

'First Dido and Aeneas came upon . . . no, they approached the shrine to seek pardon . . . ' His voice faltered. He scanned the text and continued. 'They chose ewes and sacrificed them to Ceres the Lawgiver, to Bacchus and above all to Juno the mistress of the marriage bond.'

'Joseph, you're a genius.'

'I'm no genius. I've a good memory that's all. Now you translate. Find the verb first and everything else falls into place. Off you go.'

'Dido grasps, no grasped, the sacred dish in her right hand and poured wine from it between the horns of a white . . . What's that word?'

'A white heifer. Go on. You're doing well.'

'Between the horns of a heifer? That's daft. The heifer would dunch them,' scoffed Brendan.

'Show some respect when your uncle is translating for your sister or you'll go to bed.' Mammy shook her fist at him.

Though she cooked and washed for Joseph and ordered us to get up and give him the armchair by the fire as soon as he set foot in the kitchen, we could tell she was relieved when he announced he was returning to England.

Bridie, Brendan and I accompanied him to the bus stop. He had only a small suitcase as he had got used to travelling light. We asked if he liked living in England. He said it was a foreign country and he wouldn't stay one day longer than he had to. He shook hands with us and gave us each five shillings before he got on the bus for Dublin.

The brown envelope Bridie had been watching for arrived at last. She took it from Jimmy the Post and tore it open.

She had passed with distinction in all five subjects.

'Your father would have been a proud man today.'

In October Bridie enrolled as a medical student at Queen's University. In no way did my results the following summer match Bridie's but they were enough for me to be accepted at Queen's to study English Language and Literature.

Mother Carmel thought it would be a good idea for me to have some teaching experience before starting university. For a month I helped in the kindergarten. I ate in the refectory and slept in the infirmary, next door to my old dormitory. She came to see me on my last night and asked me to pray for guidance. I had a real vocation to the religious life but if I went to Queen's I would lose it.

To pay for my help she gave me a handbag which she said was pure snakeskin. If the dents on the base were anything to go by the poor snake must have been on his last legs.

16

'Marianne.' Long arms waved, scythed through the throng on the pavement outside Robinson Cleaver's summer sale.

Alan! Alan in Belfast on an August morning.

'Marianne.' Hands pushed, shoved past handbags and shopping bags.

'What are you doing in Belfast?'

'How long are you staying?'

'I could have missed you.'

'I have missed you.'

Questions tripped head-over-heels, swallowed up answers. Hands clasped at arms' length, arms wrapped round shoulders, round waists, careless of the disapproval of a tight-lipped city. We held each other's breath, frightened to let go lest the other be whisked away on the moving carpet of shoppers and passers by.

'Re-pant, re-pant,' urged a preacher sandwiched between boards proclaiming 'Prepare to meet thy God' and 'The end is nigh'. 'Re-pant, afore yiz are cast into axterior darkness.'

We crossed Donegall Square. Trams and buses stopped to let us pass. We sat on a bench outside the City Hall, starting sentences that never finished. Memories of the last time we were together flooded over me and I was too ashamed, too shy to break the uneasy silence. He was the first to speak.

'I came over for my granny's funeral. I heard about your father.

Terrible what happened to him. Everybody in Carrig had a good word on him.'

'I'm sorry about your granny. When was she buried?'

'Yesterday. I arrived on Tuesday. I'm supposed to be catching the Liverpool boat to night.'

'You don't have to go back. Do you? Please don't go, Alan. Don't go.'

'Wild horses wouldn't drag me away. I'll get the Saturday boat. I have to be in Norfolk on Monday. I've a summer job, shelling peas.'

Two squandered years to squeeze into three summer days. I could go to the university any time for book lists. I had only come to Belfast to escape from Moynagh. I laid my head on his shoulder, close to the pulse in his neck, hoping the vinegar I had put in the rinsing water last night didn't make me smell like a fish-and-chip shop.

We had mixed grills in the Rainbow Room – chop, fried egg, bacon, sausage, liver, fried tomato and chips with slices of buttered bread. It was difficult to hold hands and cut the chop, egg and bacon. Especially the chop. I had thought of choosing the tinned-salmon salad and chips and spearing the food with the fork in my left hand, but the smell of sizzling bacon drifting out from the kitchen had seduced me and I was very hungry, having left Ballyroe on the early morning bus. When the waitress turned her back to amble off with our scoured plates, Alan kissed me. A passionate kiss that tasted of egg-yolk and bacon. He was in the final year of a mathematics degree and had a room in a house he shared with four other students. He told me the world wouldn't end if I left Ireland. Lots of students did. It wasn't too late for me to apply to study at London University.

'I need to be alone with you,' he said. We were alone apart

from the waitress who opened the door as soon as we stood up, and put a Closed sign in the window.

I felt beautiful with Alan, standing hand in hand at the Cavehill Road bus stop. He said I was a picture in my red-and-white dirndl skirt and white blouse. Had I known I was going to meet him I would have worn the green dress with a peplum Mammy bought for me in Clery's sale the last time we went to Dublin. I wore it to Mass on Sunday and Padraig Regan said he hadn't been worth tuppence after seeing me wiggle up to the altar like Carmen Miranda.

We followed the path past Belfast Castle. Alan pointed out Napoleon's face outlined on the brow of Cave Hill. His own profile was like men's faces we were taught to draw at school. A capital L for the forehead, another one for the nose and one each for the mouth and chin like the young men's faces on the front of Paton and Baldwin knitting patterns. But where most men have bullet heads that go straight to their shoulders, Alan's was globe-shaped and there was a deep curve where his head met his neck.

Below us lay the lough down which the Liverpool and Heysham boats sailed every night and where Alan would sail on Saturday. We found a hollow shielded from the wind and from anyone who might pass by. The sloping ground tilted us together. I wanted him to know that hardly a day had gone by when I hadn't yearned to feel his body wrapped around mine. That my longing for him had been so intense I thought I would die of it. But I was afraid he would think I was shameless.

'You're going to marry me, Marianne Ward. You may not think that now but you are. It's written here,' his fingers followed the lines on my palm. 'I've met dozens of girls but I couldn't get you out of my head no matter how hard I tried. I'm not going to lose you. Not ever again.'

We had rolled so close he was almost on top of me. I smelled the boghole and the Mayo man. Sweat trickling through hair. The new huskiness of his voice. Tongue pushing against my clamped mouth. Probing hands. Splash of scalding tea on my leg. Bluebottles buzzing over scattered bread.

'No. No. No. No.' I pushed him away.

'What's wrong, love? What's wrong?'

'Nothing's wrong. I'm sorry.'

'Relax, love. Lie still. I wouldn't hurt you for the world.'

Silence. Wisps of white, blown across a blue sky, pale bellies of seagulls and the smell of grass seed and heather. My neck on the crook of his arm and his fingers feather-stroking my ear and the freckled skin of my arm. Then he told me in his English-Irish voice, so soft that its ceiling was the hollow where we lay, about the room he had lived in last year. The torn curtain that let night lights in and kept daylight out. Potatoes, stews, custard and tea all tasting of the burnt bottom of the saucepan they were cooked in. How he lived like a king at the start of term on beer and chips but as the weeks went on he felt like eating the lump of cheese in the mousetrap.

He thought he had put me out of his mind. Then an Irish voice in the street or a girl's dark head in front of him in a lecture theatre, or in the cafeteria queue stirred up memories so vivid he dreamed about bombs falling in Belfast and him looking in vain for me in the rubble on blitz square. Those nightmares would only end when we were together. He would arrange for me to apply for accommodation in a university hostel because London could be a threatening city for a young Irish girl. Tomorrow we would find out about enrolling. Today was for looking at the sky.

I took his hand and twined it in mine. The rest of the afternoon lay before us. Time to linger. To uncover. To discover.

Not the adolescent tearing at layers of winter clothing of that night at Rathbeg Avenue when we devoured each other like famished calves. He kissed my lips and the hollow in my throat. Then he moved from my side and straddled me and his back blotted out the sun. Light framed his head and shoulders and gold flowed through his hair. But he was too close to the sun. He dropped out of the sky and his body fell along the length of mine. His lips were fire and his tongue was fire. In a far distance I heard an echo of the Redemptorist preacher at the women's mission. French kissing, more grievous than the 'close embraces and lewd posturing' of English dancing. A symbol and a precursor of another unspeakable intimacy. But it was only an echo growing fainter and fainter and his weight on me was light.

A ship sailed below us on its way from the docks towards the sea. A breeze ruffled the grass and the reddened sun hung low in the sky to the west. With the tip of his forefinger Alan drew a vertical line below the bend of my forearm. I held my breath as L and O and V and E appeared in pink letters on my skin, only to disappear almost before the next one was written. I wanted him to scratch with his nail. Not be afraid to draw blood. To carve an indelible message to remind me of him till we were together in October. To write 'I love you' deeper and more enduring than 'God sees me always' that I had furrowed all those wasted months ago.

I followed the movement of his finger as it printed 'you' and pressed a full stop into my wrist. The square nail, blonde hairs below the knuckle, on the backs of his hands. Hairs that curled round a silver watch and a leather watch strap. Eight o'clock, a corner of my mind registered.

Eight o'clock! Forty minutes until the last bus left for Armagh and a connection to Ballyroe.

'Don't go. You can't go. It's too soon. Stay with me. Ring your mother. Tell her you've missed the bus. You're staying with somebody. Tell her anything but don't go.'

I buttoned my blouse, tucked it into my skirt, scrabbled about in the grass for my sandals and begged him to get up and race down the hill to the tram stop.

'Phone her! We haven't a phone. We don't even have electric light or running water. No, I don't know anybody with a phone. It's the back of beyond. My mother would go out of her mind if I didn't come home. She would have search parties out. Messages on the wireless.'

We raced down the hill past the Floral Hall digging heels into the path and into steps to slow the pace I set. A mother dragging a reluctant child, apologising, coaxing, bribing.

'I'll get the first bus in the morning, I promise.' A pebble lodged under my toes. It chafed with each step but I dared not remove it till we had found a seat upstairs in the tram.

'I don't want to leave you. Honest I would give anything to stay. I will be on the first bus in the morning. We'll have all day tomorrow, I promise.'

'And all night. Tell your mother you're staying in Belfast to morrow night. Tell her anything. Only stay.'

Tomorrow night? Alan had known dozens of girls. Sophisticated, London girls. Mammy and Mrs Campbell said English girls were free and easy, hadn't the same moral fibre as us.

'Stop worrying,' He squeezed my clammy hand. 'All I want is to be with you. To hold you, to fall asleep and find you beside me when I waken up.'

Smithfield bus station was a funnel for freezing winds, an icebox designed to chill travellers to the bone. I scanned the figures in the Armagh queue, men and women hugging themselves into jackets, restraining wind-lifted skirts; tut-tutting and curling their lips in sour-faced disapproval as Alan kissed me a slow good-bye.

'Alan,' I called from the steps. 'What did you think when I didn't answer your letters?'

'I didn't know what to think. I never thought your father would burn them without telling you. Not in this day and age. I thought maybe you didn't want anything to do with me.'

'You must never think that again.'

The doors shut and the engine started.

'A quarter past ten at the Black Man. Don't forget,' Alan shouted through a tiny window.

'As if I could. Nothing on this earth will stop me. I'll be counting the minutes.'

I spread myself over two seats and rolled up the sleeve of my cardigan, willing 'I love you' to be written loud and deep on my arm. When Myrna Donnelly wrote to Eddie Jakabowski during the war, she had found a way to cheat the censors. Passionate messages were written in invisible ink which could only be read if the page was held before the fire. She demonstrated how it worked in the warmth of a lighted match.

I tasted Alan's tongue inside my mouth, so thrusting I gasped for breath and I remembered Eva who had been as innocent as a newborn child till somebody took advantage of her. Maisie had been protected from harm, kept on a leash not much longer than the rope that tethered the goat in the field behind Moynagh. Alan respected me. He would see no harm came to me.

The bus trundled along darkening roads, leaned into corners. Passengers were thrown against the walls of the bus and flung towards the aisle. The Z-bends. The hump-backed bridge, another bend and the straight road downhill to where Mammy would be waiting. Anger surged in me at the thought of her restless figure standing at the fork of the road, the lamp of her bicycle switched off to save the battery. Anger for making me hurry home like a ten-year-old child before the evening had started.

I unzipped my in-love-with-Alan face and stashed it away and I hardened my features into a scowl for meeting Mammy. For walking too fast for her to keep up with me, too slow for her to cycle without falling off. For pretending I hadn't heard her questions and announcing that I wouldn't be home tomorrow night.

A man in a black suit waited at the stop. The curate, Father Conway.

'It's your mother, Mary Ann. She's had an accident.'

The headlights of his car and of the ambulance criss-crossed in front of the house like searchlights in the blackout. Mammy was carried on a stretcher out of the house. Black lips on a dead face, one arm outside a sheet, the other under a blanket.

Doors closed in my face. The ambulance set off down the lane slicing a yellow tunnel through the night.

'She's unconscious. She's had the Last Rites, just in case. Your mother's a strong woman. With God's help, she'll pull through.'

She's not strong. She hasn't a pick of flesh on her. She's been blundering about in the dark since my father died. He was big and strong and it only took one rock to kill him. One with Michael Patrick Ward written all the way through it like a stick of Blackpool rock.

'Father Conway's going to take you to the hospital. I'll stay here with the child,' Agnes stood in the doorway. 'See if you can get in touch with Bridie. Maybe the hospital will let you phone.'

Father Conway followed the ambulance. I fixed my eyes on the rear lights that intensified to a throbbing red on the bends and glowed, constant and muted, on the longer stretches of the road.

'What happened, Father?'

'I couldn't get much sense out of Agnes. She kept saying somebody called Gabriel attacked your mother and she lost consciousness soon after. Do you know a Gabriel?'

'Gabriel's the gamecock. Agnes must have got it wrong.'

'Is it any wonder with all the trouble she's had, poor soul. It's lucky she has you to support her. You're a good girl, Mary Ann.'

No I'm not. I am a two-faced hypocrite. I confess to almighty God and to you, Father, that I have sinned. That I planned to sin tomorrow and the next day. That I lay like a pagan with a man on a hillside all afternoon. For all I know my mother is dying in that white ambulance in front of us and I can't get Alan out of my head. He shines on the road in the beam of the headlights. I could reach out and touch his image on the windscreen.

Father Conway sat beside me in the waiting room. He lit a cigarette and blew smoke rings into the air. He stood up and paced about the room, a thin, dark-haired man in his forties with a receding hairline and widow's peak. I followed the fading path of the smoke rings and tried not to stare at his legs. A piece of cooked carrot poked out of his turn-up and what looked like a lump of potato. Scraps of leek and barley clung to the bottom of the same trouser leg and greenish scum tidemarked his left shoe. Mammy always left soup out for the chickens in the tilting lids of burnt out saucepans.

Red parallel lines ran up Mammy's arm. Blood poisoning. The hand that rested on a pillow was bandaged. Liquid dripped from a bottle through a tube which punctured her right forearm. Only the rattle of her breathing told me she was alive.

'Is she going to live?'

'Now what sort of a question is that? You'll see the doctor in the morning.' The nurse recorded pulse and temperature. She pointed at the other bed in the side ward. 'Why don't you stretch out for a while.'

I shook my head. If I left my mother's side the umbilical cord which had joined me to her might snap and the last remnants of life drain soundlessly from her. If I fell asleep I might waken to find her bed empty. Strait-jacketed for the next occupant.

During the fitful night my father came and lay on the pillow beside his wife, his breath mingling with the fragile thread of hers. He had returned to look after her, to let me off the hook. To take us from the rain-sick drumlins of Monaghan back to our home in Carrig. His features blurred. Superimposed on my father's face lay another one. Young, untroubled, tanned. Alan, as I had seen him yesterday. Eyes closed against the sun, brushing flecks of dried heather from his face. Alan, on my mother's pillow as I dreamed of him lying beside me.

Mammy, I betrayed you when you were awake and I betray you again. I want to hold you in my arms and cradle you as you used to cradle me. But I'm afraid to touch you lest you break into a thousand pieces and crumble like the heather I trampled yesterday.

Washed and combed, crumpled clothes straightened, I waited from nine o'clock for the doctor's round. A brazen sun shone into the space between two wings of the hospital.

'We'll go to Bangor tomorrow. It's going to be a beautiful day,' Alan had pointed at the red sky. 'Two sunny days in a row in Belfast. Somebody up there loves us, Marianne.'

A quarter past ten. Somebody up there was playing fast and loose with us. My mother opened unseeing eyes. 'There is a Divinity that shapes our ends,' they said before the clamshells of her eyelids closed over them. The Divinity was a dirty fighter. He had thrown a kidney punch when my hands were tied behind my back.

I saw Alan waiting in the shadow of the Black Man's cape and plinth, pacing up and down in front of the Tech, moving into sunlight that flooded the green in front of Inst, scanning each bus as it came along Great Victoria Street, each figure poised in the green rectangle of its door. How long would he stand on the bad weather side of the street? Until the next bus from Monaghan arrived at half past three? Until the doctor and his cowering retinue reached my mother's bed at five past eleven and I was dismissed and sent to stand in the corridor. Until I was summoned to hear his verdict.

'Your mother's lucky to be alive. A gamecock, you say. Wicked beasts. Fight to the death. You should see what those spurs can do in a fight.' He sucked in his breath. An important man with aquiline features. 'She'll carry the mark of his claws for many a long day. Each one an injection of poison.' He propped open my mother's eye, shone a pencil torch in it. 'She's holding her own. She's a fighter too. Should pull through but she will need looking after when she's discharged from hospital. It will be six weeks, a couple of months, before she is at herself again.'

Seven weeks until the start of term at Queen's. I had the time.

I telephoned the City Hospital and left a message for Bridie before catching the bus back to Agnes and Brendan, a bus that took me further away from Alan still standing under the Black Man. He didn't know my address and all I knew was that he lived in London. A big city, the biggest in the world.

17

Betty and I enrolled on the English Language and Literature course at Queen's and shared a room in a university hostel. Tiddlers in a big pond, half-strangled by our green, royal-blue and black scarves. Our personal tutor, Doctor Wallace, said he could tell as soon as he saw us that we were convent girls. The nuns put a special mark on their pupils which they never lost.

I wrote many times to Alan care of the Mathematics Department, University of London. My letters were returned unopened but I kept on writing, changing the address a little each time.

Betty and I smoked, not because we enjoyed it. We hoped that inhaling and puffing clouds of smoke into the opaque atmosphere of the Union would make us look fast and rid us of the convent stamp we had been lumbered with. We painted Cupid's bows over our mouths and wore heels so high we had to take them off after dances and walk back to the hostel in stocking soles.

I saw very little of Bridie. She spent most of her time at the Royal Victoria Hospital or with Tim Molloy, a second-year medical student. Betty started going out with Sean Dolan who was doing Celtic Studies.

I had boyfriends too. They didn't last long as none of them could match up to Alan. I never met anyone who listened to me in the way he did. Who sent my heart into a somersault when I caught a glimpse of him. Whose touch turned my spine to jelly.

Six more letters to Alan were returned.

By Christmas Mammy had recovered, apart from her thumb, which the cock had ripped to shreds. She missed Gabriel's crowing that used to shatter the dawn. She missed watching him mince delicately about the street, tossing his angry comb. Most of all she missed the fruits of his fertile loins and she hadn't forgiven Agnes for making soup out of him. She bore him no grudge. He was male, fashioned by nature for procreation and violence.

When I returned for the long summer holidays the storm clouds I had seen gathering over Moynagh erupted in the kitchen. Words poured from Mammy's mouth, overflowed, hissed, spat and danced like milk that has been left to boil untended on the range. A kaleidoscope of words. Of wrongs and grievances. Of greed and injustice.

I gathered them from the four corners of the room and shuffled them, trying to make sense of the events that had tortured Mammy and Agnes for the past month.

The stench of death, pervasive as mustard gas, has slithered into every crevice of Moynagh. Agnes smells it too. She and Mammy climb their hump-backed hills to breathe the clean air beyond the hollow of their home and fields.

Joseph's dog, Togo, howls day and night, his head stretched towards the sky. The smell is concentrated in Joseph's room. It slips between the pages of his books, invades the pockets of his jackets, the funnels of his trousers. His sisters offer the rosary for a gentle release of his soul wherever he may be. They pray that he may be allowed to breathe his last in the home where he was born and reared, and lie in the grave at Ballyroe with his parents and Thomas and Maisie.

Jimmy the Post parks his bicycle against the wall and walks into the kitchen, a buff envelope in his hand.

'It's from Clones.' He studies the typed address, reluctant to part with it. 'Must be important.'

He waits while Mammy reads the letter. She collapses into a chair.

'Bad news, Ellen?' Jimmy asks.

She tells him and Agnes that Joseph is dead and puts the letter in her apron pocket.

Jimmy blesses himself. 'God rest him. He was a scholar and a gentleman. Too good for these parts.' He offers sympathy and pedals at top speed down the lane to spread the word throughout the townland. Mammy reads the letter to Agnes.

Joseph McKenna, husband of Philomena McKenna, of Station Road, Birmingham has died. Mr James Treanor, solicitor, wishes to see Mrs Ellen Ward concerning a matter of importance.

Husband of Mrs Philomena McKenna?

The letter is passed to Agnes who borrows Mammy's glasses to read it and hands it back to her. Husband of Mrs Philomena McKenna! All the re-reading, all the toing and froing do not delete the words. They can hold them before the heat of the fire, toss them into the flames. They will not disappear.

There has been a clerical error, a crossing of wires between England and Ballyroe.

Joseph with a wife!

Joseph scorned women, their wagging tongues, their prying eyes, their secretive bodies. Women were for cooking, cleaning, labouring in the field. He would never bring another woman to Moynagh to share the floor with Agnes. He would never have allowed himself to be inveigled into marriage with some English trollop.

Mourning for the dead brother is deferred. Mammy throws on her coat and hat, pumps the tyres of her bicycle and cycles to the office of Treanor and Lennon, Solicitors. She bangs on the wooden counter. No, she does not have an appointment. She demands an interview with Mr Treanor, Senior. Immediately. A young woman who has been typing at a desk disappears into a back room. Young Mr Treanor will see Mammy. His father is in court and Mr Lennon is busy with a client.

Dominic Treanor, twenty-five and unmarried, is at the top of Mammy's list of prospective sons-in-law. A good looking, athletic young man, he tops the lists of most of the mothers of daughters in the area.

Mammy climbs the lino-covered stairs to young Mr Treanor's office. The coffin-shaped room depresses her. The salmon-coloured wainscotting. The sooty fireplace. Dominic Treanor informs her that on the death of her brother, Joseph, the land and property of Moynagh has passed to his next of kin i.e. his wife Philomena. He tries to open a window so that Mammy may get her breath back but the layers of paint that have stuck to the frame refuse to budge.

'That is the height of nonsense,' she gasps. 'My husband redeemed Moynagh. His name is on the deeds. My solicitor in Carrig assured me it belonged to me and I have continued to pay the purchase annuity to the land commission every year since my husband died.'

The deeds of Moynagh are produced. Dominic Treanor explains slowly in non-legal terms. Had my father outlived Joseph the property would have been his. As it is, Joseph has died intestate and his widow inherits the house and farm.

Mammy's protests pierce the floorboards. Mr Lennon's secretary is sent upstairs to find out the cause of the commotion. Mammy insists that the ruling is a flagrant breach of the law. No power on heaven or earth will allow a widow woman and her children to be thrown out on the streets – not to mention Agnes who has worked her fingers to the bone every day God sent to keep the place from falling apart. Young Mr Treanor can keep his tea and his custard creams. She has come here for justice. Not refreshments. She will fight this tinker calling herself Mrs Philomena McKenna in every court in the land. She will prove that Joseph was not in possession of his faculties when the so-called marriage took place. She will go to the highest authority, the Pope in Rome if necessary, and have it annulled.

Dominic Treanor says the law is the law and he cannot alter it. He says she's upset; needs time to think things over. He will arrange for someone to give her a lift home. Mammy informs him she came under her own steam and she will go home the same way and she doesn't need a young brat, just out of short trousers, telling her how to run her life and spend her money.

She is printing the image of a cow on a pound of butter and Agnes is waiting for yellow lumps to form in her churn. They hear mooing and bawling of cattle whose voices they don't recognise and an army of hooves in the lane. A herd of bullocks is driven into the street by two strangers. One of them, a bad-tempered-looking cur with a week's black stubble on him, makes to open the gate of the broad meadow. Mammy's butter spade slams his knuckles. Agnes shows him the prongs of the graip, two inches from his face.

'Get off this land or I'll have the law on you,' Mammy shouts. Her hands are grafted to the bars of the gate. Cattle, prodded by the gombeen at the rear, jostle and mount each other. The wholesome stink of their bowels emptying over the ground and over each other smothers once and for all the smell of death.

'This land belongs to my sister. She has instructed us to graze the . . .'

The prongs of the graip on his cheek, close enough to scratch but not to draw blood, silence him. He mutters with his accomplice and they withdraw, cursing Mammy and Agnes for two hard-faced hoors, lunatics who should be strung up. They'll be back with reinforcements and show them who's boss.

Mammy is given three months to find accommodation before vacating Moynagh to its new owner and a court order is issued restraining anyone, either personally or with stock, from entering the premises during that period. Joseph's widow is not an English trollop. She's a native of the next townland. Her first husband hailed from Mullingar and she will forever after be referred to only as the Mullingar heifer or the widow woman who ran the doss-house in Birmingham where Joseph had the misfortune to find board and lodgings. And death. Her brothers will be called the Grippers.

Neither the law nor the gardaí have the power to restrain the bellowing of cattle that should be sleeping in quiet fields instead of stampeding over them. To silence the demented squealing of pigs wakened out of nightmares of knives and slaughterhouse hooks. To stop Gabriel's successor, a nameless rooster, crowing through the hours from midnight till dawn or still the frantic beating of his outstretched wings and quieten the clucking hens that should be fast asleep with their heads buried in their feathers. Mammy and Agnes take shifts to patrol the sty and the hen house and to wander over the fields, but they are always a step behind, or three steps in front of the thieving devils who torment their livestock.

A sleepless month had taken its toll on Mammy. 'Are we to spend our days wandering from pillar to post or be chased to hell or to

Connacht?' she asked us. 'The birds of the air have their nests and the fishes the sea, but we haven't a place to lay our heads.'

The rainy day for which she had saved the money from Rathbeg Avenue had come. Six weeks before the date of the eviction Bridie and I accompanied her to Carrig, where she arranged to buy a terrace house, not in the smart end where we had previously lived, but in the opposite side of the town.

'That Mullingar heifer is nothing but a thief and a grab-all. She'll get her just deserts.' Mammy's wooden spoon walloped sugar and margarine in the baking bowl. 'She is defrauding the labourer of her wages and that is one of the three sins crying to heaven for vengeance.'

I knew about mortal, venial and reserved sins but not sins crying for vengeance. 'What are the other two?'

'Wilful murder and sodomy,' announced Brendan, his eye on the mixture in the bowl.

'You know too much for your own good. Where did you learn that filth?'

'The master taught us.' He looked at Mammy, aggrieved.

Mammy hit him with the wooden spoon and ordered him to get out of her sight and go and feed the turkeys.

'The Mullingar heifer will have no luck. Just you wait and see. The mills of God grind slowly but they grind exceeding small.' She kept on turning the handle of the flour-sifter long after the last grains of flour had passed through.

We waited for the wrath of God to descend on the Mullingar heifer. We waited in vain. Word reached us that she had come home to Killnabo. One of the brothers drove her to Mass each Sunday in a brand new Rover. She wore a different New-Look costume on each occasion. With matching hat, shoes and gloves.

'Get up, get up. You won't believe your eyes,' Bridie prodded me awake. She motioned me to keep quiet. I followed her to the half-open door. It was three days before we were to leave Moynagh.

Rags of cloud scudded across the face of a phlegmy moon. In dappled brightness I made out the figures of two women bent over the dunghill. Their bodies swayed like the weights of a clock as they shifted it, shovelful by shovelful, to a spot nearby.

'Holy God, what are they playing at?' I whispered. 'Should we get dressed and go and see?'

'If they wanted us to help they would have asked us.'

We dragged open the door to the loft above the room we had been banished to when Joseph came back. From outside, almost invisible under the jagged overhang of thatch, you could see a window not much bigger than two pages of an exercise book. It looked down on the dunghill where the two women wrestled with the compacted remains of centuries. For as long as I remembered, weeds and grass had covered the midden. Nothing had ever been added to it or taken from it. Being town children we never questioned the ways of the country.

The beam of Bridie's torch picked out places where steps had broken away and the tarry blackness beneath. She threw a piece of wood up into the loft. We waited till the rustling and scurrying of whatever lived up there stopped. We tested each rickety step and we bowed low beneath rafters that sagged under the weight of thatch and crumbling scraw. A floorboard gave way, slapped its saw edge against my leg. We crawled towards the paler darkness of the window, palms and knees testing for rotten boards through which our legs might plunge to dangle disembodied from the ceiling of our bedroom. Virgin dust and near-darkness enveloped shapes that lay piled in corners or were scattered wantonly over the floor. The curves of a cradle, skeletons of limbless chairs, dinosaur remains of a harness, farm implements long extinct – the debris of generations of labourers and their families.

My hand touched the decomposing body and spoked wings of a bat or a bird that must have flown through the gap between window and wall and grown too fat to escape. I screamed.

'Shut up or go back downstairs,' Bridie hissed.

Through the circle she had rubbed in the crusted grime of the window we could barely make out the two figures digging below us.

'They must be able to see in the dark.'

'They've got used to it and they're working in a confined space.'

'Would anybody in their right mind believe us if we told them, those two, rooting in a dunghill in the middle of the night, are our mother and our aunt.'

'God, isn't it well we're getting out of here or we would all end up in the loony bin like Joseph.'

The moon glitter-edged a bank of charcoal clouds that rushed away above the house. The yard, the haggard and the women were flooded in light. The movements Mammy and Agnes made were deliberate. Unhurried. The careful searching and sifting of archaeologists. Agnes picked something out of the midden, which was now not much more than a foot high, and placed it in a sack.

'Jesus Christ, Mary Ann.' Bridie's hand was a vice on my arm. 'Are you thinking what I'm thinking?'

Mammy had said they buried Gilmour in the last place the scum from the back streets of England would look. My skin was stretched smooth with horror.

Way back in 1921, Agnes and Mammy and their mother must have dragged Gilmour's still-warm body along from the pump and the duck pond, past the house and up beside the haggard. And Maisie like a strewer in the Holy Week procession followed, spilling muddy water in their wake, covering the ground raked by his boots and the blood dripping from his wounds. Did they bury him naked or was he still wearing his clown's uniform – boots, buttons, revolver and all – when they shoved him under years of muck from the byre?

That pitch-black July night, thirty years before, they must have laboured like slaves under the whip as they filled spades and forks with dripping dung, their ears strained for the grumble of the Auxiliaries' tender. For the sound of Mary Francis racing to tell them a horde of Black and Tans was creeping up behind them.

'Yes,' I whispered.

I whispered for fear the women beavering below me would hear. Or the Mullingar heifer's brothers who skulked at night in the fields and outhouses. Or the Black and Tans or Joseph's ghost in his coffin prison between the floor boards.

What state would he be in after all these years? Would Mammy plunge her pitchfork through his eyes; through the maggot-riddled mound of his belly?

'There would only be bones left after all this time. They should have used the rest of him to fertilise the crops.' Bridie tried to sound light-hearted. Her teeth, like mine, were chattering.

'Maybe they were afraid he would cause a blight. Bring on another potato famine.'

Clouds covered the moon and we could just make out Mammy and Agnes continuing to place objects in the sack which they carried into the haggard. We picked our way downstairs and closed the brown door.

'Do you remember how Charles II had Cromwell dug up and his head stuck on a pike at Tyburn?' I whispered.

'Maybe they're going to stick Gilmour's skull on the gate at the end of the lane to frighten the Mullingar heifer.'

We were both shivering though it was a warm night. Through a window at the far end of the passage we saw Agnes raising and lowering the pump handle and Mammy bent under the flow of water.

When we got up in the morning their faces and clothes were smutted with soot from a bonfire that blazed in front of the haggard. On it perched the churn Agnes and her mother had used throughout their lives together with all the flammable objects which the neighbours couldn't use. The nuns in Monaghan had been given the paraffin cooker and the new Tilley lamp.

Into the boghole they flung three-legged pots, the bastable my great grandmother had baked bread in and the griddle that had hung on a crane over the open fire before the arrival of the range, as well as harnesses, rusted machinery and enamel chamber pots. One after the other they slurped and sank into the foetid water. I told Mammy the Russians had defeated Napoleon by burning everything when they fled their homes. She said she wasn't copying a bunch of communist atheists but she was making sure the Mullingar heifer got not one stick, not one crumb more than the house and land she stole. She and Agnes were still angry with the local farmers who had taken advantage of their situation and had conspired to pay a low price for the Moynagh livestock because the two women had no option but to sell.

'What were you and Agnes up to in the middle of the night?' Bridie asked.

'Nothing that need concern you, Madam. We were tidying up a few loose ends. Safeguarding the good name of the family from that pack of blackguards. That's all you need to know.' She fixed a gimlet eye on us and we knew that further questioning would be useless. Then she made us vow on the memory of our father not to breathe a word of what we had seen to a living soul.

There were no Redcoats with fixed bayonets on the eviction day. No furniture or pots and pans were flung out of the house which had been stripped bare. Kelly's van left with our belongings and Padraig Regan's taxi waited to take us to Ballyroe. Brendan was nowhere to be found. Search parties were sent out. Bridie discovered him behind a hedge in the broad meadow, his arms wrapped round Togo.

'I'm not going. I don't want to go to a new school,' he sobbed. 'I'll stay here with Togo and go to my own school.'

She persuaded him that Togo would be much happier with Jimmy McMahon near Moynagh than in Carrig. Brendan could come back to see him and his school friends and Mammy would get him a wee pup once we had settled down.

She and I shook the dust of Ballyroe from our feet. No regrets for the dances where the average age of most of the 'boys' was forty. Farmers' sons looking for a girl who would still be young enough to look after them in their incontinent dotage. Men who lined one side of the hall, sizing up prospective dancing partners as they did the beasts at the market, whose best offer was a ride home on the bar of a bike after a grope in a field.

Never again would we face the ordeal of Mass each Sunday. The staggered start to the journey. First Mammy and Agnes setting off on their bicycles, Brendan perched on the carrier seat behind Mammy. Then the relay race when Bridie and I picked up the bicycles they had discarded in the ditch.

Mammy said she would miss the pure and balmy air of Moynagh and Bridie told her we would all have been barmy if we had stayed much longer.

Agnes was the last to leave the house. She stood on the threshold where she had always waited when we arrived on our visits from the north and when she watched for my return from school during that wartime summer I spent at Moynagh. There was no smile on her ravaged face which surveyed the road, the duck pond, the fields and the bushy trees on the low skyline that defined Moynagh and her eyes were winter bare. When she left to go towards the taxi the door hung open behind her.

18

Mammy complained that you couldn't swing a cat in the new house. It was a terrible comedown for her to leave the broad acres of Moynagh and live in a matchbox. Through the walls poured the strains of 'They tried to tell us we're too young', followed by the *News at Six*. She said if you knocked a nail in the plaster the next-door neighbour would hang his hat on it.

It wasn't Rathbeg Avenue but water, hot and cold, flowed from taps in the bathroom and kitchen and a tug on the lavatory chain sent a shower squirting round the bowl. I looked through the window of the room Bridie and I shared. Logan's Hill and Slieve Dubh were silhouetted against the evening sky. Another face had been opened and new benches quarried since the day when work had stopped for my father's funeral.

We had come home.

Brendan slept in a boxroom at the top of the stairs but no bedroom was allotted to Agnes. No place where she could withdraw to be on her own. She slept on a put-you-up in the front room – a contraption which, after many contortions, swallowed the bedclothes and became a sofa for us to lounge on till bedtime. Her good costume and coat were squeezed into Mammy's wardrobe and the rest of her belongings hung on a nail behind the door or were kept in her suitcase under the put-you-up. She left the house each morning at eight to be in time for nine o'clock Mass and returned around twelve with her groceries.

She and Mammy talked about little but Moynagh: the 'what-if's and the 'maybes'. Agnes said she would apply for a council house and stop sponging on Mammy who said that as soon as she got her finances sorted she would see if there was enough money left to buy Agnes a place of her own in Ballyroe.

Brendan returned to his former school in Bridge Street. In the excitement of meeting old friends he forgot about Togo and his mates at Saint Kieran's. Bridie and I prepared to relaunch ourselves on Carrig.

For our first appearance at Sunday Mass in Saint Malachi's, we arranged each other's hair, checked that our make-up was visible but not loud and removed bicycle-oil stains from our New-Look green and blue coats. Mammy, who never praised our appearance in case we became big-headed, said we would pass in a crowd with a push.

The crowd we hoped to attract outside the church had already gathered round a young woman wearing a fur coat even though it was still summer.

'Bridie, Mary Ann,' she shrieked, rushed across and threw her arms round us. 'Look at the pair of you. You're enormous.'

Myrna Donnelly, back in the land of the living.

'Myrna Donnelly! You look fantastic.'

'Mrs Tiberio Zocco.' She flashed under our noses a slim hand with a wedding ring and an enormous solitaire on the fourth finger.

A foreign-looking gentleman – fifty if he was an hour – bowed a black-and-grey head with a bald patch on the crown. Both his eye-teeth were solid gold. 'He's loaded,' his wife announced to us and the throng passing up the steps. 'Ice cream.'

'Mammy said you borrowed one of my ball gowns for your first formal, Mary Ann. Which one did you wear?'

'The one with the layers of blue net,' I could have bitten my tongue off for reminding Myrna of her blighted engagement to Eddie Jakabowski.

'That old rag. You must have looked a sight in it.'

My partner had said I looked lovely. He called me Salome of the seven veils, said he hoped I could dance as well as her. I didn't know who Salome was then so I blushed and simpered instead of slapping him across the face.

'If ever either of you wants to borrow a ball gown give me a ring,' she shouted when we had reached the top step. 'We're in the book. Malone Road. There's only one Zocco.'

Myrna's fur coat caressed my face as she swept up the aisle a minute after Fr Doyle ascended the altar steps. Mr Zocco followed three paces behind. He may not have been Clark Gable but he cut an impressive dash in his fitted grey overcoat with astrakhan collar.

'For somebody who went to the bad, she's done pretty well for herself,' Bridie commented without moving her lips.

We rushed home to tell Mammy about Myrna's resurrection but Mrs Campbell and Claudette had beaten us to it.

'Myrna Donnelly can count herself lucky she found some foreigner prepared to take her on,' Mrs Campbell was saying. 'There's not a man in Carrig would have touched her with a bargepole. When it comes to choosing a wife, Irishmen don't like damaged goods.'

'Better to be an old man's darling than a young man's slave.' Mammy said. 'I hope it works out for her. I always liked Myrna. Sure she hadn't a half ounce of sense.'

'Bridie, Marianne,' Mrs Campbell stood up and shook hands with us. 'You look great. You've turned into fine big girls and the country air has done you a power of good. You both look the picture of health, don't they, Claudette?'

'Yes, Mummy. And Marianne has lovely rosy cheeks like a milkmaid.'

No one would have accused Claudette of looking the picture of health. She was a typist working for a firm of accountants in Castle Street. In a wasp-waisted black suit with peplum and a white cloche hat, she could have modelled for the front cover of *Picture Post*.

'Girls, go and make a fresh pot of tea for Mrs Campbell and Claudette.'

'Isn't that Claudette poison?' Bridie said as she poured boiling water into the teapot.

'Like a milkmaid,' I mimicked Claudette's baby-girl voice. 'Who does she think she is with that stupid tea cosy on her head?'

'Marianne, a funny thing happened,' Claudette appeared in the kitchen. 'Do you remember that boy from the Royal High you used to go out with before you went to the country? What's this his name was?'

'Alan. Alan Reed.'

'Alan, of course. Quite nice-looking wasn't he? You did well for yourself there. Well, you don't know Peter Brownlow; he's one of the partners at my office. He's not really a partner but he's very high up. He's awfully nice and very well-spoken. Well, apparently he met Alan at a meeting or a conference, some sort of get-together for accountants in London and would you believe it? Alan asked him if he knew you. Isn't it a small world and fancy him remembering you after all these years.'

Lovely Claudette, I could kiss your rouged cheeks and I could fling myself at Peter Brownlow's feet and thank him for being an accountant and going to London. Indeed it is a small world and getting smaller.

How do I know he'll want to see me again?

We have both changed. He could be married.

I don't really know him. Six months of adolescent love and a half-day on Cave Hill. Not much to go on.

'You're going to marry me, Marianne Ward. You may not think that now, but you are.'

'I'm not going to lose you, Marianne. Not ever again.'

That was two years ago.

'I'd love to hear how Alan's doing. Would it be all right for me to pop into your office tomorrow and meet Peter?' I sounded like a stranger on a crackly tape-recording.

'Alan Reed's a lucky chap,' Peter Brownlow said, taking a sheaf of papers from the top drawer of a filing cabinet.

'Thank you, Mr Brownlow.' I clutched the North London address against my blouse. 'I knew Alan years ago. We used to walk home from school together if we happened to bump into each other. I might drop him a line some time.'

'From the way Alan spoke, you did more than bump into each other.'

The dark days were over. My luck had flown back. All I had to do was to grab hold of it and hold on tight. I wrote to Alan telling him not a day passed when I didn't long for him. Though London was only a stretch of water and a train journey away, it might as well be the other side of the world.

And love was an oblong envelope with a London postmark with my name and address written in a small, square script. Three, sometimes four times a week. And plans for me to join him as soon as I graduated.

19

As the train approached Euston Station all the rows with Mammy dinned in my ears. I would rue the day I left my home to go chasing after an English Protestant, an evacuee whom I hardly knew. I needn't pretend he was half-Irish. His grandmother had been a black, Orange bigot who wouldn't give a Catholic daylight if she could take it from him. If my father had been alive he would have horsewhipped me and not let me set foot out of the house.

Suppose Alan didn't turn up. Suppose he didn't recognise me. Suppose, after one look, he took to his heels. I tried to reassemble his features from a mist of unconnected memories, seeing him in several young men who hurried past without a glimmer of recognition. Someone in a white shirt and grey flannels waved and there was something familiar in the way he swam against the tide of travellers surging towards the ticket barrier; in the way he moved, parting waves of luggage-heavy passengers. The gap between us narrowed until we stood facing each other. Alan wrapped his arms round me, gathered me up off the ground till my mouth was level with his. 'Marianne, Marianne,' he whispered into my lips, into my neck, into my hair. 'Marianne, Marianne,' trickled down my back.

I clung to him like ivy to a tree and buried my speechless mouth in his shirt. Blind hands tried to remember the hollow between his shoulder blades, the smoothness of one shoulder and the knobbled lumpiness of the other that had been broken in a rugby tackle. Then he picked up my bags and carried them as if they were filled with feathers.

'I'm going to have to pin some sort of homing device to you, to make sure you keep coming back to me.' He raised one eyebrow the way I remembered and laughed, and I knew why I had braved my mother's wrath and come to England. I walked with him towards the ticket barrier and down steps into the Underground, just air beneath my feet and for weeks, maybe even months, they never felt hard ground.

When we emerged into daylight, he rushed me to his home, the first floor of his parents' house which had been converted into a flat for him while they were in the Far East. A silent house apart from the sound of the downstairs tenant mowing the lawn of a large garden. I had an impression of heavily draped rooms, ornaments from the East and antique furniture, watercolours which Alan said were painted by his mother, but my eyes wanted only him. We held each other at arms' length and I studied the near stranger whose hands clasped mine. A flesh-and-blood man. Broader shouldered, jaw and chin more angular than in the blurred picture of the boy I had been carrying around in my mind. He drew me close until my ear lay against the thudding in his chest.

'You're shivering. Don't be frightened, Marianne. There's nothing to be afraid of.' His arms closed tighter around me. 'I'll look after you always. I promise, my precious girl.'

Precious as the sun and moon and stars.

All that freedom. Days and nights of clockless time. Him and me and years of pent-up yearning. All that weight of water straining against a reservoir wall.

'Take a long forenoon,' Mammy had advised me and Bridie. 'Enjoy your youth. There are more folk married than doing well.'

All the same, she had a dream of me walking down the aisle of Saint Malachi's church on the arm of a well-to-do solicitor, or a doctor like Tim Molloy, whose engagement to Bridie had been announced before I left Ireland. Mammy would never survive the shame of a mixed marriage, a hole-in-the-corner 'do' in the vestry of a church on her own doorstep.

'An abomination,' I heard the curate, Father Hanna, say. 'A ruinous start to married life. Two goats pulling in opposite directions. If I have to officiate at a mixed marriage, I take off my stole and any religious object I am wearing. I conduct the ceremony in the vestry without flowers, candles or holy water and I don't make the sign of the cross once.'

A priest from the north of England married us. A smiling man with a reddish-brown beard and a lick of hair spread across his balding head. He was waiting for us in the church porch, wearing white vestments.

'When I woke up this morning I felt happy,' he told us. 'I said to myself, Marianne and Alan are getting married today and the sun is shining. You know what they say. Happy is the bride that the sun shines on.' And he pronounced us, not two but one flesh.

Salty flesh that tasted of the afternoon scents blown up from the garden through the open window – carnations, musky buddleia and the China-tea smell of old roses. Alan's arms were wings folding round me and there was no telling where he ended and I began.

Evening thickened into dark blue London night and the perfume of honeysuckle, scented stock and white Persian jasmine flooded our room. I committed Alan's body to memory. Jut of thigh and breastbone, slats of ribcage, the coded message tattooed on either side of his appendix scar. He said my feet were small and dainty as a baby's and asked how I managed to stay upright and not topple over. He marvelled at the penny-sized vaccination mark on the inside of my left thigh, at the ridge of flesh that bisected it and the grainy speckling on its surface; and he thanked Mrs Bradshaw for insisting to the doctor that I was destined for the ballroom, not the back kitchen.

Alan and I talked a lot in the early weeks of our marriage. I heard about his father who taught him to play cricket and allowed him to play with the model railway which he had taken to Hong Kong with him. A happy childhood, until the Germans bombed London, when his mother took him to Carrig and left him with his grandmother, a cross old woman who hated Catholics even more than she hated dirt. He told me he was beaten up at school for talking funny, till he learned to imitate the Carrig accent. And how he had cried himself to sleep night after night, wondering if he would ever see his mother and father again.

'Do your parents get on well together?' I asked.

'Oh yes. Never a cross word. They have the perfect recipe for a happy marriage.' He smiled to himself. 'George does exactly what he likes and my mother puts up with it.'

'Were they not angry when you told them who you were going to marry?'

'Course not. My father wrote to me that Irish women make good wives. According to him they're faithful and docile.' He grinned and paused before adding, 'Which is more than could be said about him.'

'What about your mother? What did she say?'

The submissive wife. The daughter of the Orange bigot.

228

'She was delighted, with you both being from Carrig. She's going to write to you. She's looking forward to meeting you next year. You'll like her. Everybody does.'

I had seen photographs of her. She was beautiful. And stylish. A good artist and a first-class cook. I hoped my paragon of a mother-in-law stayed in the Far East for good. His father had the same thin moustache and tooth-flashing smile as Errol Flynn. He wore blazers with crests, cravats and sunglasses. What Mammy would call a 'fly-looking' type. A spiv.

I sifted and trimmed the stories Alan heard about my childhood as a mother censors books for her children. An Irishman would have understood why Gilmour had to be killed and his bones burned in the middle of the night. Not coming from a farming family, Alan didn't know the importance of owning one's own land and would have had no idea of the enormity of the crimes the Mullingar Heifer and Gilmour had committed against my family.

Belfast is a neat little city. You can hold it in the hollow of your hand. You can walk from one end of it to the other and back and still have an hour or so to spare before dinner time. The vast sprawl of London disorientated me. The sameness of endless streets – criss-crossing, stretching out, going on forever. Alan said to give London a chance. There was no other city in the world where you could walk for miles almost totally through parks. He took me through Kensington Gardens, Hyde Park, Green Park and St James's Park one sunny day. A keeper in St James's Park told us Charles II had established an aviary nearly three hundred years ago. He said the birds had their wings clipped when they were very young to stop them flying away.

Maybe my wings should have been clipped early in my

marriage. Like the flightless swans at Moynagh, I would have envied the swallows and whooper swans who came each year and flew away when summer was over. Without any option, I might have stopped longing for home and been content in London.

'Take a good look round, Paddy,' a policeman in Trafalgar Square called out one day.

'How does he know I'm Irish?' I asked.

'How does he know? It's written all over you, Marianne. The freckles, the black hair, the green coat and the way you stare. Try not to stare so much.'

Was he ashamed of me already? Did I seem like a country bumpkin, compared to those London women, mincing about in tight skirts and stiletto heels? I mustn't stare at foreign voices in the streets. At people with black and brown and yellow skins. And not ask for potato bread or soda farls or barmbrack at the baker's, or for a sliced pan or plain. Maybe I should start saying 'aitch' instead of 'haitch' and try pronouncing the first letter of the alphabet as *ay* and not *ah*. Maybe I should stop saying 'I amn't'. And maybe I should sell my soul when I was at it!

One Sunday two girls, in white-and-navy nurses' uniforms, followed me out of St Joseph's church on Highgate Hill.

'You're Irish,' the smaller one said. She had a round face and a mass of tight black curls. 'We heard you answering the prayers and we've seen you the last couple of weeks.'

'Where are you from? Have you been over long?' asked her friend who was tall and fair. As we walked towards the Whittington hospital, they interrogated me the way Irish people usually do. Maeve and Eilish were both from Dublin and had trained in London.

'You'll have to come to the Irish Club in Camden Town. Friday night. It's a gas.'

'It's great crack. There's a bar and a céilí band and you can have a good sing-song. Bring your husband.'

I hesitated. 'He's not Irish.'

'Well that's not his fault,' roared Eilish. 'Bring him along. We won't eat him.'

Alan would have stood out like a poulticed finger at an Irish club. I pretended we were going away for the weekend and promised to see them in a fortnight. They rushed off towards the hospital, calling back to me

'See you in two weeks, Marianne.'

'We'll get your address and come round to your place.'

'Give us a ring. Don't you forget.'

Loneliness, such as I hadn't experienced since leaving home, fell like a shroud over me. I would have loved to have friends like them. Lively Dublin girls, unencumbered by the puritan Catholicism of the Six Counties and I would have made lots of friends at the Irish club. I waved to them till their cloaks disappeared inside a wide doorway. Alan would have found them too uninhibited. Too noisy.

After that, I went to an early Mass in Our Lady of the Rosary.

Loneliness! Mammy says only folk with no worries and too much time on their hands feel lonely. What right had I? I should have bottled that first summer, sealed in the smell of the coffee Alan brought to bed on weekend mornings and the tang of English marmalade. The prickle of toast crumbs. Alan's arms round me and around crumpled newspapers. The sweat on our skin blackened with newsprint. Him writing ILUVYOU on the Scrabble board and claiming a bonus for using all seven letters.

And the weekend in Paris after Alan's pay cheque arrived. Him and me, part of the multitude of lovers who thronged the city, who kissed on boulevards and in cafes, in the lazy heat of Montmartre and the dusty cool of the Tuileries Gardens; whose entwined bodies swayed with the rhythm of the Metro. But above all, Paris for us was the clanking lift outside our room in the Rue Gay Lussac. Paris was yellow chinks blazing round shutters. Paris was the crack in the ceiling that meandered towards the lampshade in the centre.

'That's the Nile up there, Alan. You see where it ends in the delta at Cairo,' I pointed to a network of finer cracks near the wall. 'Where does it flow, apart from Egypt?'

'Somewhere in Africa.'

'Is that a fact? You're very clever.'

The valley of the Nile disappeared behind his face and we made love, tenderly and fiercely, till we thought we would die of love.

When Alan went back to work I spent my time cooking, cleaning and waiting. One day I moved a Chinese bowl from the top of the bookcase to the window ledge. I rushed downstairs when I heard his key in the lock. As we came into the sitting room, his arm dropped from my shoulder. He looked from the windowsill to the chest of drawers. From the chest of drawers to the windowsill. Then he picked up the bowl, studied it as though checking for damage and replaced it where it had been on the bookcase.

'It's very old. And valuable. It might easily fall or get knocked off the window. You don't mind, do you, love.'

'Of course I don't mind.' I curled up on his lap and purred to the touch of his fingers combing through my hair; travelling the length of the fold behind my ear to pin back a straying lock.

Of course I don't mind, any more than I mind living in a flat on which I may not leave a single imprint. If I disappear off the face of the earth tomorrow, your mother will still smile from her wedding photograph and the garden downstairs will go on flowering six weeks earlier than my father's in Carrig. But I often find myself comparing the silence of these lifeless rooms with the bustle of my mother's house and the constant company of my student years. And I miss the sounds and smells of home – the whistle and hiss of kettles forever on the boil, the Angelus marking each phase of the day, the floury breath of straight-from-the-oven bread, the peppery sweetness of mashed carrots and parsnips, steak charring in the frying pan.

But all that is unimportant. What matters now are your fingers tracing the lines on my palm and your fast breath on my cheek.

'Marianne, do you remember that day on Cave Hill when I said you would marry me? I didn't tell you there was nothing you could do about it.' Alan studied my opened hand. 'You see, it's all here, clearly written.'

'How did you learn to read palms?'

'Your mother wasn't the only fortune teller in Carrig.'

I stared at my hand. The life-arc curving round the thumb socket. The deep carve of the heart-line. The head-line wavering across my palm. The crease running straight from the end of the wrist to the base of my middle finger, my line of destiny. 'Show me what you see. Show me.'

'No, I have to have some secrets.' He covered my palm with his. 'After all, there's a lot of your past that you don't let me know about.'

We were wading in dangerous waters. To divert him, I said: 'I've been thinking. I don't have enough to do. I'm going to look for a teaching job.'

20

My first job teaching English was in a boys' secondary school, a red-brick Victorian building with high ceilings and bars on the first-floor windows. To my surprise my class of fourteen-year-olds didn't leap to attention when I appeared.

'Good morning, boys.' I smiled the distant smile I had been taught on teaching practice. The smile that tells them I am on one side of the fence and they are on the other. 'My name is Mrs Reed. I'm your new English teacher.'

'The top of the morning to you, Miss.'

'You can't teach English. You don't talk proper. You're Irish.'

'Who said that? Who said that? Stand up at once, the boy who spoke.'

'It was him, Miss. It was him.'

'He did. He did.'

'What you going to do about it, Miss? Hit him with your shillelagh?'

There was a knock on the door. The class fell silent as a young woman came in. Brown hair fell in soft waves to her shoulders and she had the tanned complexion of someone who spent most of her time out of doors. Her blouse was the same colour as the splashes of bright red on a calf length black skirt. When she shook hands with me a smile lit up her face.

'I'm Kitty Jackson, head of department. Welcome to Redwood. I'm very sorry I missed you this morning. Please let me know if you need any help.' She lowered her voice and said, 'Good luck with this lot. They can be a bit of a handful.'

'Miss,' a boy in the third row called to her as she swayed towards the door, 'my mum's got a skirt like yours.'

She didn't freeze him with a look or tick him off for being impertinent. She laughed and said 'Has she? You mum and I have very good taste.'

Kitty wasn't conventionally beautiful. Her nose was slightly crooked and there was a gap between her front teeth, but the temperature of the staffroom rose by five degrees whenever she breezed in. Young male teachers rushed to relieve her of piles of exercise books, to find a seat for her, to offer her a cup of coffee. Even the old fogies, usually invisible behind acres of newsprint, folded their papers, pulled in their paunches and asked her what was new, what she had been up to over the weekend or what she thought of Arsenal's chances for the cup.

When Betty and I were students we spent many hours discussing the elusive components of sex appeal, wondering if we had enough. If we had any. However you defined sex appeal, Kitty had it by the basinful.

Lunchtime in the bleak dining room with Kitty and other members of staff made the day bearable. An escape from paper aeroplanes that flew past my head when I turned to write on the board and from feet that tripped any boy I called to my desk. From the basilisk eye of the headmaster at the spyhole in my classroom door. From the din that made him burst in, stride to my desk on short, angry legs; grab a child by the scruff of the neck and frogmarch him down the corridor. From the certain knowledge that it was me he wanted to catch hold of and propel through the gates of his school forever.

During free lessons details of Kitty's life trickled out. An absent husband and two boys, aged four and two, whom she left at her mother's before coming to school.

I relayed my life history to her in instalments and she was avid for stories about Moynagh and Donegal, about Mrs Bradshaw and Eva. When I told her my mother talked to my father most nights and asked his advice, she didn't laugh the way Alan had or ask if her troubles had affected her mind.

'You were lucky to have a father you can remember,' she said. 'Mine joined up in 1939. He died at Dunkirk. Men don't last long in my family.'

Alan was sympathetic to my problems in the early days, though after a few weeks I saw his eyes glaze over when I poured out my latest woes. He wanted to make love every night but the last thing on my mind was sex. Not with Freddy Porter's pimply face grinning at me and him shouting, 'Miss, will I get Mr Moat to sort the class? Will I get Mrs Jackson?'

'Kitty, I'm so tired I pretend to be asleep when Alan comes to bed. It's wrong for a wife to refuse her husband his conjugal rights and us not . . . '

'Conjugal rights?' Kitty burst out laughing. 'You've some funny ideas. You're far too passive. You've got rights too.' She stood up, shook her hair over her shoulders and took my arm. 'You're coming home with me.'

Two whiskeys later, in the comfort of Kitty's house, I told her I had been summoned to Mr Moat's office after lunch. He said there had been complaints about the noise-level in my class and that a noisy teacher meant noisy pupils. Then he gave me a long-suffering look. The look I saw on Alan's face each evening.

'Kitty, I think he's going to sack me.'

'Nonsense. I'll sort him out. Why don't you try rolling those big brown eyes at him. He's a sucker for good-looking women. I have him right here, eating out of my hand.' She pointed at her cupped palm. 'I tell you what. I'll take Freddy Porter into my class. He's the ringleader. He's bad news. The rest will settle down without him egging them on. They're not bad kids. Not really.'

'*You* don't have problems with them.' I often saw her in her classroom, perched on her desk, a vivid skirt wrapped round her legs, laughing and chatting with her pupils.

'I grew up on the same streets as them. I speak the same language. How do you think I would fare in Belfast?'

'Irish kids bloody behave themselves. They don't dare not to.'

I came down from my high horse and relaxed with the boys, adopting the same tactics as Kitty. Listening rather than confronting. Not taking offence when they imitated my accent or laughed at some of the expressions I used. After a week or so I didn't need to look on my seat for drawing pins or apple cores and I could walk into the classroom without checking if a board rubber or wastepaper basket would fall on my head.

When I was seven months pregnant, I left Redwood with boxes of chocolates, hankies, matinée-jackets, bootees and two pram-covers – and regrets from the headmaster on losing a fine teacher!

'If we have a boy I'd like to call him Michael after my father,' I said to Alan shortly before the baby was due.

'Michael! I don't think so. Mick's a Paddy name, a joke name.'

'But it's my father's name. It would be a way of keeping him alive.'

'It would be a disadvantage for an English child. You must see that. Navvies are called Mick. Labourers and fellows on building sites are all Mick or Paddy.'

Alan called our son David. David, king of Israel. David, patron saint of Wales. A name to straddle religious divides. A name for all seasons.

21

What a reception we had on our visit to Carrig for Bridie's wedding. The fatted calf for the prodigal daughter and her English husband. A gold ring on her finger to silence gossipmongers. A fine child. Big for two months.

Mammy surveyed her new son-in-law. 'Well, Mary Ann, you can take a dry Sunday out of him. He's the same build as your father. How tall are you Alan?'

She herself had only just made it to five feet, despite having her feet and hands tied to the bed ends when she was young but she would forgive a man many faults if he was a 'decent' height.

'I'm six foot, exactly.'

'I don't like to contradict you, Alan, the first time you're in my house, but no man since God created Adam has ever measured precisely six feet, except Jesus Christ. You'll be a wee bit under or over, you'll find.'

She waited two days to give a full verdict on her son-in-law. 'I didn't approve of you marrying a Protestant and an Englishman, but bygones are bygones. You have a good husband, Mary Ann. See you look after him properly. There's not an Irishman born would change a nappy and his wife sitting resting herself.'

'You don't have to make such a fuss of him. He's one of the family. He could eat in the back kitchen the way we always did.' I prodded the potatoes with a fork before teeming them and set them on a low heat to dry out.

'He'll eat where I say. I don't want him to think he has landed himself with a pack of know-nothings. He may be a Protestant but he has better manners than most of the men round here.' She chose the biggest and juiciest steaks for Brendan and Alan. 'Give Alan another potato. He's a big man. He'll eat more than three.'

Mr Bradshaw inspected Alan as if he was a new recruit in his platoon. 'You'll do. You would have made a fine guardsman and that's a fact. Great wee baby an' all.' He shook hands with Alan and took David in his arms. 'You and me's going to the loft to see the birdies. Many's a day your mammy spent up there. Isn't that right, Mary Ann?'

Mrs Bradshaw's body curved towards her claret carpet. The old-woman smell of the parlour and her inquisition sent Alan up to the pigeon loft to David and Mr Bradshaw. Yes, I had seen the palace. Only from the outside. No, I hadn't seen the Queen or Prince Philip in person. I wasn't in London for the coronation but I saw it on the Pathé News.

Mr Bradshaw held David out of reach of pecking beaks. His birds had all come home from Scotland. Most of them lay curled in their cages, heads buried under mauve and grey and white down. Stuffed toys sleeping.

Betty sat beside me on the floor in my old room watching Bridie try on her going-away outfit – a lemon dress and jacket and matching pillbox – when Mammy came into the bedroom with Agnes to show off the hats they had just bought in Robb and Acheson's sale. Two for the price of one. Nineteen and eleven pence, the pair. Mammy asked Betty if there was any word of her and Sean tying the knot.

'We're getting married next summer and my mother can like it or lump it.'

Everyone in Carrig knew Mrs McFaul couldn't forgive Sean for being a teacher, instead of a brain surgeon or a QC.

Mammy said parents knew best what was good for their children though their opinions were not always appreciated. Then she clamped on her head a two-tone felt hat which had a raspberry crown and a mulberry brim, and skewered it with two pearl hatpins. Betty said it was very becoming and showed off Mammy's good bone structure. Bridie and I told her it would be great for the snow, but not for an August wedding.

'Agnes, you'd pass for the Queen Mother,' I said, arranging a concoction of swathed pink nylon on her crown and veiling her weather-beaten face with spotted pink chiffon. 'All you need is a summer frock to go with the hat.'

No, Agnes did not need a new outfit. The only time her eight-year-old costume had an outing was to Sunday Mass and it still looked good as new. A plait escaped from under the hat and hung down her back. She stood at the window, an elderly schoolgirl, too worried about her unoccupied cottage in Ballyroe to stay a moment longer in Carrig than was necessary. What if the Mullingar Heifer and her brothers were to take over her home in her absence? What if she was to be thrown out on the street again? We tried in vain to convince her that the Grippers wouldn't get away with taking possession of a council house.

Mammy asked Betty if I had told her that one of the Gripper brothers had lost an arm in a threshing accident and he had been seen at Mass with the sleeve of his jacket tucked up with a safety pin. Agnes shook her head and said it was no accident. It was the hand of God. Hadn't they cut and planted the long meadow and now the locals were too scared to give them a day's work and it had gone to seed again.

'An eye for an eye,' Mammy said. 'It's written in the gospel.'

'You never spoke a truer word, Ellen. And a tooth for a tooth.'

'And an arm for a farm,' Bridie and I said in unison.

Mammy said she had two very cheeky daughters. Life had been too comfortable for us and she hoped we would never have to harrow all she had ploughed.

We were about to go into McClennan's grocery when we bumped into a young man. Alan took him by the arm.

'It's Rob. Rob Nelson. Remember me?'

'Course I do. Alan. Alan Reed. Great to see you.'

'Great to see you too. This is Marianne, my wife.'

'Your wife? Pleased to meet you, Marianne.' Rob's big hands pumped mine. 'Hope you're able to control this fellow. What takes you back to Carrig, Alan?'

'We're over here for a wedding. Marianne comes from here.'

'What? You married a Carrig girl! Well I'll be damned. How did that happen? You weren't at the Royal High, Marianne, were you? I wouldn't have forgotten you.'

'No, I went to the convent.'

'The *convent*! Oh. The convent.' A chill wind whipped round the corner of Bridge Street. Rob recovered his breath after a few seconds. 'I see. Well that's fine now. Isn't it? Just fine.'

The times Alan and Rob had had together. The year the Royal High won the Senior Cup Rob scored the try that clinched it and Alan had to have his shoulder set after the match.

'Do you still play?'

'A bit. Cricket mostly.'

So much to catch up on. Must come for supper. Meet the wife. Alan knew her. Yvonne Baker. Blonde girl. Great legs. Yes, that's the one. Sat behind him in the Lower Sixth. Eight o'clock then. Yvonne would be dying to meet Marianne and old Alan.

Supper was served on a hostess trolley. Afterwards, I followed Yvonne on a conducted tour of the Venetian blinds, polished-oak floors and candlewick bedspreads of her new house in a road parallel to Rathbeg Avenue. Downstairs, over brandies, Alan and Rob bridged the gap that had widened between them in the years since they had been the toast of the rugby team And I noticed how at much more at ease Alan appeared in his friend's home than in my mother's. How his body fitted the curves of the Parker Knoll armchair, the ease with which his feet sprawled over the contemporary rug. How his voice had the same cadences and vowels as Bob and Yvonne. Their confidence. Their polish.

Alan was the only one among the wedding guests who didn't dip his hand in the holy-water font. Who stood rigid as a palace guard while knees bent before the high altar. As we waited for Bridie to arrive I dreamed of him and me and all our children filling a whole bench in the church of Our Lady of the Rosary.

Bridie arrived on Brendan's arm, her face hidden under a white veil. Brendan barely looked fifteen. His hired suit hung on his gangly frame like washing frozen on a clothes line. The organ played 'Here Comes the Bride' as they made their way to the altar where Bridie was handed over to Tim Molloy.

Mammy had agreed that giving a bride away was a stupid custom but there would have been talk if Bridie had walked up the aisle on her own. She was luckier than her grandmother who had been sold for ten head of cattle and two hundred pounds to a man she had never exchanged one word with till after the marriage ceremony, who had only seen her once in her parents' parlour to check that she had 'her shapes and her makes'.

Mammy considered Tim to be a good catch. A medical doctor who wasn't afraid to throw off his coat and do a day's work and whose body had been toughened by summers on his father's farm near Crossmaglen. The Molloy family and friends filled nineteen rows of the right-hand aisle whereas the Ward contingent on the left managed only eleven. With four of their children already married – three sons and a daughter – the Molloys were seasoned wedding-goers. They had sampled receptions in Armagh, Virginia, Galway and at the Gresham Hotel in Dublin where a hundred and fifty guests had sat down to a first course of smoked salmon and curled toast. Mrs Molloy Senior's fuchsia dress and elbow-length coatee were to feature in many more photographs than the nunnish grey and navy costumes worn by the mother and aunt of the bride. Mammy said she and Agnes had more sense than to try and look like sixteen-year-olds and anyhow Rita Molloy's dress could do with having the seams on the bodice let out.

Fr Doyle sang the praises of the newlyweds. Two fine young doctors who would bring comfort and healing to many. His one regret was that Bridie's father, Michael, hadn't lived to see this happy day.

Everyone at the reception remarked on the resemblance of Mary Ann's husband to Alan Ladd but this Alan didn't need to stand on a box for the photographs. And didn't he have a lovely way of talking once you got used to the English accent. Like an announcer on the wireless. And wasn't it really nice of him to make a speech without having to be coaxed and say how privileged he was to have married into the Ward family. When the Molloy daughters spoke to him they enunciated just that little bit more clearly, taking care to pronounce all their 'ings'.

That night in bed Alan said, 'Seeing you at home with your family and friends makes me realise how much you gave up for me, and I'm afraid Ireland will always draw you back and away from me.' He put his forefinger on my lips and continued. 'I feel very guilty depriving you of a wedding like Bridie's. Poor Marianne, all you had was a hole-in-the-corner do, without one of your family to wish you well.'

I held him tight and kissed him. 'Don't talk daft. Our wedding was perfect. I wouldn't have changed it, any more than I would change my life with you.'

There are times when it's better not to tell the whole truth.

Without Bridie, it was as if a light had been switched off in the house. Little was said on our last morning. Mammy rocked the borrowed pram where David lay between sleeping and waking. 'Your sister would have been eighteen if she had lived. She would have been going to Queen's in October,' she said.

I caught my breath. No mention had ever been made of the baby who had been buried in unconsecrated ground. A memory almost obliterated by time. One of the many taboo subjects in our family. Like Gilmour and Joseph's spell in the mental hospital.

'I thought the baby was a boy. Eva told us it was.'

'Poor Eva, she always got hold of the wrong end of the stick.' Mammy sat down beside the fire and stared into burning coals. 'She died just before she was born. Before she could be baptised. The nurse said she was perfect.' She gazed at David's face. 'Perfect, apart from being dead. She put a cloth over her. Wouldn't let me see her and we weren't allowed to mark her grave.'

'Did you not think that was terrible?'

'It was the law of the church.' Mammy spoke with such finality I thought the subject was closed. 'I'll never see her,' she went on. 'Her soul will stay in Limbo for all eternity.'

'You don't believe all that stuff about Limbo, do you?'

'I believe what the Church teaches and so should you.' Her eyes raked my face. 'I hope you aren't losing your faith, living over there in a pagan country.'

'It's not a pagan country. There's good people over there. Same as any place.'

Arrivals and departures, landmarks that signpost the life of the emigrant. I told myself I was luckier than my father's three brothers and sister who sailed to Boston when they were barely grown and never saw their family or homeland again. But as the taxi pulled away from the kerb, I felt as though salt was being rubbed into my heart. Mammy banged on the window and ordered Brendan to go back into the house for something.

'You forgot your wheaten bread and your meat. She'd forget her head if it wasn't screwed on to her, Alan.' She passed a bag of warm bread and a parcel containing two pounds of fillet steak, a sirloin roast and three pounds of Jimmy McDonnell's beef sausages through the window. She wedged two ten-pound notes between David's hand and jumper. 'You're as welcome here as the flowers in May, Alan. You know that. Any time. Don't leave it too long before your next visit. Sure maybe you'll come back for good.'

The image of my mother stuck in my head throughout the journey to the airport. A tiny figure in flapping clothes, clutching her skirts against the breeze. A rush bowed in the wind.

Dear God, look out for her. Don't let the wind blow rough on her. Don't let it break her in two. I'll be back soon, Mammy. I don't think Alan will. We're too much for him. We crowd him. He needs more space than we do.

'Why does your mother give us meat to take back with us?'

'Because you can't get decent meat in England, stupid. You don't have lush Irish grass over there. That's why.'

I told Alan I had never tasted offal or pork till I went to England. 'Mammy says the Jews and the Arabs have more sense than Christians. She wouldn't have pork about the place because the pig's an unclean animal. When Our Lord cast out devils he chased them into swine.'

'How come you have bacon every morning and cooked ham most days?'

'Bacon and ham don't count. They're not real pork.'

'Oh, I see. Fancy me thinking they were. She's some woman. I like your family very much, but it will be good to be in our own home again, just you and me and David.'

Home?

The Isle of Man lay below us, white edged on an azure backcloth. An island painted on the page of an atlas. The clod of earth, flung by Fionn Mac Cumhail at a Welsh giant, that fell short and landed in the Irish Sea. I looked back through the window but no matter how I twisted and craned my neck all I could see was the grey expanse of an aeroplane wing.

22

It's a little girl,' said a masked voice level with my arched knees.

A nurse raised my head. The man inside the mask held up a slippery baby.

'Those are marks of the forceps.' He pointed at red dents on my daughter's head. There were bruises on one temple and cheek, black and swollen like week-old blows and out of her middle grew a grey snake, smeared with blood and mucus. Yards long. 'She was lying on the cord. It was wrapped round her neck. The discolouring and the swelling will disappear in a few days.'

Pethidine sleep. Champagne sleep. Woozy. Bubbly. I am in a narrow bed floating round and round. Soon it will move out through the window and up to the place where aeroplanes fly above the clouds.

'Mary Ann. Get your mammy.'

I try to block my ears but my hands won't budge. I bury one ear in the pillow. 'Go away, Eva. I want to sleep. Go away.'

'Mary Ann. Please, Mary Ann. It's awful sore. Awful sore.'

The bed glides down close to Eva. She's sprawled in a pool of blood on the floor below me. A baby lies between her legs. Tied round his neck is a string of pork sausages. Pink and fleshy. Twisted so tight that his black eyes bulge. His blue face bulges. Terror bulges Eva's face. Sweat has matted her hair and gathered in beads above her lips.

'I'm coming, Eva. Hang on. I'm com . . . ' But I can't wake up. Can't open my eyes. My limbs won't stir. I'm a ton weight on a weightless bed.

'Get your mammy, Mary Ann. I'm scared. I want your mammy. She said she would come.'

'I'll go and get her, Eva. Don't move. I'm going to get her. You'll be all right. Mammy'll see to you.'

I shift to one side. Slither off the bed into blood that carpets the floor and flows through the gap below the door. My feet slip and slop in warm redness and I trip over my sodden nightie.

'I'm scared, Mary Ann. My insides has fell out.' Eva's roar splits my ears. Not a human sound. The bellowing of cows in the byre in Moynagh before calving.

'Mammy's coming. I'm going to . . . ' I crawl towards the streak of light under the door but my eyes have shut without me knowing and I can't stop falling flat out on the floor.

Yellow lights. Voices calling. Haemorrhage. Haemorrhage. Send for the doctor. Quick. Hands lift me on to the bed. Pull off my nightie. Thread my arms into a backless gown.

I tell them about Eva and her little boy with the cord knotted round his neck. They won't look. Won't listen to her screaming. They stuff pads between my legs. I can't hear her any more. Only their whispering and the tsk-tsk of shoes on the wet floor. Maybe she's asleep. A white apron moves to pick up a syringe from a tray on my locker and I see them. The blood has frozen into a lake over Eva. Red ice over her and her baby lying motionless between her legs. They tell me to stop crying. I have lost a lot of blood but I will have a transfusion. They still won't look at Eva. I grab a bare arm and say I have to go to the shop for a blue romper-suit and white furry coat for the baby. He can't be left without a stitch on his back. A woman laughs, tells me I have a little girl. I can't put her in a blue suit. It wouldn't be proper. I'm still crying, still pointing at Eva when a needle pricks my arm.

Eva, I could have untied the cord round your baby's neck. I could have bitten through it and let him breathe. But I fell asleep and let you die again. I'm sorry. Oh Eva, I'm sorry.

'David was straightforward. It's supposed to get easier. Marianne nearly bled to death.'

Alan sat on a chair beside my bed. His mother Sally, a misty figure in shades of moss, patted his arm. Her delicate perfume drifted across to me. Still on the edges of sleep, I imagined her as a cool and slender lily of the valley.

'She's on the mend,' Sally whispered. 'She's in the right place.'

'I nearly lost her. What would we have done without her, especially the baby?'

'Everything's fine now. Relax. You have a perfect family. A boy and then a girl.'

Alan and his mother communicated in a language audible only to each other, like bat sounds or dog whistles. I had learned to lip-read.

There would be no more babies. What was good enough for the Royal Family was good enough for us. The Queen and Prince Philip had stopped at two, set an example to the man in the street and to an over-populated world. So had the Queen Mother and King George. If everybody kept on reproducing like the Irish and the Africans we'd be standing on each other's shoulders before the end of the century.

I didn't nearly die, Alan. Forceps deliveries are two a penny. Women don't die of a uterus infection any more. Not in hospital in 1958. Eva bled to death. I had a blood transfusion. Somebody slipped the cord from my baby's neck. Eva was on her own.

'Have you thought of a name for my granddaughter? What about Fiona? Fiona Reed. What do you think, Marianne?' Sally inquired. 'The first time I heard the name was in *The Highland Twins at the Chalet School*. Flora and Fiona they were called. I thought what a beautiful name. I wished I had had a little girl called Fiona. As well as Alan, of course.'

I liked my mother-in-law and wasn't jealous of her as I had feared I might be. Like me, she had lived in Carrig till she was sixteen. Over here in England similarities mattered, not differences. She had helped me choose the Victorian semi we lived in. Told Alan that the wife was the homemaker. All he had to do was pay the mortgage, do repairs and sort out the long west-facing garden, make it fit for the children to play in and me to plant flowers.

Fiona. The fair one. 'I like the name, Sally. It's easy on the ear. We'll call her Fiona.'

'Farola!' I accurately predicted Mammy's shriek from the telephone kiosk on the corner of Castle Street and Main Street. 'What sort of a tomfool name is that to saddle a child with? I suppose the next one will be Tapioca. Or Sago.'

As soon as my stretch marks disappeared and my bust shrank I would go shopping for the mud- and sand-coloured clothes Sally wore. Skirts and jackets that skimmed her body, hinted at its curves. Blouses made in Hong Kong from pure silk, and narrow court shoes which enhanced the slimness of her legs. Maybe I would persuade Alan to let me have my hair sculpted like hers in a style that would suit me much better than the waist-length hair of my teens. He liked to brush it at night and gather it up in a noose above my head, to let it fall in a curtain over my face and breasts before parting it.

'Promise me you'll never cut it,' he'd say.

Fiona was two weeks old before I was allowed to go home. Home to Sally and George and to David who climbed on my knee, touched my nose and cheeks and chin, counted my fingers and buried his face in my jumper when we tried to persuade him to look at the baby. Home to Tessa, my next-door neighbour, who arrived with a bunch of tulips and a pink sleeping bag. Home to my lovely house, bright with daffodils and March sunlight. To the William Morris curtains on the window looking out at the yellow of the forsythia bush and the deep pink of the flowering currant.

Alan took David from me and crouched beside him. 'This is your baby sister. You're going to help take care of her. You and me both.'

Their two blonde heads level with the baby's dark head. My share of the world.

David leg-clamped himself to me and together we hobbled down six steps to the kitchen where Sally was spreading cream over a peach Pavlova. There was a vase of daffodils on the scrubbed table and the cream cupboards were free of handprints and tea stains. Even the sunless dining room glowed in the blaze from the log fire which George had lit. He carved a leg of lamb while Sally served roast potatoes, mushrooms and French beans.

'Great to see you've got your figure back, Marianne; curves in all the right places.' George's eyes roved over me as he slid four slices of meat on my plate. 'Very tasty. Very juicy.'

I wanted to like George. He was Alan's father and a loving grandfather. It was George who had supervised David's first steps, who took him to the swimming baths every week and who spent hours in the garden showing him how to use his miniature cricket bat. In fairness to George, he was always in good humour, flashing an ear-to-ear smile no matter how I tried to put him down. He reminded me of smart alecs you saw in war films selling black-market nylons or alcohol out of the back of a van. Same glad eye. Same glib patter. He was always pleasant to me. Too pleasant at times, always managing to squeeze up close when he passed, to say I was all woman, or a bit of all right. If he sat beside me at mealtimes, his thigh pressed against mine. If he sat opposite, I spent my time dodging his active toes and there was a leer on his face when he told his smutty jokes that made me want to slap it with a wet floorcloth. According to Mammy, he had the look of a bad character and no female between the ages of eight or eighty would be safe alone with him. Kitty said lots of Londoners were like George. It was second nature to them and harmless. I shouldn't let him see that it bothered me.

The first time he met Kitty, he offered to teach her to play golf. He stood behind her in the back garden, arms tightly round her as she leaned into him to practise her swing. When he refused to release her, she wriggled out of his embrace. 'Down, Fido! Down, boy, down!' she said with a laugh, dancing round him, prodding him with his club.

Sally took David to buy an ice cream.

'That woman's poison where men are concerned,' Alan said to his father when Kitty had gone. 'Why can't you act your age and stop making a fool of yourself?'

'He's jealous of his old dad, Marianne,' George chuckled. 'All those years with that Bible-thumping granny of his have turned him into a stuffed shirt. I feel sorry for you living with such a spoilsport.'

I could have learned a lot from both Tessa and Kitty on how to handle George. Maybe if I had, we would have been spared the tragedy that was to darken all our lives. But Alan wasn't the only stuffed shirt in the family.

'Open the neck of your nightie. I've a present for you.' Alan propped me up on two pillows and clasped round my neck a chain from which hung a moonstone in a gold setting.

'It's lovely, just lovely. Move the mirror a bit so I can admire myself.'

The milky blue stone on the crevice of milk-swollen breasts. The creamy warmth of the bedroom. Alan's gold tiepin on the dressing table, his rolled up tie, cobwebs of gold on his hairbrush and our infant daughter asleep beside the bed in a blue carrycot

'I was afraid I'd never see you wearing this – ' He touched the warm moonstone. ' – that it would stay in its box in a drawer. I wondered every night you were in hospital if I would ever lie beside you again and hold you like this.'

'You can hold me closer than that. I'm not made of glass. I won't break.'

I put my arms round him, round the dried-grass smell of his skin, round the roughness of his night-time face and his fleecy pyjamas and I held him until the sobs that wracked him grew silent.

Tessa and her husband Trevor had moved from the North East to Hawthorn Road a year before Alan bought our house. Their daughter Vanessa was six months older than Fiona. Tessa was no longer the slim girl in the wedding photograph on the sideboard, dwarfed by the sombre figure of Trevor in a grey morning suit. Her plump face was framed by dark auburn hair – burnished copper, she said, unless the bottle in the bathroom cabinet was lying. During those years when I was at home with the children, I probably saw more of Tessa than anyone, except Alan. Her life and mine were bounded by the rectangle between Hawthorn Road and the nearest clump of shops, the church, the library and the small park where we pushed our prams or sat when the weather was warm. She talked a lot about her birthplace. A city built on an almost-island in the river Wear, dominated by a castle and a Norman cathedral with steps leading through the city walls to path ways round the river.

We fed each other's nostalgia. I learned about the Miners' Gala, the event of the year in Durham City. How her father carried her on his shoulders to the big meeting in a meadow by the river. And the procession back to the cathedral. Brass bands playing and streets filled to bursting with hundreds of miners walking behind their colliery banners. I told her that whenever a band played in a park or on the street in London, a shiver ran through me and I heard the pipe and flute of Orange processions, the thud-thud of Lambeg drums and the tramp of marching men.

Tessa's father sent her the *Northern Echo* and Mammy posted the *Belfast Telegraph* and the *Irish News* every week. Alan accused Tessa and me of being professional exiles who took no interest in what was going on around us.

'My mother was just as much an emigrant as you,' he said one night as we were getting ready for bed, 'but she adapted to a new life and put the past behind her.'

'Well bully for her.' We seldom argued. Only about things that really mattered. 'I don't ever intend to put my past behind me. Not for you or anybody. Besides, what past did your mother have? She's not really Irish.' I slammed the bathroom door, but not before I hear him shout, 'At least she didn't turn into a boring Irish bore.'

Bridie lay full length on a lounger, a sunhat dipped over her face. Her son, Hugh, and David made castles in the sandpit and pushed each other on the swing while Vanessa and Fiona played with

Bridie's baby on a rug on the grass.

'Alan really pulls his weight in the house,' Bridie said. 'Tim Molloy could learn a thing or two from him. You're very lucky. But then, you always were.'

As I chopped some more lemon, apple and cucumber in the kitchen and refilled our glasses with lemonade and Pimm's, I thought how I would like to reminisce with my sister over our childhood and adolescence, instead of chatting about the present which was centred on domesticity – children, meals, Mammy's health, her squabbles with Brendan. So it was to Kitty, not Bridie, I confided my dread of Alan's silences and the sensation I sometimes had of living with a stranger.

'You and Alan really get on well together.' Bridie heaved herself out of the sunbed and checked that the men hadn't come back from the pub. 'The trouble with Tim and me is, we see too much of each other during the day with working in the same surgery. And then of course his lordship has to relax on the golf course and at the bar after a hard day's work but it's all right for me to cook the dinner, wash up and see to the children.' She patted the bulge under her navy and white spotted maternity smock. 'Tim likes the idea of a big family. Gives a man status, he says. What he doesn't like is the noise and the mess kids make.'

Tessa called to collect Vanessa who was playing with the baby.

'Mammy, can we have a baby? Please, Mammy.' Fiona and Vanessa held the baby's arms and frogmarched her over the grass towards us.

'For God's sake be careful. Do you want to pull the child's arms out of their sockets? Put her down. She'll fall.'

'Stop fussing, Mary Ann. She hasn't far to fall.'

'I'd love another baby,' said Tessa. 'Trevor says he was an only child and it didn't do him any harm. He says there's only one way to make certain we don't have another one.' She rolled long-suffering eyes skywards before continuing. 'Marianne doesn't know how lucky she is with two lovely children and a husband like Alan.'

'Can we, Mammy? Can we have a baby?'

'Come and have some orange juice, you two, and call the boys. Here, give the child to me.' The baby put her arms round my neck and her sticky face against my cheek. She smelled of powder and milk and oranges, the sweet smell of warm, fat baby.

'Can we, Mammy? Ask Daddy if we can.'

I didn't need to ask Alan. I had heard his answer. Many times.

The happy years of David's and Fiona's early childhood slipped seamlessly by. My son, an English boy, moulded in his father's image. My bright-eyed daughter, vibrant as Bridie but with the old-fashioned wisdom of my mother. A pigeon pair, as Sally and George could be relied on to say, whatever the occasion. Yet below the unruffled smoothness of our lives, I was aware of a current of discontent, a weariness with what I condemned as milk-and-water blandness. Was it something in my upbringing that made me need the turbulence of Ulster summers? The vulnerability. The unbelonging. And what perversity stopped me weighing my family's trouble-free existence against the deaths, evictions and straightened circumstances that had darkened my mother's life?

'I was thinking,' Kitty said one day as we walked with our children on Hampstead Heath. 'I don't often envy other folk but you're really lucky. If I weren't one hundred per cent anti-men and if Alan weren't your husband and didn't dislike me so much, I could quite fancy him myself.'

'Alan doesn't dislike you. He thinks you influence me too much. That's all. And I do know I'm lucky.'

'The luck of the Irish,' she smiled. 'I'm not moaning. Barring accidents, we make our own luck.'

My father said that if I fell out of a tenth-floor window I'd land on a load of hay. Luck ran in the Ward family. Same as TB did in other families and misfortune in the McKennas.

'Better to be lucky than rich,' he told us. 'Mary Ann's like me and I've been lucky all my life.'

And so he had been.

Mammy said true happiness could only be found in the next life. The prayer she recited each night after the Rosary reminded us that we were 'Poor banished children of Eve, mourning and weeping in this valley of tears.' I was glad I took after my father.

But I knew that luck could run out any time as it did for him in Slieve Dubh quarry at midday on Halloween, 1948.

23

I am an accomplished liar. My cleverest lies are the ones I tell myself. I tell myself I ran clean out of luck early one morning, on my knees on the black-and-white lino squares of the cloakroom, near the bottom of the stairs. I say that was the moment when the carpet of air on which I had built my house burst and deflated like a bicycle tube pierced by a nail. Air that had slid below my feet and cushioned my step ever since Alan lifted me up at Euston Station and swung me round and round as if I was ten years old.

Sometimes, as Bridie and I rode our bicycles round Carrig, a tyre would go flat. Not suddenly but over days. A slow puncture according to my father. It could be caused by a pinprick, too minute to be visible to the naked eye. Indiscernible even after he turned the bicycle upside down on the garage floor and removed the tube from the tyre. Or a small thorn might have lodged in it and leaked air like a faulty valve. He passed the newly pumped tube slowly through a basin of water, eyes peeled for tell-tale bubbles oozing from the spot where he would place a plum coloured patch. You could still ride with a slow puncture. You just needed to pedal that much harder and pump the tyre halfway through each journey.

I was afraid my children would grow up unaware of their Irish background. Alan said there was no chance of that with me ramming it down their throats night and day. 'Stop smothering them with bloody Ireland,' he'd say.

Fiona beamed down at her grandparents and us in the front row of the parochial hall in Kilburn. She was born to dance. Her grace and fluent movements made the two little girls on the stage with her look like carthorses. It was her third competition and as she performed I knew she was on course for another medal. Even Alan, who disliked what he called the stiff, robotic movements of Irish dancing, smiled and tapped his feet to the music. I imagined the headings in Irish and English newspapers.

'Daughter of former champion sweeps the boards at Dublin *Feis*.'

The child beside her started to dance wide, to force Fiona to the edge of the stage towards the space above the third step. She danced to her right. I grabbed Alan's arm as her leg poised for what seemed an age before she toppled and fell. Not a bad fall. A twist, more like.

'Get up,' I shouted. 'You're not hurt. Get up and finish the dance.'

She didn't step back on the stage but ran past me to her father and buried her face in his shirt.

'Go back,' I hissed. 'You're the best. You can still win.'

Whitened knuckles clung to his lapel and my only answer was her muffled sobbing.

George stroked her head. 'You stay here with Grandpa, Fiona.'

'She's my child,' I snapped at him. 'She'll do what I say.'

I couldn't speak to her on the journey home.

'Fiona doesn't want to go to Irish dancing any more,' Alan announced during the evening meal. 'She would like to do ballet with Vanessa.'

'Oh she would, would she? Can she not speak for herself? Has the cat got her tongue?'

'She's six years old and she's scared of you. She's afraid you'll make her go back.'

I coaxed, bullied and pleaded. What would we do with her new costume? What about all the medals she would win?

'I don't want to go. None of the girls talk to me. Nobody from my school goes.' Tears streamed over her face. Over untouched ham and salad.

'Anybody can fall. I used to. All the time. You just have to pick yourself up and start again.' I reached my hand out to her. She ignored it and moved closer to Alan.

'You don't have to do anything you don't want to, sweetheart.' Alan dried her eyes.

'She's an Irish child. Dancing is part of her heritage. You've no right to interfere.'

'I'm her father and I have every right. She is half-Irish and she lives in England. Stop brainwashing her. The children go to your church with you. Is that not enough for you? Let her choose what sort of dancing she wants to do.'

'Choose! She's too young to choose.' The louder I shouted the calmer he sounded. I rushed to the bottom of the garden, out of earshot of his patronising voice and my daughter's snivelling. I seized a pair of shears and sliced dead heads off roses, together with some perfect blooms and buds that had barely opened.

I didn't accompany Alan and Fiona when they bought a pink tutu and fleshy tights. Trevor took her and Vanessa to ballet class every Saturday morning. George said little girls looked great in ballet dresses and big girls looked even better.

Soon after Fiona's sixth birthday Alan moved to a new job near Harrow. A job with prospects and a chief accountant nearing retirement.

'We hardly see him,' I moaned to his mother. 'The children

are in bed when he comes home and even then he only wants to sleep or work on the papers he's brought back with him.'

'It was the same when George was looking for promotion. He ate, drank and slept work. I often wondered what I was doing, stuck by myself all day on the other side of the world.' Sally examined her wedding ring, eternity ring and five-star engagement ring with the intensity of a prospector searching for gold. 'I developed a thick skin and learned to turn a blind eye. Maybe you should do the same for a while.'

Would Sally have turned a deaf ear had I told her about George's pawing hands and lewd tongue? How he used to dare me to squeeze past him in the narrow passage down to the kitchen. Just a bit of fun, he said, when he grabbed me from behind. I shouldn't act like a tight-arsed Irish virgin. He knew I would say nothing, wouldn't rock the boat.

George.

You can't pretend he never existed. Can't bury him in that nailed-down corner of your mind where you stashed Eva years ago. He won't disappear as she did. He's still here and he will be every day for the rest of your life.

Sally had gone home with a migraine and Alan was seeing a client in Reading when I returned from the parents' evening. On my way upstairs to check the children, I heard George's footsteps but paid no attention. You don't in your own home, in the room where your son and his grandson lay sleeping. He came into the bedroom and stopped behind me. But it wasn't a terrified child of nine he spreadeagled against the wall. Take away the aftershave and the sweet stink of gin, and he could have been the Mayo man. Same slobbery flesh, same hands snatching fistfuls of breast and thigh. The thwack of my knee in his groin curled him into a whimpering ball, a blow meant to cripple not just George but the Mayo man and the GI or British Tommy, or whoever it was, who had taken advantage of Eva.

I closed the door, picked up David's clothes from the floor and laid a clean shirt, shorts and socks on the bedside table.

The door opened. George stood silhouetted against the long, stained-glass window of the landing.

'You shouldn't have done that, Marianne. It was just a bit of fun.'

'You're drunk. Get out of my way,' I whispered, afraid of wakening the children.

'Ask me nicely.' A leer that was both maudlin and threatening covered his florid face. 'You shouldn't be so rough. You could do a chap a serious injury lashing out like that.' He braced his palms against the doorposts and shifted his weight, a boxer anticipating his opponent's next move. 'Ask me nicely. Go on, ask me nicely.'

'Get out of my way.'

I pushed him once. And again. Not hard. The second punch caught him off balance. He reeled, swayed for a moment, then toppled backwards into the stairwell. His body thudded on the six treads to the half landing. His skull crashed against the wall.

I willed myself to put my weight between him and the next flight but he tumbled over the edge of the half landing and rolled, topsy-turvy. His head banged against the bookcase at the bottom of the stairs and he lay quite still, splayed out over the floor.

'George, George,' I screamed. 'Get up, George. Please.'

The rag-doll figure didn't move.

'What's wrong, Mammy? Why are you shouting at Grandpa?' David called out.

'Nothing's wrong, love. Go back to sleep.' I closed the bedroom door.

George's face was ashen. Low moans punctuated his laboured breathing. Blood trickled from one nostril. My left hand steadied the telephone, guided my right index finger. Nine. Nine. Nine.

A convulsion shook his body. Then a rumble of thunder. I held my breath as he inhaled, listening for the roar and rattle of the exhaled breath that said he was still alive, that he could be all right.

Humpty Dumpty sat on a wall.
Humpty Dumpty had a great fall.

Nobody pushed Humpty Dumpty. He just happened to be the wrong shape for sitting on a wall.

X-rays showed a fracture at the base of George's skull and another on his temple. Tests revealed a considerable amount of alcohol in his blood and all the king's horses and all the king's men couldn't put him together again. Alan and Sally took turns to sit by his bedside till the following evening when he opened blind eyes and his life seeped noiselessly away.

The police who came on the night of the accident listened while I sobbed my version of events. I had heard George come up the stairs. Probably up to the top. I couldn't be sure. I was tidying my son's clothes. The curtains were closed but there was some light from the landing window. They took measurements at the top of the stairs; remarked that the loose carpet might have caused George to trip. One of them made me a cup of tea.

The detective inspector, six feet four and hands to match, who came on the evening of George's death refused my offer of tea. He cross-examined me as though I was already in the witness box. What had been my relationship with my father-in-law? Had I given him alcoholic liquor? Had he access to alcohol in my home? Did he normally help himself to gin? What communication had I with him prior to going to my son's bedroom? What period of time elapsed between the fall and my telephone to the emergency services? Distances were measured. From the door of David's room to the top step. Length of each flight of stairs. The space in the hall where George had lain.

For days I shivered at the sound of each step on the drive. The telephone or doorbell rang and I was certain the police were coming to cart me off to the station. What if the inspector had discovered discrepancies in my statements? What if the autopsy report declared that the bruising on George's groin couldn't have been caused by his fall? What if scraps of fluff under his fingernails matched the woollen jumper I had been wearing that night?

I dreamed I was dragged to the morgue. A shape lying on a slab under a green cloth moved and George's alabaster corpse sat up, pointed at me and said, 'She pushed me. She pushed me.' I woke up sobbing. 'It was an accident. It was an accident.'

'Go back to sleep, love.' Alan held me close. 'Of course it was an accident. He'd had too much to drink. Poor Marianne. There, there, don't cry.'

He, Sally, Tessa and Trevor smothered me with devotion and concern. A stranger might have thought I had only just managed to survive the disaster which had cost George his life.

A verdict of accidental death was recorded.

A hearse conveyed George to the crematorium. Solemn strangers, wearing identical black clothes, carried the coffin into the chapel to the strains of 'Abide with Me'. Only a handful of mourners attended the service. Sally, Alan and me, Sally's next-door neighbours, Trevor and Tessa, Kitty and friends from the golf club. The clergyman, who read from notes, told us George had been born in Muswell Hill, had served his country in the Royal Navy from 1939 to 1945 and had been a devoted husband, father and grandfather. Dark blue curtains parted, the pine coffin with brass handles glided out of sight and George was expedited with sanitised precision. I thought of my father's and Maisie's funerals. The comfort of a crowded house and packed church. The men of the family and friends shouldering the coffin to the graveyard. The slow leave-taking. The fond remembering. And I thought how cold and cheerless an English cremation was by comparison. Surely George had deserved better than two days alone and unmourned in an undertaker's chilled parlour, but when I asked Sally if his body would be taken home for his last night on earth, I might have been suggesting she share her home with a victim of bubonic plague.

Afterwards at Sally's house there was a choice of coffee or tea or sherry and pale chicken or ham sandwiches and raspberry gateau.

'Poor George, I'll miss him. He was full of fun; loved a cuddle and a dirty joke. There was no harm in him though.' Tears brimmed Tessa's eyes. She might have been a mother complaining of a mischievous child. 'Maybe he was different with you, Marianne. You being Alan's wife and a bit strait-laced.'

'You're right there, Tessa.' We hadn't seen Alan come up behind us. 'He would have known better than to cuddle my wife. I've seen her give him looks guaranteed to freeze at fifty yards.'

George's clothes were sold or given to charity and Alan and Sally divided his golf clubs between them. His name was rarely mentioned till the evening, a month or so later, when David blurted out, 'Did Grandpa die because he wouldn't let you out of my room, Mammy?'

The walls of my throat thickened and closed. Alan's eyes bored into my head. A tap dripped, each drop an explosion on the metal sink.

'Grandpa had a dizzy spell and fell down the stairs, David. It happens when people get old. Sometimes at home he had to reach out and hold on to a chair to steady himself,' Sally said calmly.

'But I heard Mammy shouting at him.'

'That was after he fell. I woke you shouting at him to get up.'

After supper Alan went upstairs with the children. Sally picked a plate from the draining board and cradled it in a tea towel.

'Strange how things turn out, Marianne,' she said. 'Many a time I felt like pushing George down the stairs when I used to hear him coming up in his sock soles in the early hours of the morning. Poor George, it wasn't that he didn't care about me. He couldn't help himself where women were concerned.'

I longed to throw my arms round her and confess. To reassure her that I had lied only to protect the family. During the minutes of waiting for the ambulance, tabloid headlines had flashed before my eyes. 'Attempted rape of daughter-in-law ends in death of 64-year-old man – Woman admits pushing lecherous father-in-law down stairs.'

'I miss him,' she went on. 'I miss him coughing and belching round the house. We'd been getting on much better since we came back. Having you and the children meant so much to us both. A real family at last. He thought the world of you, Marianne. But you know that.'

'Oh Sally, I'm so sorry.' I put a wet hand over hers.

'If only I'd stayed here with him, it might never have happened.'

'You mustn't think like that. You weren't well. You needed to be in your own house.'

'What did happen that night? David says you had a row with Dad.' Alan had come quietly into the kitchen. His voice was steel.

I struggled to speak but no words came.

'What way is that to talk to your wife? Anybody with half an eye could see the strain Marianne has been under for the past weeks. Show her some sympathy instead of cross-examining her.'

'Why would he make up a story like that? That's what I want to know.'

'And why do you believe him instead of me? He's only eight, for God's sake.'

'Children make up stories. You used to tell terrible lies to your granny about your father and me. She always believed you instead of me and gave me hell afterwards.'

That night in bed Alan apologised and tried to take me in his arms but when he touched me it was George's flesh-crawling fingers I felt. George's head lay on the pillow beside me, sweat on his meaty face, a wet smirk on his mouth. And whenever my husband loomed above me, wanting to make love, I saw George, his hands braced against the doorposts. Alan's fast breathing was the wheezing and gasping that had heralded his father's death. I pushed him away, turned my back and clutched the edge of the bed.

After a week or so Alan turned his back too. We lay as far apart as possible in our double bed, snatching back a straying toe or elbow as if we had touched an electrified fence.

I chose my confessor with care. North London bristled with Irish priests. From the darkness of the confessional box in Westminster Cathedral, Fr Cedric Hirst's cultured tones assured me I had committed no crime. I had not premeditated George's death. His raised hand traced the shape of a cross. *'Ego te absolvo'* and I was washed free of sin. But every time I went downstairs George tumbled helter-skelter in front of me and when I came into the house I stepped around his body with the thin line of blood trickling through his moustache and over his waxen cheek.

I wasn't guilty, yet because of me George was dead. My grandmother had killed Gilmour and got away with it, as had my mother, Agnes and Sister Mary Francis, all three accomplices in his murder. Thirty years later they felt no guilt. But what about the weeks, the months after the Tans left Ireland when they no longer quaked with the fear of being burned alive in their home or of finding Joseph's mangled body lying on the street? How many buckets of water did they go on pumping to wash Gilmour's blood from their hands and clothes, his smell from their skin? How often did they whisper to each other about the killing and remember each blow on Gilmour's head? My grandmother had taken her secret to the grave and Mammy and Agnes had lived with theirs till Bridie and I wormed it out of them. They had burned what remained of their victim to safeguard the good name of the family. As for me, I had protected my precious honour from a harmless old man, my children's grandfather.

Horrors of the night haunted me. Jumbled nightmares. Switched images. My grandfather's frenzied whip flailing the bloodied flesh which had been his wife's face, lashing Bridie's bent head. My grandmother's spade striking till George's skull was a bone-flecked pulp. Gilmour's head banging against the bookcase in my hall. My mother and Agnes separating duck eggs from hen eggs, sifting through Gilmour's bones.

My father often said I had the gift of the gab, that I could get away with murder. He never told me the price I would pay.

24

Kitty and I sat near the castle at Hastings looking out at the spindly pier perched on stilts in a still sea and at the great bulk of Beachy Head on the western horizon. The children had gone to buy lemonade and chips from the cabin behind us. Gulls spun in the wind, slid sideways down the air, stalled and hung like pictures painted on the sky, while beside us huge, brown baby gulls snatched food from their parents' beaks. Over the noise of their squawking, I told tell Kitty exactly how George had met his death.

She stared at the sea for what seemed a long time. 'I don't think you should tell Alan. Not now. After three months. To you and me George was just a dirty old man who couldn't keep his hands to himself but he was Alan's father. He may not have known that side of George or may have chosen not to know. If you tell him what happened, he could hold it against you for the rest of you lives and wonder what other lies you had told him.' She looked me straight in the eye. 'It's no good you going to Confession if you can't forgive yourself. You're the one putting up barriers. You have to tear them down.'

'I can't talk to Alan any more. I do try.' I paused, then blurted out: 'I sometimes wonder if he really works as hard as he claims or if he's found someone who appeals to him more than me.'

Kitty lit a cigarette. 'I don't think you're right. There would be signs. I'm a bit of an expert on these matters.' She inhaled, the way a real smoker does, and breathed out slowly. 'Alan's a straightforward bloke. Anxious to get on. You must relax and stop torturing yourself.'

On our way down to the sea we stopped to watch a group of men cleaning their nets and throwing unwanted fish to screeching gulls. A fisherman wearing black oilskins jumped out of a boat which had docked on the shore and attached a cable which inched it up on the beach. The children raced about following the cable to a black wooden hut, asking questions of the crew.

'That's what they miss living in London,' I said. 'I was lucky. I spent so many summers near the sea in Donegal when I was young.'

'Why don't you take them to Ireland for a holiday? It would do you all good.'

'Alan doesn't want to go. He can't stand the bigotry. Besides, when my family get together we can be quite overpowering. We stifle him.' I picked up a stone and tried to skim it over the sea but it sank without trace. 'It's a shame because I need to see my mother. She's not getting any younger and she won't come to England again.'

'You and Alan could do with a break from each other. These last months have taken their toll on you both. You and the children could go while he's at work. He seems perfectly capable of looking after himself.'

Carrig! Light years away from George and from Alan.

'I'll see what he thinks. It's a good idea. In fact it's an excellent idea.'

'And perhaps one day you'll take me to see if Ireland's half as great as you say it is.'

'Maybe next year we'll all go, when things are better between me and Alan.'

If Kitty had had a permanent or semi-permanent man in her life I would have asked her, but she had a succession of lovers. As she said, men didn't last long in her family. Women friends were far more important. Mammy would welcome her in Carrig for a few days, a week even. She saw divorced women as man-eaters and would worry about Kitty trying to lead Brendan astray or getting her claws into any decent Irishman she clapped eyes on. Though Mammy had never met a divorcee in the flesh, she was an authority on the Duchess of Windsor and Rita Hayworth, dismissing them both as immoral tramps from America.

We rounded up the children and walked through the tall shadows of wooden net lofts towards a fish-and-chip shop. I stopped as we reached the kerb. 'Do you know something, Kitty,' I said. 'I feel as if a pall has been lifted from me and I've remembered. Ghosts can't cross the sea.'

You go away and those you leave behind stand still, frozen in the time you last saw them. You dash on and off boats and trains. You whirlwind round relatives and friends and the part of you that you didn't know had fallen asleep is joyously awake for the first time in ten years. You take your children to see the big house where you grew up and are surprised how it has shrunk. You tell them how your father used to stop his car coming back from Warrenpoint and you believed him when he pointed at the windows of your home and said they had turned to solid gold. You say the front garden was much bigger and talk excitedly about the games you and Bridie played when you were young.

The children don't accompany you on your search for Eva's home. This is your own, personal Calvary. Neat pebble-dash houses with pixie gardens and playing areas have sprung up where she used to live. You walk through Fern Court and Fern Close and Fern Park Avenue and find no trace of the gate or the cracked path where Eva's waters broke the last time you saw her. But it's George, not Eva, you find on that new estate. He's in the skinny figure of the man watering plants in his garden. In the grandfather holding the saddle of a child's wobbly bicycle. In Carrig, he's among groups of unemployed men hanging around street corners, leaning against the Post Office and the Bank of Ireland.

Ghosts may not be able to cross the sea but they cast a long shadow.

You visit Uncle Dan in an old people's home in Stranorlar and tell him you'll see him next year. Bridie said the same thing to Uncle John when she was last here. It's seven years since Aunt Annie's body was taken from the women's ward for burial in the shallow family grave in Kincasslagh where John has since joined her. You tell Dan the sore on his lip will get better. He nods in agreement, knowing full well that the cancer which killed John and the men he fished with won't spare him. Outside, you and Bridie rinse your lungs and nostrils of the smell of urine and the smell of old men dying, and find Tim and the children waiting in the bar. The barman laughs when you ask what time the pub closes. 'Sometime in December,' he replies and wants to know if living in England has made you forget your own country.

Two of Dan's great-nephews sleep in his bed in the space above the kitchen. David and Fiona race over hills to the port and along Arland's Banks and Keadue Strand as you and Bridie did long ago but there are no voices telling stories in Irish round the fire at night and no Kitty Peadar contorting wool round knitting needles in the empty house next door.

Now a mother of five children, your sister's glow has dimmed. Most evenings after supper, her head nods and she falls asleep by the fire. Then, as if a genie had rubbed the tarnished surface of a lamp, the young Bridie reappears, bright as the angel on a Christmas tree.

The years in exile have carved bitter lines into Agnes's face and pursed her once smiling mouth. Her two-roomed cottage in Ballyroe is a stone's throw from the chapel and from McMahon's grocery and pub and you wonder why she's not grateful for her inside lavatory and hot and cold taps in the kitchen. She chats briefly to the children, asks about life across the water; then all her talk is of getting back the house and fields the Mullingar Heifer plundered from her. She is waiting till 'the child' is big enough to take up the cudgel on her behalf, drive out the invader and restore her to her rightful home. Brendan, the little brother I hardly know, is a young version of my father. At twenty-four and fully grown, he's more interested in Anne who teaches with him in Carrig and the fortunes of his football team than in restoring a few sour acres to an old woman who claims to be descended from the kings of Ulster.

Your mother has eyes and ears in the back of her head. You allow her to believe that George fell in his own house. She asks had he been hitting the bottle. She prays God to have mercy on his soul, but says he had a roving eye and his unfortunate wife had not had her troubles to seek.

'Is his wife on the lookout,' she asks, 'or has she landed herself another man already? And don't you look at me like that, Mary Ann. I listen to *Woman's Hour* and I read the English papers. From what I hear, women in England don't let the grass grow under their feet.'

You telephone your husband a few times and hear the phone ringing in the empty house that is your home. You imagine him bent over sheets of figures at a desk or on a golf course. A shadowy figure on a shadowy landscape.

On the train from Liverpool to London I tried to put flesh on Alan's bones. His children, exhausted by an early start, slept on either side of me. The Irish Sea I had crossed last night still separated our worlds and the song Betty sang at my farewell party crowded my head: *'Tabhair ar ais an oíche 'réir* – Give me back last night'. The anxieties and misgivings I had experienced on my first train journey in England overwhelmed me but none of the excitement, and Mammy's last words weighed on me like a ton of bricks. 'If you wait another ten years you'll come back for my funeral.'

Alan was waiting where we had left him a month previously, his arms stretched wide to close round his children and me.

'You've got to come next time, Daddy. Everybody was asking where you were. Can we all go again? Soon. Soon.'

He persuaded David and Fiona to release his hands. He tied my hair in bonnet strings under my chin, kissed me and said I was a sight for sore eyes. I told him there had been a lot of speculation about his absence. Some of the gossips in Donegal had asked was I not worried my English husband might run off with a twenty-year-old blonde. He laughed, picked up our suitcases and said chance would be a fine thing.

'Say we can all go to Carrig every year, Daddy. Brendan says I can be in his under-twelve team next year. We played football on the beach every day in Donegal. Even in the rain.' David reached from the back of the car and hung his arms round Alan's neck. 'Daddy, can you skim stones over water?'

'Of course I can. I used to get six or seven bounces like the Dambuster bombs.'

'Brendan can do seven, sometimes eight. I only ever did five.'

'Well we must all go to the seaside and see if I can do as well as Brendan. Not so tight, there's a good lad. You're strangling me.'

The car pulled into the noise of London traffic and headed along Euston Road and away from the city till we reached the familiar red-brick houses and gardens of Hawthorn Road. I wandered from room to room, marvelling at the neatness of our house.

'You must have slaved for days. You deserve a medal,' I said to Alan. Then, in the kitchen, I spotted the dishcloth draped over both taps, instead of lying in a ball in the sink. 'You cheat, Alan Reed, Kitty helped and you weren't going to let on. There was me thinking you'd been slaving for days.'

'Oh yes, she called for a few minutes yesterday to find out when you were coming back.'

'She mustn't have got my cards. I'll give her a ring.'

'Marianne, you've been away for a whole month.' He replaced the phone on the receiver and kissed me. 'There's plenty of time to talk to her. What about talking to your husband?'

Later that evening he said, 'I thought I'd enjoy the peace but I couldn't concentrate. The silence was terrifying.'

'I did phone but you were never in. Did you go out much?'

'Not much. Here and there. You know how it is. Don't talk any more. Let me look at you.'

He pulled down the bedclothes and kissed my neck, my armpits, my breasts and belly. I wanted to tell him how much I had missed him but there was his weight stretched over me, the tip of his tongue doing a tooth count in my mouth and a fire racing along every nerve of my body.

That night I was certain George's ghost was finally laid to rest.

I couldn't see the morning sun when I woke, only its reflection on wet, moss-agate leaves of a tree whose name we'd never learned. Something white moved among the foliage in the long garden behind us and out of the pages of a storybook stepped a unicorn, his single horn hidden by overhanging branches.

'It's a llama,' Alan corrected me. 'The chap who lives there got it from Peru.'

'Peru? Is that where unicorns come from?'

'It's a llama and it's cream.'

Well, it wasn't the time to argue. Not with his arms open wide to embrace me. I lay beside him till the sun moved round and a hundred, thousand sequins twinkled on the dancing tree without a name and I thought how wonderful it was to look into a high blue sky and not the low ceiling of cloud that hangs so often over Ireland. And to have a unicorn playing ring a ring o' roses round the apple and pear trees near the bottom of my garden.

'I love you, Alan. I'll never leave you again. I promise. Not ever again.'

The following year the children and I spent a month in Ireland.

And the year after that.

And the year after that as well.

Until July 1969.

Passions that had been simmering for years in Northern Ireland came to a rolling boil. By the end of the month, Belfast blazed nightly on the television screen.

'You're not going this year. You wouldn't even consider it,' Alan announced as though the subject was closed

'It's very localised, Alan. A long way from Carrig.'

'Do what you want to, but my children aren't going. It's time they spent a summer with me.'

Mammy had other ideas. 'You're not going to let a bit of trouble stop you coming,' she shouted down the phone. 'Things will settle down. They always do. Marching's a pastime in Ulster. You know that. If it's not one lot, it's the other.'

'But . . . '

'Anyhow, the rioting won't reach us. Let me know when you're coming.'

The phone buzzed. Mammy didn't indulge in greetings, good byes or chit-chat. Ringing England was expensive enough.

At lunch three weeks earlier at Sally's, Fiona and David had dominated the conversation with plans for their annual trip to Carrig while Alan consumed roast beef, runner beans and potatoes with the concentration of a robot programmed to hoover his plate in silence.

'Please, Daddy, can we go to Carrig for good and have a house near Granny?' Fiona looked at the glazed faces of her father and grandmother. 'You too, Grandma.'

'Come and help me serve the pudding, Fiona, and give your tongue a rest or your ice cream will melt before you find time to draw breath.' Sally collected dinner plates and cutlery and put a bowl of fruit salad on the table. 'We'll have coffee on the patio.'

Alan buried himself under the Sunday papers in the conservatory while the children tried to coax a black-and-white cat off the garden wall.

'Marianne, I hope you won't think I'm speaking out of turn but is it a good idea leaving Alan alone every summer? I know you like to keep in touch with your family and the children appear to have a wonderful time.' Sally arranged white cups and saucers with gold rims on a tray. She wore a flowing white dress and open sandals that showed off scarlet toenails. She had started to paint her toenails the summer after George's death. 'I'd better put some orange out for the children.' Her hands shook and a tray containing ice tubes slipped through her fingers. 'Silly me, I should watch what I'm doing,' she muttered, stooping to mop the floor.

Why couldn't she keep her nose out of my business? What had she done during her married life but swan about in the East attended by an army of underpaid servants? What did she know about going out to teach and running a home? At least George hadn't been moody. I could never be sure who would arrive home in the evening – the man I married or Mr Hyde with a scowl on his face that would stop the clock. But Sally wouldn't want to hear about that. Mammy was right. When the chips are down, blood's thicker than water.

'Alan doesn't mind. He's very capable, you know. He learned how to look after himself at his grandmother's in Carrig and here in London, years before he married me.'

My dart hit the raw nerve I had been aiming at. Sally's face paled once the crimson flush receded. She closed the kitchen door. Closed out the sound of children shouting. Closed out her son, the *Financial Times* and the *Sunday Times*. 'I was trying to say it's not always a good idea to leave a husband too long on his own. Not at Alan's age.'

She offered me a cigarette, steadying her hand holding the lighter. I half-turned from her and looked through the window at David climbing a chestnut tree at the bottom of the garden and Fiona still trying to tempt the cat to come down out of its branches.

'Women often have to make choices that tear them in two.' Her eyes in the back of my head pleaded with me to look at her. 'I was criticised for leaving Alan in Carrig after the war and going to Singapore with George. My mother was very bitter. Said I put my husband before my son and her.' She stubbed her cigarette in the ashtray; ground it till pale tobacco threads burst from their paper casing and mixed with ash. 'If I hadn't gone with him, Marianne, he would have found plenty of women to comfort him. Women you would never suspect. Even my friends. Especially my best friends.' She paused. I refused to take the bait. 'I saw it happen too often and I don't suppose George was any worse than most men.'

I shrugged my shoulders. She lit another cigarette but didn't smoke it. A tube of ash toppled into the ashtray.

'You and Alan used to be so happy together. I'm worried for you. That's all.'

'You mustn't worry, Sally,' I reached across the table and patted her hand. 'Alan's far too busy to look at anybody else. He's married to his job, grooming himself for promotion. He's a good husband and a good father in his own way.'

'I'm sure you're right.' Sally blew her nose, stood up and smiled back at her reflection in the mirror.

I didn't tell her that since my last visit to Ireland George slipped into our home daily with Alan. His shadow fell across us during the day and at night he occupied the sullen space separating us in bed. I didn't say that we seldom made love. Love! As if our silent fumblings in the dark had anything to do with love.

The prospect of promotion came sooner than even Alan expected. I sensed it in the jaunty turn of his key in the lock, in his light footfall devouring the space between front door and kitchen, in the excitement which belied the sobriety of his city suit.

'Old Knox is throwing in the towel at last. And about time too.' He put a bottle of champagne on the table, filled two glasses and beamed round the table at me and the children. 'He's having a big send-off. I'm in with a very good chance. Maybe not his job but a step up at least. So, there may be good news for this family before long.'

'Will we be rich, Daddy, really rich?' asked David.

'Can I have as much pocket money as Vanessa and a new bike?'

'That's terrific news, Alan. You'll get it. Nobody could deserve it more than you'.

'The firm's having a dinner and dance in some posh hotel. We're expected to bring our wives along. To be vetted as a couple, I expect. You will come, won't you?'

'I'd love to. I don't remember the last time we went dancing together.'

'What will you wear, Mum? That green dress you bought last summer?'

'No. No. Nothing casual. I want your mum to look really smart. It's very important for me. Something dressy but not showy.' His hands described a female figure in the air.

'Don't you worry about a thing, Alan. Leave it to me and your mother. Maybe Kitty will come too.' My delight bounced off green and cream kitchen tiles, half smothering the thought that it was a sad state of affairs when Alan and I needed three glasses of warm champagne to create a kind of harmony between us.

'Kitty doesn't really have much idea about fashion. She's still a bit er – a bit sort of casual. I want you to look like a top executive's wife. Elegant and – sophisticated.'

'Don't worry. Your mother will keep me right.'

Sally spotted the outfit in a boutique in South Moulton Street. A black-gowned creature with the figure of a famine victim slid the dress over my head. She closed the zip from buttock to neck and I was moulded into cream lace over silk. It was one of those rare garments that transfers something of its own beauty and style to the wearer. A dress that caressed the skin, smoothed away bulges and flattered the lines of the body.

'It's fabulous. Perfect,' Sally said from a cream-satin sofa. 'You look a million dollars.'

I studied my six reflections. 'Do you know something, Sally? I'm inclined to agree with you.'

'And very versatile, madam.' The assistant helped me into a matching coat with mandarin collar. 'For a wedding. The theatre. Cocktails. That special occasion.'

Sally draped herself over sofa while I paid the bill. 'Marianne, you'll be a knockout on the night.'

We returned from the dance shortly before midnight. Alan sprawled beside me on the sofa, running his fingers through my hair.

'You were a big hit with everybody. Especially the MD and he's the one that matters.' He clinked his whiskey glass against mine. 'I was so proud of you. A bit jealous too when he asked you to dance for the third time.'

'He was only doing his duty. He thinks very highly of you. Told me you'd go far. What do think of that?'

'I've an appointment with him on Tuesday morning. This could be it, Marianne, and you will have helped clinch it.' He refilled our glasses. 'He sang your praises to everybody, said you were not only beautiful but highly intelligent.'

'What did he expect? Some sort of moron?'

'He said I was a very lucky man.'

'He was half-cut. Anyhow, I'm far more interested in pleasing my husband than some guy who's old enough to be my father.'

'You do please me. Tonight's the beginning of a new life for us, Marianne. A better life. I haven't been very good to you lately but it's all going to change. All going to change. You wait and see.' He enunciated each word very slowly to counteract the slurring in his voice. 'It's important for a man in a senior post to have the right wife. Very important.' He stood up, stretched his hands till our fingertips touched. 'Finish your drink and I'll show you how you please me.'

Arm in arm we lurched upstairs, whispering, giggling, pressing fingers against lips as we passed the children's rooms even though David was staying with a friend and Fiona was at Sally's.

Never was our lovemaking so sweet, so slow, so wild. Shouting-out-loud love in a blaze of electric light. Sweeter for the squandered years. Slower for the promise of our future. Wilder for the hunger to be satisfied.

26

I am on my knees in the cloakroom near the bottom of the stairs. Black-and-white lino reels. My arms grip the lavatory seat. My mouth hangs open over the bowl. I try to retch quietly not to alert him, to stifle the long roar from my guts, the explosion as last night's supper hits the water and spatters the bowl. I try to retch quietly but the devils inside me are rowdy.

The door is wrenched open. Alan hasn't stirred the other mornings.

'You're pregnant. You're pregnant.' His anger slams the nape of my neck. 'Go on, admit it. I heard you yesterday and the day before. How long did you think you'd get away with it?'

Thin toes flex and relax through the pile of the hall carpet. Tense and relax. The veins on his ankles quiver.

A yellow stream spurts into the bowl. I cling one-handed to the seat, fumble for paper, wipe drool from my chin. The scar on his knee is aubergine against last summer's tan. Blonde hairs curl over his thighs.

Nausea thickens my cheeks, gags my throat. Nostrils pricked against the stench, his eyes travel down the open front of my nightdress to the bulging veins on my breasts. Breasts distending into old stretch marks, swollen beyond the cup of his hand.

'You did it on purpose. We agreed after Fiona that two was enough, but you decided to have another go. We can't afford it. You're in England. Not bloody Ireland. Get rid of it. It's legal now. And quick. Do you hear me?'

I hear you, Alan. I'm pregnant. Not deaf. Trevor and Tessa can hear you too, and the children. You and your mother agreed on a family of two. Nobody asked me. I can't speak. Bile and puke will pour from my opened mouth. Not words. Go away. Please. I don't want you to see me like this. Ugly and stinking.

He kneels beside me. His hand fans over my back. His voice is gentle, coaxing. 'We're too old, Marianne. I'm forty. Past all that caper. We can't start that over again. Look at you, spewing your guts out at your age. You're not fit to have another child. It could kill you. What will the kids think?' His hand rubs my back, snags in my hair. I press the knob on the cistern and clear water rushes round the bowl.

'When you're ready, go upstairs and lie down. I'll bring you a cup of tea and we'll find out how to deal it. How far on are you? A month? Two? It's nothing. Only a blob. It will all get sorted and we can forget about it.' He pats my back, calls me a good girl, says I must see the reason of it.

I wrap both arms tight round my belly, look him in the eyes and shake my head. Right to left. Left to right. Right to left.

'No! No! No! No!'

'We'll see about that.' He stands up, bounces on the balls of his feet. 'Either it goes or I go. I mean it. There's more to life than slaving to feed a crowd of children.' His feet move like a dead hen's when you pull its tendons.

The sides of my stomach meet in a last tearing retch. I wipe the back of my hand across watery slime hanging from my bottom lip.

'It's your choice. Me or it. Understood? Me or it. Your choice.'

The words tear at the linings of my brain. I know Alan. He won't give in.

The treads above the cloakroom ceiling echo to the thump of his soles. Me or it. Me or it. A scuffling of feet and two doors close.

Given the choice between her husband and her son, Sally chose George. Nobody asked her to murder her son.

I, Mary Ann Ward, have no choice.

'Alan, Alan,' I scurry up the stairs after him. He turns on the half-landing. My head is level with his feet. 'I'll do anything for you but I can't kill my own child. Our child. I can't do it.'

'Relax, Mrs Reed. Everything is fine. Your baby could be here for Christmas.' The doctor had a thick grey moustache and bushy eyebrows. My father grown old. 'Of course you're not too old. I'd far rather see a woman in her late thirties who already has children having a baby than some wee lassie of fifteen or sixteen.'

I stood up to leave.

'You seem very tense. Any problems at home? I take it your husband is pleased?'

I shook my head.

'Don't worry. He'll come round once he sees the baby. They always do. No other problems?' His pen hovered above a prescription pad.

I shook my head. 'No, thank you, doctor.'

The waiting room at the clinic brimmed with expectant mothers. There was no point telling him what had happened the afternoon I took the Lower Sixth to a matinée of *Hamlet*. No prescription could cure that.

I am on the upper deck of a bus inching its way along Baker Street. The pavement is a sea of colours. Raspberry, royal blue, crimson, green and orange; the white and pale blue of mens' shirts. A splash of yellow. Yellow hair on a globe-shaped head. Alan's head. Alan, tieless in shirt sleeves, his stride slowed by oncoming crowds. By the crush and jostle of briefcases and shopping bags.

'Look up, Alan. I'm here and you're down there,' I knock the window pane. 'You and me both in the middle of London on a Tuesday afternoon.'

An Indian skirt and a purple blouse are thrust against him. The bright purple of aubrietia. I tap again on the window. And again. A woman moves at the same pace as the bus. At the same pace as Alan. I see that her arm is linked through his. She tosses long brown hair, throws back her head and smiles up at him. Up at me. A decapitated face on a purple plate. The face that shatters my life in one single moment. Alan bends his head over the half-open mouth. My knuckles are glued to glass. My hand against the pane is cold as death. Shadows without substance move past me and nothing exists but the couple on the pavement below. Alan and Kitty, Siamese twins, joined at cheek, shoulder and thigh.

Another person might have hurled his belongings pell-mell into a holdall. Not Alan. Each garment was removed from its coat hanger, folded and placed in a suitcase besides his newest underpants, some of them still in cellophane wrapping. If it was his tan, his summer-bleached hair and the razor creases on shirtsleeves and trousers that caused resentment to stew inside me, it was the socks that brought it to a spitting boil. Eight pairs – black, navy and white rolled into their partners, nestling into each other on top of his cricket jumper like a litter of kittens.

I wrenched out the drawer and emptied into his case the pile of odd socks that had been waiting for months, maybe even years, for their other halves to turn up. 'See what your whore makes of that lot.'

'You've got it completely wrong, I told you I'm going to stay at my mother's till you see sense but you don't want to listen. You're hell-bent on splitting this family.'

The self-righteous tone of reproof. Deft hands folding a pale blue V-necked jumper against his chest. I snatched it from him, threw it to the floor and stamped on it.

'You're hysterical.' Detached. In control. Like Sister Paul the day her cane split the skin on my wrist for my own good.

I thought he was going to hit me, so I raised my arm to parry the blow. He grabbed it in mid-flight, picked up his suitcase and left. The marks of his fingers reddened my flesh and out of nowhere came a memory of my first visit to Lyons Corner House shortly after I came to London. Not traffic crawling round Eros, the marble stairs or the food, but his hand brushing my cheek as he leaned to tuck a label inside the neck of my dress, his touch soft as swansdown.

Bridie or Mammy would have deluged Alan and his car with old suits and discarded shirts. They would have festooned the windscreen with grey underpants and vests and parted his hair with golf shoes and rugby boots but I merely looked down as he reversed out of the drive and drove off without a backward glance. How many years was it since Kitty accused me of being passive?

Late that evening when David and Fiona were asleep, I emptied boxes, envelopes and albums of all the photographs Kitty appeared in. Black and white and technicolor faces, him and me and the children. And her. All smiling as if we hadn't a care in our lives. And I questioned every one. The staff photo way back in the early days at Redwood School. Her and me in the front row, in summer dresses with flouncy skirts, our legs crossed in the same direction. With our four children in Cheltenham, arms round each other, laughing fit to burst. Last Christmas, she and Alan pulling the wishbone, paper hats askew.

We didn't have open fires any more, so I made a pile of her photographs and set fire to them on the crazy paving outside the kitchen. Each square, each rectangle curled, blistered and bubbled as if the heat had brought some latent suppurating disease to the surface. The flames, which took an age to spread, sputtered and died and had to be rekindled before my foot ground cobwebbed ashes into dust. Snatches of the letter she had sent a week previously fanned my fury. – You have got it all wrong, Marianne: Alan and I were only having a bit of fun. – You know what I'm like. – It meant nothing. – It's you Alan loves.

'Hell roast her,' I willed myself to roar at the black sky but the only sound to emerge from my throat was the hoarse whisper you hear in a hose pipe after the water has been turned off.

'When's Daddy coming back?' David asked during Saturday lunch, between mince stew and rice pudding. As good a time as any. No rush, no deadlines. No red eyes to explain away.

'Daddy's not going to live with us any more.'

'But why? Where's he going to live? When will we see him?'

'He's going to stay at Grandma's but you'll still see him every week,' I told him, three weeks too late.

He put the pudding dish on the table without a word. Fiona and I listened in silence to the sound of his feet on the stairs and the click as his bedroom door closed.

'He's not going to live here. Where is he going to live? It's going to be awful not having a daddy,' she howled.

'Don't be silly. He's still your father,' I put my arms round her and hugged her. Vanessa tapped the kitchen window with her tennis racket.

'Daddy's left home. I'm an orphan,' Fiona told her between mouthfuls of rice pudding. 'Can I have my pocket money, Mum? We have to hurry or all the courts will have gone.'

I did the washing-up and tidied the kitchen. Only David's

brimming bowl remained on the table. His sobs stopped when I knocked on his door. I asked if I could come in but there was no answer. He lay on the bed, his face resolutely turned from me, his body stiff in my arms.

When he came down he found me crying at the kitchen table. 'Don't cry, Mum. I'll make you a cup of tea and you'll be all right. You'll see.' He opened a packet of Gipsy Queens and munched through four while the water boiled.

David was almost two years younger than Alan had been when we first met. Old enough to dash across a windy street to pick up a young girl's hat. Old enough to send her heart cartwheeling up to the roof of the Alhambra Picture House when he kissed her hand. Too young to know that sorrow can't be switched off like a boiling kettle. That it can't be drowned in two mugs of tea, even if they are sweetened with Gipsy Queens.

'Keep yourself looking nice, Marianne. It is very important for a woman in your condition to make the most of herself. There's some very smart maternity wear in the shops. We'll have a look afterwards,' Sally said over ham quiche and salad in Harrod's, 'and when Alan comes back he'll realise what he's been missing.' She dabbed her lips with a napkin. 'He's stubborn, like George. Like most men but he misses you all. He'll give in when he's ready, so make sure you're always made-up, even in the house, and have your hair done every week.' Hand on chin, she scrutinised me. 'It's a pity he likes it long. One of the short styles would really suit you.'

'Brendan and Anne are getting married when they get their summer holidays. I told them schools in England don't close till near the end of July but they've made all the arrangements and nothing I can say will stop them.' Mammy's voice rattled down the phone. 'She wants a very quiet "do", on account of her mother. Wouldn't you think she could have waited till the full year was up?'

'Anne did nurse her mother for six years. She's a very nice girl.'

'Nobody's saying she's not. Since they waited that long, another few weeks wouldn't hurt them. I might have known you would take his side. Well, are you coming for the wedding or are you not? And I think it's time that husband of yours showed his face over here or people will think he's left you. If they don't already think that.'

'I couldn't get time off so near the end of term. We would have to fly and come back the next day. It would be very expensive.'

'So you're not bothering to attend your only brother's wedding. We're a small enough family without you opting out.'

'It's not . . . '

There was click as she hung up. I held the buzzing receiver way from my ear and called Fiona.

'That was Granny. Brendan and Anne are getting married on Saturday week.'

'Terrific. Can I be a bridesmaid?'

'No, we can't afford to go just for a weekend. We'll go later.'

'The day we break up?'

'I've an appointment at the hospital on the first of August. We'll go after that.'

27

If you chose to arrive in Carrig the day after internment you couldn't expect to be the centre of attention.

'Where was the prime minister of England while Belfast burned?' was Mammy's greeting to me and her two grandchildren when we arrived from the airport with Brendan and Anne. The answer was delivered in the same breath. 'Well, I'll tell you. He was sailing the high seas in *Morning Cloud*. *Morning Cloud*, I ask you! That's what John Bull cares about this place.'

Bridie sounded weary and anxious. 'I can't wait to get to Donegal and out of this place. Most of the women round here are swallowing tranquillizers like dolly mixtures. Another night like the last two and I could be on them myself.'

Since I last saw her, she had lost the bloom of youth that auburn-haired people often keep well into middle age. Her hair, which usually fell in shining waves, looked dank and lifeless. There were dark pouches under her eyes and varicose veins bulged under the elastic stockings she wore most of the time since Mary's birth two years previously.

Mammy had arranged with Agnes to do the three-day pilgrimage to Lough Derg, so Bridie was instructed to drive her to Ballyroe while Tim, Brendan and Anne took the children to Donegal.

Mammy informed the soldiers at the border that it was a sad state of affairs when Irish people had the pistols of a foreign army pointed at their heads before being granted permission to pass from one part of their own country to another. As we drove away from the border post, she wound down her window and shouted that a woman of her age should be treated with respect and not called 'love' by a whippersnapper in a khaki uniform.

Agnes's cottage smelled of Moynagh. The tangled stink of cabbage and broth. We ate cooked ham, tomatoes and soda farls at her kitchen table which was covered with a red-and-white checked oil cloth. A serrated edged strip of the same material had been tacked round the high mantelshelf where the Infant of Prague perched in his glass dome. Pope Paul VI on the balcony of Saint Peter's raised his hand in benediction from the front of a 1966 calendar and Miss Fisher and my grandmother's portraits hung side by side above the put-you-up. Since the eviction from Moynagh, Mammy and Agnes had become mirror images of each other. A foreglimpse of myself and Bridie thirty years from now. A smile broke over Mammy's mouth on learning that the Mullingar Heifer was crippled with rheumatism and had been seen limping up the aisle at last Mass on a stick. And her face glowed when she heard that one of the Gripper brothers had been operated on in Dublin for trouble in his private parts and was still having trouble 'down there'.

'God works in mysterious ways.'

'Chickens always came home to roost.' Agnes nodded in agreement.

'Those two would put years on you. The same old guff day in, day out.' Bridie said as we washed up. 'Come on, we'll go for a spin.'

She turned left at the crossroads beyond Ballyroe taking the road to Moynagh, which had been lying empty for the past few years.

'Did you know that the Gripper's wife, the one who took possession of Moynagh, had a nervous breakdown. Apparently a ghostly face kept appearing at the window whenever she was alone and unseen hands hurled stones and clods down the chimneys.'

'Was it our grandfather with an empty whiskey bottle looking for a drink?'

'More like Jimmy McMahon with a full bottle of whiskey inside him. Call it a coincidence but hardly had they taken themselves back where they belonged, than the bold Jimmy rented most of the fields for grazing. For a song.' She stopped the car and looked at me with a straight face. 'Naturally Mammy and Agnes aren't speaking to him any more for consorting with the enemy instead of making them hand the place back to Agnes.'

A rusty chain was locked round both gates at the end of the lane leading up to Moynagh.

'I'll go over first and help you.' Bridie guided my feet over the bars and helped me land as if I was a small child, and we walked along the potholed track where my admirers used to wait to escort me to Saint Kieran's school. Grass and weeds grew calf high on the street in front of the house and sprouted through crumbling thatch. The pump rusted headless beside the murky puddle that had once been the duck pond. Planks, nailed together in the form of a cross, had replaced the rotted handrail on the steps to the hayloft. The doorway and windows of the house were boarded up and slippery moss coated the step and windowsills. *Buachalán* grew rank in fields where Jimmy McMahon's cattle chewed the cud and swaying grasses hid all evidence of the Grippers' ill-fated attempt to mow the long meadow.

'Bridie, do you see what I don't see?' My goose-pimpled arm pointed at the haggard.

Her eyes searched the lush semicircle of grass where the dunghill had been. 'My God, the burial mound's gone! Mammy and Agnes sure knew what they were about, the night they cremated Gilmour.' She tugged my arm and we moved towards the lane. 'Come on, this place gives me the creeps. Too many ghosts. Too many spying eyes.'

'Dear God in heaven, who would believe a dump like this could cause such hatred and such heartache?'

'Don't you let Mammy and Agnes hear you calling their ancestral home a dump.' Once more Bridie helped me over the gate. 'And don't let on we came here or the interrogations at Castlereagh will be a picnic compared to the grilling we'll get.'

Early next morning we drove to the shore of Lough Derg and waved to Mammy and Agnes as a boat took them towards the island known as Saint Patrick's Purgatory. Out of the water rose the basilica, a slate-coloured building, stark against a slate-coloured sky. Alcatraz, surrounded by dormitories that could have passed for the wings of a prison.

'It doesn't seem right for two old women to spend three days climbing over sharp stones in their bare feet,' I said.

'You've seen grannies far more ancient than them hobbling round the beds and going back year after year.'

'True enough. I wonder what they're going to pray for.'

'What do you think? That the Gripper brother catches his other arm in a threshing machine.'

'And that the Lord will smite every first born in the house of the Mullingar Heifer.'

'First born! You're joking. Those two won't be content till every last one of that family is in the grave or banished to England.'

We headed out of Pettigo. It was fair day in Donegal and the packed town smelled of porter and farm animals. 'My Wild Irish Rose' blared from loudspeakers fixed under the eaves of several shops, almost drowning the din of conversation and the squeals, grunts, mooing and neighing from pens in the market.

'I'm glad you decided to come over, Mary Ann. You've cheered me up.' We squeezed on to a bench at the end of a deal table with our two cups of tea and Paris buns. 'At least Mammy and Agnes have a fine day for the pilgrimage.'

'My memories of Lough Derg are rain, rain and more rain and huddling in the cold outside the church door during the night, trying to stay awake.'

'What about the time the tops of your feet got burned and you couldn't hobble round the beds.'

'That was the year I did Lough Derg to find Alan again.'

'Somebody was listening to your prayers. I thought you were mad at the time but you have a good marriage and it must be a lot easier rearing a family in England than in Belfast. How is Alan? Is he pleased about the baby?'

I paused before answering. 'Not exactly. He thinks it's irresponsible to have more than two children.'

'Two! A real Protestant family. Don't worry. He'll be as daft about this one as he was about the others.'

He says; he thinks. What do I know what he says, what he thinks. We only discuss practicalities when he comes to see the children.

He and Kitty have flayed me. Pared me down to the bone. Their names whizz round and round my head but gag my throat. He's in my thoughts every waking hour. There's a lump in my throat when I rush up the drive, hoping he's come back to stay, dreading to discover he has taken the rest of his belongings. But even as my key turns in the lock I know there's no one inside, like the times you dial a number and can tell from the first ring that it's sounding in an empty house.

I fall asleep towards morning and he's there. And her. Together. I'm chasing a runaway pram. It doesn't career headlong away from me but moves just fast enough to stay beyond the reach of my fingertips and the hammering in my chest. Wherever I run, they are there along the roadside, a hairsbreadth from the pram, their hands which could bring it to a standstill fused to each other's waists and I waken up sobbing into a pillow still redolent of him.

Last night I decided to read in bed. A snap I had taken of Kitty at Hatfield House fell from my book. Head and shoulders against hollyhocks and the red walls of the Royal Palace. I cowered against the pillows as if a mouse had scurried across the counterpane. Then I tore it in two, in four, in eight jagged pieces. The fire was dead and there were no matches to be found so I threw the scraps into the lavatory. I looked in the bowl before flushing it to see her beautiful, crazy-paving face almost reassembled and smiling up at me. Memories of that day darted like minnows through my head – the stroll through the house and the garden where Elizabeth Tudor had walked as a young girl, lunch in a pub nearby, the usual exchange of confidences.

Count your blessings, I told myself but however I counted, I ended up staring down a well of gut-wrenching loneliness.

I could tell Bridie my pregnancy had given Alan a perfect excuse for leaving. I could tell her he never wanted to see the baby. Bridie had her own troubles. She'd learn soon enough about mine.

As we took the road through the Rosses she said how she

worried about the children every time they left the house. Especially her eldest son Hugh. 'Parents don't know what their children get up to, once they're out of their sight. They can so easily get involved in the Troubles. Especially since that eejit Faulkner has taken it into his head to bring in internment.'

28

Anne chased into the waves after the ball, a slim girl in a blue, sleeveless dress, long brown hair blown over her face. Then like a water nymph she emerged from the sea. Her shot hit David on the leg as he ran between a picnic basket and a black anorak.

'Out, David, you're out,' she called, her heels sinking in wet sand. She squeezed water from the hem of her dress and raised her arms above her head.

'Isn't it great to be young?' Bridie and I were sitting with Mary on a rug at a safe distance from the rounders game.

'Just listen to you. You played rounders last year and there's nothing to stop you now. You're not a cripple. Tim looks more pregnant than you.'

A handkerchief, knotted at each corner, protected Tim's balding head as he panted between second and third base and was caught out by Kathleen.

'Poor Tim, he never did get his figure back after the first pregnancy.'

'And five more babies haven't done much for him either. The only exercise he enjoys is lifting the elbow. Talking about exercise, you should take a walk and not lie about resting yourself.'

I wandered along the edge of the sea, curling my toes through sand scalloped with froth left by each wave of the ebbing tide. In a cove at the end of the bay, a baby staggered a few yards from his father to his mother's outstretched arms. The girl wore a dress of flimsy pink material. Her husband's trousers were rolled up to half-mast and the skin on his shoulders and around his braces had been burned a fiery red. They followed each faltering step the child took. When he tripped and collapsed on his bottom, both parents rushed to pick him up, to soothe him, to watch over him as he tottered off again. I chatted to them for a while about their son and we told each other where we were staying and who we were related to, the way you do in this part of the world.

I walked slowly back to where Bridie was building a sandcastle with Mary, my head swimming with memories. David's and Fiona's hands lost in Alan's, while they walked up the beach at Studland Bay to the ice-cream van. The four of us going into the sea, Fiona perched on Alan's shoulders. Myself and the children burying him; their laughter as his toes wiggled through the buckets of sand we piled on them.

Fat raindrops splashed my arms as the heavens opened and started spilling the rain they had been hoarding for the past week. Not soft Irish rain to curl your hair into tight corkscrews and put a bloom on your cheeks but stabbing rain that turned the bright morning into dusk and pitted the yellow sand. Bridie picked up Mary, her handbag and the picnic basket at third base. Both the rounders teams grabbed their belongings, bats and balls, buckets and spades. David and Hugh ran along the beach, their faces stretched into the downpour.

It was a day for forgetting about barnacles and beaches, a day for bringing in enough turf from the stack to keep the fire going till night and staying safe and dry inside. Our bodies bent against the driving wind, big hand clutching small hand, we staggered home through the teeth of the storm.

After Dan's death a new kitchen, a bathroom and two

bedrooms had been built where the byre and the hen house once stood, but the old house was exactly as it had been when we were small. In a way we didn't mind the rain. The heat of the previous days had been unnatural in a county that gets the first blast of wet winds off the Atlantic. There was nothing to be seen outside, for the sky had fallen halfway down the hill opposite the house and the noise we were making inside blocked out all sounds of the storm.

Brendan and Anne were jammed together on the creepy inside the hearth. He played the tin whistle and she sang 'Glory O, Glory O, to the bold Fenian men'.

'That's a terrible dirge for this time of the day. Give us "Slattery's Mounted Foot", Brendan,' said Tim. He took a mouth organ from the dresser and accompanied his brother-in-law. We all joined in, stamping feet, thumping the table:

Down from the mountains came in squadrons and dragoons
Four and twenty fighting men and a couple of stout . . .

At first you could hardly hear the knocking. There it was again, timid but insistent. A woman stood close to the door. Hands clasped at her throat, she anchored a headscarf that the rain had sculpted to her head. Wind billowed her coat and whipped the hem against her legs. She stepped into the porch. Water dripped in a circle round her before running into cracks in the floor. She could have been any age from twenty to forty, for the rain had blurred her features.

'I'm looking for Maggie Charlie Rua's place. I was told it was in these parts. Do you happen to know where she lives?'

Bridie and I exchanged glances. We knew Maggie Charlie Rua all right. She lived about half a mile from the house. An evil-minded woman who interrogated us and the children whenever she saw us.

'Do you have a man at all, Mary Ann, or was it the fairies brought those two childer of yours?' she would ask. Then she'd nudge Bridie and cackle, 'Sure maybe it's more than one man she has over there in England and nobody to keep an eye on her.'

This summer she had been more persistent than ever, dropping in every morning on her way from Mass and staying till we made tea for her. We would have liked to tell her to clear off but it was said she would put the evil eye on you, as soon as look at you. She had a habit of grabbing hold of any strange man she met on the road and running her hands over his startled face and body to check if he was the lover she had met at the herring gutting in Lowestoft thirty years previously. Maybe we could have been more tolerant. For the past twenty years she had been nursing her bedridden mother, a cantankerous old woman with a tongue that could clean corn and Packie, her only child, wasn't the full shilling.

That was Maggie Charlie Rua and what could this poor, half-drowned creature want with her? She said she had walked six miles from the town after visiting her sister in hospital and she had been told that Maggie would put her up for the night. We looked at each other. Visiting hours at the hospital were strict. Wednesday and weekend afternoons and evenings only. But what business was it of ours?

Brendan and I took her by car down the rocky lane that led to Maggie's place and watched her squelch along the rutted path to the door. There was no mistaking her reception. The older woman's squat body was a frenzy of rage – mouth jabbering, arms flailing, finger pointing.

'You're nothing but scum, filthy tinker scum. You're Cromwell's spawn. Get off my land or I'll take the graip to you.'

The woman walked away and stood with head bowed, abject,

in the driving rain. Maggie stomped to the car, careless of the storm gusting round her.

'Let you be taking nothing to do with her, if you know what's good for you. She'll bring the wrath of God down on you, you mark my words.'

The woman flinched, got into the car and returned with us.

'Do you have an outhouse, a shed, any place where I can spend the night and I'll be on my way the morrah. I'm that worn out with the walking.'

We said we could make room for her, brought her in and gave her dry clothes to change into, for she had nothing with her but a battered handbag.

Anne doled out potatoes and Bridie ladled stew on plates. She said we could 'eat on our knees' at the hearth because it was so cold. A fire blazed in the old kitchen with its dresser filled with delft – bowls, plates and mugs criss-crossed by a thousand cracks, lustre jugs and teapots. On the wall opposite a picture of all the popes, from Saint Peter to Pius XI, hung a picture of St Patrick driving a mass of writhing snakes into a sea as angry as the one we had left this morning.

Our visitor joined us wearing her own shapeless, black dress, the headscarf still clamped to her head. Tim, who is the most good-natured of men, offered her a plate of stew. 'You need something in your stomach after your long walk,' he said. She shrank from him and fumbled for cigarettes in her bag.

'Here's a cup of tea to warm you up and a piece of bread,' Bridie put a cup and plate on the table beside her. 'You eat when you feel like it.'

We asked her name and where she came from. She had a way of not answering that was disarming without being offensive and there was a sadness and a remoteness about her that inhibited any further questions. Her presence cast a pall over us. We could neither ignore nor include her, and something of her misery gradually seeped over us all. We looked forward to the time when she would be gone and the black rain that came with her, but all afternoon it fell muffled on the thatch and drummed unnerving on the corrugated roof of the porch.

In the evening the rain turned to a drizzle. The adults and older children went to the *Ostán na Farraige* and the small ones were in bed. I sat with a book, opposite our visitor, resenting her uninvited presence, annoyed that it was my turn to stay at home, away from the music and the company. She fell asleep in the heat and silence.

She didn't stir when Maggie Charlie Rua came rat-tat-tatting at the door. When I saw her turn towards the house I moved into the shadows. She pressed her nose, flat as a snout, at the small windowpane. Her black eyes swivelled, devouring every object within their range. I heard her go to the back to peer through the windows; then she went out to the road snarling curses and prophecies of damnation.

I studied the woman's face, round, young and soft, for sleep had smoothed the daytime lines and tensions and the shadows from the fire merged with and dimmed the dark pockets beneath her eyes.

And then I felt a movement. Sudden. Slight. The fluttering of a butterfly wing. The quiver of a tiny foot. A miniature finger stretching. Shadow boxing. I sat stock still. Listened and waited. And there was nothing in the kitchen but silence and waiting. Silence pure as ether. Another movement. An eyebrow twitching. Coiled spine unwinding. My precious baby had held on. It stirred and stretched in liquid darkness.

The woman twisted in her chair and anger flared in me. Raw

anger at her existence. At the unwashed woman stink of her. The nicotined fingers. The cracks in her plastic shoes. I eased the weight in my belly away from her and willed her to walk through the door and disappear into the damp evening as noiselessly as she had come.

The sleeping fingers of her right hand probed under the edge of her scarf. They burrowed in rhythmic massage, easing polyester towards the crown of her head. She moved against the chair. The headscarf slid down and circled her neck.

I stared at her in horror. Jagged clumps of short, stiff hair stood out on her skull like an old scrubbing brush when the bristles start to fall out. Black gunge was embedded in her scalp and there were deep, cruel cuts all over her head. The exposed parts of her scalp glistened raw and red. Scabs had come unstuck on her headscarf and blood oozed quietly from newly opened wounds.

She woke with a start, sat back for a moment on her elbows, then clapped her hands over her ears and temples. I had never seen blind, speechless terror until that moment and I don't know how long it was before I tore my eyes from the hopeless eyes that held mine and from the cowering body shrinking deep into the armchair.

'I'll make some tea for us. It's high time you had something to eat.' I turned my back on her nakedness and went into the new kitchen. The knife sawed through wheaten bread and a thick slice fell on its side. Red jam slid over butter.

When I came back, the headscarf was tied under her chin and she was smoking, silently tapping ash into her left hand until there was enough to throw on the fire.

'Have some home-made jam. It's been a great year for the raspberries.'

'They'll find me. They always do.'

'Who's they?'

'There's nowhere you can go that they don't find you. They always find you, no matter how far you go.'

Her voice was flat, resigned to the inevitable.

'Have you no one to help you? No family? A husband?'

'I'll keep moving but they'll find me. They always do.'

'Surely there's somebody could help you. Take care of you.'

She smoked another cigarette and gazed into the fire, her face expressionless.

'I had six childer but they tuk them all away from me.'

'God help you. Where are they now, your children? Who's looking after them? Do you see them? '

'Said I'd never see them again. Said I wasn't fit to rear them. Youngest's only eight months. A boy it was.'

Once more she drifted into her own thoughts.

Then, in a voice as void of emotion as if she was asking the time or if it had stopped raining. 'Will you tell on me?'

'No I won't, I promise. Sure what's there to tell?'

Without another word she went to bed.

Two cars stopped outside and the family burst in. Hugh sitting on the bottom step of the stairs, put his flute to his lips and played 'The Streets of London' followed by 'The Hills of Donegal'. I closed the doors between the old kitchen and the woman's room, hoping she had fallen asleep. Then Tim and Brendan played the tin whistle and the mouth organ and it was long after midnight when they went to bed.

'We had a great night. Pity you missed it. How did you get on with yer woman?' Bridie smiled as we washed cups and glasses.

I told her what had happened.

She slumped into a chair. The cup she had been drying lay

on its side on the table, the tea cloth still half inside it.

'I don't want to know.' The anxiety I had noticed in Belfast a week previously clouded her face. Her fists pounded the table. Slow, almost inaudible thumps. 'Why did she have to come here of all places? Could we not have a bit of peace for two weeks?' She stopped staring at the table and looked up at me. 'It's not that I don't care about her. I don't want to have to care. Not right now.'

'I didn't want her any more than you but she came to us, God help her, and nothing can change that.'

After a few moments silence, Bridie spoke in the same listless voice as the woman. 'A couple of weeks ago a girl was tied to a lamppost in one of those backstreets near the surgery. They shaved her head down to the skull and poured tar over her and then they stuck feathers on it.' Each word was squeezed out as if it hurt to speak. 'She stood there all night. Nobody dared untie her till morning. Her mother brought her to the surgery. Tim said she was a pitiful sight.'

'What was she supposed to have done?'

'God knows. Gone out with a soldier. With somebody else's husband. Maybe they just didn't like the look of her. There doesn't have to be a reason. Not these days.'

I filled the kettle, took a bottle of milk from the fridge, warmed the teapot and when the tea had drawn I poured it into two mugs.

'You don't know you're born till you meet somebody like that poor soul.' And I told her about Alan.

'Oh Mary Ann.' Bridie sat upright and took hold of my wrist. 'What must you think of me for being so wrapped up in myself. Mammy said that you weren't yourself and, God forgive us, we both thought you were annoyed at being pregnant.'

When she asked would I have Alan back I said I wasn't sure. Most days all I wanted was to turn the clock back and us to live happily ever after.

'Can you not find it in your heart to forgive him? We all make mistakes but they don't wipe out the good times.'

'I know, but the longer he stays away the harder it is. Besides, we come from an unforgiving people.'

'You're an educated woman. Don't you think lack of forgiveness is what's wrong with this country?'

I didn't answer, though my sister's words were to scratch at the surface of my mind many times in the coming months

'Marriage isn't easy for anybody and none of us is perfect,' Bridie said, looking through the window where the glow from the unrisen sun was lightening the sky. 'Look at the time. You should have been in bed hours ago.' She rinsed our cups at the sink while I put bowls and plates on the table. 'I'll have a look at yer woman's head in the morning. Whether she likes it or not.'

When I got up I saw her leave the visitor's bedroom with Tim's black bag. 'I've seen to her. She should be all right, as right as she can be.'

'Did she tell you anything?'

'I asked her nothing and she told me nothing.' Her tone said the subject was closed.

The morning was bright and sunny, as if the storm had never happened. The woman ate her breakfast and we waited with her for the bus. Tim and Brendan each gave her a fiver and I gave her a couple of pounds. She climbed into the bus and sat down in the first vacant seat, her face, half hidden by the headscarf, empty as a mask. And I saw not her but Mammy, after Kelly's van emptied our house, her eyes fixed on the bottom of Rathbeg Avenue. And Mammy and Agnes straight backed as Padraig

Regan's taxi rattled over the potholes on the lane out of Moynagh, neither sister casting a backward glance at their birthplace, their pride, the last possession of the dispossessed, intact. And Eva, a headscarf glued over her gone-wrong perm, standing in the puddle of water that had gushed from between her legs. We waved to our visitor but she was looking straight ahead and the bus took her past the lake, round the high rocks and out of our lives.

Bridie, her daughters and Fiona hurried to prepare a picnic to take to Aranmore, while Tim and Brendan busied themselves packing the cars. Anne and I re-sorted sleeping arrangements for five adults and eight children. As we stripped and remade the bed the woman had slept in, we talked about Anne's new house, names for my baby and whether she should keep her mother's twin-tub or buy an automatic washing machine. If it hadn't been for the pile of cigarette ash in a saucer on the bedside table, our visitor might never have existed.

I was glad we had never learned her name. Without a name she had no identity or definition, and might perhaps be easily forgotten. But her memory haunted me for months. Her aloneness. She and I had both breached the codes of our societies. Though unlike her I had not been physically branded, I had paid, and was continuing to pay, a price for my defiance.

LANDING

In the seconds between dreaming and waking the darkened bedroom begins to take shape. My mother stands in the doorway and Michael sleeps in a carrycot beside me. The smell of paint and fried bacon wafts over us. 'Go back to sleep after your breakfast. I heard you up half the night with the baby.' Mammy puts a tray on the bed – porridge, bacon, egg, tomato, fried bread and two cups of tea – as she used to every morning when I was a schoolgirl. She opens the curtains. A tiny woman with restless energy, her waist-length hair, now grey and sparse, is plaited and wound into a bun as it was in her girlhood.

Sally dyes her hair ash blonde. She wears knee-high boots with the midi skirts that are worn this year. She's only eleven years younger than Mammy.

I get up when Mammy returns from Mass and search for a space for the carrycot. The front room is piled with furniture, stacked newspapers and rolled-up carpets. A red bulb in the form of a cross glows below a picture of the Sacred Heart. It has replaced the heart-shaped oil lamp of my childhood. A square of velvet drapes the television that Bridie, Brendan and I bought to keep Mammy company. Visitors sometimes ask if there's a parrot sleeping in a cage under the cloth.

Jim Ferguson has arrived and is painting the ceiling of the back room. 'Great to see you, Mary Ann, looking younger than ever. Mrs Ward, you should have told me Mary Ann was coming home with the wee baby. I could have come some other time.'

'Indeed you could not, Jim. Your time is as valuable as hers.'

I say I'll go to the shop round the corner for baby food.

'No, you won't. I wouldn't give any custom to that pack of bigots. You sit there and read the *Irish News*. I bought an English paper for you as well. I'll get the baby food from O'Neill's when I'm shopping for Jim's dinner.'

In England, I don't buy South African fruit. Different sanctions apply here.

Mammy returns weighed down with food for the dinner and clothes for her English grandchildren. I am instructed not to get under her feet. I watch her paddle from stove to sink, from fridge to cupboard, treading an unerring path between the five shovels of coal she keeps on the floor. Jim Ferguson needs a good dinner. Young women these days don't know how to attend a man.

Chairs for Jim and me are carried into the echoing room which reeks of paint, wallpaper paste and white spirit. I carry in two plates piled with fillet steak, potatoes, parsnips and carrots. Mammy sets the table for herself in the kitchen and switches on the one o'clock news.

Jim eats half his steak and one potato, puts a forefinger to his lips, closes the door and opens an empty paint tin. With the speed of a pickpocket, he slides the remains of his meal into the tin. Mammy collects our plates and places our pudding before us.

'You enjoyed your steak, Jim? I like to see a clean plate. Your mother always said a working man needs a bit of kitchen.'

'That was lovely. You make a great dinner, Mrs Ward.'

Three quarters of his custard, pears and cream join the meat and vegetables in the tin.

'Why don't you tell her she gives you too much. It's a shame to waste all that food.'

'Your mother's a great wee woman, one in a million. I wouldn't offend her for all the world. She's in her element cooking for somebody.' He puts the tin in a plastic bag and hides it in the cupboard. 'It's awful hard for her all on her lone, and you all gone. Mind, she's fairly cheered up since you arrived.'

Mammy goes into town for cream buns for our afternoon tea. I can't leave the house as there's no pram for the baby. Besides, she doesn't want me to talk to the neighbours. She locks the front door behind her. The back door is already bolted against thieves and terrorists. I put three plates, pudding bowls and glasses in an enamel basin. The same number as I wash at home, though I often forget and set four places. I rinse a tumbler in hot water and slide it up and down the draining board, holding the warmth in my hand. By applying for jobs over here I thought I was taking control of life. Putting the Irish Sea between me and my troubles but my head is swimming and I've had enough of decision-making. Of balancing the plus and minus on already weighted scales. How much easier it would be to drift along any path Fate chooses like a glass gliding over a Ouija board.

The scullery window looks out on a rectangle of uncut grass. A half-bald privet hedge has grown so tall it casts a permanent shadow over the drizzle-soaked garden. There are cream flowers on the Christmas roses in my London garden and the winter jasmine has been bright yellow since December. Yesterday morning I saw daffodils and crocuses growing in swathes over the wide verges of Durnsford Road. My unicorn loves the winter. I often see him from my bedroom window stepping around trees and bushes. Sometimes he raises his neck to look at me.

I had forgotten how long winters last and I realise that the scene outside the scullery window is reality. As it always was. As it will be. Not the rose-tinted, summer-holiday postcard of Ireland my children and I carry in our heads. Of cousin packed outings on timeless days. Of empty beaches. Of August sunshine itching to burst through cloud.

I wish I were back in my own home where Alan's books are still on the shelves I helped him put up. Where his feet are printed in the shoes he left in the bottom of the wardrobe. Where his smell lingers in his jumpers, fooling me that he lives with us, that he will park his car in the drive and I'll hear his key in the door. My home where I am queen of the castle.

The teapot jumps and spits on the gas flame. Jim Ferguson sings out of tune to pop music on the radio. The walls of my mother's house close in and the smell of paint and stewed tea stifles me. Tomorrow and the day after will be the same as today. Mammy will attend me hand and foot and dictate my every move. I'll eat a half-pound of steak and Jim will carry his food away in a tin. I won't go out gallivanting but will eat fruit cake and drink treacle-coloured tea every two hours. And then Friday. The interview for a job in a school for eleven plus rejects. The job for which Mammy is pulling strings.

The tumbler clatters across the ridges of the draining board, like an alarm clock shocking me out of sleep. I am not drifting. It's my finger on the moving glass; my heat has warmed the air inside it. I will take the plane to Heathrow on Thursday.

Mammy has bought gravy rings and chocolate éclairs. I heat the gravy rings under the grill. Each night of our stay in Paris, Alan and I bought hot doughnuts from a kiosk outside a cafe, near where the Rue Soufflot meets the Boulevard St Michel. I see us shifting them gingerly from hand to hand, making our way past the Luxembourg Gardens, turning towards our hotel, our lips smothered with sugar, smothered in smiles.

'In the name of God, Mary Ann, are you trying to burn the

house down?' Mammy opens the window to let the smoke escape. She tells me not to worry. I have a lot on my mind. She and I eat charred gravy rings and eclairs and rest our cups on the night storage heater.

'We'll knock that wall down and put the dining table in here.' She points at the wall between the back kitchen and the scullery. She seems to have shed years since she went out. 'I know you'll want units like Bridie's but the whatnot and these cupboards will do you fine.' She studies the marble-topped whatnot and the dark brown cupboards and adds quickly.,'Unless, of course, you really have your heart set on units. Would you want cream, like the ones you have in England?' She doesn't wait for an answer. 'I went into Charlie McGreevy's. He says he'll install central heating once the good day comes. This yoke would have seen me out.' She taps the night storage heater 'But the children will have to be kept warm, especially the baby.' Patches of red glow on her cheeks. Excitement stretches her crêpe-paper skin. She is a woman with aims and projects. A woman with a stake in the future.

'But Mammy . . . '

'I nearly forgot to tell you. I ran into Mrs Donnelly down the town.' She closes the door into the hall, draws her chair up close to mine and whispers, 'I told her about your trouble. You don't have to worry. She won't breathe a word to anybody. She had enough bother herself with Myrna and yon Yank. Myrna's coming up on Friday. She'll call to see you after your interview.'

How do I tell her I have been travelling for too long at a different pace and on a different track? 'I'm not going to the interview on Friday. I'm taking the plane on Thursday morning. I'm sorry, Mammy.'

I wait for her outburst but she doesn't speak. On her way to the scullery the dishes in her hand clatter as she stumbles and almost falls over the shovel of coal near the kitchen door. She stands hunched and rigid at the sink scouring months of tea-stained grime from the porcelain surface.

Bridie and Tim and their two eldest daughters arrive at the same time as Brendan and Anne. Car rugs are spread over floorboards, I sit beside Brendan on a rolled-up carpet. The table is crammed with sandwiches, cakes, cups and glasses. Mammy's granddaughters tell her she's to sit still and be attended like the queen. Michael is passed from lap to lap. Anne refuses to part with him, says she needs all the practice she can get.

'So have you decided how long you're staying, Mary Ann?' Brendan asks.

'I'm going back in the morning on the half-eight plane.'

'But what about your interview on Friday? Father Doyle has arranged a time specially to suit you.'

Mammy's face darkens. 'Well, you will have to tell him your sister has decided to suit herself and to pot with everybody else. Mary Ann doesn't know whether she's coming or going. She'll rue the day she turned her back on her own country.' She refuses an offer of sandwiches. 'And I'm to be left on my own again. I might as well be in the Sahara desert for all the company I have.'

Bridie rolls her eyes at me.

Then the chat turns to family reunions, birthday parties, the dinner dance they will attend at the end of the month. They discuss the papal encyclical on birth control, the education system, the recipe for the meringues Anne made. And politics. Everybody talks at once. A broad spectrum of opinions.

'The schools should be desegregated,' I say. 'If Protestants and Catholics got to know each other when they were young there would be a lot less hatred and bigotry.'

'Desegregated. You talk like a West Brit.'

'Nobody would think you were reared here.'

'Leave her alone. Mary Ann's been away too long. She's forgotten what things are like over here,' Bridie snaps at Brendan.

'But things are getting worse every year. You don't have to live in Ireland to see that. They're not going to settle down now. Not after Bloody Sunday.'

'And what's that supposed to mean?'

'Well, only this morning I read in the paper that there is an average of four bombings every day. It can only get worse.'

'You don't want to believe everything you read in the papers,' says Brendan.

'Things always seem worse than they are. Everything has changed since you left and nothing has changed at all. The Troubles will have blown over by next year. People get sick of fighting and want a normal life.'

'You're talking through your hat, Tim,' says Mammy. 'I'm an old woman and there have been nothing but troubles all my lifetime. They will end when Ireland is free and that won't happen till Cromwell's bones and coffin have melted away.'

'Is that right, Granny? Where's Cromwell buried?'

According to Mammy, Irish soil had rejected Cromwell's body. The men in charge of disposing of his putrid remains were at their wits' end and had dropped his iron coffin into the depths of the Irish Sea. That's why crossings from Ireland to England are so rough.

'Well, even if the Troubles do end there's still the discrimination and the obsession with religion. It's a pretty poisonous atmosphere for children to grow up in.'

'You don't know what you're talking about.' Brendan pays no attention to Anne, who tells him to stop shouting at me. 'We have the best education system in the British Isles. Second to none. There's discipline in our schools and respect for authority, not like those hooligans across the water. This is God's own country. You couldn't beat it with a big stick. Bridie's right. Your trouble is you've been away too long.'

One evening, I was in the pigeon loft with Mr Bradshaw waiting for the last of his birds to return from Scotland. A neighbour called to say he had seen a mauve-chested fellow with red feet strutting about in a garden two doors down from his.

Mr Bradshaw shook his head and said that selfsame bird was a pain in the ass. He had had to fetch him back twice before. Last time he was perched in a tree out the Belfast Road. He had felt a right eejit rattling a corn can at a pigeon that only came down when the notion took him

'What will you do, Mr Bradshaw? How will you get him back?'

'I'll wring his neck. That's what I'll do.' He made a slashing gesture across his throat. 'Mrs Bradshaw will make soup out of him. A pigeon that doesn't know his own home is no use to man or beast.'

Betty and Sean arrive with a bottle of whiskey.

'It's like the last night of Paddy's wake,' Sean says. 'Mrs Ward, if I'd known you had to pawn the furniture to keep the bailiffs at bay we would have brought a few chairs round.'

Betty glares at him and says that remark is not funny.

Mammy says not to mind. Sure there's no harm in Sean and she expects a song from him once he has had his supper.

Then we lean against new wallpaper or dusty plaster and sing and talk till midnight.

Michael has turned night into day. He wakens to be fed at three o'clock on Thursday morning. I listen to the heavy breathing of my mother's drugged sleep and tiptoe into her bedroom. A thin rectangle of moonlight filters through partly opened curtains, silvering my mother's gaunt face and shoulders and her hair lying loose over the pillow. On the dressing table beside her bed are hairpins, an alarm clock, sleeping pills, a crucifix and a glass of water. Green mould has formed in the bottom of a bottle of water she brought from Lourdes four years ago.

On wet days Bridie and I used to stand in puddles and rain-filled gullies till our shoes and socks were soaked. Mammy sat us in front of the fire, our feet in basins of hot water and mustard, bowls of soup in our hands. I want to lie beside her, to hold her as she used to hold me but I must not disturb her. The sleeping pills will wear off soon enough and I'll leave her today with only a ticking clock for company.

I stand by the window. Moonlight glistens on the hoar-frosted roofs of a housing estate that was slapped up a few years ago. I used to look out morning and evening at the flat stretch of Slieve Dubh and the lower slopes of Logan's hill. The near horizons that cradled my childhood. I picture them beyond the frozen rooftops. Outlined against a navy sky. But the houses have linked arms and crowded together. Not a chink between.

And I hear again the song Betty sang before the party broke up. The song I always ask her to sing on my last night in Ireland. What she calls a dollop of Celtic twilight for the emigrant.

A rúin mo chléibh, nár mhilis ár súgradh croí 's nár ghairid!
As Ó Rí na glóire gile, tabhair ar ais an oíche aréir.

(O love of my heart, wasn't our lovemaking sweet and
    wasn't it short!
O King of bright glory, give me back last night.)

Thick gauze has covered the moon's face and a band of mist drizzles its edges. I dry my eyes with a corner of the curtain.

In ten hours Michael and I will be in our own house where Sally will have prepared a meal for us. Alan phoned yesterday. He will be waiting at Heathrow. We will travel along the A4 and the North Circular and on the journey I will tell him how and why his father fell to his death, exactly as I told Kitty six years ago. When we will arrive in Hawthorn Road, he will either stop the car on the road or he will turn into the drive outside our house. Whatever. My feet will be planted on firm ground and my eyes will be open wide.

At half past seven Brendan arrives to take me to the airport. Beside my suitcase is a bag bursting with wheaten loaves, potato bread, a Christmas cake and four pounds of raspberry-and-black-currant jam. Billy McDonnell, the butcher, opened up early this morning for me to collect the meat Mammy had bought for me: two pounds of fillet steak, four pork fillets, a leg of lamb and two pounds of sausages.

Mammy brushes away my attempt to kiss her goodbye and stuffs a roll of ten-pound notes into Michael's sleeping bag. From the gate she calls as we drive off. 'Next time you come, it will be to my funeral.'

She has a busy day ahead of her – Jim Ferguson's dinner to shop for and prepare. He's having apple tart for pudding. She has made the pastry already.